In Search of The Crystal Planet

The Star Crystal saga: Book 2

DC Daines

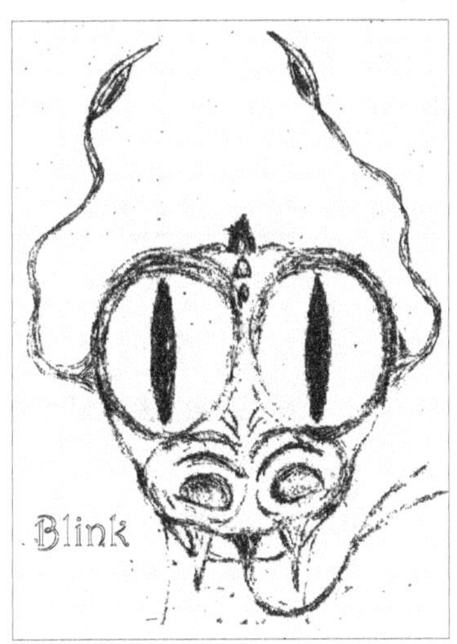

Illustration by DC Daines

All the characters, events and situations portrayed in this book are fictional. Any resemblance to actual persons, living or dead, events, or locales is entirely coincidental.

IN SEARCH OF THE CRYSTAL PLANET
Copyright © 2014 by DC Daines
All rights reserved.

Cover art Toonlancer
Book design, DC Daines

No part of this book may be reproduced in any form or by any electronic or mechanical means including information storage and retrieval systems, without permission in writing from the author. The only exception is by a reviewer, who may quote short excerpts in a review.

Website: www.thestarcrystal.com
Facebook: the star crystal

Toonlancer artwork: http://toonlancer.deviantart.com/

Author portrait by Daryl Olsen
https://www.facebook.com/ASourcePhotography

First edition: June 2014

About the Author

I do not write the stories. They write themselves, the voices within my head directing my fingers to the keys. Though I am finding my footing in this world of words, I am proud to say that I have many projects that I am participating in. The 'Secret Santa Initiative' being one that has enriched my understanding of the written word. But now, amongst all the other things I want to do in life, I am waiting for the day when I can sit down with Captain Scrycher and his crew and try me some pickled rat's nuts.

Illustration by Toonlancer

Acknowledgments

I will not go into how many hours I have funneled into my writing. But simply put, 18 hours a day of late has become a normality rather than a rarity. It has taken an awful lot of work to get the novel this far and I would like to thank all those that had a hand in it. I know I have to have missed someone, so if it is you, this is your thank you.

Special mention to:

Ellie. Sarah and my mum who helped with the original edits.

Linda and Owen for your countless suggestions and Philip for being my grammar maniac and teaching me a trick or two.

Toonlancer for being an awesome guy, great friend and an awesome artist.

Dane Richter, a fellow author for his awesome advice, getting me on the right track and his no bull attitude. You have been a massive help.

Daryl Olsen for the great author pic for the covers.

My wife and kids, I believe they may have thought that the book had swallowed me whole as they have barely seen me during the process.

Dedicated to

Bron for being my Guardian Angel, my direction
and allowing me to be Tokyo Underground's 'nutty professor'.

Without which, this would not have been a reality.

Blink, by Toonlancer

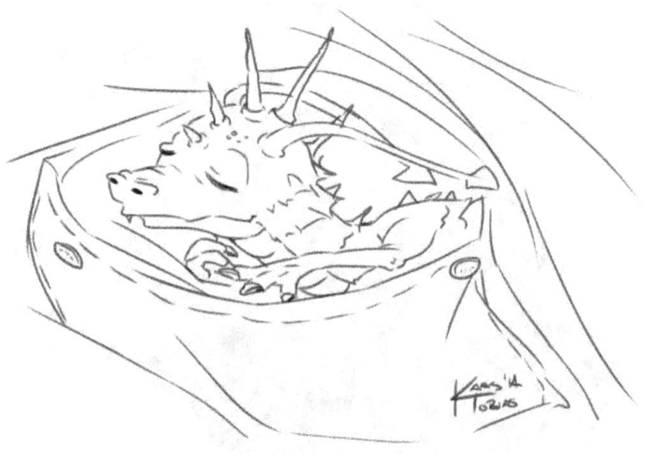

Blink Lineart by Karis Tobias
DA: minti-fresh.deviantart.com/
tumblr: coolmintifresh.tumblr.com/

Prologue

The Story Teller of the Strays' demise has become another victim in his peoples sordid past. The casualty of an event that would have been held within the memories of his crystal. But alas, the crystal is shattered, splintered into his flesh, its broken form still clutched by the dragon Blink's tongue. Amongst the corpses of his friends and foes, the Teller's body lies still. His heart beats no more, his lifeless body, frozen upon the ground. A pool of blood is all that remains of his life force. Once expelled it had frozen within the earth. It now pulses in the depths below. Blink's little form spasms slightly, the crystal shifts in his grasp, catching the eerie light of the Stray home world. Their life forces have entwined, working their way deep into the ground beneath these empty shells. The Three sought each other in life, on the battle field and, finally, in death. Yet, even in their last moments, they have found the resolve to fight for their destiny. These three have melded, their life forces waiting patiently. It has taken thousands of years to find their home world, but in these final moments, they have lost it again. Yet they pulse, waiting, as time is of no concern to them in their non-corporeal form.

The blood and life force that had come from and was known as the Three was now glowing and pulsing in unison with the dome, which glowed and pulsated in turn. The Three oozed through the dome. They dropped down, deeper into the dark unknown. They were stopped, their descent halted by something deep within the earth. They moved along this object in the darkness, trying to find a way past, coating the length of it until they were extended to their limits, now just a thin film. Knowing no urgency, they ceased their attempt to go lower. Resting in the darkness they absorbed the energy from around them, growing brighter and illuminating the space they occupied. They had a realization as they lay there, somehow seeing the crystalline branch on which they waited. After all this time they had reached their destination and in that instant they woke the tree from its slumber. The tree lit up in brilliant light, absorbing the blood and life force of the Three. The tree came to life dramatically as images flashed forth, filling the room, illuminating the many chambers on its walls. Images flashed from the crystal's memories, of pain, death, wrong choices, of ships in battle, fighting, snow, blizzards, ships falling, falling, then finally red, blood red as the tree tapped into Teller's memories and his life drained from his body, his mind waning away. Teller's consciousness fought back, his conclusion was not his destiny. Blink fought too, his primitive mind screeching at the coldness of death. Together the Three fought back. Their life force overpowering. Their need for conclusion strong. The red flashed more intently; blinding, like the sun itself, intense beyond belief, burning all in its way. Then nothing. As quick as the light appeared it was diminished, *blinking* out the last hope, last life, to be gone forever. Leaving the tree as it had found it…

In darkness!

The figure trudged through the snow aimlessly. After two thousand years, there seemed no point to this existence; but he could not die…

He was known by many names.

The founder; The creator; The first one...
God…

His body, once blue, was charred like a burnt corpse. His skin was no longer the brilliant, and beautiful blue, it once was.

He did not care. He did not worry. He was broken.

His heart and soul had grown cold over these years of self-imposed exile. His children were gone from this world. Massacred in the explosions. He felt only grief for the loss of his gentle children.

His mind had snapped when they were killed. Now all that remained was the cold loneliness of a father without a child.

A father should not outlive his spawn. How could life be so cruel? He did not know. He created life, someone else took it.

My children, my favored child, what can I do without you?

His thoughts were always the same!

Power!

He felt it pulling at him. He tried to resist. He was tired.

"Just leave me alone."

He was too weak, his will broken. Starving himself for so long, he had no energy; no power. Nothing left to resist this magnetism.

He allowed himself to be taken as he traveled whole; not caring where he went.

His mind; his body; his soul.

Taken into another place, he traveled with three others, none of whom were whole. They were only part, unlike him. In this place, a place much lonelier than before. The blackness concealed him. Protected him. Nurtured him. This new realm empowered him. Replenished his soul. His life, his purpose.

But still this place was so cold no mortal body could survive. It changed him. It allowed him to alter himself further, change his DNA, and his own body so it was cold like this realm; cold, like his heart!

His purpose grew; willing himself now to get back. Back to the reality from which he came. To avenge his children. To destroy the one who betrayed him, abandoned him in time of need.

All this, he thought, for millennia it seemed. His mind became corrupted, twisted and warped until finally he was released.

He did not need a vessel like the others, but he required more power as he was whole. He entered this realm, closing the link to the place from which he'd come. This was his reality, but not his time. It was earlier. How much earlier he did not know. He did not care. Revenge was all that mattered.

He looked at the others trapped in the nets below. Broken as he once was. None to see him. None to worship him. They could only feel the cold disappointment he felt as he saw these broken shells on the ground beneath him. Their fire almost extinguished under his anguish, the tear in his eye falling into the fire below. The tear's power tried to extinguish the fire as he mourned. His creations were broken. They had been changed beyond their God's image. He left quickly and quietly.

Seeking death…

It found the fire, itself, and the other. It had searched for so long, an eternity, waiting. It had waited for the moment to come back, to re-enter this realm! Here the emotions were strong, stronger than ever before, the rift had opened, allowing the past and present to become one. Now, in the past, their past, it had to come back. Back to the one, the one it was linked to, the one that it was with. The one that needed it! One of the Three.

One other was here, the Creator, his life force unknown and unfamiliar. The Creator had created the rift, had opened it, but not controlled it. The entity known as the Three controlled it, driven by desire. It had to enter through the rift, there was no other way. It could not, they could not, let it happen again. The pain, the suffering and the hope lost. The tree; the tree of life. So close but so far. This time would be different. The Three would change it, change the past. It would be unwritten, they would re-write the new past, their future. They would prevail. They would win. The Strays would be returned to their birth place, the place of their ancestors. Entering the crystal, the life forces rejoiced. Finally the Three felt whole, their emotions, their memories, now images exploding before them, none able to control the other. The crystal rejoiced as it welcomed itself; it in turn displayed the future, their past! Images of pain, death and wrong choices, of ships in battle, fighting, snow, blizzards, ships falling, falling, then finally red, explosive red, red like the light from the sun. Too many minds, too many images! The crystal could not hold them, they were too complex. They needed to escape. As Teller touched the crystal, it…they… all tried to flee, simultaneously, into this vessel. Teller, who was this vessel, was large and free, much larger than the crystal had been! The life forces were explosive and forceful, entering Teller for the first time together, the force slamming him into the bulkhead. While he lay there the Three worked, they changed, they became, they were now him and he them, their genetic make-up combined, twisted, changed. They had to do this, to the one they entered, to do this thing to save him, to save them, to SAVE… US ALL!

Chapter 1

Scrycher's legs ached as he knelt down, allowing the darkness of this place to conceal him. From his vantage point of many hours, he had been observing the actions happening before him, while waiting patiently for all to arrive. He had observed the crowd coming sporadically from all across the station in this time, but the flow of bodies had now stopped. *It is almost time!* he thought.

All the children were now sitting or kneeling around a fire before a cloaked figure. The figure was also kneeling, mostly concealed behind the fire. He was like a statue. *Until now!* The figure at the fire gracefully arose in an effortless motion that made his body look as though it was floating, and he addressed the crowd before him. The fire was burning brightly in this dark place, illuminating the area around him as though an aura of his person. He continued to rise as he spoke, moving with the same passion as the fire, the fire's light and flames in turn mimicking his gestures. The children around the fire stopped fidgeting and listened intently as though watching a play unfold before them.

Scrycher had never seen anyone command such attention as this figure in front of the crowd. This figure, a storyteller, drew Scrycher into the tale of the Stray lineage and their blight. Scrycher's legs were still aching, but this did not bother him. The tale was so intense it made the world and his pain seem distant.

"Come closer and I will show you, the beauty, the truth, the loss, so you may know too well the pain of trusting those we once did."

Scrycher watched intently as a box was delicately lifted from out of the cloak of the story teller. *Dutanium?* Scrycher thought; this metal was very rare and expensive. His sensitive ears heard the *CLICK, CLICK, CLICK* echoing across the bulkhead as the box opened; he did not see nor hear the box dropping to the floor near the side of the fire. His attention was now drawn to the crystal floating above the story teller's hands. All other thoughts were completely lost to him as the crystal shone its light out in all directions, hypnotizing all who gazed upon it.

The illuminations were magnificently projected into the air. The colors then transformed into images, moving into a continuous film now being played back for all. All who watched were mesmerized. Images of beautiful trees; the trees made of crystal. The lands of glass grass, and bizarre looking insects swarming around them, or were they insects? Scrycher looked closer. These insects, larger than he first thought, reminded him of Blink. Smaller and obviously not as fat. They were, after all, flying. Scrycher allowed himself a little laugh at the thought of Blink flying. In his years of traveling he had never seen anything like this place. The picture changed to images of elf-like children, naked but for the natural fine fur covering their bodies. Something clicked inside him as he put the two images together, he sought Scrags out of the corner of his eye. He could also make out the indent that was Blink in his mess of hair. A warmness filled his smile as his thoughts returned to the images of the children. Their bodies glistened in the dim light of the planet, lighting their Stray facial features. These children were playing by themselves, while longer, sleeker forms of them lay under the trees. These older Strays seemed content, smiling at their playing young. This place, this planet they were in, seemed like paradise to all who watched.

Scrycher sensed a longing to find this place; a planet he had been searching for, for what had seemed his whole life. He felt connected to it, and the crystal. He hoped that this man was the last piece of the puzzle he needed. He had gathered the information for years on how to find this lost place. Now he had an avenue to use it, to check its details. Scrycher wondered, *did this man before them control the images within the crystal or did it control him?* He now knew the rumors about this man, as exaggerated as they seemed to him in the past, were simply understated. No words could have done this display justice. It was purely magnificent.

Scrycher was ripped out of his trance by a hand shaking his shoulder.

"Boss! Boss!" Chelsea's voice was low as she shook Scrycher, a slight desperation obvious in her voice; demanding his immediate attention.

Scrycher turned. Through the darkness he could barely see his three comrades standing behind him, waiting impatiently for his response.

"The Prof just called. Scans show Company pigs comin' our way. They just got off their ship, 'bout five minutes ago."

"How much time?"

"'Bout forty minutes boss. If they know where they are goin' to, 'tis doubtful."

"Is it the same ship? The one that has been tailing us for weeks."

Chelsea whispered into a black square box resting in her closed hand. "Prof, they the same ones been chasing us?" The replying voice came back gurgled.

"I-I-I d-do n-not know, th-they look t-the s-same. P-p-p-poss-sib-b-bly."

"Captain, we don't know. Don't reckon we can take that chance." Chelsea looked at Scrycher, trying to anticipate his response.

Scrycher thought for a second. This figure before them at the fire was the one he had been searching for. They needed him on their side. If they performed the capture now then this would jeopardize his cooperation.

The communicator sparked up again. "G-G-G-oo-oo-oon F-f-force-ce, G-get ou-out n-now!"

"How fast?

"Th-The sh-sh-ship is c-coming in h-hot. Th-they w-will n-not b-be as l-long as-s the others-s. Th-They l-look l-like th-they kn-know wh-where th-they are g-going."

Scrycher knew what this meant. The Company Goon Forces were on their way. Coming in hot meant that they were not going to stop for anyone, not even officials, not even Company pigs. They must have known the Strays were here and they were going to get them no matter the cost.

"Boss, we need to go now. For the sake of the Stray children." Chelsea's voice was straining now as she pleaded with him; she did not want to get in a fire fight with Company men, especially not a Goon Squad.

Scrycher looked up, signaling Chelsea, Rod and Jaxter to take position. As they left, he put his hand softly on Scrags' shoulder, ensuring he did not wake little Blink. The boy was not a full Stray, rather a bit of both breeds. Ironically, the term 'Scrag' was the actual word used to describe the offspring from the crossbreeding between human and Stray.

The boy of maybe nine or ten looked up dazed, as if being pulled out of a trance. Quickly regaining his composure, he loaded a large net into the cylinder Scrycher was kneeling beside. As Scrycher raised the cylinder onto his shoulder he yelled, "Strays!" He knew that the confusion to come would allow them the opportunity they required to keep all the Stray children trapped within the circle of the fire, stopping them from getting to the safe haven of the darkness. "Get 'em, now," he commanded the others as he pulled the trigger, shooting the first net, controlling the huge recoil so it hit home. His target, a small Stray boy was pinned to the hull, the net's magnetic cups ensuring there was no escape.

Scrags scrambled to reload the net gun, as more of the children around the fire started to break their trances, leaping out of the fire's and the crystal's light, only be thrown back to the deck they had sprung from, captured in these nets. This team had done this many times. They had information, much information, and they used it well. Getting these children before the Goon Squads did, and trying to relocate them, was top of their list of priorities. They were indeed like a crack unit themselves, well oiled and precise in their execution of the capture. One after another the Stray children fell to the ground; defeated, laying there, terrified. As Scrycher netted another, he thought of the children and how he wished he could do this differently, but he never wanted a repeat of the first time.

They had started these campaigns years ago. Their first assignment had been a complete disaster. They had come across a group of teenage Strays that absolutely did not want anything to do with humans. They could not be convinced. Scrycher had felt disheartened and beaten at their attitude and had left without an argument. He soon realized that was a fatal mistake as he heard a Goon Squad deploy.

He had watched from a distance as the Goon Squad hunted the Stray children, killing their leader that had resisted, taking the rest forcefully. Scrycher had watched, unable to do anything. After all the mess a lone boy was left, accompanied by a vulgar man who had stayed behind to have some 'fun'. Scrycher snapped at the sight of this man's actions, shooting him in the head. He then broke this cover to rescue the young boy from under the man's corpse. Both the child and Scrycher barely escaped with their lives, as the Goon Squad returned. They had been hunted for months. Thankfully, the Squad eventually had enough of the chase and gave up searching for them. Unable to change anything at the time, Scrycher vowed he would never let anything like this happen again. He had never let Scrags from his sight since then, and they had not allowed a Stray child the choice of refusal either.

Scrags' attention was drawn to the crystal again, his job of loading the nets no longer required. Scrycher signaled to his team, allowing them to rest as he lowered his arm. Looking around at the carnage, his eyes were drawn to the teller. The teller's eyes started weeping, and he was looking at something in the midst of the children, as if trying to signal something or someone. Scrycher looked into the pile of bodies and nets. Movement! Raising his net gun as the small Stray leapt from the fire, Scrycher shot and the boy was slammed down to the ground.

Scrycher noticed a dramatic change in the teller's eyes. The tears were gone, now replaced with hatred. This Stray would be hard to convince to help them after this, if he did not try and kill them first. The crystal's light changed dramatically, drawing Scrycher's attention back to it. The images were now dark and evil, almost morbid. They became those of barren wastelands and corpses on the ground. Many graves scattered the landscape, the air and ground was filled with red dust, and red dust clouds thrashed about in the swirling winds. There was no light. No life, only death. Snowstorms and blizzards blew across the fire. These seemed so real that they almost put out the flames of the fire before them. Then the pictures of the landscape became covered in snow.

The teller's body arched forward violently, hissing as Scrycher watched. The teller grasped at the crystal in desperation. His emotions of pain, aggression, and hatred all touched the crystal too.

In this heightened emotional state Teller forced the crystal and its contents open to all.

This one act allowed a passage to open into the crystal from another realm, another time. It allowed all of the Consciousness, DNA, and memories of the future, Blink, Teller and the Crystal itself to enter, into the crystal's shell.

One other came from this realm to theirs. His cold heart almost extinguished the flames as he sailed over the fire into the darkness. His power so intense, the rift closed behind him.

Scrags' jaw dropped as a swirling black vortex opened above the crystal. Coming forth from the portal were three entities encircled in light whirling around each other, yet connected. Each form of light looked different from the other; each one a life force; one red wisp, that of Teller; one black, that of Blink; and one white, that of the crystal itself. They darted around the fire as though lost, stopping momentarily as if the Three were unsure of what to do and of where to go. Decisively they all traveled into the crystal, and into its shell. Scrags could not believe what happened next. A hand reached forth from the vortex. The hand was covered in ice as it grabbed at the vortex's edges. Pulling itself out; contorting its body to fit through the small rift. First the arm, then the head, followed by the shoulders, chest and waist until finally the legs and feet were removed. This figure completed his movement out of the vortex, now free to stand over the fire below. He levitated above the fire as he looked down at the children below. His old features were enhanced by the wrinkles now on his brow. His body was neither thin, nor plump but that of an average man. However, below the frost, his skin had been darkened to a charcoal color and cracked as though it had been badly burnt. As the figure searched through the forms below him, the air became cold. The figure looked up, a tear dropping from his eye as he looked around. The tear dropped into the fire. As it hit the fire, it exploded, the coldness almost extinguishing its flames. In one quick motion he was gone, flying off into the darkness.

A feeling of pain, of death, of tragically wrong choices waved out of the crystal, its light making all around it feel as it felt. Images forced their way out of the crystal, images of ships in battle, of people fighting, the images of these people were somehow familiar to those still watching. Finally, back to snow, a planet covered in snow, then blizzards. It was as though the crystal had regained some control of itself. Then suddenly and dramatically the images changed. A ship was falling, then a pod, falling and burning as they went. The light became fire, then red. Blood red now stained the snow. The final image was fire red again. The crystal looked as though it exploded in a light so intense it seemed to be a sun itself.

The new occupants of the crystal cried out in pain, this space was too small, they were being crushed. Their memories and thoughts changed as they tried expelling them. Expelling the most emotional of all at first; then he came; their knight, their savior, touching them. Allowing them to touch him! To escape this shell!

The teller's body glowed. The five onlookers stood in awe as his body rose above the fire, arching back as though he was going to fly over them in an attempt to escape. Rod pulled out his gun, aiming at the teller. Chelsea saw this out of the corner of her eye. Without another thought she ran over to him, punching him in the jaw before he could take the shot.

"What the hell are you doin' fool? Don't use your gun!" she screamed.

Turning, Rod looked her up and down with pure evil in his eyes as she returned to her position. "You will get yours, hag! Just you wait." He spat the words, and blood, onto the deck, while intimately fondling the large knife on his side, and his tongue probed his aching cheek.

Jaxter's jaw dropped with the explosion of red light. He felt as though the light was trying to burn him, as a furnace would do to a corpse. The teller's hood was thrown off, and a masculine Stray face was bared for all to see. This face seemed older, and more mature, than most Strays Jaxter had seen, the fine fur covering the face a silvery gray. The teller's eyes opened, exposing his soul to all. The bright light beaming out sought the souls of those who watched, trying to touch them and occupy their shells. The crystal, now in the teller's hand, diminished to a mere torch light in comparison.

The three forced their way back out of the crystal; they could not go back to the realm from where they had come. That way was now closed. Their only choice was to enter Teller himself! They knew this would be dangerous, but they decided together. Simultaneously. Explosively.

Chelsea turned her head away at the sight of the storyteller being thrown into the bulkhead. "That must've really hurt," she winced. Turning back, she ordered the crew into action. "Round 'em up, and be quick about it. We're in a hurry!"

Scrags, who had just witnessed the wisps entering the teller, snapped himself out of his daze as he took his cue, walking out of the darkness and into the fire's low light. He paused at each child briefly, with Blink breaking the tension by bobbing up and down, flapping his little wings, stretching out his neck, and generally entertaining the children, who giggled slightly at his antics. Speaking softly, Scrags told them to be still and co-operate, so that they could be safely removed from the nets that held them. Each child was then picked up from the ground, and carried to a wagon. The children were being piled on the wagon like sacks of grain. As the last child was loaded, Chelsea turned to Scrycher. "What we gonna' do with 'im?" she nodded towards Teller. "Can't leave 'im here or he'll get Gooned for sure."

As Scrycher walked over to the unconscious story teller, he replied. "Leave him to me. I am sure I will find a use for him." Picking him up by the arm, Scrycher effortlessly threw the story teller's body over his shoulder, the weight barely registering on his masculine body. The crystal fell from the teller's grasp and clinked to the metal deck. It went unnoticed by all but Scrags, as Scrycher did this. Scrags ran over, picking up the crystal, its dim glow increasing in his grasp. Placing it in his pocket, Scrags followed behind Scrycher, as they made their way back to the ship.

The small dragon, Blink, nestled in Scrags' hair; he had seen this crew perform missions like these many times before. He was not interested, he just wanted to rest. As the crystal clinked on the deck, Blink's attention was diverted from his attempted nap. His eyes enlarged so they looked as though they were all that was on his head. Searching for the source of the pretty sound, his head rotated back and forth, looking. He did not see the crystal until Scrags had it in his hand, its light getting brighter as it was placed into Scrag's pocket. Blink's head curved over Scrags little head and down towards the pocket and the prize.

"No, Blink, not yours," Scrags lightly tapped Blink on the nose. One finger was all he needed to get his point across to his little pet. As Blink accepted his master's wish, his eyeballs returned back to their normal size. This acceptance did not stop him from skulking back into the mess of hair, combing it with his claws, to make it fluffier, before drifting to sleep. Colorful images of beautiful crystals filled his dreams, these dreams flowing over into memories. These memories were of glass grass and crystal trees with other little dragons flying around. Small and young Stray children chased these dragons playfully, laughing as they did. The happy gurgling, as Blink was caught and tickled by one of the children, was the only part of these memories that reached Scrags, as he listened curiously to the little dragon nestled on his head.

As Blink slept, so did Teller. The three entities now sharing this shell with him started working on his body.

The crystal's future consciousness; changing his body to absorb and amplify more of the power that was produced by the crystal.

Blink's future consciousness; changing Teller's DNA, modifying it to serve a purpose.

And Teller's own future consciousness changing his mind; allowing it to tap into his thoughts, their memories, to show him the path to their salvation!

Chapter 2

Lance was excited; he had started the chase only weeks earlier. Now he was almost at his goal, his latest tip putting them less than an hour behind this band of criminals. Hopefully he would get to them prior to any of the Stray children being taken. He knew his mates would be proud of him now, crossing the lengths of space and dealing justice to those breaking Company law, by swiftly capturing them. This Captain thing was not as bad as he thought; maybe this form of punishment was not all that bad. It was better than a hanging anyway. He had been given the title of Captain. Captain of a Company vessel, the same vessel he was using to chase these criminals now, their crimes against the company appalling even for the worst of criminals. As his vessel docked at the station he thought back to that fateful night that had put him in the situation he was in now and forced him to Captain this vessel …

Two and a half weeks earlier...

The laughter rose over the sound of clunking feet, as the five men laughed and slapped each other. Each one hugged the other in a one armed manly embrace as they celebrated.

"Finally, Lance me boy, you have become a man. Thrown off those shackles you call education and joined the real world like the rest of us working men." The large man's mouth was wide as he bellowed out laughter that sounded like thunder. He joked as his highly polished bald head sparkled in the light from the street lamp just above him, and he stroked his clean shaven face. "Maybe you can get Viny out of the predicaments he keeps finding himself in?"

"Hey, Hammer, I thought the deal was legit. How was I supposed to know the kegs were stolen?"

As the men stopped to enter the establishment before them, Lance turned. Facing the tall and lanky ginger headed man, Lance spoke eloquently. "Do you think that the fact that you were buying the kegs from a hooded figure in an undesirable part of the neighborhood in a dark secluded alley might have given it away? Or, did you just think these three things were just coincidences?"

Viny's light complexion flushed the color of his hair as he turned his face in embarrassment, the others staring him down. Roaring in laughter, each of them broke off their glare, and slapped Lance on the back. Lance faltered under the onslaught of the much larger men, but corrected his posture quickly once it was complete.

Viny waited until the laughter died down and turned back to walk through the door as the smell of brew assaulted his nostrils. The bald man could not let Viny pass without a further embarrassing comment. "That education will be worth every cent, hey Viny?" The laughter started up again only to die down quickly as they readied themselves, straightening their appearances, the thought of ale on all their minds.

The five men quietly entered the establishment in an orderly fashion, Hammer ducking his head to enter the small doorway, and Viny's face still blushing red from the embarrassment. As they entered, a cute, mousey blonde barmaid winked at Lance.

Viny dug his elbow into Lance's ribs giving him a goofy grin, the embarrassment now gone from his face. "She wants you, eh?"

Lance turned, giving a look of disgust in reply, as he looked around in search for a spare booth. The smoke filling the room made it hard to see Viny's embarrassment returning. Unfortunately for them all, it also made it hard to see the booths, so they stepped further into the room, pushing their way through the raging crowd as the music and lights blocked most things from their minds. "Hammer, do you see a booth for us?"

The bald man, almost half a body taller than the others, looked past the multitude of heads, but before he could reply the mousey-haired barmaid returned, grabbing Lance's elbow and affectionately leading him and his mates to a booth in the corner. A pitcher of black colored ale and five glasses were already positioned on the table waiting for them. "Congratulations Lance, maybe you can take me out now you are not so busy?"

It was Lance's turn to blush as he turned and whispered something sweet into the barmaid's ear. She left, smiling from ear to ear, not bothering with the podgy man before her, as he shook his hands feverishly above his head in an attempt to get her attention.

Hammer sat down, the bench creaking under his weight as he reached over to pick up the pitcher and sculled it. Wiping the broth from his mouth, he bellowed. "Thanks for the ale love, but you'd better get me mates one too." As he spoke, he slapped a large hand on the bench beside him, beckoning Lance to sit.

Acknowledging the gesture, Lance sat on the edge of the bench before giving him a big cheesy grin as he slid back off the limited space. Together, these men's appearance was amusing, worlds apart but best of friends nonetheless.

"Get in here," Lance called to the other three men, who easily fitted into the other side of the booth as the blonde waitress delivered another pitcher. Viny ogled the barmaid before he quickly grabbed the ale, pouring himself a drink, and placing the glass to his lips before anyone else could get to pour one...

"To my mate Lance and his accomplished career, or what will be one!" Hammer slammed the empty pitcher to the table as the others started stories of their recent missions, filling Lance's head with tales of grandeur...

"What I would give to be you guys," Lance said as he finished his sixth ale, his speech slurred, and actions slow.

"I am sure that when you start crusading against the slaughter of those poor defenseless rats all on your own, you will not have time for the likes of us, or our tales." Viny was well and truly drunk, sloshing around his beer and spilling it over the others as he slurred Lance's profession.

"Can he help it if he is so righteous? I am sure you will not be so pompous when he bails your ass out of jail." Hammer was not as drunk as the others even though he had now finished his fourth pitcher. "Plus every woman needs their white knight to save them from the dragon." Hammer laughed again winking at Lance and nodding towards the barmaid. "And I am sure she will be saved tonight!"

Lance looked at the direction of Hammer's nod, the barmaid catching his glance and giggling gleefully.

"Yuk!" the voice was heard over the chatter in the room and had originated from a table to the side of them. A lone figure leaning over her ale, sat alone, yet to taste a drop.

"What's your deal, lass?" Hammer inquired. "Your man dump you at the altar? Or just stand you up? Oh what the fool he must be!"

The young woman lifted her posture, her brunette hair flowing down the length of her back and onto the chair seat as she spoke. "It is because of prats like you that I cannot get a job on a Company vessel. You're too busy womanizing that you would not know a good pilot if they bit you on the nose." The lady pursed her lips as she put the glass to her mouth. Opening wide, she sculled the glass and wiped the ale from her mouth with her silken sleeve.

The men on Lance's table all stopped their chatter, the image before them unbelievable, as the pretty lady sculled her beer, slammed down the glass and called to the barmaid for another.

"I would love you to bite me." Viny chuckled.

"Stop your chatter, daughter, you embarrass yourself and me!" The podgy man was still sitting in the seat he had been in hours before, a dozen empty glasses before him. "Go home to your mother, wench, and cook my dinner. Forget about this dream of yours. You flying a Company vessel is a foolish whim. It is a man's job!"

As the barmaid walked past carrying a glass of ale, the podgy man grabbed at her behind, squeezing it. "And you had better be in my bed tonight you whore." Spit sprayed over his table as he spoke. The barmaid attempted to swing at the man with her free hand. Catching the action mid-way he latched onto her arm, pulling her into his lap. With her forced into his lap the man licked the barmaids face, covering her cheek in alcoholic slobber.

"Father, you are a pig!"

"Watch your place woman, and don't use that tone with me."

The young lady calmly removed herself from her table, as Hammer attempted to get up, his large muscles flexing, his fingers ripping through the solid plastic backs to the bench he was sitting on. Lance calmly laid a hand on Hammer's arm, cautioning him down as he spoke quietly.

"Do you not know that he is on the Company Councill?" Hammer, taking notice of the warning, allowed himself to relax briefly.

"I believe this is mine?" Taking the glass of ale from the waitress, the young lady turned quickly, throwing it in her father's face.

The man let go of the barmaid, raising his hand to strike his daughter. "Who do you...?"

He did not get to finish. Lance had bounded out of his chair in his drunken state and hurdled the table and chairs, landing between the young lady and her father, catching the offending hand before it struck her.

"I, Lance Anthony Dragoon, believe that it would be an injustice to this lovely lady's face if you were to continue with this action. I would suggest that you apologize to your daughter for your actions, then go home, have a cold bath, and apologize to your wife for being a womanizing fool." Lance, proud of his speech, turned to his friends in his drunken stupor, bowing as they cheered. As he turned away from the man, he did not see the glass being swung, but he did feel the glass smash across his head, knocking him to the ground, a gash opening on the back of his head.

Hammer, in his haste to assist his friend, ripped the table from the steel decking, the table's bolts snapping like straw before he threw it to the side, quickly separating a crowd of drinkers in its path as they moved to dodge the debris. "How dare you? You podgy little fool."

Hammer's question was answered as the crowded room quietened, and the mass of bodies moved from the immediate area. All eyes now turned to the six large muscular bodyguards jumping in between Hammer and the man.

"Look what you have started now, Wench. When will you learn to hold your tongue?" The Councill member was red through the exertion of hitting Lance across the head, his eyes lit at the promise of a brawl. "Oh well, better get me money's worth. Sick 'em boys!"

Hammer stood his ground, barely an arm's length from Lance.

"Father?" The young lady played with her hair as she spoke, the bodyguards getting closer to Lance all the time. "Maybe you should apologize to these men, and call off your dogs, before they kick your ass."

"Leena you disappoint me." The Councill member turned to his men. "Beat that wench too, and don't be gentle on the account that she is my daughter."

Leena turned to look at her father, her eyes showing her disgust in his actions, as the bodyguards all stared blankly at each other, questioning the unusual order.

"Get to it, or do you want to be jobless?"

Leena turned to the first guard that approached her, his stance showing his hesitation. "You wouldn't hit a lady, would you?" She tossed her long hair around by swinging her head while she planted a massive kick in the man's groin. As he dropped to the floor he grabbed at his crotch, and covered the Councill man in vomit. The guard lay there huddled like a child as Leena grabbed the dazed Lance's arm, swinging him into Hammer's waiting reach.

"Thanks, love." Hammer easily slung Lance's body onto the bench chair they had been sitting on before turning back to the fight at hand.

"Do I have to repeat myself?" The Councill member was trying to rapidly wipe the sick off his silken shirt with a silken handkerchief he had pulled from his shirt pocket, while gagging at the smell. Yelling, he looked up. "Get them now!"

Hammer took two steps forward placing himself beside Leena, looking down to give her a wink as he did so. His stature dwarfed her so that she took the appearance of a mere child standing next to him. "Hammer time!" He joked.

Lance had regained some of his composure. As he sat there holding his head, he called out to the Councill member. "How say we deal with this like adults, Sir? Come up with an amicable agreement. One like; if you back down we will not need to kick your bodyguards' behinds, and then your chubby one. You can at least leave with your dignity intact."

"Ha, Ha! This man is not only a spineless whelp, he is a comedian too! Sit down boys, these children are not worth the effort!" The Councill man's voice was full of humor, as he held his round stomach, laughing aloud.

The tension in the room died down and the chatter started up again; no one saw Viny get out of his seat or even paid attention as he walked around Hammer and Leena, heading towards the bar. Everyone did pay attention as Viny turned back quickly, spitting in the Councill man's face. "Who are you calling children, you fat pig?"

Two of the bodyguards bounded into action, grabbing Viny's skinny arms.

Viny had anticipated this and flipped himself upwards and backwards, kicking himself into motion. Using the table before him and the men's hold on him to his advantage, he came down behind them and used the momentum of his somersault to simultaneously kick hard into the back of their knees, dropping both men to the ground before the Councill man. Two more guards joined the fray, smashing into Viny's back with their fists, knocking him to the floor.

The four bodyguards stretched Viny's body out, each taking a limb as the Councill man continuously kicked him. The other two guards stood ready to keep Hammer and Leena at bay.

"Just try it, wench, and I will do more than beat you," the guard grabbed his groin in his right hand, "I will ensure you have not broken these."

Hammer turned back to Lance, who was getting up from the chair, still holding the back of his head. "Unhand him! You have had your fun."

"Not until this skinny whelp is dead." The Councill man drove the point home with another kick to Viny's ribs, adding to the blood now coating the floor from the beating he had received.

"B-boys," Lance stammered, as he staggered over to Hammer. The other two men from his table got up.

Hammer nodded to Lance. "Freddy, Boiler, you mind giving us a hand?"

"Of course not, why would we want to do anything else?" Both men spoke in unison, as though they knew each other's thoughts. One man as black as tar and the other as white as a ghost, neither man huge, but neither small, for that matter. They walked confidently to push past Hammer and Leena and the white man turned to the other; "Boiler, you want the right or left?"

"Well, the right of course Freddy, why would I choose the left? Or maybe I should choose the left. What do you think, left, right? I don't know."

The two guards before the men looked at each other puzzled. Were these men just going to talk all day?

Freddy slapped Boiler in the face. "Shut up you fool, and fight."

Boiler in turn slapped Freddy in the face. "Idiot!" Both men continued slapping each other like women, finally grabbing each other's shoulders and wrestling, building momentum, spinning each other in a circle.

Leena turned to Lance who just did one thing; he pointed back at the two men as they spun themselves one more time. This time both men got airborne at separate times. First Freddy kicked one guard in the chest sending him sprawling onto the floor; then Boiler got airborne smashing his legs into the other guard's chest sending him sprawling into the first guard, both guards now lay winded on the floor.

Boiler and Freddy stepped aside, one left and one right, bowing and gesturing their hands outwards to the other three. "After you," both men said simultaneously, a smug smile on each face.

Both men smirked at Leena, as she looked on, not knowing what to say.

"Thank you muchly, young chaps. I think we can take it from here." Hammer walked past Boiler and Freddy, grabbing the first two unsuspecting guards by the scruff of their necks, flinging them out of the way. The two guards quickly regained their footing returning to brawl, occupying Hammer, as he went blow for blow with the two men.

The Councill man was still kicking Viny, who's eyelids were barely open, and spitting blood at each new blow.

"Father, enough!"

The two remaining guards turned to their new challenge, releasing Viny, allowing his body to slump on the floor, as he moaned in pain.

Both guards threw punches towards Lance and Leena at the same time, the two defenders quickly dodging the first attack to land blows of their own, Lance with a punch to the guard's stomach and Leena kicking the man in the leg as he motioned past her. The two guards looked at each other as if hatching a plan, both coming in again, this time feigning a blow, countering the oncoming attack, and landed a winding blow to both Leena and Lance.

"Oh crap. Help!" Lance called as he tried to regain his breath.

Hammer turned in order to help Lance but stumbled, as his assailants landed large kicks to his back.

Leena was still crouched over as the two guards went to swing again.

The guards were cut short in their attack, as Boiler and Freddy came out of nowhere, jumping on the guards' backs. The guards flailed their arms around, trying to remove the two men from their backs.

"Hey, Boiler, what you reckon to this?" Freddy stretched out one of his arms, *poking the opposite guard in the eyes with two fingers.*

"'Bout the same as this!" yelled Boiler, as he copied the action on the other guard. Boiler then slapped his hands across the ears of the man he was riding, the man dropping in pain. "I reckon that worked better though."

In anticipation of Freddy copying the same move, the other guard covered his ears. "I reckon this will work just as good." Freddy laughed, as he placed two fingers in the guards nostrils, turning them until the guard also dropped to his knees in pain.

"Group hugs." Both Freddy and Boiler yelled as they joined hands pulling themselves together, ending in a hug, and the cracking of the two guards' heads together.

As the two men removed themselves from the limp bodies, they wiped their hands on the guards' uniforms, their cheeky grins returning.

"Good job Fred."

"Good job Bo."

The crowd of onlookers roared in laughter as both men stepped over the bodies to return to their booth, and to their drinks.

Hammer had two red faced guards in headlocks with both men gasping for air. Leaning a little more, he closed their windpipes, only removing his grasp on each man as he felt them lose consciousness. "Never mess with the Hammer." He laughed as he got up, the downed bodyguard count now at six.

"See Father. Told you so!" Leena was smiling as her father hastily got out of his seat, anxious to escape the room. The room around her slowed as Leena watched Viny, battered beyond recognition, jump slowly into the air. His feet seemed to come alive and swing around very close to his body to extend slightly, contacting with her father's head. "Nnnnnoooooo." Leena called as her father's head was snapped sideways, still in slow motion as it dropped, hitting his temple on the side of the table, the impact knocking him unconscious, or worse…

As soon as Viny's feet hit the floor, he bolted off, out of the establishment and down the street. The others turned to each other. "What has he done?" Lance asked as Leena bent down, now cradling her father's head in her lap. The

Councill Guards did not take long to reach them, mere minutes passed before they entered, taking the four remaining men away at gunpoint, leaving Leena to mourn for her father alone.

Lance sat still, his hands covering his face, as he tried to control his breathing. He knew their fate was sealed if the Councill man had died. The long wait had drained them; the three other men sat quietly, none of them showing an ounce of the life that had been in them two days before.

"I want to see the murdering scums. It is my right. Let me in now." The voice was Leena's, it was strong, decisive and would definitely not take 'no' for an answer. She entered the room and the door closed behind her. "You bastards' you…"

Lance stood up. His eyes were red and tired, his natural bravado no longer apparent in his stance, his shoulders dropped as he came to terms with the cold fact that they were now all dead men. "All I can say is I am sorry, I will assume full responsibility, but please spare my friends." Lance moved toward her, gesturing to his friends as he spoke. As Lance got to the bars, Leena whispered.

"There is no time to lose. My father is dead, and the Councill has called an emergency session to decide your fates. Rumor is that it will not go well for any of you. I will not have you hang for my father's pigheadedness." Leena concentrated as she spoke, rummaging through her pockets. She handed a key through the bars. "Use it to escape. I will see to it that you get away."

"No, I cannot let you do this. I know the law; you will hang in our place, even if he was your father." Lance pushed the key back towards her as he spoke, only to think of his friends, if for some reason this went wrong he needed a way out. "OK, I beg of you, can you do me another favor? Tell the Councill that I give myself over as the sole participant, and that I will forgo the proceedings, to be hanged on the morrow."

"But it was the red haired man, not you."

"Have they found him?"

"No, but they are looking."

"They will not find him, he is too skilled at evasion, he has had too many years of getting himself out of trouble to not be."

"Why do you…"

"These men are the only family I have known, I will not let them die because of my mindless chivalry. They are good men with lives to live."

Hammer peered over from the bench as he spoke, oblivious to what his friend was about to do. "Lance, what you doing over there boy? Nothing stupid I hope."

"Go now, please, and tell them. Don't let us all die for this accident."

Leena's gown flowed over the floor as she shuffled off. "Guards."

"You can have this Hammer character's head; I have no need for him." Lord Dragoon was getting impatient, the Councill wanted Lance's head and there seemed to be no way around it.

"What would we want with this character, when we have your son's head already?" The rotund man placed another grape like fruit into his mouth, the juices flowing down his triple chin as he smiled. He was very happy at this moment. Ever since he had come into the Councill, he had wanted Lord Dragoon dethroned, this was almost as sweet.

"Why do we have to kill anyone? We all know Marcus Pratt was a womanizer and a swine. Why would we press charges when even his daughter objects?" The voice was quiet, but powerful, commanding the attention of the other twenty-two Councill members seated around the table who were listening intently to the argument.

"Why? You have never liked poor old Pratt, why should we listen to you? You blue witch." The rotund man spat out the words aggressively as he spoke.

Parting her veil, the woman raised a clear glass of water to her blue lips, drinking it as though it were wine as her skin glistened beautifully in the dim light that emanated from the center of the table. Putting the glass back on the table she spoke, "Insults are so you, Gremell, as they were Pratt. I believe the *way to a harmonious relationship is through love and giving. Maybe if Pratt was of the same belief he would be here now,"* as she gestured in a flowing motion to the empty seat to the left of her.

"Paleen, you would not even be on this Councill were it not for your... uniqueness, shall we say." Gremell stroked his long gray hair away from his eyes as he placed another piece of fruit into his mouth, spit from his chewing spraying the table as he spoke. "And I can vouch that Pratt gave away his fair share of loving." The vulgar remark came with a smirk as Gremell finished chewing, and licked his lips suggestively.

Bang! Everyone's attention was drawn to the large man as he got up from his chair and slammed down his fist on the table, shaking it violently. His chest puffed out, the veins on his neck bulged, and his muscles clenched and unclenched under the mild effort. "Enough! We need to get this matter sorted, and you two bickering will not help get it done any quicker. Dragoon, what have you that you can use in your son's defense."

Lord Dragoon saw his chance to play his hand. "Lance is willing to die for his friends, even though he did not commit the act of murder. You need a Captain like him to save our Company, one to help stop the uprising of the Strays. A Captain you can control, not one controlled by me, one with integrity that is not corrupt. One to stop an uprising that has been happening under your noses; developing for years, while you played happy Councill."

The members of the Councill all stood up in shock, chattering amongst themselves, all asking the same questions, the tension in the air electric. Taking a deep deliberate breath the large man spoke in response. "What can he do that anyone else cannot?"

"He can carry my name through the ports and stations, chasing down this ship. If I am seen to be taking control of the situation myself, these Strays, and others like them, will see how confident we are of our forces and it will scare these Strays back into their holes. No one needs to know it is not me."

"That's very manipulative, even for you, Dragoon! How do we know that you did not hatch this plan to save your son?" Gremell had stopped stuffing himself with fruit and had stood with the others, hands now placed on the table as he accused Dragoon.

"Oh, but I did have this plan to save my son when I entered, but could I

have fabricated this beforehand?" Lord Dragoon raised his hands. Removing his gloves he directed his blood red palms, devoid of skin outwards, towards the center of the table. "Let me show you." Small images made of light formed above the table; the images started as picture of solid light then formed moving pictures; a movie playing before them. These images showed small gatherings of Stray people, then larger, and larger gatherings over a period of time. An image of a ship with an airplane-like design entered a station, leaving with many Stray children hidden in a wagon. "Need I remind you what happened last time we dropped our guard to the Stray people?"

Raising themselves from the hard benches, Lance and his friends stood as the guards entered the cell area.

"Been nice knowing you all, I could not think of better men to die with." Hammer grabbed the three men, embracing them, winding them with his brute strength.

Lance broke off, stepped away and corrected himself, straightening his crumpled clothing the best he could before he spoke, "I could not think of better men to die amongst either. It has been a pleasure knowing you gentlemen. Hopefully you will remember this day and have a chuckle over something so silly." Lance hoped for the best. If the Councill accepted his proposal then all the other men would be let off with a warning, hopefully.

"You did not do something very silly, Lance, did you?" Boiler removed himself from Hammers hug, looking Lance directly in the eyes to gauge his reaction.

Freddy stepped back also, gauging Lance's reaction by just a glance. "You bloody pompous fool, what makes you think your life is worth more than ours?"

Freddy and Boiler moved as one, hugging Lance intently. "Your father can't even get you out of this one, you know?"

"Lance Dragoon, you have been charged with the murder of one Marcus Joseph Pratt, how do you plead?"

Lance turned to the guard who was reading from the small screen in his hand. *"Guilty."* Turning to Hammer he patted him on the shoulder, slyly passing the jail key to Hammer's hand as he shook it. *"If this does not work and they come back to execute you, get out and run."* Hammer looked curious. *"Compliments of the lovely Leena."*

"But why would you not have used it before?"

"You are all my friends; I would not want to lengthen this friendship if I were to break the thing I vowed to uphold. Plus, we were not meant to be running all the time looking over our shoulders, only to be killed anyway. This was the most sensible course of action for our predicament."

"Fool, we would follow you half way around the galaxy if it meant you would live." Hammer hugged Lance intently as a small tear formed in his eye.

Click. *The door to the cell opened as the guard stood, weapon raised. "Lance, please step outside."*

Hammer saw this as an opportunity to help his friend as he rushed past Lance and slammed into the first two guards, knocking them to the floor. The room lit up blue, as the sirens blared; the two guards behind the first reacting fast. Small handguns at their side were raised to shoot pellets at the man coming crashing towards them. Pop, Pop, Pop, Pop. Hammer fell to his knees, then slowly raised himself again. Pop, Pop, Pop, Pop. Both guards waited, their hands shaking. Hammer raised his head again. Pop, Pop, Pop, Pop. Hammer could feel the darkness creep in as he dropped to the floor beside the first guard and watched as Lance stepped over him, raising his hands as he reached the guards.

"I am ready."

Lance was led down the steel corridors of the citadel. This was one of the many citadels in this part of space, more significant than any other because it housed the Councill. He had always wanted to see the Councill; he had just never envisioned it would be like this. He had dreamt of being a barrister or judge, who would have been asked before the Councill and asked for a "favor". Now this dream would never come true. He knew what the men had said was right, even his father could not get him out of this.

Lance knew his father was important but had never had much to do with him, the man was very busy. All Lance knew was that he was very high up in the Company, and was also very powerful. No one was as powerful as the Councill though. Everyone knew this; and he and his friends had been directly involved in the killing of one of their members. An example needed to be made of someone. With his father in the highest rank, he knew this someone had to be him, Lance Dragoon.

They had made it to the Councill chambers quite quickly, the guards having kept a steady pace. Yet this pace did not lessen as they walked past the chambers, the guards outside the doors not blinking as they passed by.

One of the guards leading Lance glimpsed the perplexed look on his face and spoke harshly, "Your fate is far worse than the Councill." With this they lead him away into an unknown part of the citadel.

The chamber was huge; the doors leading into it were ornate with intricate pictures of dragons and knights carved into them. Lance stopped, studying the shapes in more detail.

"Get in there. The Lord waits for no one!" With a shove, the guard launched Lance into the room. Regaining his balance, Lance looked around, his eyes taking a minute to adjust to the dimly lit room. An unnatural light seeped from what appeared to be an even larger chamber behind this one. The door to this second chamber closed quietly as Lance tried to peer around the door frame to see its contents.

"What makes you think you are better than a Councill member, in that you can kill one without consequences?"

Lance made his way around to an oaken table, thousands of years old and worth half a fleet, its legs and top carved in some ancient art form. As he studied the table he conversed with the man in the room. "Lord. I do not believe I, nor any of my party to be better than the next man, nor do I believe a Councill man to be better than you; or you him. The death was a mere accident, for which I am deeply sorry."

"Are you willing to suffer the consequences for the actions of the others, even though you did not kill the man?"

"Yes, my Lord. I have stated that as counsel to the party accused of the death, I will take full responsibility for the matter. My only regret is that the

punishment is death. I have yet to start my career and my first case seemed to have ended with a hanging, unfortunately my own!"

"Your father cannot help you out of this one. He is not powerful enough to overrule the entire Councill."

"I do not expect my father to bail me out nor, have I ever. I stand on my own feet; if he has intervened it is of no fault of mine."

"So you say you have never required your father's assistance?" Curiosity crept into the voice.

"I never said that, merely that I have never asked for it. This table and the carvings on your door are fantastic; can I ask how long you have had them?"

"Longer than you would believe, boy. The door is but one piece of a puzzle to that which comes to me in my dreams, waking and sleeping."

"Why am I here?"

"You are here to see if what they say is true."

"And what would that be?"

"That my son has finally transformed into a man worthy of my time. A man that would put others before himself."

Lance had missed the subtle change in the tone of the voice as the cloaked man stepped out of the shadows, a tone symbolizing a slight admiration for the man before him. The cloaked figure stepped over to Lance, the silken black gloved hands stretching out to greet him.

"Nice to meet you, son! I wish it was under better circumstances."

"Father." Lance stretched out his arm shaking the hand before him firmly.

"Here is what I think. I need a Captain to command my ship. I have a mission. A mission requiring someone who holds your integrity for the law, for your crew, and for the others who you will be chasing. I would expect you to hold yourself to the same standards you do now, and not falter. I need to know what they are doing, how they are doing it, and why they are doing it. They cannot be killed, I need them captured. All my other Captains would kill first, ask questions later, if they were not bought off first."

"But I am not a Captain; your crew would not want me there."

"My crew will do as you command."

"I do not want this responsibility."

"Do you want the deaths of your friends on your conscience?"

"What do you mean?"

"If you do not take command of my ship, the Councill will execute Hammer. A shame, I hear that it took twelve shots of our strongest tranquillizer to take him down. Four shots can kill a lesser man. I would love to keep an individual like that on my payroll. But if you insist on not taking the Captain's job then I will just have him executed beside you."

"Why?"

"Because I can, and the other two, Boiler and Freddy, I think their parents will owe me a large favor after this, and that is a favor I intend to collect. I do not think that a mere farmer's son like Hammer would get me what I wanted. Maybe I am wrong. You can be the judge of that."

"Who am I chasing and with what crew?"

"Well, my crew of course, never can be too careful. The mark is a ship we have been tracking quietly for some time. The Captain is a smuggler of sorts, Stray children, I think. His first in command is a woman, she organizes the slave trade of those Stray children fit enough. And then there is a large black man. Some say he sells the meat of those Stray children they kill or are too weak, to any one that will pay. I believe there may be a small Stray child on board too. By last report the Captain is somewhat inclined to never let the boy leave his sight."

"Why have you not stopped them yet if their crimes are so terrible?"

"We need to find out their plans and then capture so we can interrogate them. We were hoping they will lead us to their drop points, but so far they have evaded us. They have acquired great wealth in their years of smuggling, arms dealing and thieving. I believe they have been paying my men off, to say the least"

Lance leant on the table before him, his mind swarming with the evil acts this crew had done, and the possibility of it continuing. *"You will guarantee Hammer's safety?"*

"Of course, Son, you have my word."

"I do not really have a choice then, do I, Father?"

Chapter 3

Paleen stood under the dim street light, her pale blue complexion amplified in its ambiance. She was not accustomed to the harsh weather at this end of the citadel. It had only been a matter of minutes standing at the outer area of the citadel, but her thin silken robes did nothing to cover her erect nipples on her ample bosoms. Her delicate, thin, and long hair flowed over her shoulders onto these silken robes, the hair not quite black, more purple, as she ran her fingers through it. She looked around nervously. She did not want to be here, but this meeting was a necessity.

"Pardonn meee missuss, you reckonn wee could have a little lonvinnn?" The drunken man was sloshing a half full glass of ale around, as he swayed from side to side, trying to court the lovely lady before him. "Wellll, how bouttt it loveee?" He questioned again as Paleen tried to turn away, now covering her face with a small silk scarf. "I Saiiid how bouttt somee love. Loveee." The man's voice and hand shook angrily, spilling his beer over the metal decking.

Paleen's face hardened, turning a deep blue and her slender lips curled into a scorn, as she turned to the man. Lowering her scarf, she spoke. "I am not interested, nor are you. You will put down your beer, walk away and forget you ever saw me. Understood?" Paleen's voice was strong and musical, commanding the man. Kneeling down, the man placed his beer on the metal deck, then got up, turned, and left without a sound. With the threat passed, Paleen's complexion softened to a light blue.

"Paleen, you have not lost your touch." The voice was also very strong and musical, but masculine as its owner walked out of the shadows, his blue features glowing. His features, matching Paleen's but being darker in coloration, changed subtly as their eyes connected.

They did not speak in words, just in pictures, each one in the other's mind. It was as if a dance took place, a gentle waltz with neither one leading but following each other into a mutual embrace. Pink colored their cheeks as they became more intimate.

"You know what to do?"

"Yes, it is clear."

"You know what is at stake if you fail?"

"Yes, you have made this clear."

"Do not trust Dragoon, he is still his father's Son."

"Yes. I understand."

The two turned from each other, affection still in their eyes as they left each other's embrace. The man began walking back into the shadows, from whence he had come. He turned slightly at the shadows edge, before blowing a kiss and disappearing into the cold night.

"Good luck, Lallone, my love." Covering her face with her veil, Paleen turned to head back to her home. Back to her lonely existence! Exiled from her people and the ones she loved. She knew Lallone, her husband, was taking great risk in seeing her, but it was time. A necessity. He needed to find them, to save them, before it was too late, again.

"Get me Captain Phillips; his vessel should have landed by now."

"He is waiting outside your chamber, Lord." The guard kept his glance down. He did not want to anger Lord Dragoon. No one ever did.

"Get him in here, fool! What, are you stupid?" Lord Dragoon made his way around to his desk. The desk, one thousand years old was more of a status symbol than useful furniture, left by the past Lord, four hundred and eighty years before. He much preferred to work in the chamber behind this room, the room in which he could be himself.

The guard ushered in an old, short man, badly dressed and drunk, made obvious by the way he stammered into the room.

"Kill me now if you must, Dragoon, do not let them come in the night for me." The Captain slurred as he threw his arms around, trying to emphasis his words.

"You have it wrong, my dear Captain. I merely want to borrow your vessel. My Son is to Captain it for a small while, and after, you can have it back."

"If it is in one piece when he returns. What's to say I want it back?"

"If it is retirement you want, then I can accommodate you. After all, you have given many years of loyal service haven't you? No skimming off the top, no letting smugglers go for a bribe? You are too honorable a drunk for that, aren't you Captain?"

The man started shaking, his face now pale. His eyes, glazed. "Whatever you decide is more than fair by me, Sir."

Dragoon reached for the desk, opening a draw to the side of it. The Captain started to stumble to the door, thinking he was about to be retired. He stopped as Dragoon called out to him.

"Take this as payment, and let me not see the likes of you around again. Or I will do what I should do now. Retire you permanently." Dragoon threw the bag of coins to the man across the vast chamber, finishing the conversation. "Do not spend it all at the tavern, as you may lose your tongue, or you may find yourself dead in the gutter."

The Captain dropped to the floor, scrambling for the bag of coins before scurrying out of the room. The guard opened the door at Dragoon's direction to release the pathetic worm.

"Send word to Lance. He now has command of a vessel. Tell him to be there by tomorrow morning, ten o'clock, and tell him not to be late!"

As the guard left the room Dragoon turned back to the desk in front of him. Pushing a button in the side, he activated a hidden monitor, now rising out of the desk. The screen was in stark contrast to the old desk it raised from.

"Councill." The monitor blinked on. "You can hang Hammer tomorrow; make sure it is at midday."

"As you wish, Lord Dragoon."

"End." The screen blinked off. "Informant fifty-two." The monitor clicked on again, Dragoon waited for a minute then spoke. "Using your money well I see."

The voice from the monitor was casual but surprised. "Yes Sir."

"I need you to complete a special assignment for me. It will mean enough funds for a comfortable retirement for you, and still allow you, 'your pleasures'."

The voice became more exited. "Yes, Sir."

"You are to make sure that your new Captain does not capture the vessel you are going to be chasing. Wound them, but do not kill them."

"Yes, Sir."

"I repeat under no circumstances are you to apprehend or destroy the ship you will be chasing!"

"Understood, Sir."

"End." The monitor blinked off.

"Hey, how 'bout we see how much the prisoner can take again."

"You reckon we can get more than twelve tranqs in him this time?"

"Don't know, but I don't want to be under him this time. I am still aching from last night."

"How you going to wind him up to have a go at us?"

"Tell him he is too late to save that mate of his, I suppose. Lance wasn't it?"

"Of course, we will not open the door this time, will we?"

"Are you stupid? I just wanna have some fun. I don't want to get trampled by that man again, just see him hurt a lot. Especially after the whipping he gave us yesterday."

"Anyway, he is to hang at midday, so if he dies we just hang a dead man."

"Ha, Ha, Ha," The two men laughed cynically as they made their way to Hammer's cell.

Sitting alone in the cell, Hammer's head pounded as he fondled the small key in his hand. He had woken to an empty cell. He had no clue as to what had happened after his attempted escape, or how long he had been unconscious. What if Lance was hanging now, would he be able to save him? Well, he was *going to give it a go, even if it killed him. Standing, he palmed the key and walked to the cell door slipping the key into the lock and turning it. The latch clicked, echoing through the cell block. Bad timing he thought, as two guards walked in through the doorway in front of him.*

"Hammer, do not try to escape again." The guard was shaking as he removed his tranquillizer gun from its pouch and aimed at Hammer.

"Why would I do that?" Hammer questioned. Might as well play with them before I break their necks, *he thought.*

"To save your friend. But it is too late." The guard laughed slightly as he spoke. Hammer reacted to the news, slamming the cell door into his face in fury, breaking the man's nose. Swinging himself nimbly out of the cell, Hammer grabbed the arm of the other man, snapping it in two. The guard dropped to the floor in agony, screaming as his arm hung limply by his side. The first guard stood up, blood gushing from his nose, and raised his gun at Hammer. Pop, Pop, Pop, Pop, Pop, Pop, Pop, Pop, Click, Click, Click, Click.

Hammer stood, grinning. "You got none left, boy." His adrenaline and hatred fueled him on as he head-butted the man, smashing his already broken nose into pieces. With blood splatter covering his face as if some tribal war paint, Hammer grabbed the man by his neck and snapped it like a twig. As the guard fell to the ground the other man started firing, Pop, Pop, Pop, Pop, Pop, Pop, Pop, Click, Click, thump, *Hammer punched the man in the side of the face, knocking him against the wall. "When will you learn?"*

"You do not want to escape." The man managed to say before Hammer crushed his windpipe with his boot.

Two more guards came running in to see what the ruckus was about. Hammer grinned, "More toys."

"Stop."

"Why? What you going to do? Pop me with your toy gun?" Hammer was already making his way towards the men, bloodlust in his eyes.

"No! Because if you are not here to hang at midday, then that friend of yours will die in your place." The guard turned to his co-worker, nervously awaiting Hammer's response.

"These two just told me he was dead."

"They were wrong. Lance is to go free, unless you escape of course." The guard's voice became more confident as he saw Hammer's hesitation.

Hammers shoulders dropped as he sighed, Lance was alive. *"What do you mean, die in my place?"*

The second guard cleared his throat as he babbled the words out. "Lance's father is high up in the Company. He cut a deal with the Councill; your head in a noose in exchange for Lance's life."

Hammer turned, returning to his cell, and slumped to the seat as the two guards regained their courage, laying their boots into him. Hammer did not struggle as he fell to the ground. Well, at least Lance was all right, but if I ever get my hands on that Viny! *he thought as he let the tranquilizers take effect.*

In the early hours of the morning, Lance made his way to the military vessel, escorted by two armed guards. "You think we could stop off and have a talk with Hammer before we go?"

"Our orders are to take you straight to the ship. No stops."

"But what if I will not go, until I see Hammer first?"

"He is still sleeping off the tranqs, I heard. Even if we let you go, he would be in no shape to talk."

The other guard piped up as they rounded a bend and headed towards the hangers. "Do you want to live, boy?"

"Of course I want to live. I am here now, aren't I?"

"Then do not disobey Lord Dragoon, or you will not live long."

They could see a ship; military class, two cannons and laser equipped; bulky, but well-armed for a fight. Eight crew members stood in front, coming to attention as they saw him. The look of disgust in each of their faces was obvious as he walked closer to them. He could not blame them; after all he was taking away their captain and invading their ship.

The Commander stood out of line, greeting Lance with a nod of his head; this was more than an unproven Captain could have hoped for. The

Commander knew who Lance was and how he had got the position. *Lance will have to earn my respect;* he thought, *which was something this boy before him seemed incapable of doing.*

As Lance stood in front of the men, he nodded to each in turn, gauging their expressions for a minute before moving onto the next. One man seemed more relaxed than the others. He held his glance longer.

"Gunnery it is, Sir. Pleased to meet you. If you need anything please ask. I hope I can be of assistance."

"Thank you Gunnery. I appreciate your straight-forwardness. In return I will do the same. As you all know I am your new Captain, a position I did not seek, nor want. As you would not have actively sought out myself, I apologize. Unfortunately, we all find ourselves in an unwanted situation."

The Commander turned to read this man's body language before him, his expression genuine as he contemplated his new Captains fate. Maybe he will not be too bad after all. Anyone would be better than that whining alcoholic that had commanded this ship before him.

"To make this a whole lot easier on us all, I will say this, this is a one mission job. Once it is complete I will be gone, and you can all return to your normal lives, and Captain." Lance could see the postures of the men before him relax slightly as he continued. "We are to apprehend a smaller ship; one crewed by thieves, slavers and worse. I do not expect it to be easy, nor do I expect it to be hard. I do expect that there will be enough problems to challenge us all. I have heard that we adequately out-gun and out-man them, so we have this on our side."

The Commander allowed a smile to slip onto his face. This is going to be real easy. We can take out any smaller ship with two shots, and be home for dinner. *The appointment of this Captain was sounding more and more like a cruel hoax.*

The rest of the crew also let themselves think the best. After years of doing it hard, it was time for a break and they were all happy for the change.

"We are to capture them, not kill them. This vessel's crew has important information Lord Dragoon requires, and we are to deliver it to him in the form of a living, breathing crew."

The Commander blew his top. "Damn!" *he cursed. They never took prisoners; they didn't even know how. The law of space was kill or be killed, everyone knew that.* "What a load of crap. First we baby-sit Lord Dragoon's boy. Then we have to capture and baby-sit some criminal scum."

Lance turned to the Commander. "I am sure I can count on you to baby-sit me, and deliver these scum to my father, or do I get myself a new Commander?"

The Commander stopped short. This man had some balls; maybe he is indeed all right. *"No, Sir, I will do my best to baby-sit you, Sir!"*

Chapter 4

"Captain, Sir, we are here. What are your orders?"

Lance had been caught up in nostalgia, forgetting about his crew. "Have we landed yet?"

"No, we are docking now. We just have to get through the official docking channels."

Lance was very new to this, he did not know the first thing about commanding a ship and it showed. "Can we not avoid the channels?"

Coughing, the Commander piped into the conversation before anyone else could reply. "Only if you want to be found floating in space any time soon. These people do not take kindly to others enforcing their power around here, even a Company ship such as ours."

"Very well then, let me know when we are docked. Commander, get two of your men prepared, and get me when we are ready to search for these criminals." Lance strode off to his chambers, doing his best to hide his embarrassment.

"Garath, how far is Lance from capturing the ones he seeks?" The voice originating from the monitor in the dark room sounded concerned. The monitor was flashing as the figure on the screen moved slightly; every movement from the dark figure, no matter how small, changing the amount of light radiating into the room.

Garath sat with his legs resting comfortably on the desk in front of him, answering eloquently, almost like a teacher would to his student. "He is close I believe, but you need not be so restless. We have it under control."

"But I need these criminals to take us to the planet, or at least show us they know of its location. You should be keeping closer tabs on Lance." The voice from the monitor had an edge to it.

"You dare question my competence after all these years? Do not forget who I am, what I am, or what I know!" The tone in the voice had changed to an aggressive one and the man's legs tightened, the muscles flexing under the silken pants.

"I apologize. You know we are after the same thing. You must understand I have been searching for a long time."

"I do not understand how two hundred years would seem long to someone like you, but I do not care for waiting that long either, so we have that in common. I am, after all, only carrying half your DNA, and I have been exposed to only a small amount of this crystal's energy in recent years. I do not command a position of power, allowing me to horde the crystals as you do. As such, I have been aging much quicker than you." Garath raised the mirror sitting on his desk, looking at his features in it. His face was young, maybe thirty years, his brown hair, thick and curly and a cow's lick hung down onto a chubby but masculine face. Immaculately preened and presented hair covered this face, a beard of ten centimeters all over and a long mustache, curled at both ends. He played with the mustache as he admired his features.

"You look splendid for eighty years, if I do say so."

"Not as good as you for five hundred… I know what is at stake and I will make sure we find it. I want eternal youth as much as you." Reaching over the desk the man turned off the monitor. In the darkness his voice chuckled. "Yes, Lord Dragoon, I will find it. Then I will take the crystals and your place on your throne."

The monitor blinked back on revealing a clean shaven man. He stooped to be seen in the monitor as his jet black hair glistened, given no sign of graying or revealing his true age of forty something. "Garath, I am almost there. We are getting ready to deploy now."

"Good. Make sure you come in hot. Don't let them miss you and definitely make sure you clash with Lance. Ruffle his feathers a little."

The voice from the monitor was hard and military-like and now answered with slight pleasure in it. "I would not have it any other way now, would I?"

"Do not kill him, Zackory! We need him for our plans."

"If you told me what those plans were, we would be on the same page and I would not need to do things on my own." Zackory's brow curled in frustration as he lent forward to fill the screen with his face.

"Don't forget your place for now. When the time is right you will be given enough information to do what is required of you. Once this is done then we can take our rightful places." Garath leant forward in turn, but before he could turn the screen off, Zackory finished his movement and shut off the screen, leaving him in darkness yet again.

Garath leant back in this darkness, relaxing. His hands flexed before he placed them behind his head. It was easy to relax and enjoy these moments of peace when you knew that you would live another hundred, or so, years. His incredible life expectancy was mostly due to that unusual accident. He removed his beard and mustache, placing them on the table before him. No one could see the scarred and horrible lower face that was revealed in this dark room, the scars a direct result of the incident that had transpired more than sixty years ago.

Sixty Years Earlier...

"Captain Garath, we are nearing the location you indicated on the charts."

"Can you spot it yet man, or not?" Garath was young and brash. He had no time for small talk with this officer.

"No, Sir. We are near the location that the disturbance was recorded but have yet to see anything." The young officer was looking into a monitor showing the vast area of space around them. All appeared empty.

"Well get to searching man. Something must have triggered the alarms. We need to find the source of power, so I can take it back with us or claim it for the Company." Garath was sitting in the Captain's chair, with his feet up, but he was not relaxed. His muscles were tense as he sat proud. His face was clean shaven and his chin distinguished. All in all he was a very handsome man.

"But Sir, we can't find what is not there! Maybe there was a glitch in the system?" The officer was clutching at straws. He knew a power signature as large as the one they had recorded must have been made by something huge, and very powerful. It would have to have been a ship many times the size of their vessel; there was no question about that. But it was not here, and this was the spot from which the power had originated.

Garath stood from his chair, flexing his large shoulder muscles. Linking his fingers, he stretched his arms in front of him, cracking them. "Do I need to persuade you to look harder?" His voice had a sick joy to it as he thought of disciplining his crew member.

As if by the mere thought of this punishment, the vessel stopped abruptly.

"What is that?" Garath yelled as he regained his balance.

"Not sure, Sir. Still nothing showing up on the screen." The officer wiped off the sweat beading on his brow. He did not want to get a beating for this disturbance as well.

Garath was searching through the crystal window at the front of the room when he noticed a shimmer in space. The shimmering continued as though an area of space itself had shifted. Walking to the window, he searched for the shimmer again, not daring to blink. He quickly pointed as he saw it reappear. "There it is!"

The shimmer grew outwards from its origin until a complete ship appeared before them. It was small and sleek. Much smaller than the large military vessel Garath commanded. It was unusual with two small wings and a very small bridge area. It appeared that that was all that it seemed to have. From the bridge stared a man. Not just a man, a dog man. The two men locked gazes as they stood squaring off against each other. Neither knew quite what to do. Both men now waited for the other to make the first move.

"What was that? Why have the engines gone off line?" Lallone stood beside the dog-like man, and next to the console of the small vessel.

"Dogny not know, will go find out. Will do that for you, master. Not let you *down. Find out now." Dogny scampered away quickly, dropping down into the pit in the middle of the floor. The bridge was small, maybe two men long, and there was little room to move as Dogny foraged. Throwing one thing after another over his head, Dogny continued; "Screwdriver, ratchet, clamp, wrench, spanner. Oh well, better than nothing. He raised himself out of the pit with a screwdriver and a spanner.*

Returning to the console he dropped to all fours and started working under it, removing this panel and that, as he pulled out wires and other items. In one swift movement he pulled a mass of red wires from the base of the console. "Nope, not right. Master you do something wrong. Dogny not know what is wrong. Master never wrong. Dogny never wrong." As he reached in further, his shoulder pushed up against the console, causing him to stop talking momentarily as he hit his head whilst straining. "MMM cosmic scrambler. That should not be here." As he spoke, he pulled a large red box from beneath the console and the ship surged, lighting up brilliantly before it powered down.

"What is it, Dogny?" Lallone looked concerned.

"Dogny sorry. Did not mean it. Sorry master. Dogny sorry." Dogny's face pouted like a child that had been scorned as he knelt on the floor, the red box still held in his hand. "Someone planted. Dogny should have found. Found before this. Found before we stuck." The ship was now dead in space as its engines powered down completely.

"Can we get them back online?" Lallone was now sitting under the console with Dogny, trying to remain calm as he conversed with his friend to see if they could fix the problem and get the engines back online.

"Better if we not have to cloak. Dogny could work much quicker if not getting..." As Dogny spoke he placed his hand back in the console, yelping as he got yet another shock. "Shock!" Dogny pulled another electrical panel out of the console. The panel sparked as it was removed, and placed back. "Poo, poo, poo, poo. Dogny sore."

"Sorry, Dogny. You know we cannot risk being seen. The Founders do not want us out here. We cannot turn off the power. It will remove the cloak." Sympathy filled Lallone's voice.

"Brrrrrrrrmmmmmmmmmmm" The engine kicked in. They purred as the ship started moving and both men attempted to get up from the floor. The ship

lurched suddenly as though the engines had stopped and both men were flung back onto the floor.

"Sorry, master. The engine must have overheated. Must have been a cooling coil. Will see to it straight away master. Right now master, don't have to ask twice. No you don't, just once you need." Dogny leapt up from the floor as Lallone raised himself, using the console to assist him. As he regained a standing position, he stopped moving. Lallone now stood with his eyes wide open in shock, looking out of the window. Dogny was right next to Lallone in front of the console, looking at his master in confusion.

"What, master? Dogny not..." Dogny ceased speaking as both men now froze. A well-presented man was on the bridge of a vessel before them. A vessel they had crashed into. A vessel with a crew that could now, possibly by all accounts, see them and their ship. It became clear that the man could see something as he stepped closer and closer, shouting orders to his crew and pointing at Dogny.

"Dogny, get us the hell out of here." Lallone's eyes screamed the words as loudly as his mouth did. Before them was a large military class vessel. He recognized it well. It was a Company vessel. As he screamed again the cloaking shimmered. "Now, Dogny!"

It was too late. The cloak dropped as he stood there at the console with Dogny beside him. Both men still stared at the daunting vessel as it loomed before them. Lallone's jaw dropped in shock. He had never bumped into another vessel before, nor had he ever been uncovered. This is bad. Real bad! *He thought, as Dogny stood staring at Garath, and Garath in turn, stood staring at Dogny.*

"What the heck is a dog doing on that ship?" Garath was still staring at the ship in dismay as he had when it first appeared. The dog-like man did not move as he stared back. Turning to his crew, he screamed at them, "Get a boarding party and get me that ship." Garath returned to staring at the dog like man. His thoughts soon turned to wondering how powerful this ship must be to cloak itself.

"Yes, Sir, we will get right on it, Sir." Two of the men standing on the bridge left quickly, headed for their small shuttle craft. "We will try and board her immediately."

Garath did not hear the men, so did not respond. Instead he smiled wickedly as he thought. With that much power and the ability to disappear integrated into this vessel, I would be unstoppable. *He thought of all the wealth he could amass by conducting secret raids on the Company strongholds. He had to get this technology at all costs.*

"Captain, the shuttle is exiting now."

Garath looked away from the dog man for a moment, and watched his two crew members pilot their shuttle around the back of the uncloaked ship, trying to locate a docking clamp to attach with. He looked back, just as the dog man turned and scampered three steps to stand in the middle of the ship. He seemed to continue walking, getting shorter, but he was moving no further. Garath contorted himself awkwardly to look under the small vessel. If his eyes were not deceiving him, the dog man should have had his knees and feet in space by now. As he straightened again he caught a last glimpse of the dog man's head, disappearing as though swallowed by the ship or space itself. Oh well, this is going to be easy, *he thought.* A ship without a crew makes for very easy pickings.

He watched his shuttle swing around again, yet to find somewhere to dock on the small vessel, and he turned to yell at the communications officer. "Tell them to get in that ship now. I don't care what they have to do. Just get in that ship."

Dogny could not believe his eyes. "Poo, poo, poo, poo. He has seen us he has seen us, he has seen us."

Lallone waved his hands in the air as though signaling Garath. Garath did not respond; instead he looked away. Lallone looked to where Garath was looking. "Dogny, he only sees you. He cannot see me. And he has sent a shuttle over to try and board the ship."

Dogny turned from Garath to head down to the pit in the middle of the ship. One step, two steps, three, he was at the pit's entrance. One step, two steps, three steps, he was gone; his body concealed in the darkness of the pit. As he disappeared he yelled back, his voice echoing as though he was in a vast cavern. "Dogny fix this. Dogny fix good." There was silence for a minute or two as Lallone stood there, watching as the man on the other ship got angrier and angrier, now yelling at his crew. There was a loud clunk as something large smashed against the floor. "Hi Ho. Hi Ho. Hi Hooooo, and off to work I go hi ho hi ho hi ho hi ho hi ho hi ho, and of to work I go." Clang, Clang, Clang. *All the sounds echoed through the ship.* Clang, Clang, Clang.

"Mmmmmmmmmmmmmrrrrr." The ship rumbled as it shimmered again. This time the sound continued as it reset and proceeded to re-cloak the ship.

Dogny walked with a slight dance as he came up and out of the chamber. A large hammer was in his hand, resting over his shoulder as he sang. "Hi ho, hi ho and off to work I go hi ho, hi ho."

Lallone took a step to Dogny giving him a big hug, raising him above the ground as he spun him around.

Dogny smiled, as he jumped up and down. Lallone stepped away from Dogny trying to avoid the excited man's movements. He did not succeed as Dogny accidentally let the hammer go, dropping it onto Lallone's foot as he spoke excitedly. "Dogny good. Dogny great. Dogny fixed and did not break."

Lallone wiped a tear from his eye as he hopped around the small ship.

"Master, what is wrong?"

Still hopping, Lallone replied a small smirk on his pained face. "Nothing, my dear old friend, nothing. Let's get out of here."

"Right away, master. Better not be rude. Bye-bye, little fly." Dogny waved to Garath's ship as the cloak completed, watching the anger in the man's face as it turned red.

"What is that damn dog doing?" Garath watched as the dog man re-appeared on the bridge of the ship. He watched as the dog rose off the ground,

and spun around, and dropped the large hammer on the ground. This was in itself odd at best, besides the fact that the whole time it looked as though he was talking to himself. This was going to be easier than he thought. The dog man must be crazy, and a crazy man is easily parted from his goods.

"Captain, the crew on the shuttle have found a docking port and are going to dock with it." The young officer smiled a little in relief.

Garath turned violently to the man speaking and scorned him harshly. "Well, took them long enough." Garath turned back to the ship to see the dog man waving at him as the ship shimmered and disappeared again. "Smart ass little! Where the hell has he gone now?" His face was red and his mood near boiling point, but he was still clear headed. He watched closely, studying the space in front of him. As he made out the shimmering mass moving away from his shuttle-craft, he pointed, yelling, "There. Shoot it down. Shoot it now."

"Where, Sir? I can't see anything." The ships gunnery was extremely worried, his tone betraying him. He could not see anything except their own shuttle now turning to return to their vessel and he did not want to hit that.

Garath stormed over to the weapons console and pushed the gunnery off his seat with a hefty shove that sent him crashing to the floor. Sitting down quickly he grabbed the controls. He squinted his eyes, scanning the space again. The space seemed to be still now. He had almost given up hope when he noticed the space shimmer a few hundred meters in front of them. Excitedly, he aimed and pulled the trigger, sending a volley of cannon fire out of each cannon.

There was a massive explosion mere meters from their left cannon. The shuttle pod from their own vessel was in the line of fire. It exploded into pieces, showering the larger vessel with debris. The vessel lurched and shuddered as its left cannon was ripped from its hull. The first volley from the right cannon exploded around the cloaked ship. The shimmer was obvious for a small time before it re-cloaked. "What the...? What, are they firing at us?" Garath had no idea what he had just done. With debris flying in all directions and the left cannon off line, Garath shot the right cannon again. The second set of volleys followed the first. This time they hit something. The ship before them shimmered as it stopped and became apparent again. "Oh yeah! That's what I mean." In his haste, Garath pulled the trigger again as he sent a third set of volleys at the now uncloaked ship. Another explosion erupted as the cannon fire hit debris that had been thrown from the shuttle pod. This new explosion took out the second cannon. "Heck, what was that? Are they still firing back?" Click, click, click. Garath stopped pressing the cannon trigger as he realized they were no longer functional.

"Get our shuttle on the line. I want them to get me that ship before they repair it again." Garath was red-faced but relatively happy barking orders. The smaller vessel seemed to be dead in space and he could not see any crew. The charred remains of one of his crew floated by the window.

"But Captain, you just shot down our only shuttle. There is the crew." The officer pointed as the second body floated past the window.

As the man spoke, Garath watched his dead crew float past. He turned his attention to the damaged ship, looking on as the dog man stood up at the console and madly pushed buttons. In one fluid motion Garath flicked open the red case on the weapons control panel before him, revealing a switch. He flicked the switch eagerly. Wrrr Wrrr. The bay doors did not open. They were jammed as a result of the two close explosions. He tried flicking the switch again. Wrrr, Wrrr. "If I cannot have this ship no-one can." He screamed, slamming his hand onto the panel. Wrrr, Wrrr, clunk. The two laser bay doors jutted out, moving the debris that had been in their way as they opened. The laser cannon extended out as it charged. As he lined up the uncloaked vessel, Garath thought of the wasted technology he was about to destroy. Well, maybe they would be able to salvage some of the wreck. It was more than could be said for his own shuttle.

"Up, up and away, I say." Dogny's spirits had risen since the ship was cloaked, and they were headed away slowly from the attacking ship. They could not travel quicker as they would give away their location. The small vessel lurched and shuddered as a volley of cannon fire hit them. The force of the volley knocked both men to the floor. Dogny was dazed and sat there for a second getting his bearings. "Well got our cloak still, we have." The second set of volleys hit the little ship. The hull creaked and buckled under the volley. Bzzzzzz, Bzzzzzzzzzz. The cloak dropped as power was diverted to structural integrity. "Dogny bad. Jinxed I did. No cloak." In a very fluid motion, Dogny *jumped off the floor to the control panel. Frantically he pushed and pulled several levers and buttons, to no avail. The ship stayed uncloaked. "Dead in space we are. Dead in space!" His face drooped as he looked at Lallone.*

Lallone had not got up, instead he nursed his forehead. He could feel the presence of the two that had died. He felt their pain as they burned for seconds in the cold darkness of space before they died of asphyxiation. "When will they leave us alone? No wonder the Founders do not want us out exploring. If all the species are this hostile, we will be killed before we find Paleen." As he spoke, a new sensation came over him, a presence that seemed very familiar. Looking at Dogny he spoke quietly. "They are using the crystal to supply their weapon. If I can contact it, I can ask it to power down. Will that give you enough time to get us away from here?"

"Dogny get us moving, get us running again. Dogny won't let us down." Dogny stopped looking at the console. As he walked towards the black pit in the middle of the ship, he grabbed the hammer again. "Hi Ho, hi ho, and off to work I go; hi ho, hi ho." Clang, clang.

Lallone closed his eyes, holding his temples as he concentrated. His mind searched for the crystal's presence that he had felt moments earlier. As he found the crystal, images flashed from his mind to that of the crystal, showing it the truth of the act it was about to commit. To fire at them would be to destroy two of the Creator's creations. To murder one that was created in its Creator's image.

The crystal did not respond well to these images. Its reaction was severe, blocking itself from being harnessed as it had been many times before. As it got angrier it continued to horde its own power, keeping it from the Company vessel, refusing to let it be used for such an act. Over time it got hotter and hotter. Its core burned, a sensation that touched Lallone's mind. Lallone stooped over as the pain intensified. In desperation, he broke the psychic bond between them, as he tried to prevent getting mentally damaged. Lallone did not need to be connected to feel what happened next. The crystal burnt through others. Their souls cried out to him, to anyone, and then its thoughts became muffled. Its emotions leveled out, as its burning pain lessened. It had lost its fight, and its will to survive. Its life force sparked up momentarily and Lallone allowed himself a fleeting hope. His heart sank as the spark dulled and against its will, its life force was sucked out of its shell. Then there was nothing. The crystal was gone from Lallone's mind, as were the two souls.

Garath had seen the light illuminate on his panel to show the laser was charged. Now all he had to do was flick the switch. He smiled as he waited for the explosive blast that would mean the end of the small ship in front of them. Click, click, click… "Why will this laser not fire? Damn it. Get back on your seat, boy, and fix it." Garath was fuming, all he had to do was fire on this ship with the charged laser, and it was not working. He moved off the chair to hunch over the gunnery that he had pushed off the chair moments earlier.

The gunnery was now re-seated and frantically working to find the problem. "Sir! We are getting a large overload recorded from the crystal that powers the laser."

"How can that be?"

"Maybe the debris damaged the power regulation of the crystal when it hit our vessel." The officer was only guessing. He had no idea what the problem was.

"What can we do about it?" Garath was more than annoyed. This small ship he was trying to capture seemed to have more lives than a cat.

"We need to abandon ship, Sir." The gunnery's voice betrayed his fear. He knew the consequences of a crystal explosion. There would be nothing left of the vessel they were on.

"In what? If I recall correctly I was told, not so long ago, I blew up our only shuttle, doing your job as you could not see the target." The thick sarcasm dripped from Garath's mouth as he spoke. "I may suggest you do your job now and work out what we need to do so you do not get us all killed."

"Sir, we need to get the crystal cooled, and quickly." The young officer had removed himself from his own console and made his way to the gunnery's station. He now pointed to a red display lighting up on the panel before them. The panel showed three full bars as they watched the red line climb further. "When this fills, we are dead."

"Get to it, boy. Now!" Garath followed the officer as he turned from the gunnery and his station and ran out of the room.

"Sir, we have four bars left." The gunnery's voice echoed through the corridors as the two men worked.

"Are you sure this is going to work, boy?" Garath was again standing over the officer.

"Sir, the only way to get the crystal stable is to cool it. Do you have any other suggestions?" The young man was talking while trying to remove the panel, fumbling in his nervousness. The large, heat-resistant gloves added to the awkwardness, making it hard to remove the metal plate from the wall that was housing the crystal. A thousand colors seeped out of the gaps as the crystal inside glowed intensely, ready to explode at any moment. A long glass cylinder full of a green cooling liquid and a pair of long tongs were positioned beside him.

"Three bars left."

Opening the cover, the officer fell back screaming, as a wave of heat exploded through the area around him and burnt his face and eyes. Garath, quick to react, swung his body up against the wall, his back now hugging it as the heat wave blew past him.

"Two bars left."

Kicking the officer's body out of the way, Garath ripped the large heat resistant gloves from his hands. As he put on the gloves, he watched the heat expelling from the small cavity. Kneeling down he grabbed the tongs, reaching with them into the chamber, and fumbling to get hold of the crystal.

"One bar left."

The heat from the compartment was still intense, burning his hands even through the gloves. He reached further and further but he just could not reach it. As the heat became more unbearable he did the only thing left to him.

"The meter is full."

He plunged his whole arm into the chamber with the lower part of his face exposed directly to the heat. He could hear himself scream silently as the heat seared through his jacket and clothes and burn his lower face. He did not dare to open his mouth in fear the heat would melt his insides. He felt the tongs lock onto the crystal and he felt the pain. It was too unbearable. He screamed aloud as he pulled the crystal out of its cavity. The cooling liquid bubbled as he lowered the crystal into it, the fluid spitting all over his already burnt chin.

"The meter is dropping, well done." The gunnery's relieved voice echoed through Garath's pained mind as he felt the crystal's power flow through him, searing his insides. His tongue and vocal cords melted through the intense heat, his mouth now wide open, seared in place. He had no voice left to scream. The power flowed out of the crystal into his mouth and into his body. The body that had already been partially changed to absorb the crystal's power. His body was half modified at conception, as he was the son of the altered Lord Dragoon. He had no choice; he dropped to the floor, falling on his side. His body had given up. His last vision before he blacked out was that of the cooling tube shattering and the crystal falling to the floor beside him. His wide mouth absorbed the power of the crystal and the power repaired and fixed what it could of his damaged body while he slept. The crystal blinked out as all its energy was depleted. Its shell now just that, a shell, as all its life was now gone. The power had been completely sucked up by this man. This leech.

"No Lord Dragoon. We do not know how much longer he will be in a coma."

"Get me when he awakes." Lord Dragoon's voice was anxious. He had waited three months, and his son had not completely recovered. It seemed that everyone with an opinion was saying it was a miracle that Garath was alive, and most of his wounds had healed. Dragoon knew better. His son had absorbed the power of the crystal as he himself had done those many years ago. Dragoon watched as Garath continued feeding off the energy around the room, as he was doing. He had, over many years, trained his own body to absorb what power he could, from that around him. He also knew that his son had absorbed too much energy from the crystal, and his body must expel it in order to find a safe level. Then it would need to be maintained. So every day he placed his hands on his son, funneling a great deal of power from him. He would leave him enough energy to repair his broken body with, but not enough to kill him.

Like clockwork, each day he came back to find his son had replenished the energy, and was again dangerously close to death. Dragoon could not understand how he was absorbing so much power in such a short period of time. He had to be the first to speak to him. To uncover the truth of this immense power and to ensure no one else would find out what really happened.

"Father." Garath awoke groggily as he reached his arm out before him. Pain burned through his body so intensely he could not distinguish where it originated. Lord Dragoon grabbed his son's hand, and with the other, ushered everyone out of the room. "What has happened to me?"

Lord Dragoon pulled a mirror from the night table beside him. Garath looked at it. He could not recognize himself. His face was hideous. His lower face was covered in welts and sores. He pulled his father down to him and whispered, "Kill me."

As his face was pulled close to his son's, Lord Dragoon felt the energy being drawn from him. He could see the energy as it entered Garath through his damaged skin, and Garath's skin glowed as he lost consciousness again.

"So simple," Lord Dragoon whispered, "the skin is a barrier, limiting the amount of power I absorb."

Garath woke. The room was dark and quiet. His face felt unbearably painful. As he tried to touch his face, his arms stopped abruptly. The manacles attached to him clinked as he strained against them. He lay in the darkness for what seemed like years, screaming…

"Patience my son. You will be freed in good time."

Chapter 5

The Commander interrupted Lance's thoughts, as he entered his quarters, "Lance, we are ready," with two armed men waiting slightly behind him.

"Very well, 'Commander', let us get to it then." *Cannot even bring himself to call me 'Captain'!* Lance thought, as he emphasized 'Commander', *see how he likes it.*

The four men exited the ship, as the landing bridge opened onto the metal hull of the station. As they walked down its length, Lance glanced around. The docking bays were full of ships, hundreds of ships, and many configurations he had not seen before. His inexperience overwhelmed him as he turned to the Commander whispering, "How are we meant to find their ship in this? We are not even sure if it is here?"

The Commander was walking quickly and with purpose, his rifle over his shoulder, as he answered the question with little enthusiasm. "My informant was very clear; the ship we require was seen heading to this station mere hours ago. We will not apprehend their ship, though. We will try and apprehend them whilst they are in the act of Stray smuggling, which will help you better try your case, and get you off my vessel, and possibly stop my vessel from being damaged!"

"But we do not know any of their appearances."

"How hard is it to find a Stray boy, black man, a woman and a dozen Strays piled into a wagon?"

Lance quietened at this comment. He really felt silly now. Concentrating on the chase at hand, he spoke sternly, "Well we had better not chat all day, off to catch the criminals."

The Commander smiled at the pathetic attempt of Captaincy, continuing on his quick descent into the crowds of people massing around the docking bays. As he talked, the Commander asked subtle questions, ones that could be interpreted but not lied about. Within thirty minutes they were hot on the trail of the criminals they sought. Turning to Lance, the Commander spoke, ensuring he gave him his full attention. "We are maybe ten minutes away from their destination at most. It is rumored that there is a gathering of Stray children a short distance from here. No doubt our criminals will be there as well."

"Well done, Commander. I can see why my father placed me-" Lance was thrown off balance as a large man crashed into him. Lance turned, forgetting about his conversation, shouting at the man that had just hit him. "Hey you! Stop!"

The figure stopped and turned slightly, the weight of the bag on his shoulder shifting slightly as he did so. The crowd stopped their jostling and quietened as they waited for a fight, while the Commander and his men closed in on Lance, covering him with their weapons in case of the worst.

"Yes, you." Lance pointed at the man that had stopped. "A little manners goes a long way, or were you dragged up?"

The figure turned to face Lance, making it obvious that a body was slung across his shoulders. "Sooorry, Siiir." The man swayed as he talked. "I waas trying too geet myy mate home before the wife knooows he is goone. Had a few tooo many, and she is a feisty oone. If you knooow what I mean." The man winked a sloppy wink as he lost his balance, catching himself before he fell to the ground.

"Be on your way then, but be careful next time."

The man did not need to be told a second time, "Yees, Siiir. Thank yooo, Siiir." He left, stumbling off into the crowd that was now dispersing again.

"Can we go now, Lance?"

"Yes, Commander."

The Commander leant into Lance whispering aggressively into his ear so no others could hear. "You ever heard of discretion boy? Now they will undoubtedly know we are here." The Commander's nostrils flared as he stormed off, leaving Lance to straggle behind. This was going to be a lot harder than he had originally thought. Lance's face returned to the all too familiar blush of late.

They had taken no more than ten steps when they saw that the area before them opened into a dark expanse, with a small, barely lit fire, glowing in the distance. Lance bustled through the Commander and his men who had stopped and were waiting in the darkness at the extremities, assessing the area in front of them before entering. They did not follow.

"If it isn't the little puppet, Lance."

Lance turned, his eyes trying to focus as he peered into the darkness. "Show yourself."

A tall man with jet black hair stepped forward and into the fire's light. "Better, little puppet?"

"Why do you call me a puppet, Sir?" Lance was trying to be polite, yet his fists clenched and unclenched in frustration.

The tall man swung his arms around the area before them as he spoke. "Were you not sent here by your father to apprehend… That's right. You're too late to apprehend anyone, aren't you? Look around, they are long gone. Well, you at least talked the ear off one of them." The man laughed an evil laugh that echoed through the darkness.

"The bloody drunk!" Lance turned to run back in the direction that he had come.

"Not so fast! As I said, you are just a puppet. I do not like puppets. I am hunting those you seek. If you get in my way, I will…" The man gestured with two fingers as though cutting something. "Not hesitate to cut… your strings, shall we say?"

Lance returned his gaze to the man's eyes as he spoke. "If you know my father then you will not interfere. I will be out of your way soon enough." Lance went to make his way off again.

"Sorry, I don't think I can let you do that." The man placed his hand on his pistol, holstered to his black pants, and patted it.

Lance looked back to the fire, took a step towards it, then turned, running in the direction he had come. *Thump.* Straight into the frame of a shorter man, built like one big muscle. The man's immaculate appearance was in contrast to the rough beard covering his face, although the beard was artistically shaped. Lance raised himself onto his knees, only to waver and drop to all fours as the man spoke.

"You're a little inexperienced at this Captain thing, aren't you?" The man leant forward, giving Lance a hand as he preached to him. "You need to make sure you hold all the aces. Say, have two or three of your men keep a close eye on their Captain, so he does not befall foul play."

Lance grinned as the man helped him to his feet, remembering that the Commander and two others still waited in the darkness for his word. As Lance stood, he studied the man's features. They seemed very familiar but he was not sure where from.

The black haired man turned to the other. "What are you doing here, brother?"

"Could not have a family reunion without me, could you Zackory?" The man wiped his hands together, removing the dust after letting go of Lance's hand.

"Or is it that you do not trust me? Don't trust me to baby sit our little brother, do you Garath?

Lance looked at both men in astonishment. These men looked familiar as they both had his features, in one way or another. Each man was born from a different mother, but their resemblance to each other was still there.

"Zackory! What would have stopped you from shooting our poor brother where he stands, if I was not here to?"

Zackory did not have time to respond as Lance cut in, "This." He clicked his fingers as he spoke. *Click, Click, Click.* The Commander and his two men released their safeties on their guns, still not revealing their positions.

Zackory drew his gun in response, removing the safety and pointing it at Lance.

Garath took two deliberate steps to place his hand on Zackory's gun, lowering it as he spoke. "Bravo, brother. We may yet make a captain of you."

"If you live that long, little brother." Zackory spat out the words as he holstered his gun.

Lance knew the men he was searching for would be gone by this time so he watched the two men as they walked into the darkness; arguing amongst themselves about who was right, and who was wrong on how to handle Lance. As their final whispers died down he turned to the fire. As he walked over to it, something caught his attention, a glint, but it was suppressing the light, not reflecting it. A box lay behind the fire, its black exterior continuing to catch the small flames from the fire as he picked it up. Fondling it with his fingers, he thought of the coincidence of meeting another two of his family members in such a short time. This was peculiar indeed. As his thoughts of family and coincidences died off, he again returned to the chase at hand. Searching the area he noticed the scuffed patterns to the decking. Obvious signs of a struggle, *the poor children*. Blood stained the ground behind him. *Murderous scum*, he thought. "Any day now I will have you, any day now."

As he left with purpose in his stride he let the box he was holding fall into the fire, the fire's flames sparking up slightly as they tried to engulf the object.

"SSShhhhh." Scrycher stopped suddenly, holding his finger to his mouth as Blink awoke from his slumber. Blink's scales were raised and he was hissing violently into the crowd of people massing before them.

Scrags grabbed Blink's nose harshly, closing the jaw in the middle of a hiss. Delicately, he used the other hand to caress the little dragon's back. Blink calmed slightly, now purring, but those big eyes continued to comb the crowd before them, with his scales raised.

"What ya think? Company?" Chelsea glared at Scrycher as she asked the question.

"Yes Chelsea, I know. If I had listened we would be back at the ship by now. We cannot dwell on that at the moment. There are four Company men, and one Company Goon." Scrycher pointed the men out in the crowd. The five men were positioned such that Scrycher and his crew could not get through the crowd unnoticed by them. "I want you to go that way, through that gap, and meet me at the ship. Do not stop, and for no reason do I want you to turn around, or come back for me. Do you understand?" Scrycher's face was concerned but solid, the expression telling Chelsea that she had better do as he said.

"But how-?" Scrycher cut her off. "I'll flash them. What do you think? Just get going."

"Yes, boss." Chelsea spoke quickly to the others before leading them to the opening. "Good luck, Scrycher." She called as she left.

"Luck ain't got nothing to do with it." Scrycher mumbled under his breath as he strode off, quickly gaining momentum. He dodged the people in the crowd until he slammed into an arrogant looking, slender, blond haired man. The man went sprawling sideways, struggling to stay on his feet. Scrycher did not stop his own momentum, which carried him further into the crowd.

"Hey you! Stop!" The voice matched the man's presence; arrogant and bold. Scrycher had picked his mark well. Turning while still in motion, he staggered, partly to balance, and a lot of acting, as he turned to the man, ensuring the face of the storyteller thrown over his shoulder could not be seen. "Yes, you."

The crowd shifted making way for these men to have their showdown. Scrycher knew his performance was critical as he glanced sideways, he could see the wagon and his crew edging their way quickly through the distracted crowd and sighed in relief as he continued.

"Sooory Siiir." Scrycher swayed as he talked, emphasizing his slur as though drunk. "I waas trying too geet mee mate home before the wife knooows he is goone. Had a few tooo many and she is a feisty oone. If you knooows what I mean." Scrycher then winked a sloppy wink, directed at Chelsea, who had turned to check on his progress.

Chelsea was concerned. She had not taken her eye off Scrycher and the

Company men through the whole drama. The fifth man, a man in black, seemed to be enjoying the show. He now wore a cynical grin as he brushed his jet black hair from his eyes. The three Company men were now in a defensive position around the man Scrycher had collided with. *Smart,* she thought. Scrycher must have realized this man was the leader, and played his hand accordingly.

As Scrycher winked he feigned a fall, acting like he'd lost his balance, sloppily regaining his composure a moment before he would have hit the ground.

The man replied just as Scrycher had hoped, his crew now through the crowd and safely heading towards the ship, increasing speed to a slow jog.

"Be on your way then, but be careful next time."

Scrycher did not have to be told twice. He spoke as he turned again, fumbling as he entered the crowd. "Yees, Siiir. Thank yooo, Siiir." As he rectified his stance, and strode off quickly, he could see the crowd dissipating, and with it the Company men; but not before one of the men leant over to the other, and whispered. Scrycher's heart quickened. Were they found out? The young man's facial expression changed to that of a schoolboy that had just been scolded by his teacher. Scrycher allowed himself to smile as the other Company men left in the opposite direction. His heart beat slowed, as he wiped the sweat from his brow. "That was too close."

A small, solid man dressed in black walked into Chelsea. She froze, her jaw dropped. This was another Company man, finely preened down to his peculiar mustache.

"I would stop gawping if I were you. The others won't take long before they realize they were fooled. Well, they shouldn't anyways."

"What?"

"Off with you before I change my mind, and capture you for myself. Nice prize you'd be. And I can imagine as a reward for your capture; your head sitting on my desk... at the head of the Councill! MMMMMM." The man looked up as he stroked his mustache. Turning, he left towards the others as Chelsea regained her composure.

"What the? Chelsea, you all right?" Jaxter had stopped the wagon and turned to aid Chelsea, only to have the man leave.

"Weird little man. Let's get out of 'ere." Chelsea looked towards their destination, not wanting to think what would have happened if the man had wanted them taken prisoner, or worse.

"What we waiting for? Capture!?" Scrycher had come up on them fast and was now motoring towards the ship.

As they approached the ship, Scrycher stopped, giving Chelsea the story teller to carry the remainder of the way. "I have a little business to attend to."

The others went about loading their cargo of Stray children onto the ship, and Scrycher made his way to the guards' mess located just outside the hanger.

"Phypee! How are you, my old friend?" Scrycher smiled, his eyes glowing as he addressed the tall, skinny man, who was comfortably dressed in the green uniform of an inspector.

The man turned, running his fingers through his immaculately preened silver hair. He peered at the man before him, stroking his clean shaven chin, and then his eyes lit up. He spoke with a slight accent, as he hurriedly traversed the two steps to Scrycher, grabbed his arm, and pulled him into a hug. "Been too long, I have not heard that name for so long, my friend. I had not seen you for so long that I thought that the job may have finally caught up with you. Especially after giving you my intel on the story teller." The man gestured to Scrycher, "Sit, have a drink, and tell me what ails you."

"Sorry, Philippe. This is purely business. I am in a pickle." Scrycher's grasp on his friend's arm tightened. "We are carrying the normal load, but that tip of yours worked out, we have the story teller, unfortunately he has come with two separate Company crews as a bonus. A minimum of one Goon and one Military. They are hot on our tail."

"Oh, you've pissed someone off a great deal since I served with you then. Never thought you'd be able to cope without me, proven me right, I see."

The man laughed slightly, knowing the extent of the situation that Scrycher and his crew were still in. "Tell me, my Chels' still on the crew?"

"Yep, and she still has a way with words." Scrycher let go of Philippe's arm. "You have certainly done alright by yourself." Scrycher gestured around the room, ornate in different things the guards had acquired from vessels docked at this station. Scrycher stopped looking around, grabbed his friend by the shoulders and shook him slightly. "What do you say, can you help us?"

"No probs. Boys, we've got a couple of Company vessels to inspect." As he spoke, a little joy sprung into his eye. "Be the most fun we have had in a while."

Scrycher dragged the small framed man to him and hugged him again. "I owe you one, Father."

"You'll owe me more than one, Son."

"Patience was never you forte, was it Zackory? We will have what we want, soon enough." The bearded man was again, stroking his mustache, as he walked and contemplated the actions of the last few hours.

"You are a fool, just like our younger brother there. You prance around like a puppet, and don't even see it." Zackory was red faced from being outwitted by his younger sibling, and was not afraid to show it. "We could have taken them down where they stood. But no, you want them followed. What are we to do, when we lose them again?"

Garath reached into his pocket, pulling out a black box. Extending its aerial, he flicked a switch. Beeping in time with a little red light, the box came alive. A grin crossed his face as he spoke, "Why would we lose them, little brother? I have them, just where I want them. Courtesy of the young lady, now carrying my locating bug in her jacket." Garath thought back to the bump and plant that had worked so easily on the girl, Chelsea.

"You are definitely the planner." Zackory's demeanor did not change as they neared the hanger, and he raised his voice.

"I still say, we should have killed them all."

"Stop!" Philippe stood before them, hands raised. "We have orders to search your vessels, as you may be harboring fugitives." Philippe smiled at this little thought. He had thrown in the fugitive comment as a little irony. He was, after all, helping the fugitives to escape.

Zackory walked up to Philippe, placing his arm on his shoulders. "Now, we can work this out, can't we?"

Click, Click, Click. Philippe's men raised their rifles, removing their safeties as Philippe winked at Scrycher's ship, to let him know he had the situation at hand.

"I am sure we can, once we look through your vessels." Walking to the hanger, Philippe led the men to their vessels. Their vessels were located side by side, with another two of Philippe's guards, positioned at each vessel's entrance.

Scrycher watched from the cockpit as he gave the order. "Get us out of here, Chelsea."

Philippe had made his way up onto the landing platform of Zackory's ship. He stood there, two guards now positioned before him, three behind, with Zackory in the middle. He was not taking any chances. Garath stood on his landing platform, with two guards guarding him.

"Well, let's enter then, shall we?" Philippe was excited. He had not entered a vessel of this caliber before, and was anxious to see what was inside.

"You have made a grave mistake. I am normally a very patient man. You have miscalculated my patience, and my contempt for misuse of authority. I will, indeed, teach you a lesson. Unfortunately for you, you will not have the chance to learn from your mistake." Garath called out, nodding to Zackory as he swiftly raised his hands. His large hands grabbed both the guards before him, their fragile necks now in his powerful grasp. He squeezed on their throats, crushing their windpipes slowly. Raising their bodies above the deck, his powerful arms flexed and the men's legs flailed about as they tried to get some sort of footing. They dropped their guns, their hands grabbing at those massive hands around their necks. Garath's face was stern, as he positioned a thumb on each of their jaws and quickly flicked his hands to snap both men's necks. He flung them from the platform, onto the deck below.

He turned to Philippe, who had raised his fire arm, and was now pointing it towards Garath. There was a flash, as Zackory's arms subtly matched Philippe's actions. Philippe felt a cold pain shoot through his left hand, before it dropped to the floor, and the front of his weapon fell to the deck. Blood spurted from the stump remaining, and Philippe dropped to his knees. Dropping what was remaining of his rifle, he grabbed at his stump, trying to stem the bleeding. Zackory's arms stretched outwards as he launched two hidden blades from his sleeves. These knives lodged themselves into the windpipes of two of the men before him. The three men behind panicked, and in the confusion, faltered. This was all Zackory needed. Two thin and razor sharp blades extended out of his sleeves, one covered in Philippe's blood, the other clean. One step backwards was all it took, his arms seemingly never moved. All three men dropped, their heads rolling across the floor, and under the vessel.

Zackory turned back to Philippe, who was still struggling to stem the bleeding from his missing hand. Withdrawing the blades into his sleeves, Zackory extended his hand. In his dazed state, Philippe accepted the hand and rose. With Philippe upright, Zackory tensed his arm. His other arm moved from his side, the sword extending for seconds as it severed Philippe's arm at the elbow. Zackory's foot planted in Philippe's chest, launching him from the vessel's platform, to land with a 'splat' on the deck below to bleed out.

Zackory looked curiously at the arm for a moment, as he turned it over in his hands. Looking up at the fleeing ship, and Scrycher staring back, he skewered the arm. Scrycher stared back with glazed eyes as Zackory waved the hand from side to side, exaggerating the movement as he smiled. His sickly smile continued, as he used the arm to prod the other bodies. Seeing no movement, he kicked them aggressively from his platform to the deck below. He flung the severed arm onto the limp body of Philippe. Slowly looking up, he licked the extended blade that was covered in blood, his movement exact and exaggerated again, as he taunted Scrycher. His face contorted into a wicked, evil smile, his mouth now covered in blood as his eyes glistened. *Nothing like killing your surrogate father to keep me in your thoughts until we can finally meet in my little trap... my worthy mouse*, he thought to himself.

Sirens sounded, lights flashed and the bay doors started closing. "Get us out of here. Now!" Scrycher was racked with guilt, but he could not throw away the only advantage he had obtained. The ship turned and glided out of the bay as the doors were closing, leaving his dear friend to rot on the deck of the hanger below.

"What happened, Boss? Philippe sort them out for us?" Chelsea tone was light as the hanger doors closed behind them.

Clearing his throat, Scrycher replied, "Yeah, Chelsea, he got them sorted for us." Turning, he headed to his quarters. "Call me when we get to the location. Rod, you know the drill. To the galley please!"

"But Scrycher." Rod was pleading as much as Rod could.

Scrycher's voice was hard and cold as he spun around, "Don't test me, or I'll space you." His fists clenched and raised as if to knock Rod's head off. His jaw locked, and he ground his teeth, as he stared through him, barely checking his rage to leave; every step now echoing through the ship as he stomped to his quarters.

Chapter 6

It had been many hours since the alarms had started. The flashing lights had been turned off, and the guards had allowed Lance access to his vessel. Any hope that he had of capturing the criminals was now dashed, and Lance was having trouble thinking over the sirens. Both his brothers stood on their vessels' platforms. Neither had been fast enough to get out of the hanger before the doors closed, but neither man looked concerned. They were clean and well-dressed, nodding slightly to him as they returned to their ships as if nothing had happened.

Lance stood, watching as the clean-up crew put the last of the body parts into the carts, then wheeled them away to be spaced. *No man should have to die like that,* he thought. He turned as his brothers departed. Their sleek and stealthy vessels packed three times more fire-power than the one that Lance commanded. He was glad they were on his side, well, sort of.

As Lance turned back to enter his vessel, he noticed a shimmer out of the corner of his eye. As he focused on it, he could see the shimmer grow and lowered onto the deck. A tall, blue figure stepped gracefully onto the shimmer, and the gown it was wearing flowed with him, mimicking his movement. Lance stood, mesmerized, all other sounds and movement like a distant dream. Could it be? He had heard of this race, older than time itself. Supposedly, they had one of their species serving on the Councill. She was at least two thousand years old; having joined the Councill just after the Stray home world was destroyed. She had not aged in this time, or so the rumors told.

As this figure lowered itself to the ground, by what could only be described as levitation, another creature came from the shimmer. In stark comparison to the first, this one was erratic and its snout pointed to the sky as it walked, sniffing as it went. Even over the sirens, he heard cracking as it twisted its neck sideways in a flicking motion. Lance had never seen this type of creature. This was nothing unusual. After all, the Company occupied a large part of space that covered over a hundred other species that were not native to the Councill's home planets. The creature spoke in rapid spurts that matched his movement. The blue man stared at the dog man as he spoke to him, and then walked off.

Lance watched as they left, a strange feeling coming over him, *is someone searching through my mind*. As he thought this, the blue man turned to him. He looked directly into Lance's eyes, as the dog man bounded off. Lance buckled, reaching for his temple; the pain like a hot needle inserted into his head.

"What was I doing? Where have my brothers' vessels gone?" Lance looked around. The area in front of him was clear, and ships were now taking off by the dozens. The little incident of the death of the security guards on the station was enough to scare some of the more desirable inhabitants from this station. He did not remember that he had just witnessed one of the race known as 'the Founders'. Confused, he turned, the slight headache he had developed, blurring his thoughts.

Lallone gracefully glided down his transparent ship's platform, and onto the deck below. A slight shimmering was obvious below his feet as he moved, with the gown he was wearing concealing the fact his feet never touched the floor. He did not like these places; they were for the lesser species to inhabit. Unfortunately, this task was important. Otherwise Paleen would not have sent him on it.

A dog-like human exited the craft behind him, with none of the grace or beauty of Lallone. The creature raised its head, its snout pointing upwards. Sniff, Sniff, Sniff. The creature then flexed its shoulders backwards, flicking its neck from side to side, its neck cracking as it did so. "So happy." Flexing its neck from side to side again, the creature continued, "All cricks are out, master. Time to search."

Lallone stared into the dog man's eyes.

"Yes master, the trail is fresh. Close they are, not many hours now. We should find them today, should we not? Weeks gone by very close now." The dog man was throwing his head all over the place; from side to side, up and down, as if he could not control it. Sniff, Sniff, Sniff. "Scent found, follow me. Off to see the wizard, the wonderful wizard of Oz lala lala lala the wonderful wizard of Oz." The dog man bounded lightly into the crowd that stood before the hanger doors. His skipping stopped abruptly. "Master!"

Lallone was standing, looking at a neatly dressed young man on his ship's landing platform. "He cannot know I am here." Lallone was mumbling to himself. "Paleen was wrong about this one; he is indeed special; we may be able to trust, but not yet." Lallone squinted as Lance reached for his temple. "He cannot know I was here." Lance stood dazed, looking out towards Lallone, seeking him, but not seeing. Satisfied, Lallone turned and headed towards the dog man, patting the back of his neck in recognition that he was back in the chase.

"All right master, everything all right?" The dog man looked worried, his head turning sideways as he asked the question. Lallone nodded as the dog man raised himself. The two, even though so different, seemed to be very similar. The dog man, standing upright, was of the same stature and height as Lallone. Their masses were of equal standing, though Lallone carried his like a feather and the dog man carried his like a lead weight. Lallone's blue skin glistened in the dim light as did the dog man's fine coat. The eyes were also different, but similar. The shape was the same, but the dog man's eyes were dark with a black luster to them and Lallone's were bright as though full of joy, but emotionless at the same time.

Dropping his stance once more to the hunched position, the dog man bounded off into the crowds, Lallone easily kept up as he glided behind him. The dog man was scorned repeatedly as he bashed his body against others, but everyone seemed to move out of Lallone's way, even though they appeared not to see him.

The dog man stopped for a second, sniffing at the air again, and speaking as Lallone caught up. "Off to find them, we are. Off to find the profited ones. Will go down in history, you will. Me too; Dogny the great.

Found them, we will. Find the Fabled three."

Lallone touched Dogny again, signaling him. Dogny bounded off across the decking noisily, as his master glided. What a wonderfully weird sight if anyone could see. "Off to see the wizard…"

Dogny pushed through the streets, the smell of urine assaulting his keen sense of smell. "Dirty animals these are. Not clean at all. How survive this long, me not know." Stopping abruptly, he froze, his outstretched hand, pointing towards a small area in the distance. Smoldering ashes lay in the center of the area. The only light came from the small red sparks that tried to ignite the charcoal in its heart.

Lallone placed his long, slender fingers into his gown, removing a small crystal, one similar to the story teller's. Raising it before him, it glowed brighter, dispersing a white light that touched Dogny's coat. His fur started to glow in response, slightly warming and lighting the area around them.

The two walked together to the embers of the fire. "Here they were. Lots and lots. And the ones we seek here too, I hope. All at once!" Dogny sniffed the air and stopped speaking, a look of concern in his eyes.

Lallone moved to his friend, placing a hand on his shoulder as he questioned. "What?"

"Feline Stray, Dragon, and crystal."

"All here at the same time?"

"Yes."

"But no dragons exist outside our realm."

A slight wind blew as Dogny raised his snout again, following the path until he reached the pool of blood near the bulkhead. "Strange this one! Injured blood. Not smelt this before, not in long time."

Lallone was looking perplexed as he stared into the embers, he thought, *it could not be*.

"Much worse than that, master, this one. All together they are." The dog man shivered at the thought.

Lallone tried to place the pieces in the puzzle as he rubbed his hands together. "Together…"

"Mixed, combined as one. The three in the one. None separate from the other, master."

Lallone stared at the ground as he kneeled near the blood, looking into its genetic make-up. "This is not possible. Not here. They are in stasis. No one else has the means to do this. Dogny. Can you smell duratanium?"

Dogny sniffed around. Stopping, he faced the fire. Reaching his hand into the embers, he searched, ruffling around until he drew back his hand, a small box in it; the box in which the story teller housed the crystal. "Just one, no other..." he started juggling the box as though he had suddenly realized that he had removed it from the hot embers. "Hot, hot, hot! Oh cold!" Handing Lallone the box, he continued sniffing. "Many others were here. Bad, bad men. Ones whose smell is foul. Hope we are not too late. Our people need us, them. Bad for all, we were too late."

Lallone fondled with the box in much the same way the story teller had. The latches released, clicking as they opened to reveal nothing inside. Closing his eyes, he concentrated.

"Master!"

Lallone raised his hand in a gesture to stop, as his blue appearance became lighter, a glow illuminating under his skin. His eyes blinked open, showing only blue as his mind searched. Rolling back and forth, his eyes searched the darkness of space. Blackness; a wall. Lallone slumped forward, his eyes returning to their prior color. "I am being blocked by one much stronger than they should be. Let us continue our journey. When I am close, I will try again. Our journey is almost over, my friend."

"Just begun, master. Just begun. Places to go, people to see. Yes, yes we have."

Philippe stirred from the pain induced sleep. He had been oddly positioned. His body was now propped up against something hard, and something soggy. Both objects caused different sensations on his back as he sat slumped over. He could not see his arms. His eyes were looking at his legs laid out in front of him like someone would do for a mannequin. He knew his body was in shock, as he was shivering, and the skin on his face felt clammy. Worse of all, his arms hurt. He glanced left and right, looking towards his arms, realizing at that moment that they had been amputated. He was missing a hand from one arm and from the elbow down on the other. He had no hands. Not one.

Philippe tried to scream, but his mouth was dry, and his weak body would not respond. Instead, he searched the area. His eyes were the only part of his body that seemed to work, limiting his vision around him. He was in the garbage; this he knew by sight and smell. Multiple bodies were strewn around. The uniforms on these bodies looked familiar somehow. It did not take long for the cold realization to hit home. These were his men; the men that he had used to try and board the Company vessels. All he remembered was that face. The sick look of joy on it when he felt the pain. A clean pain, one you would get from a paper cut. How did he end up in this place? Something must have gone wrong. After everything he had done for this station. Years of service, and he had been thrown out like trash. Bitterness stirred in his heart, which was now barely beating.

The air in front of him grew cold. His breath steamed the air before his face as it exited his mouth.

"Do you want to live?" The voice was raspy, the breath freezing cold on his ear as someone whispered to him.

Philippe panicked. Fear filled him as he tried to see the body belonging to the voice. He could see no one.

"Do you want to live?" The voice was more aggressive now, angry, like it was not going to ask again, spitting ice into his ear with the question.

Philippe tried to nod, but nothing happened. Blinking, he tried to signal to whomever spoke.

The area around Philippe became colder. A line of ice formed from his throat to his belly button on his clothed chest. His clothes peeled away as if by magic, or the fabric was cut by an extremely sharp blade. An invisible blade? He watched in horror as his flesh opened where this line had been. The skin peeled back as though being cut by a scalpel. His ribs creaked as the invisible blade cut deeper, cutting through the bone. He could still see no one and no knife, no blade. He could feel every incision, every movement. He tried to scream again. His throat, still dry, would not scream, would not even gurgle. He knew he would die here in this place, like a piece of garbage.

He felt something resembling fingers work their way between his ribs. In an explosion of flesh and bones, his ribs were ripped apart. If Philippe could have been sick, he would have. His organs, still barely functioning, were now open to the air. He could feel the cold on them. Th-Thump, Th-Thump, Th-Thump, Th-Thump… His heart beat. How he was not dead yet, he did not know. How he had remained conscious, was even more of a mystery to him. He watched on as his heart became frosted. Then he felt it. The cold touch as the invisible fingers compressed around his heart, freezing it, stopping it from beating. His lungs deflated as he took his last breath.

Something brushed over his eyelids. Frost formed on his eyebrows and eyelashes as it did.

Slowly, cautiously his heart began to grow, the other organs shifting to make way for its bulk. It stopped growing; its bulk now twice what it once was. Bo-bom, bo-bom, bo-bom. Philippe's heart started to beat strongly, stronger than ever before as it thawed. The lungs inflated and deflated as they too grew in depth with every rise and fall. Their mass stopped growing when they were also twice the size they once were. The chest closed as the ribs re-molded themselves to the shape of the newly sized organs. A second set of thicker ribs formed over the first, making the chest much more pronounced than it once was. The skin and flesh were no longer enough to cover these wounds and began to grow, filling in the gap.

Philippe's eyelids flicked open, as the skin on his chest closed and healed. His eyeballs were pure white. No iris. No pupil. Just white. Coughing, he awoke from his nightmare, his dream.

Carefully, he raised his head. Looking forward, he saw his reflection in some scrap metal by his feet. His eyes colored like the rainbow. The colors swirled until they settled. His eyes were now a light blue. He lifted his head further. In his line of vision he saw a frail old man, who was covered in frost. His skin beneath this frost was charred as though it had been in an intense fire. The skin, and the clothes, on the old man looked too big. They could have fitted a man five times the size of this frail figure before him. Philippe looked at the stumps on his arms, void of hands. As he watched, small things emerged, bubbling from the wound on his hand-less arm. *Worms writhing through my flesh!* he thought, as he screamed in panic. Repulsed, he tried to rip them from his flesh, forgetting he had no hands to do so. Unable to do anything, he starred, horrified. His eyes swirled in colors again, until they settled, bright red, and the worms turned into baby fingers. Then a baby hand. The hand grew bigger, and bigger, until it had replaced the one he had lost. The other arm started growing. A long thin extension bubbling out of his arm. Then fingers, and finally, a hand, until it too was grown back, replacing the old.

Philippe held his new hands and arm up for the world to see. As he raised his arms, he could see the muscles rippling within them. The muscles changed before his new eyes. His eyes were now black, their life force dark as the muscles in his arms became stronger. Stronger than any man could have thought possible, or ever dreamed. The transformation continued as he hunched over. The pain of all his muscles increased intensely. He did not scream. Changed beyond the man he was, he now welcomed the pain, and the change to come.

As Philippe's transformation completed, he stood, flexing his body that had become one giant mass of powerful muscles. The frail old man before him studied Philippe inquisitively, and smiled proudly. Grinning, the old man thought to himself, *I have not lost my touch! Creating is as easy as ever.* His thoughts were cut short, as his stomach rumbled. He was hungry and he needed to eat now! Turning, he looked into the human remains that were scattered around him. "This will be a feast." He said, as he rummaged through the bodies, pulling out a plump, headless one. Extending his index finger, he cut through the leg. His razor sharp finger made short work of the meat and bone. The man's mouth opened, and his jaw jutted forward, as his head tilted back. Feeding down the leg, he closed his mouth. A gurgling sound came from his stomach, and then a burp, as he opened again to eat another leg. The ritual of eating like this went on until all the legs from the headless corpses were gone. "Nothing better than a nice drumstick to start the day." The voice, no longer raspy, had an air of insanity to it as he belched.

Philippe was horrified and disgusted by this man's actions. He had, after all, eaten all his dead friends' legs. *Though they have no use for them now*, he thought. His stomach rumbled as a hunger attacked him.

The man before him spoke, as he licked his fingers. "Eat, my child."

The man was now chubby and large. His features were unusual. His face looked human, but was blue in color, very dark blue. His ears were pointed with a circular lobe under each. Gone was the frail old man, and the black scarred features.

Lifting a carcass with two fingers, the man spoke, as he threw it to Philippe. "Here you go."

Philippe's instincts kicked in. Opening his mouth, he bit down on the flesh of the body, his eyes now showed the blood-lust through the white, as he frenzied. His razor sharp teeth made short work of his meal, as he tore the flesh from the bones, devouring it. Content with his meal, he spoke as he rose from the bones beneath him. "Who are you?"

The plump man had adopted a seated position to watch Philippe as he had fed over the corpse. Now stood up, he replied in a proud, pitched, insane tone. "You may call me, Father, Creator or God. Whichever name you prefer."

Philippe dropped to his knees, with his head and hand now resting on the ground before him. The Creator hovered over the ground, quickly covering the distance between them. He placed a finger under Philippe's chin to lift it. Philippe's eyes were now a light blue, and were welling up. Placing his face near Philippe's, he spoke in a matter of fact tone, "You do not worship me. You serve me. I want a General, not a slave."

Philippe looked upwards, awe in his now black eyes as frost covered his face. "A General! But what do I command?"

The Creator looked around for a second. The rubbish beside him moved. His reflexes were lightning fast, as he reached in, withdrawing a rat. The rat squealed, biting and clawing at him as it tried to escape. He looked at it tenderly, then snapped its neck quickly, before it could inflict any damage to his new skin. He sliced open its chest with his blade-like finger, until he exposed the heart. He then grabbed one of the whole corpses, one that had a broken neck. Laying this corpse flat, he cut open its chest too.

Philippe looked on at this spectacle, his eyes full of swirling colors. He watched as the Creator grabbed both the heart of the rat, and human, joining the two creatures in a horrific display. Rat and human features now mixed into the one creation. With this change came an unexpected side effect that Philippe gawked at. The Creator withered. The mass he had given to this transformation was taken directly from him. Famished, the Creator then returned to eating more flesh, with the rat man now animated, doing the same beside him.

This rat-like creature before Philippe resembled more zombie than the person it once was. This thing, that was once his friend, was now a monster. The four corpses still with heads attached were soon transformed into rat-like men, and the headless corpses that were left, devoured.

"Let's go find us a chariot, another General or two, and a few more soldiers." The Creator spoke as though he was going on a shopping trip, as he glided off. The five, unusual looking men, now followed their God, with Philippe at the lead; his eyes, emotionless, and jet black, as he obeyed.

Chapter 7

Rod stood in the galley, shaking his knife in disgust at the brig door, as he spoke; "How's come every time we drop a shipment of Strays off, he makes me stay in the galley." He returned to skinning the rat in preparation of their next meal, as Profitor replied.

"Y-you were e-employed as th-the c-chef, were you n-not, R-rod?"

Rod gutted the rat skilfully with his knife, as he answered; "Yeah, but it still don't make it right. We've got as much right to know where they taking the Strays, as the rest of them."

Profitor looked up quickly from his specimens that were methodically laid over the galley's table, tweezers still in hand, as he returned the conversation. "Oh! I th-think y-you h-have got it w-wrong. I ch-choose to s-stay in h-here when they d-deposit the S-strays. Anyways I-I like the time a-alone w-with my sp-specimens."

"You not even the bit curious? I know I am."

"N-no, I am n-not, n-not even in the s-slightest. You h-have to u-understand, th-they h-have been t-together for many y-years. You h-have only been h-here for two." As he finished explaining, Profitor returned to the probing of insects and other creatures on the table before him.

The door from the brig swung open quickly, with Scrycher yelling out from behind it in a happy go lucky tone. "Well how's this for a sample, the one you wanted I hope, Prof?" He threw a glass jar to Profitor, as he cleared the doorway, a large cheeky smile plastered across his face.

As if by complete reflex, Profitor agilely raised his hands, catching the jar easily before it could hit the table. Turning the jar around to study the specimen, he allowed himself a boyish grin. Excitement was evident in his voice as he nodded, "Y-Yes, S-sir. Th-thank y-you."

"My pleasure. Hope dinner is almost ready Rod? I don't want to go to sleep on an empty stomach."

Rod's mood was not improved by the Captain's dramatic entrance, he never received anything and he did not feel like part of the crew. His voice was like venom, striking out at Scrycher in a matter of fact attitude, "Yes, Scrycher, we would not want you to go to sleep on an empty stomach, now would we?"

Ignoring the comment's sarcasm, Scrycher left the galley without another word. In response, Rod slammed his knife through the chest of the rat that he was still preparing, splattering blood over the preparation area, and leaving the knife sticking upright in the cutting board. Seeing no reaction from Profitor, who was deep in thought over his new specimen, Rod removed the knife and sneaked onto the bridge, one thing on his mind; revenge…

"Chels, did you pack those nuts I bought from the last stop?" Jaxter was leaning over the galley table, as he spoke to Chelsea, who was busy sorting through a box of trinkets. He knew he needed the nuts to fasten the grating on the cooling system, for their Gatling gun. The Captain had been on at him for weeks to get it fixed. Now he had bought the nuts, he would get it fixed, leaving the Captain something else to complain about.

Not looking up from the table, Chelsea replied in a matter of fact tone, "Didn't you pack em, Jax?"

He thought back to when he purchased the box of nuts. The man handed them to him, and then, what did he do? "Nuts…" He remembered the lovely lass that walked past, and that he had put the box down to follow her through the street, and into her small stall. "Nuts, nuts, nuts," he cursed. "Forgot to pack 'em. Left 'em where I bought 'em."

Rod was back behind the galley's bench, preparing the last of the meals, as he called out. "The Captain is gonna have your balls man. I hope she was worth it."

Jaxter thought back to those lovely legs, thighs… A gleeful smile made its way onto his face. Rod jumped over the preparation bench, and took two steps before clumsily slamming his bum down on the dining table seat, next to Jaxter.

"Tell me all about it. Was she blonde, brunette? Was she flat chested, toothless?"

Jaxter turned to Rod to address the inappropriate comments, an expression of concern on his face as he replied. "You are weird, man."

"You just workin' that out now? I knew that from the moment he crawled onto this ship." Chelsea continued to sort through the box of trinkets she had on the table before her, not raising her head to see Rod's expression at her insult.

"You know you want me, Baby. Ever since you met me, you can't take your eyes off me. I seen it." Rod was grabbing his groin as he leant back on the bench seat.

"All you 'seen' was me making sure you did not knife me, or someone else, you weasel. Wouldn't look at you otherwise. You repulse me."

"Oh man. I rest my case. You need help. You keep getting whipped by Chels over there, and then come back for more. Weird, weird, weird."

"At least I will not be as whipped as you, when the Captain finds out you forgot your nuts again." Rod smiled evilly, leaving the table to return to the preparation bench, as Scrycher entered the room on cue.

"What's this I hear about nuts? Hope there's some in my stew. Nothing better than a rat's nut stew, my mother used to say." As he sat down, he pulled out the chair beside him. Scrags had entered the room behind him, no Blink to be seen. "Sit down my boy, Rod here, has made us some lovely rat nut stew." The crew laughed at the Captain, as he joked, all thoughts on the meal at hand as Rod started serving the bowls of slop.

"Hey Prof, mind moving that crap off the table whilst I serve? Rod nodded at the jars and the other equipment sprawled over the table in front of Profitor.

"S-sorry R-rod I w-was just so excited over the Pupa the Captain brought, that I got a l-little c-carried away." As Profitor scrambled to put away his specimens, he kept his head down, nervously trying to get his specimens back into their correct jars. Scrycher could see that Profitor was nervous, so he thoughtfully reached over the table, giving him a hand to place his tools in his little pouch, in an effort to gently hurry the process.

"Thanks, Captain."

"Here you go." Rod placed the last bowl of slop down in front of Profitor. "Hope you enjoy."

Scrycher noisily cleared his throat, getting everyone's attention. "Are you forgetting something, Rod?"

"No, Captain. I don't think I am." Rod eyes darted over to where Chelsea sat. He had deliberately, not served her a meal.

"I thought I was paying you to serve meals to the whole crew?"

"Yes, Captain."

"Well don't let me down then. You are one short."

"Sorry, Captain, I must have made a mistake."

Chelsea sniggered, "You'd better add that you can't count, to your resume."

Scrycher held his solid facial expression as Jaxter and Chelsea laughed heartily. Though he wanted to laugh with them, he still needed this man to trust him. "Thank you, Rod."

At this comment, Rod left to head back to the preparation area, leaving his own bowl of slop on the table.

"Hrrrr, ppppp." Rod snorted and spat out a green booger into Chelsea's plate. He then stuck his pinkie finger up his nose, before stirring the slop with it to ensure no one could see the spit. Returning to the table, he smiled, his crooked teeth making him look all the more creepy as he pushed Chelsea's open box of trinkets, off the table with the bowl.

"Oops. Sorry, didn't see it."

Scrags ducked down and around as his sharp reflexes allowed him to easily catch the box and all its contents, before it could smash on the floor.

Chelsea bent down, affectionately looking Scrags in the eyes, while he raised the box to her. The same affection was carried in her voice. "Thanks, sweetie."

Scrags blushed, as he placed the box in her hands, Chelsea ensuring she delicately touched his hand to show her appreciation. A touch like a caring mother would give to her child.

"He's bit young…"

Scrycher stopped sipping his soup with the spoon, and dropped it to the table, the clanking, getting everyone's attention. "Rod, do you think you could get me some salt? This seems to be a little bland. Did you use both nuts, or just one?"

Disgusted, Rod stood up, yet to touch his own meal. As he turned his back, Scrycher quickly swapped Chelsea's bowl with Rod's.

"On the other hand, Rod" Scrycher chewed loudly. "I think I found the other nut." Scrycher's chewing became louder as he spoke in jest with his mouth full. "This seems to be a little better than I thought. This slop might not need any salt."

Rod snarled as he turned to return to the table, but before he sat down, Profitor spoke.

"I-I w-would l-love some s-salt while y-you are th-there, R-rod." Profitor looked up from his bowl, an innocent look on his face as he waited patiently for Rod to retrieve the salt.

"What you think I am, your slave, Prof?" Rod stopped, reached out as he took a step and grabbed the salt from the bench. He then turned, and slammed it down on the table, as he returned.

Embarrassed at Rod's response, Profitor dropped his stare to his bowl. He reached out for the salt, but misjudged the distance, knocking the container over. Seeing Profitor's embarrassment, Jaxter picked up the salt, placing it in his hand. He patted Profitor's hand gently before letting go. Profitor did not raise his head as he sprinkled a little salt on his meal. "Th-th-th-thank y-y-you, J-Jaxter."

"No prob's, Prof, you just enjoy that slop." Jaxter spoke, as he lifted up the spoon from his plate, letting the slop ooze back into the bowl, small bones plopping into the liquid.

As Rod started eating, he grinned wickedly, looking up at Chelsea who was digging into her plate of slop. "Was it worth the wait?"

Chelsea grinned, as Jaxter winked at her. "Worth every minute."

Scrycher observed that Scrags waited patiently, not wanting to start his meal whilst the antics were playing out before him. "Bog in boy. Food waits for no-one."

Scrags needed no further instructions. He grabbed the bowl, lifting it to his lips to slurp the meal down.

"He'd eat anything, that one." Jaxter laughed. "Even Rod's slop."

Scrags stopped momentarily, looking confused as he watched the others, but quickly returned to slurping his meal as they all laughed.

The friendly banter was cut short by a crash in the preparation area. Rod jumped up, rushing into the small area to find his cooking pan and slop on the floor. Leaning over, he picked it up. Blink was under it, gnawing at the head of the rat, and covered in slop. Blink looked up just as Rod tried to slam a large frying pan down on top of him, the pan hit the floor with full force as Blink blinked away. The pan pounded onto the metal deck, making a jagged edge. It sent a ringing vibration through Rod's arms and ears as he cursed. "Bloody lizard!" His face boiled red as he got his knife from his side, and headed back to the table, brandishing it menacingly in the air. "I am going to skin you, and cook you for dinner."

With hackles up, Blink hissed, baring his teeth to show that he would protect the skull in his paws, from his vantage point of Scrags' head. His eyes widened, and he screeched again, not removing his stare from Rod.

Scrycher's voice showed how drained he felt as he raised himself from the chair. "No thanks, Rod. The rat slop was quite enough for today. You have outdone yourself." With this, Scrycher walked out of the galley, and towards his quarters.

After the meal of rat slop he had just eaten, Scrycher felt drained and sleepy, not at all like himself. He thought of his crew that he had left in the dining area, the tension now broken by his exit. The others joked again over the meal Rod had prepared for them, none of them knowing of the stress he felt inside. Every little decision seemed to grate at him, as if eating him from the inside out. What if he made the wrong decision... had he? What if he, or one of the crew was killed? Philippe! *Why, why did I have to involve him?* After all this time, why had he involved him now? He was like a father to him. He was the only father he could remember, and he was dead. Dead because of some foolish errand, a destiny he could barely remember. Was it all worth it, the loss of his father, and the loss of his friends? It was one thing to be a smuggler, and to help the Stray children. Watching their every step and trying to ensure the Company did not catch them. It was another to be chased vigorously by the same Company vessel, over and over again, the crew oblivious to the agenda behind the chase. Even he did not know what it was.

Hisss, Bang! An explosion echoed through the ship, stopping Scrycher in his tracks. He turned sharply and hurried back through the galley towards the explosion. Profitor and Rod were still eating at the table, and looked up as Scrycher stormed back through the galley, neither man giving him a second glance as they returned to their meal.

Chelsea, Jaxter and Scrags were all in the cockpit area trying to assess the damage through the billowing smoke. They were all huddled outside the Gatling gun compartment, looking into the rectangular grating. It was laying open, leaving the corrugated cooling hose for the gun exposed. Blink was keeping Scrags amused by blinking into the smoke. He would return moments later to blow it into funny shapes and creatures.

"Jax, what do we have?" Scrycher said, crossing his arms over his chest, his mouth distorting into a scowl as he tried peering through the smoke.

"Me hose has been chewed again, Boss! Possibly one of Rod's rats?" Jaxter looked comical as he stood, holding the tiny, crimped hose in his giant black hands. He knelt on one knee, investigating the gaping hole in the hose, the damage, jagged and random, looked as though it had been chewed.

"Will your gun work without it?"

"No, Boss, it is essential to the cooling, it will overheat after maybe five minutes without it. And then-"

"Huh, Sounds like all the men I've had." Chelsea moved away from the gun, and walked to the communications console. "Captain, there are no ships around us. We will be safe for now."

Scrycher leaned forward, his nails biting into the worn backrest of the Captain's chair, yet the seat was in good condition as it had rarely been used. He did not like sitting, and he did not like being caught off-guard. Turning back to Jaxter, he fixed his disapproving gaze upon him. "I thought I told you to fix those grates, so the bloody rats could not get in?"

"I tried, Boss!" Jaxter's voice lowered, he had not seen the Captain this strained before. The Captain's temper boiled and his face flushed red.

"Well, you did not try too bloody hard, now did you?"

"But, Boss." His voice raised a little and he stood, his impressive stature dwarfing even Scrycher as he continued through gritted teeth. "I told you, I needed the nuts; the ones to do the joining. But we have not got them yet." Jaxter did not like conflict, but he did not like the tone in the Captain's voice either.

Blink, blinked in front of Scrycher, balancing oddly on the back of the Captain's chair, with both clawed legs positioned in between his hands. His head darted from side to side, trying to get Scrycher's attention. His big eyes opening wider as he realized, he could not hold his breath much longer. Unable to get his attention, Blink was looking into Scrycher's face as he desperately exhaled, and gasped for air. A large puff of smoke, that would have been a marvelous animal shape designed to break the tension, blew directly into the Captain's face. Blink did a little giggle, with his tummy wobbling, a laugh that stopped abruptly when Scrycher's face reddened from holding his own breath. Blink looked to the others in the room. No one else was laughing. The three others stood staring, with their jaws hanging open. Seeing this, Blink frantically fanned his wings, trying to fan the smoke away, and then shrieked at Scrycher's expression when the smoke cleared. He dropped to the floor and ran into the corner, with his tail between his legs.

Scrycher's muscles rippled in his large arms and neck, with the redness of his face now flowing into them. He rocked the chair slowly from side to side, then quicker with each motion, loosening it from the floor. In one huge movement, Scrycher ripped up the seat and its base from the metal mooring and raised it above his head. The three others ducked prior to Scrycher throwing the chair at the wall behind Chelsea. Blink, blinked into the security of Scrags hair, as it hit the wall. The chair smashed on impact. Scrycher walked sternly over to the mess, placing his foot on the crumpled seat as he ripped the base from it. The base was buckled, but the four bolts and nuts on it were still serviceable. Scrycher walked over to the petrified and shaking Scrags, still standing between the two men. Blink was now nestled on his head, with both front paws over those big eyes of his, sheepishly peeking out. Blink closed his eyes completely as Scrycher raised his arms. Scrycher paused. His instinct to make a point and smash the chair over Jaxter's head was still running through his mind. Taking a deep breath, he rethought this course of action. *Not going to get the right reaction*, he thought. Without looking up, he gently handed Scrag's the base of the chair, using the young boy as a buffer. "Here are your NUTS; would you like anything else before I go and get some rest?"

Scrycher strode off before Scrags could answer. The rhythmical scuffing of his torn black jeans was obvious in the silence that had fallen over the ships' crew, his path taking him back through the galley, and to his quarters. Neither Profitor, nor Rod, dared to raise their heads this time, as they continued slurping at their meal, a dirty cup of slop, possibly a beverage, now positioned next to each of their plates. As Scrycher passed the men, he paused and waited till both men had stopped slurping, and were staring into their bowls, attempting not to be noticed.

"And 'get' me up when sleeping beauty in there decides to 'stop sleeping!'" Scrycher nodded towards the brig. His eyes stayed fixed on the cloaked figure lying with his back to the cell bars, and continued walking.

"Yes, Boss!" Chelsea had her head buried in the control panel in concentration, but answered loudly. Without acknowledging the reply, Scrycher opened the door into the crew's quarters, walked through, and slammed it behind him.

Profitor's mouth was wide open. He closed it and sighed, the relief evident on his bearded face as he turned to Rod, who had continued to eat his slop. He stuttered heavily as he spoke, "Th-th-th-that w-w-was a c-c-close one, d-d-don't y-you th-think!"

Rod slurped his soup, "Nothing to worry 'bout, Prof." *Slurp*. "He don't bite." *Slurp*. "Much!"

Scrags turned shakily to Jaxter and handed him the base of the chair. Gently, Jaxter took it. Turning it around, he looked at the nuts and tried to hold back a smile. "Don't tell the Boss, but these are the wrong size."

The tension slipped away as Blink returned to blowing smoke creatures, and the occupants of the bridge broke out in fits of laughter.

"Where did they come from?" Scrycher's voice was harsh, yet controlled, as he leant over Chelsea, to stare at her control panel.

"Don't know."

"I thought we had outrun them, Chels."

"Sorry, Boss. They must've headed straight out. Philippe mustn't have delayed 'em as much as we thought. By dropping off the Stray children, we gave away any advantage we gained." Chelsea was flicking switches, and watching as the blip on her screen changed shape, and color.

Scrycher's train of thought clouded as he thought of his dear friend Philippe, and his unnecessary demise. *The children*, his mind screamed. "Did they see us offload the Stray children at the holding station?"

"Nup. It's been hours and we cover our tracks too well. Plus the dampers kill anything that can track us when we're close, they'd get a general direction, but nothing solid till we left the field."

"Good." Scrycher stood straight, opening his lungs to bellow orders for all to hear; "Battle Stations!"

Chelsea flicked a switch before effortlessly gliding over to her position on the flight stick. "Rod, take over."

The faint clanging of feet signaled Scrags running out of the galley, while carrying a steel crate. He slung it across the floor, Blink appearing on it as he let go, riding it, screeching in joy as it traveled, skidding along the deck, to land with a clunk in the Gatling gun compartment. Scrags followed behind, sprinting and jumping into the Gatling pit, right onto the crate, as Blink disappeared again. This series of actions left him standing ready on the crate, so he was tall enough to man the huge gun.

Scrycher moved into the center of the cockpit, standing where his captain's chair had once been, and turned to Rod, who was now manning Chelsea's console. "Rod. Open a channel."

Rod flicked a small switch, and a slight buzz filled the room.

"Company vessel. What do you want?" Scrycher's voice was direct and emotionless. There was only silence in reply.

Blink reappeared in front of Scrycher, grabbing at the air in desperation with his claws, fanning his little wings wildly as he tried to keep himself in the air. With his normal perch—the captain's chair—gone, there was nothing stopping him from falling onto the deck with a *PLOP.*

"Cannon fire, left side." Rod's voice was calm as he spoke, grabbing the console before him as Chelsea quickly veered the ship right, leading it out of the path of the projectiles. Small explosions caused waves of energy to wash over the ship, helping Chelsea steer further to the right until they were face to face with the offending Company vessel. Blink stopped, rolling head over tail, his claws now gripping the floor grating as they slowed. Scrycher briefly acknowledged Blink, as he shook his body in disapproval at the removal of the chair, then attempted to straighten himself from his own fall.

"I know. Bad idea. We can discuss this at another time." Blink's hackles rose up, and he hissed at Scrycher who replied sharply, almost hissing back. "Another time." Blink dropped his head, as he skulked away. A loud hiss was left echoing through the cockpit, as he blinked into his small bed in the crew quarters.

A proud and eloquent voice broke the scene as it was broadcast over the speaker. "Surrender now and I will spare your lives. You will be tried, and convicted fairly by the Councill." Scrycher raised himself from off the floor. He realized exactly how bad an idea it had been to rip the captain's chair from it. After all, he had never commanded from a sitting position before. He also realized that he knew this voice. It was from the man he had bumped into at the space station. This must be the Captain of the vessel that had been tracking them for weeks. "The Councill knows not of fairness. We will not surrender, to be hung like rats for the slaughter." Scrycher paused for a moment, waiting for the comment to be registered by the other Captain, before continuing in a slightly less aggressive tone. "We have some money, or resources that you may find useful. Can we come up with, some sort of compromise?"

The Company Captain returned the answer quickly, disgust evident in the voice. "I am a man of honor. You disrespect me with your offer of tribute. I will not take your bribe, but will take 'Your Surrender'."

Scrycher looked at his crew in turn, as they turned to him, signaling Chelsea and Scrags before he continued. "If you will not take a bribe, maybe you would take lead?"

Chelsea swung the ship slightly as she accelerated, allowing her movement in all directions if she needed it. Scrags had both hands on the gun before him and focused on the task at hand, as he swung it into action.

"Make it count, boy. We have less than five minutes before it overheats."

"What are they doing? Gunnery, can you wound them?" Lance sat upright and to the front of the captain's chair, with the excitement in his voice evident. He had never been in a real fire-fight before. This was exhilarating.

"Certainly, Sir. We have superior fire power." Firing volley after volley, the Gunnery attempted to look genuine, as he aimed for the small craft headed towards them. The little ship was making his secret mission very easy to follow. Each volley of cannon fire was met with a corresponding hail of bullets, exploding the projectiles before they reached the little ship. Whoever was firing the guns was extremely skilled, and accurate.

"Whoa, we're good!" Chelsea loved the stimulation of the fire fight, and the redness of her cheeks showed it, as she maneuvered the ship to dodge a cannon volley. "This is the most fun I've had with a stick in my hand for years."

"Well, you've not had mine yet love. Then you'd know what fun was." Rod turned his head towards Chelsea, the toothy grin repulsive, as he drooled over the thought of her.

Chelsea spun the ship, avoiding another volley. She replied without moving her sight from the space before her. "Over my dead body, lil' man."

"If that's what it takes, I'm all for it." Rod's smile grew wider as he leant over the console, looking into Chelsea's top and at her breasts.

"Take that! And that! You cannot touch me!" Scrags pulled the gun from side to side in a boyish way. He smiled from ear to ear, as he pulled the trigger on the Gatling gun, to destroy the oncoming cannon fire. Scrycher stood beside him with a proud, but cautious look in his eyes.

Rod quickly turned his attention to Scrags, as he replied to the innocent comment. "You wanna bet, little man?" Rod's smile now covered his face, a sickening grin.

Scrycher's voice was hard and unforgiving as he replied, "Enough!" He did not take his concentration off of Scrags. "We need to do damage now, the gun is heating up too much." He placed one hand on the boy's shoulder and the other in front of him, pointing at the vessel before them. "If you can hit them there, and there, you should disable their propulsion. What you think Chels, reckon you can get us close enough?"

"Can't see why not, Boss."

"Well take us in then."

"Aye, aye, Captain." Chelsea pulled hard on the stick to maneuver the ship so she could get in position, while Scrags shook his head excitedly, with Scrycher ruffling his hair fondly.

"Are you purposely trying to miss them?" Lance was now, literally, on the edge of his seat. His elbows were raised off the arms, and his hands were clenched into fists. Lance's lip was firmly planted between his teeth as he half stood. "Aim for that annoying gun." Lance threw one hand out, pointing at the Gatling gun that was causing them so much trouble.

"But, Sir, if I get anywhere near that gun, we will breach their cockpit. Bye, bye, crew." The Gunnery could not believe Lance's stupidity.

"Alright, Gunnery, what do you suggest?" Lance allowed himself to sit back in his chair nervously as he waited. The Gunnery did not hear Lance as he spoke as he was too deep in thought over his retirement and his actions just before this mission.

The Gunnery walked through the cold night, his thin uniform doing nothing to insulate his chilled body. He was not worried; he would soon find someone to warm him. He had been called back from active duty, Not a day too soon, *he thought. He was missing a little lady action every now and again, and tonight was the night to rectify it.*

The polluted smell of home was familiar to him and he breathed it in as though smelling perfume. This smell did not deter him in this seedy part of the Councill's station; it drove him on.

He peered eagerly at the women displaying themselves on the path before him, not stopping as he perused their ranks. Their clothes, also not made for fighting off the cold, allowed him ogling rights, as he looked at their breasts. No imagination was needed as their nipples showed through their gowns, lingerie and other tacky costumes. He felt like a handful tonight. Not too much to waste when it comes down to playing with them, *he thought.* Not as costly either. *He chuckled.*

A short, large breasted woman pushed aggressively past the others, and walked up to him. He stopped as she placed her hand on his groin, squeezing it aggressively as she opened her mouth. Her four remaining teeth, black and rotting, were all that was left of an awful smile. "You up for a little lovin' tonight, darlin'?" Her voice was croaky and her smile removed as she coughed into the Gunnery's face. The Gunnery looked her up and down. "For the right price, love." He did not have the perception of the haggard crone before him but perceived an image in his mind, an image of a buxom beauty waiting for him to take her.

As she rolled up her ripped pants, to show her wrinkled legs, she also rolled a goober in her mouth. Thwatt. She spat it out aggressively onto the deck below. "Well, we can work that out when we work out the particulars. I do everything for a price, you know."

The Gunnery led the lady of the night to his quarters with the comment 'anything for a price,' ripe in his mind as he opened the door to his small room. He grabbed her, throwing her onto his bed, and closed the door behind him.

The whore removed herself from the bed quietly. Her face was barely recognizable, now black and swollen as she limped from the room, grabbing the money from the nightstand as she left. She gingerly, and quietly, closed the door on the way out, ensuring she did not wake the Gunnery.

Gunnery rolled over, looking at the door as he uncovered himself. His bare chest was blanketed in the gray hairs of a man of many years.

The room was lit as the monitor on the far wall was on. "Using your money well, I see." There was a tone of sick pleasure in the voice.

The Gunnery sat up, startled, but did not bother to cover his nakedness. "Yes, Sir." He had heard from this man many times in the past, but never by monitor, and never here in his quarters. He had always heard from him on the ship, and always from the room while they were on missions.

"I need you to complete a special assignment for me. It will mean enough funds for a comfortable retirement for you, and still allow you 'your pleasures'."

The Gunnery could not conceal his excitement as he spoke. "Yes, Sir."

"You are to make sure that your new Captain does not capture the vessel you are going to be chasing. Wound them, but do not kill them."

"Yes, Sir."

"I repeat, under no circumstances are you to apprehend, or destroy the ship *you will be chasing!"*

"Understood, Sir."

The monitor blinked off. The Gunnery raised himself from the bed and walked over to a cracked mirror on the wall, near a small, filthy, washbasin. He turned slightly, peering sideways into the mirror to look at the large, bloody scratches down his back. Turning back, he stooped to lean on the washbasin. He looked into it, as he washed his hands in a brown liquid that trickled from the outlet. Observing his appearance in the mirror, the Gunnery pulled down the bottom of his eyelids and looked for some time at the redness in his eyes. As he let his eyelids go, he looked deeply into the mirror. His graying hair, wrinkled features, and huge bags under his eyes, were all that greeted him in the reflection. He had to make this last assignment work for him. After all, he was a man aged beyond his years in this terrible existence.

The first pass of Gatling fire missed its target, as Chelsea veered out of the way of the oncoming cannon fire. The little ship spun around again, under her unwavering control, and handled beautifully under her guidance, as she feigned the ship to the left. Cannon fire exploded from the company vessel, and Chelsea's concentration hardened. She systematically pulled the ship around, getting so close to the Company vessel that she barely missed the large hull before them.

"Now!" Scrycher was holding onto the cage of the Gatling gun, heat from the gun radiating around him and Scrags, sweat beading on them. Scrags pulled the trigger; the excitement in his body was evident as the bullets were released. They blazed through space like red, angry, insects on a mission to sting their prey. On impact, Scrags let go of the gun, throwing his hands in the air, and squealing at the fact that he had hit his target. Scrycher watched, concentrating on the spot they had hit as their bullet's lights extinguished. "Damn, I was sure that would work." He looked over his shoulder, wiping the sweat from his brow, and called out in a mixture of disappointment and concern. "Chels, get us out of here!" Chelsea continued her trajectory away from the Company vessel, as it exploded, the little ship buffeted by the force. Scrags was thrown from his stool. Scrycher's muscles barely registered as he reacted, grabbing the boy by his collar. As he lowered him to the deck, Scrycher praised the boy, ruffling his head of hair. "I knew you could do it, boy."

The hull creaked and murmured under the strain, as Chelsea's muscles tightened, her hands clenching the stick. The Company vessel was down an engine. Off balance, it was sent into a spin. Rod laid sprawled on the floor, his grip on the console lost, as echoing footsteps clanged through the ship, and Jaxter bounded to the cockpit. The ship jolted, and he planted his large foot to keep balance. *Crunch!* "Is everything alright?" Jaxter's eyes were wide as they darted around the room, his breathing erratic. He looked down in response to the girly cry at his feet, and gingerly stepped off Rod's hand, allowing Rod to cradle his throbbing hand to his chest. "Oops."

As Jaxter stepped off Rod's hand, and towards Scrycher, he spoke jovially. "Huh, I see that the makeshift fix on the gun worked out fine."

Scrycher turned and looked at Jaxter sternly. "What do you mean?"

"Ooops." Jaxter looked sheepish as he turned, mumbling under his breath as he left. "I must have forgotten to tell you. I jerry-rigged a new cooling system so that the gun would not overheat for at least 10 minutes or so."

"Jaaaaxxxxxxttttttttteeeeeeerrrrrr!"

Lance jumped from the Captain's chair, screaming as the engine exploded. "Do something." The ship started spinning, sending the young Captain flying into the center of the room in mid order. His body sprawled face first into the decking. As he lay there, licking the blood from his split lip, he sighed.

The Commander pulled back on the control stick. Reaching forward, he flicked a switch aggressively. The remaining engine stopped firing. Flicking another switch in the same manner, the Commander started two secondary thrusters to slow the spin of the vessel. As the vessel came to a halt, he flicked these switches off. His face flushed as he turned to Lance who was still on the floor. "Captain Dragoon, I have done something, we are stationary. Are you now alright with me doing nothing, whilst the ship repairs itself?"

Getting up gingerly, Lance swayed. His glance was swapping between the Commander and the Gunnery. Unsure of how to react, his face flushed. Pulling down the two bottom corners of his jacket sternly, he turned, his voice croaking, "Dismissed!" and strode out of the room.

"Pompass Ass!" The Commander called out after him…

Chapter 8

Teller lay on the floor bruised, battered, and woken from his slumber. His gray and furry face now pressed up against the bars from the last of the erratic movements. Gingerly he pulled himself up the bars, using his superiorly strong arms to raise his body with ease. *Th-Thump, th-thump... Th-Thump, th-thump.* The vein in the side of his head felt enormous, as his temple pounded. Off-balance, and limping from the pain, he made his way to a metal bench, attached to the side of the cell. He could not think. His vision blurred, his focus shifting as he looked around. Lying down, he stared at the bars of the cell he was in, then nothing, as his sight blurred again. With his vision gone, the other sensations, unfamiliar to his body, were amplified. His skin felt as though hot embers were stuck all over it, burning his body, and his fur felt somewhat different on his skin. It also seemed to be burning as he listened to the voices in the other room.

"C-Captain, I-I am not sure b-but is that not th-the crystal from the drawings on the t-temple wall? Th-the one in th-the r-ruins?" Profitor's voice was very shaky as he asked the question.

Scrycher's voice was much deeper, and confident, almost booming through the partly open doorway in response. "That's your field of expertise Prof, not mine. You tell me."

"W-we w-will have t-to get back on th-the planet and e-explore the ruins a-again, b-but I would th-think th-that it is."

"Well that's settled. Off to the ruins. I just hope this Company vessel got the hint and leaves us alone to do what we need to."

Teller dropped out of consciousness, only to be drawn back by the sound of a screaming girl.

"You big lug. Look at the size of me hand."

Teller's vision cleared, as he watched a dark man, several times the bulk of himself, enter the room.

"Sorry, Rod. How was I supposed to know you were taking a nap on the floor of the cockpit?" The man sounded genuine in his apology and explanation, unlike the feminine voice that echoed through the doorway.

"Nothing unusual, hey, Rod? Always doin' somethin' so you don't have to pull your weight. To lay down in a fire fight though, wouldn't have even thought you were capable of that one." A woman of maybe thirty years walked through the door as she looked behind her, exposing the shape of her ample bosoms, bulging from her tank top for all to see.

Teller's vision blurred again as others walked through the door, all laughing at this Rod's expense...

Jaxter moved towards the far end of the brig, turning sideways to clear the entrance as he studied a crystal in his hand. The crystal seemed no bigger than a small child's toy as he continued to turn it, studying its shape as he leant against the wall. "I don't know what to make of this crystal, Captain. Maybe we should give this to Prof to study further?"

Chelsea's head lifted up at this disconcerting remark. "You mean you studied that thing for the last day and didn't find a thing?" She turned her attention to Teller. Noticing that he was rousing and the shape of his muscular frame apparent under his cloak, she leant upon the wall, and found herself staring, and tongue-tied. "You never don't know what makes things work, or how it does it, Jax."

Scrycher made his way to a small table setting in the center of the room and pointed at Teller as he spoke. "Talking about working, nice to see sleeping beauty managed to sleep through that." He raised one leg onto the bench.

Jax shook his head and shrugged his large shoulder as he threw the crystal towards Scrycher. "Nope, don't know a thing about the crystal. Not even where it keeps drawing its power from. It is almost as if it draws its source from the environment around it. Maybe Sleepy in there can let us know how it works?"

Scrycher caught the crystal, cupping it, to ensure that it did not drop. "Where's Rod gone? I want him to start looking for the planet that we picked Blink up from. I want to see if this thing sheds any light on the ornament in that pool of sludge."

Rod snuck through the doorway to slink against the bars in the back of the cell area. He wiped his large knife across the bottom of his pants, leaving a green coolant stain on them, which he quickly rubbed in. He looked around cautiously to see if anyone had noticed. Realizing they were too occupied with the crystal, he relaxed, and proceeded to clean his nails with the knife as he spoke. "Scrycher, what planet?" His swollen hand was clumsy and he cut himself, the blood not bothering him one little bit, as he looked up.

"I'll give you the co-ordinates. Just give them back when you have loaded them in. It is a ruined temple, and is where a lot of our information on the home planet has been obtained from."

"How come I never heard of it?" Rod sucked the blood off the finger, his eyes rolling back into his head at the taste and texture. He then returned to cleaning his nails, giving the appearance that he really did not care.

"Cause Scrycher has the only key to its location." Chelsea spoke up. "And I would not try anything funny, little man, or you will have more than a sore hand to deal with." Chelsea removed her pistol from her side holster and started cleaning it in an affectionate way.

Rod's eyes sparked up. "Oh baby, you promise? If you rubbed me like that, I am sure I would have something else sore."

"Enough! Take these co-ordinates and load them in." Scrycher reached into his pocket, pulled out a small memory stick, and handed it to Rod.

Rod grabbed the stick and placed it in his pocket as he spoke, pointing back to the cell with Teller in it. "Not goin' anywhere. Sleeping beauty is up." Rod wiped the sweat from his brow and gave a sideways glance at the cockpit area. He sighed deeply in relief as the others diverted their attention towards Teller.

Teller's mind was clear, as he watched the interaction between these people. However as he stood, the clarity turned to fog, and he felt like throwing up. *Th-thump, th-thump, th-thump* His head throbbed. The room started spinning. He could focus only on one thing. A crystal hovered before him. His crystal. He walked clumsily, crashing into the bars but still held focus on his crystal.

Scrycher walked slowly towards the cell. "Well, who have we here? Joined the world of the living, I see." He held the crystal before him as though a token of his non-aggressive intent. "Can you tell us about this crystal and how it works?" Scrycher took one more step to stand within arm's length of Teller.

Teller's cloudy mind could think but one thought. He had to get his crystal back. His crystal, that now floated in an aura, was within his grasp. Lurching forward, he grabbed at the crystal, his claws coming out to lengthen his reach. As his hand hit the mark, his shoulder hit the bars, twisting his hand sideways. He felt the crystal within his grasp, then the warmth. He pulled back in shock.

Scrycher grabbed at his wrist in agony as a razor sharp claw chipped the crystal and cut deep into his hand. "Friggin' hell!" A crystal shard now embedded in his palm glowed intensely, almost blinding those in the room for a split second. "You want it? You have it, you furry piece of crap!" Scrycher dropped to the floor, grabbing the crystal, unintentionally coating it in his blood. He flung it at Teller through the bars. The crystal's light diminished as Scrycher's blood encased it.

Teller panicked as he saw the crystal being flung at him. Stepping away from the bars, he watched in slow motion as it navigated its way through the bars and into his hands. Now covered in blood, it sat, pulsing lightly in Teller's hand. Slowly, the blood covering it pooled in the area that had been chipped. As the blood did this, it was converted by the crystal, repairing the chip.

"Prof! We got an emergency." Chelsea had been quick to jump up and grab Scrycher by the shoulders, leading him into the galley where Profitor was working on his specimens.

"Friggin' space the Stray." Scrycher was gritting his teeth and holding his wrist as he screamed, blood pulsing from the deep cut in his palm.

"My pleasure." Rod's sickly grin returned as he leant forward, only to be blocked by Jaxter.

"You not going anywhere, fool. Unless you want me to space you too."

Profitor was erratically scooping his specimens into his duffel bag, to make room before him. "D-down h-here." Scrycher grimaced as he lowered himself, guided by Chelsea.

Gritting his teeth, he yelled again. "Chels. You spaced the Stray yet? You'd better, 'cause if I get to him, he will wish you had."

""S-stay s-still." Profitor grabbed Scrycher's hand and held it down with his thin fingers, barely half the size of the large man's. Dabbing the wound with a work cloth he had on the table, Profitor gasped. "P-part of the c-crystal is l-lodged in o-one of your a-arteries. I-I n-need to g-get it out a-and r-repair the d-damage. C-Chelsea have y-you seen my t-t-tweezers?" Chelsea tried to gingerly look through the samples left on the table as Profitor sprawled them out in a panic. Many of the sample jars spilt off the table, onto the floor, and smashed. Letting go of Scrycher's hand, Profitor dropped to the floor, searching for the tweezers under the table and chairs. Sweat poured off his head, as he threw anything in his way across the room, be it sample jar or rubbish. "C-can't find them. J-Jaxter g-get me s-some needle n-n-nose p-pliers." Jaxter's stomping sounded like thunder as he came running, rummaging through the small pouch on his waist, as he got to the table.

As Jaxter went to hand over the pliers, he noticed something in Profitor's hand and pointed as he spoke. "Prof, aren't they your tweezers?"

"Get this bloody thing out of meeeee!" Scrycher's face was blood red and boiling hot; he groaned, and rocked back and forth, as he squeezed down upon his wrist, blood still pulsing out of the wound.

Profitor's face was equally red, with embarrassment, as he spoke. Chelsea pushed down on her Captains shoulders, stopping the rocking motion as Profitor went to work. "S-sorry C-captain. D-do n-not move." He reached for the crystal shard. As the tweezers touched the shard, Scrycher screamed in pain, jolting up, and throwing Chelsea backwards into Jaxter's waiting arms. Profitor jumped back and out of the way, barely avoiding a smack in the face. He wasted no time and grabbed Scrycher's hand again, studying it. "Wh-what the?" As Profitor watched, the crystal shard melted into Scrycher's artery, closing the wound behind it. The damage to Scrycher's palm now resembled a flesh wound, and seemed no more serious...

Teller stood in the cell as Scrycher returned with a bloodstained cloth, clenched in his palm. "Now who are you, you mongrel?"

"I have no name, just a purpose. I am the Teller." Teller was holding his head with one hand, trying to dull the sound of the blood beating through his body. With the other, he held the crystal. The crystal's power was working slowly, allowing its energy to sooth him, to calm his nerves. He used this as an anchor, pulling himself out of the fog, allowing him to concentrate on something other than the throbbing of his head. Scrycher replied in a very agitated tone. "What did you want with half my bloody hand?" He held up his hand so Teller could see.

"I did not mean any harm. I was disorientated and confused. I reached for the crystal and my vision blurred. I was not trying to hurt you. As I said, I am a man of storytelling. In this role I am not capable, nor am I allowed, to inflict pain. It is part of the order of things." Teller stretched his hands out in a circular motion as he spoke, encompassing the area around him, as if he was telling a story now.

"Well, Mr Story Teller, what can we do for you today, that would stop you from attacking me again?" Scrycher's voice had calmed a little, and the look in his eyes showed cunning.

Teller's reply was as deep and demanding as it was when he was telling the story on the station. "You can start by letting the Stray children go. Set them free to do as they want. Do not leave them caged like animals."

"Done! Anything else?" Scrycher stepped closer to the cell. His head tilted sideways as he spoke further. The look in Teller's face showed slight confusion. "Well, while you are making demands, is there anything else you so desire?"

Teller could see the strap of a rifle over Scrycher's shoulder. He did not want to anger this man and end up dead, but he wished to remain true to himself. "I do not wish for anything for myself. I wish for nothing for myself, as I have no need. I wish for those that this life have been unjust to, to be allowed a life of belonging, not a life of exile."

Chelsea spoke abruptly as Teller finished, "Spoken like a true prophet. Hey Boss, this one's a real catch. Maybe we shouldn't throw him out the airlock, after all."

The crew sniggered briefly at this comment, before Rod continued the conversation. "This one's a real blowhard. How 'bouts we do as Chelsea says, and stick to the original plan. Cut our losses and throw him back to where he came?" Rod's eyes glinted.

"Hate to say it, but I couldn't agree more, Captain. Let's just get out of here, and get as far away from that bloody ship as we can. We don't need anything else to slow us down."

Scrycher looked at Jaxter's posture as he spoke. This large man never said much, but he was very adamant about this. *Maybe I should rethink my plan?* "Point taken, big man. Now, everyone out, while I have a chat with our prisoner alone."

"But where are the children? When will you release them?" Although Teller wanted the answer, he was mainly trying to stall the exit of the other crewmembers. He did not want to be left alone with the man that he had injured.

"They are released." Chelsea's voice had softened slightly as she admired this man. This man that had been given a choice to ask for his freedom, but instead, he had asked for the freedom of others.

"Where? How do I know you are not lying?" Teller's response was quick and cutting.

"Yeah, where are they?" Rod pushed the crooked end of his nose in the air as he spoke. "I'd like to know that."

"None of your business, little man." Jaxter gave Rod a look that told him to shut up, but Rod as usual did not heed the warning. Instead he grabbed his groin in a vulgar manner and replied.

"You're just jealous that you're not as much a man as me, big man. Or is that, big man with a little-"

"Enough, children! We have more important things to deal with, other than your manliness. Now get out!" Scrycher raised his bloody hand and pointed towards the galley. They needed no further instructions, and his crew quickly exited.

Teller looked on at these actions, like a filmmaker assessing everyone as they interacted. He looked back at Scrycher. His features seemed familiar. Then the image came to him. That of a young man about the same age Scrycher was now. The man had been working in the mines, organizing the families to fight on the home planet. This was all in the crystal; Teller had seen it during his exploration of the archives. How this man had come to be in the crystal's vast storage, he was not sure. The image would have to have been before the mass destruction, two thousand years before. Teller was torn from these thoughts as Scrycher's voice boomed at him.

"Now, alone at last." Scrycher smiled as he took his rifle from his shoulder. Teller cringed at this action and shrunk back further into the cell with caution, but no fear showed in his eyes.

"You reckon he's for real?" Chelsea queried the others as she sat on the edge of the table, her small pistol in her hands as she cleaned it. "He's kinda cute, don't ya think?"

"S-s-sorry, I d-did not get a g-good look at him, w-with h-having to p-patch up the C-Captain, and a-all." Profitor had gone back to playing with his specimens on the table, tidying up the broken glass jars, and swapping them out for new ones. Blink was also on the table, chasing one of the jars back and forth, as he pawed it from one side of the table to the other.

"A bad move on Teller's part, but I reckon they're sorting it out right now." Chelsea looked back at the doors as though wishing it to be true.

"Chelsea just wants a pet to play with. She's even named the pussy Teller, after all." Rod was pacing, sweat on his brow, as he rubbed his hands together, and his eyes darted back and forth to the cockpit.

"What do you care what I want, rodent?" Chelsea looked down the barrel of the gun as she spoke, aiming it at the pacing Rod. "What's it to you if I want to play with the Teller?"

Rod made his way to the table, placing his hands on it in a menacing stance, spitting into Chelsea's face as he spoke. "You tart! You'd bang anything. You know you'd have two pussies between your legs with that one?" Rod shrugged his head towards the cell doors.

"I could live with that." Chelsea winked at Profitor who fumbled with his tweezers, dropping them on the floor with a *clink,* in his nervousness.

"Wouldn't you rather a real man, Chels?" Rod looked at her with a sick longing in his eyes as he went for his crotch, grabbing it yet again.

Chelsea gave her whole body up to a laugh as she spoke. "Can't see one here to do. Otherwise, I might say yes." Chelsea turned to Profitor and Jaxter, "Sorry, boys."

The two men mumbled under their breaths. "No offence taken." Jaxter leant forward from the wall, as he waited to see if Rod had a comeback.

Rod turned from Chelsea. This mark was always too hard. *Just you wait,* he thought.

"What is wrong with us pussies?" Scrags sounded offended as he asked while walking past Rod; to make his way to the galley for a small snack.

Rod's eyes lit up with a menacing look, as he grabbed Scrags by the shoulder. Rod spun him around so he was facing the table, and then, with a small shove, pushed Scrags forward. As Scrags grabbed the table to stop himself from falling, Rod pulled down the young boy's pants, speaking in a sick and evil tone. "Bend over pussy while I check." Undoing his belt in a bold fashion, Rod watched as the scared Scrags froze in the forced position. As he slid the belt from its seating in his pants, Rod drooled out of the side of his mouth. So focused with his current actions, Rod did not see Jaxter straighten up and take two steps to Scrags' location. Lifting the little boy by the scruff of his neck, Jaxter moved him to the other side of the table as a mother cat would a kitten.

Jaxter dropped his pants. Placing one hand on the table before him. He turned to Rod and spoke strong and boldly. "You will have to go through me first, little man. If you dare!" With the other hand he slapped one of his black cheeks.

As Jaxter's black bum glistened in the dim light, he placed his other hand on the table, winking at Scrags with a playful expression. Rod's smile was now gone, turned into an evil grin as he placed his hand on his knife, slowly drawing it from its sheath.

"Do not kill me. It will do you no good." Teller's face was full of stubbornness as he spoke.

As the door to the galley closed, Scrycher laughed. "Now why would I do that, Teller? We have the same goal in a twisted sort of way." Scrycher laid his rifle on the table as he knelt on a stool. "Now where do we start?"

"Why do you appear in my crystal?" Teller opened his palm, projecting a small image from it. The image was that of a man who was identical to Scrycher in appearance. The image then faded. "He... You, appear throughout the crystal's history. How can that be?"

"So the crystal is a map to our history?" Scrycher raised his eyebrows at the vocalized thought.

"No. It is more than that. It is a living memory of all those that have touched it before." As Teller talked, the crystal glowed brighter, feeding off his passion. "But again, how did you get into the crystal's memory?"

"I think, I can explain that. My family has been hunted for years. We often had to run and hide in the middle of the night, until finally my parents were taken. Through what I remember of my mother's stories, and what I could gather from around the stations, it goes like this: My family is from a long lineage of human-Stray descendants. My great-great-great... grandfather, I am assuming, is the one in the crystal. He was one of the first people to start working on the home-world. He was also, one of the few to take a Stray wife."

"Before it was outlawed." Teller's voice was somber, "We are not animals; we have as much right to love as the rest of you."

Scrycher continued, "There was an accident at one of the facilities, where many workers were killed. My grandfather was injured, and was pierced with shrapnel of crystal shards and rock. No one thought he would survive, but he did. Once he recovered, he fought for better rights in the mining facilities. The Company would not hear of it; they did not, and do not, care for life, other than their own. Therefore, he led the uprising, which eventually ended with stop-work strikes, and some catastrophe that affected the home world. There are rumors that shock troops and military were sent down to get the employees to go back to work, but to no avail."

"Then, tales of the worst. Some tales tell of explosions from the heavens, others of explosions from a chain-reaction between facilities. The end result; the same. Millions dead and most others left infertile. The Company banned all entry into the space around, or near the planet, not hard as the planet was, is, in the middle of nowhere. Finally, the home world was lost. How much is fact, I do not know. I have been searching my whole life for the reason my parents were taken, now I know it is all true. Because of my family's legacy, we were hunted until only I remain. This rifle is all I have to link me to my past."

Teller had glazed eyes as he spoke, "That is why your image is in the crystal. I remember now. The images are of a man, bravely leading my people against vast odds."

"And from what I have been able to find out, he never forgave himself for it. But we can be different. We can try and undo the wrongs of the ones before us. With you, and that crystal, I believe we can find our home planet, and hopefully re-establish it as a place of peace for our people. We have thousands of Strays scattered in facilities hidden across the system, safe and out of the reach of the Company. For now! But with nowhere to call home, we are just putting off the inevitable. I put this to you; you can either be the Teller of our dark and disturbing past, and an even darker future and death; or join me, and my band of misfits, to become the Teller of our bright future."

Teller grabbed at his head as he fell forward, resting on the bars. The fogginess was gone, but the pain was still there.

"Are you alright?" Scrycher opened the door to the cell as he spoke, concern slipping into his voice.

"No. I have these pains in my head that I have never had before." Scrycher helped Teller out of the cell and onto a stool.

"Well, you did hit your head pretty hard on the bulkhead. Maybe that is all it is?" He had never seen a Stray in this much pain before. They were a proud and powerful race, even if they were downtrodden.

Teller raised his head, looking deep into Scrycher's eyes, "I will help you. But if I find out that you are working for the Company, or your own selfish gains, then I will see to your demise. This is our ancestors' planet we are searching for, not another place to profit from. Understood, smuggler?"

Scrycher laughed as he stood up and extending his hand, he replied, "I'll hold you to that, even though you do not seem to be in much of a condition to follow it through. Teller stretched out his hand, shaking Scrycher's, "Ouch! Are you trying to break my other hand too?" Scrycher winced as his hand was crushed under Teller's grasp.

Teller released his hold, turning his hand over as he stared at it. "Sorry, I do not know my own strength at the moment."

Holding both hands together, Scrycher spoke as though to a long-time friend, "Well, enough damage for one day. Let us go and meet your new crewmembers. And while we are at it, we will get you some food, and a bed. You might not need the bed for some time though, sleeping beauty." The two men laughed as they opened the galley doors.

"Whoa! Am I missing something guys?" Scrycher's eyes were wide with disbelief as he entered the room.

"Ah-ah yes, Rod. That is the correct measurement for a rectum of a man the size of J-Jaxter. J-Jaxter, you can r-replace your pants now. Thank you. Oh-Oh s-sorry C-Captain, I did not mean to o-offend." Profitor did not look up as he spoke. He just kept looking at his specimens, as though nothing had happened.

"I know you wanted to welcome our guest, Jaxter, but do you think this is at all appropriate?" Scrycher could not help but plaster his face with a large smile as all the other crewmembers' jaws dropped at Profitor's comment.

Chelsea winked at Teller as she spoke. "Not yet Captain, maybe when I get to know 'im better." From the corner of her eye, she could see Rod re-sheathing his dagger as he slowly crawled back to the food preparation area.

Scrycher turned. "Guests do not get this kind of royal treatment normally. Well, what do you think?"

Teller was quick to reply. "Not yet thank you. I am sure a meal and a bed to sleep on, will do for now. I appreciate the thought though."

Jaxter face blushed as he tried to pull his pants up, struggling to get them over his bum cheek. "Put that hairy ass away, man. I don't want to be thinking about that whilst I am eating my meal." Scrycher walked past Jaxter as he laughed, slapping his bum cheek heavy-handedly.

"Anyone else want to bare their ass, except Chelsea that is? Or can we get to eating our meal?" Scrycher grinned as he sat.

Blink turned his attention from gnawing on a rat skeleton, to hiss violently at Teller, as he got close to Scrags. He raised his hackles and his color blended in with the ship, so all that could be seen were his round, white eyes; then, he was gone, blinking into Scrags' hair in the same menacing pose. Blink's body color changed quickly to match Scrags' hair as he messed it around, making sure his small body was concealed.

As Teller spoke, the small dragon clawed downwards. His eyes were red and his body tense.

"Enough, Blink. You are hurting me." Scrags' voice was so commanding that Blink allowed himself to relax as Scrags continued, "Are you the teller of our past?"

Teller spoke quietly as he raised his hand, "Yes I am, my son. What would you like to know?" Teller's hand lowered on Scrags' head and Blink screeched. His small mouth opened and snapped at the hand. *Th-thump, th-thump, th-thump.* Teller grasped at his head as an intoxicating pain crashed through him, starting from his temple and radiating thorough his body as he fell to the ground and into unconsciousness.

"Bliiiinnnnnk…"

Teller was woken from his forced slumber by an explosion, so loud, that his already throbbing head was compounded by ringing in his ears. As he regained his footing, he stood, looking at the cockpit, smoke now billowing through the doorway.

"On it, Captain." Jaxter jumped, sliding over the large table as he ran for the extinguisher. Grabbing it, he continued the momentum into the cockpit. Chelsea was just behind with another extinguisher in her hand, as the second explosion sounded through the ship. This explosion, twice the force of the first, knocked Chelsea backwards, her head crashing into the floor. Screaming exited the cockpit, and seconds later, Jaxter's leg followed, flying over the table and slamming into the wall behind Scrycher. Other small amounts of flesh splattered over the room and its occupants.

A huge, whooshing sound followed, sucking their precious air out. The blast door shut in front of Scrycher, who had run from Teller's side, screaming, "Noooooo!" He slammed, face first into the door; ignoring the pain, he beat his fists upon it. Finally, covered in sweat and the blood from his own hand, he slid down the door. Bloody tears now streamed from his eyes.

Chelsea regained her bearings, crawled over to Scrycher, and allowed herself to collapse onto him as she too, burst into tears. The emotions were so intense. Teller grasped for his head again and fell to the floor.

Th-thump th-thump, th-thump, th-thump... Teller's blood coursed through his temple, his world spinning as the Three fought to stop history repeating and he slipped back into his past self.

"Teller, you alright man?" Jaxter took one step towards him, allowing a hand to rest on his shoulder.

"What?" Teller was pushing away the fog as he heard an explosion, so loud, that his already throbbing head was compounded by ringing in his ears. He stood, confused at the repetitive nature of the scene before him. He tried to focus as he looked at the cockpit area of the ship; with smoke now billowing through the doorway, again.

"On it, Captain." Jaxter turned towards the table very quickly, and leapt towards it, only to fall flat on his bottom. Teller had grabbed Jaxter's arm that had been resting on his shoulder, pulling him to the ground as he tried to leap.

"Teller!" Scrycher's eyes widened in shock.

Chelsea turned around at the sound of Scrycher's voice, dropping her newly acquired extinguisher, and drawing her gun to aim at Teller. "Don't know what you're doin' Stray, but, let him go before I blow that mangy head off your shoulders."

Teller took his hands from Jaxter and raised them. Jaxter looked up gingerly, rubbing his sore behind. Teller watched and as Chelsea lowered her weapon, he leapt forward. A second explosion resonating from the cockpit, smashed into Chelsea's back, slamming her forward. Teller hit the grating with his knees and caught her between his legs, stopping her head from hitting the grating on the deck. *Whoosh, thump!* The blast doors closed before the air was pulled from the room.

Chelsea's head was in Teller's crotch; she rolled her frame over so she was now facing him. She spoke and looked softly at him. "You did not have to be so dramatic. You could've just asked if you wanted it."

Teller blushed as he spoke, "Well, I did not think you would say yes. Can you forgive a man for taking advantage of the situation?"

Jaxter fidgeted on the floor. "Reckon you two love-birds could give it a rest, and give me a hand to get up?"

Scrycher stopped staring curiously at Teller, and leant over Jaxter, giving him a hand off the floor. "Everyone else alright?" Scrycher looked around the room, counting heads as he spoke. "Rod!" Rod was nowhere to be seen. "Rod!" Scrycher's voice rose as his eyes darted around.

Rod popped his head out of from behind the preparation counter. "Scrycher."

"See, told you he was a rat. Like the rat he is, he crawled back into his hole." The crew broke into fits of laughter at Chelsea's jest.

Chelsea got to her feet, looking around the room, "Well, can't lay here all day with you, Teller. We've got a ship to mend. Jaxter!"

"Yes, Ma'am."

"Rod, get out there too and give them a hand," Scrycher's voice was serious as he shouted the order. Chelsea and Jaxter moved quickly through the galley doors and through the prison cells. They knew where they were headed; the tail section of their ship and the external airlock.

"Nope, not my job. That's what Jax and Chels are for." Rod grabbed his knife and started cutting rats. "You need me in the galley. After all that space walking, they'll be awfully hungry now, won't they?" Rod grinned at Scrycher, as he stormed off, following Scrags and Teller who had already hurried off after Chelsea and Jaxter. Profitor turned to Rod, his eyes rolling back in disgust, before he followed the rest of the crew.

Rod was left alone, smiling to himself, "Pity that explosion did not take out one of those bloody losers."

By the time Scrycher reached Chelsea and Jaxter, they almost had their suits on.

"Next time we do this, I hope you're undressing me, not putting clothes on me," Chelsea smiled at Teller, as he placed the helmet on her head, and secured the latches.

"Just make sure you are careful out there, and when you come back in, I'll consider it a date, and undress you," Teller smiled back at her in an assuring way.

"It is a date then."

Scrags dragged a crate along the floor, climbing on top of it as he grabbed the large helmet. He went to place the helmet on Jaxter's head as Scrycher spoke, "Jax, out of the suit. I will go." Scrycher had seen the beads of sweat gathering on the large man's brow and knew something was wrong.

"No, Boss. This is my job, and I will do it," Jaxter's eyes showed the fear he felt, as he let Scrags put the helmet on him, and he panicked.

Scrycher put his hand on Jaxter's shoulder in a reassuring manner, "I can take your place. I know you do not like confined spaces."

Jaxter allowed his eyes to close and his breathing slowed, although the beads of sweat now traveled down his face. Opening his eyes, he spoke, "I am OK, Boss. Turning to Chelsea, he spoke quickly, "Let's get in and out, Chels. Don't want to be out there any longer then we have to be." Chelsea and Jaxter grabbed the large piece of hull plating they had got from storage and attached a drill apparatus to their belts. These belts also held large bolts to attach the hull plating with. Stepping into the airlock, they looked at each other, and then back at the crew. The door was swung closed, and sealed by Scrycher via the large wheel in front of it. Once secured, the airlock de-pressurized, allowing the outer door to be released.

"You up for this, big man?"

"You bet, wouldn't miss this. A romantic space walk with you." Jaxter moved, ensuring one boot locked to the hull before releasing the other, his body shook and his breathing became erratic. The trek was arduous and both of them were physically exhausted by the time they got to the cockpit area of the ship. A large hole and damaged metal was the only sign of the gun that was once there.

The cockpit was de-pressurized, and placing the sheet was easy as they leaned over to put it in place. Chelsea knelt down, drilling the first bolt into place. Moving along, she drilled another, and another. Looking up, she noticed Jaxter had not moved. He was just standing there, frozen, his drill in his hand. She feverishly worked to get the other bolts attached, as she watched the crazed look on his face converging in his eyes. As she pulled the last bolt from her belt, she fumbled with it. It floated away from the ship as it escaped from her grasp. Standing up quickly, she reached up before it could float too far. The momentum she had used to get there deactivated her boots from the hull, propelling her body with great force away from the ship. In an instant, she saw her life flash before her. Then she felt her acceleration stop suddenly, banging her head on her helmet.

"Teller, what made you stop Jaxter?" Scrycher was not messing around. The two were alone. Scrags had run off to the other end of the ship to play, while they waited for the cockpit to be repaired. Scrycher was not waiting for answers. He wanted them now.

"I saw him die in the second explosion. A gory death." Teller held his head again as the throbbing increased once more. *Th-thump, th-thump, th-thump.*

Thinking back to the dramatic death of Philippe, Scrycher spoke quietly, "Pity you were not with us a while ago."

Teller did not hear this over the throbbing, but as he spoke it stopped, his voice low and fear in his eyes. "What is happening to me?"

"Need a hand?" The voice was that of Teller's. "Scrycher thought you were taking too long. Thought you might need a hand or two." Teller gently pulled Chelsea's body back onto the ship's hull, ensuring he did not rip either suit. Jaxter was still standing in fear, and did not move, nor did he register the rescue, as his eyes darted around madly. As Chelsea's boots locked to the deck, she lowered herself. Not wanting to waste any time, she drilled her last bolt and leant over, removing Jaxter's bolts and placing them in her own belt. As she took the last bolt, Jaxter's eyes lit up as if awakening from his fear. Realizing what had happened, he started running on the hull of the ship towards the airlock.

Teller looked at Chelsea, who just pointed and yelled, "Save him!" Teller did not need to be told twice, as he turned and followed the bounding Jaxter. Teller's feet barely touched the hull before his other foot left, as did Jaxter's. They both knew that this method of space running was extremely dangerous, but they did not care, each with a different goal in mind. Jaxter rounded the wing section and tripped, losing his footing to send him sprawling along the deck. Teller could see no choice but to change direction. He ran along the length of the wing like a wildcat, and then dropped to all fours, launching himself into space towards the ship's hull. He hoped with all his might that he had estimated correctly. Sailing through space he traveled at high speed, hitting his target dead on as he slammed into Jaxter's legs that were still soaring away from the hull. Teller's helmet cracked on Jaxter's boot, air hissing slightly from it as he slammed his feet down. This quick thinking was all that stopped his helmet from smashing completely on the hull. He stood, dazed, as both feet latched onto the hull, a mere meter from the airlock hatch. With the force and angle of the impact, Jaxter's boots did not latch, but bounced, jolting Teller's body. His suit stretched to its limits, stopping Jaxter from flying into space. The seams stretched further, the suit ripping at the arms as more air hissed from it. Holding his breath in desperation, Teller pulled on the large legs he had been holding, to attach Jaxter's feet onto the hull. Teller panicked as his air leaked into space. Jaxter, still in shock, took the two steps required to get to the safety of the airlock. A peace came over Teller as Jaxter disappeared into the ship. He relaxed, allowing his body to float back to a standing position.

Th-thump, th-thump, th-thump. Teller closed his eyes as he let out his last breath allowing him to be one with the space around him.

Th-thump, th-thump, th-thump....

"Don't leave me now. You have to undress me!" Chelsea looked into Teller's eyes affectionately as he regained consciousness.

Teller winced in pain, his lungs burning as his head lay in Chelsea's lap. He looked up at Chelsea who had not yet removed her space suit, "It's a date…"

"Well, we can't get to the ruins like this. We need to get the parts to replace our gun." Scrycher patted Jaxter on the shoulder as he left, "You've done well, Jax."

"But Captain, I really let you down," Jaxter was looking down at his feet as he talked quietly, his embarrassment evident.

"Jax, we are space worthy again and that's thanks to you repairing the inside of the cockpit. That is all that matters. And anyways, if it had not been you freezing up out there, it might have been me. After all, we are both claustrophobic." As he turned, he looked at Chelsea who was still leaning over Teller. "Chels, get us to the Syndicate."

"But boss, the Syndicate!" Chelsea knew that he must be desperate.

"Just get us there. I will do the rest." Scrycher headed to his quarters. He could feel his blood pulsing through his body with more strength as though his heart was pumping more efficiently as he walked. He did not know that the crystal was still changing his body, integrating itself into his blood.

"Wh-what is b-bothering y-you, T-Teller? Y-You seem to b-be holding y-your head a-a lot." Profitor looked up from his specimens and broken jars that he was sorting through. Some specimens were damaged, others fine, but he handled all with care as he spoke. Teller was massaging his temples and slurping up some of Rod's slop, as he sat.

"I have had this awful pain in my head since I awoke. It is that bad it appears to be fogging my vision, and clouding my judgment," His voice strained with the pain from the pressure of the blood pounding in his head.

Profitor reached over to Teller to remove the spoon from his hand and removed his hand gently from his head. He gingerly closed Teller's eyelids; the light gray fur covering his face glowed slightly as he tried to relax. Teller was in too much pain to argue, so he allowed Profitor to continue. "I-Imagine your feet are getting h-h-heavy, h-heavy, h-heavy… This heaviness is working its way through your body. Your legs… your bottom, your chest… your shoulders… your stomach… your arms… your hands… your neck… your head. N-now your heart, heavy, c-concentrate on your b-breathing, d-do not c-control it, let it c-control you. F-Feel nothing, s-see nothing, j-just your b-breathing. Sl-slow methodical c-controlled. Feel your blood slow, the pressure drop, the pain diminish. *Th-thump, Th-thump, Th-thump, Th-thump, Th-thump…*

Chapter 9

"Everyone got their cloaks? This is one nasty planet. Under no circumstances, do you upset the locals. We have more than enough to worry about already." Scrycher was stressed, and his voice betrayed it. He did not want to come to this planet, but he had no choice. The Gatling gun was destroyed. The only parts remaining were the connectors, and these were the only people close enough from whom they could get a replacement.

The ship door lowered, and they exited, allowing the crew to see the vast, uninviting area before them. The sky was dark and dreary; only lit by the continuous lightning that plagued the skies. Speech would have to be made between thunder bursts, and loud enough to get over the constant drumming of the rain. But Scrycher already knew this. This was not what he was worried about. It was the Syndicate that bothered him. This planet was home to the most cutthroat and unpredictable crime organization in the system. They did not take kindly to others, unless they brought lots of money; something Scrycher did not have.

The uninviting atmosphere of the place did not end there. As they walked off the platform, they could smell the decay of the rotting flesh of those that dared cross the Syndicate. The Steamers were in action. Massive men, carrying a steam canister on their backs, covered in silver suits, steamed unfortunate souls into the gutter. Their bodies mixed with the other bodies already disposed of. The Syndicate liked this form of punishment. What better way to ward off the people like themselves? Thieves, murderers, and undesirables.

As they got closer to the Steamers, their senses dulled, and their hearing numbed due to the *hiiiissssiiinnng* of the machines. They made their way through beggars, and other undesirable characters, until they reached the city. Well, if you could call it a city. The planet was covered in rectangular metal containers. Many of the containers were the size of Scrycher's ship or bigger, and all were full of goods and merchandise. A great deal of these items were rare and exotic, most illegal, and almost all, were stolen.

The gates to the area before them were formidable. Old and rusted, yet they could withstand an assault if one were to come. Beyond these gates was their destination, and the parts required so desperately. Scrycher, against his better judgment rallied his crew. "Let's do this." Scrycher flipped his hood over his head, stooping in the storm to make his way through the alleys.

A small, old man peddling his wares was calling out, trying to get their attention as the four comrades walked past him. "Buy meeat on a steek, Sir. Beest meeat on the planeet." The aroma from his small stall pleasantly wafted from under the large umbrella that was protecting his wagon and wares from the elements. Liquid burned inside an ornamental jar that was positioned in the middle of his cart. The heat cooked the meat that was rammed onto wooden sticks.

"Give me one." Rod was quick to throw a dollar note to the small man as he took the stick of meat. Fat dripped down his chin as he chewed one of its multiple pieces.

"H-how do you kn-know what m-meat that is?" Profitor was pointing at the stall and shaking his head in disbelief as Rod tore more of the meat off the stick.

"Tastes a crap load better than the bloody rats I cook up. So why should I care?"

"D-Do you know h-how many stomach infections you can get from bad meat?"

"Don't care, don't wanna know. That stuff don't float my boat, like it does for you, Prof."

As the small man removed another stick of meat of the small fire, he turned to Teller, "You want meeat on steek, Sir?"

"GGGRRRRRR." Teller's aggressive growl was obvious to even this pushy salesman who pulled the stick of meat away from Teller hastily.

"Sry, Sir. Sry, Sir. Mee keep meeat." The little man placed the stick back on the fire that still burned strong and smokeless on his wagon, even though the wind howled strongly through the street.

Teller raised his nose, sniffing the air, his keen sense of smell told him there was something concerning about this man's meat. With this in mind and the little man's stick of meat out of his face, Teller moved off quickly, removing himself from under the man's umbrella and away from the peculiar smell.

"Settle tiger. Don't want to scare the locals." Scrycher chuckled to himself at Teller's actions. This Stray never ceased to amaze him. As he continued to chuckle, a large man walked into Profitor, knocking him to the ground. Scrycher leant down and pulled him off the ground. "Profitor, get back to the ship. I don't think you should be out here."

"B-But C-Captain."

"Don't but me. I need to know you are safe with Chelsea, Jaxter and Scrags! Sorry."

"H-Hey g-guys where y-you going? S-Scrycher h-has just s-sent me b-b-back to the s-s-ship t-to s-stay s-safe w-with you g-guys." Profitor was in a tizz, as he walked behind them. He had seen them walking away from the ship as he went back to it, so thought he may as well tag along. After all, what harm could it cause? Scrycher was always too overprotective.

"Bloody hell, Chels, the Boss is goin' to kill us if he finds out that we went out." Jaxter cautiously looked around him, the area before them barren and uninviting, "You reckon we can get some nuts from here while the Captain is not watching us?"

"Hope so. Not in the mood for another chair smashing moment." Chelsea was walking beside Jaxter, with Scrags, sulking in the rear. "C'mon Scrags. Scrycher didn't take you because he was worried 'bout the men he was going to see. Otherwise you'd have been by his side." Chelsea stopped, allowing Scrags to walk in front of her, while she stroked the back of the boy's head gently.

They walked around an alley, and Blink stood up excitedly on Scrags' head, his large eyes bulging. The marketplace before them was in stark contrast to where they had just walked through. It was bustling with different stalls and characters. The chatter and excitement of the crowd soon dispelled Scrags' mood, as he watched in amazement at the cages of weird and ugly creatures on the booth before him. Blink turned his head sideways, looking at a rat-like creature in a cage. He licked his lips with his long tongue. As the tongue darted out of his mouth and towards the creature, Scrags' small hand and fingers intercepted with lightning fast reflexes. "Blink!" The little dragon retracted his tongue, moping, as he snuggled back into the hair.

"I-I-I need s-some more j-jars f-for m-my s-specimens. I w-will n-not be long."

"But Scrycher will…" It was too late. Profitor was making his way through the crowd, and out of their sight.

"Ah well. What have we here?" The voice was chirpy and high, as the dog-like man spoke. The dog man did not wait for a reply; instead, he continued talking, "Well no matter what you want, Dogny got it. You want a lolly for the boy?" He grabbed a large gooey-looking ball on a stick from his stall and handed it to Scrags, who eagerly took it. Scrags eyes lit up at the ever-changing flavors as he licked it. Looking at Chelsea, the man continued, "Maybe a necklace for the wife?" As he spoke again, he looked at Jaxter and Chelsea's hands. "Mmm, no wedding bands. Maybe a necklace for your lover? No? Yes?" Dogny stared into Chelsea's eyes deeply, probing, feeling, exploring. Dogny blushed as he turned back to Jaxter, "If she not your lover, you need to make her your lover, wowee." Jaxter tried to speak as he reached into his pockets, fumbling around for the bolts that he needed the new nuts for. "Ah, that is it. You need nuts, lots of nuts. These nuts the best." Dogny fumbled through a draw he had just opened, jingling parts as he went, "Nup, Nope, not at all. Oh yes, this one, that one, that one and this one." Reaching forward, he grabbed Jaxter's open hand with both of his, placing something into them as he searched Jaxter's eyes. Deep he delved to find nothing, "On the house, I say. No cost, nothing at all. Just remember where you got them from, who you got them from. Maybe you pay me another way, I say." Jaxter looked into his open palm as Dogny removed his hands. In his palm lay four nuts of the exact size he required.

Dogny turned back to Scrags, who was still lapping into the lollypop. "Little man, let me see, what else do you want?" Blink hackled up this time, those big eyes, boring into Dogny. Dogny looked at Blink, faltering, as he stuttered. "D-Dragon…"

Scrags stopped licking his lollipop to speak, "No, Sir. He is just a lizard. Hee hee." As their eyes locked, Dogny froze. He had no choice; he was drawn into Scrags' intricate mind.

"This small boy. Could this be one of the fabled?" Dogny's mind raced as he searched. The boy's past was open to him. He searched back further and further until he was in the womb. Blue! Blue, how could it be? He needed to get further back to see why. Further back still until he was conceived, the mother's face blue and familiar. "The future teller?" But Dogny did not stop there. He went further back to when Scrags was thought of by his father. His father's face was like a picture to Dogny, one he knew all too well. "Jarel!" he shouted, as he tried to claw back to the future, Scrags' mind fought back. A dragon's head exploded out of Scrags' mind, sending Dogny sprawling to the ground, kicking his feet and thrashing his arms. He tried to fight off the internal attacker, as though it was attacking him in the real world.

Chelsea grabbed Scrags' shoulder, "Let's get out of here. This one's a freak!" she said as she led him away. The attempt to invade his mind had angered Scrags. He growled as he turned back to Dogny, the growl turning to a purr as he watched Dogny fighting for his life.

"Frank, we need the cooling rod and Gatling gun for our ship. You know the one." Scrycher was trying to play it down. He had entered the store blasé. He knew he needed the part desperately, but he did not want Frank to know it.

Frank was a chubby man. He was unsightly and crude, as he popped a long, thin meat ration into his mouth; the fat dripping down his face into his unkempt beard. As he licked his greasy fingers, he spoke softly, his voice barely audible over the thunder and rain outside. "What happened to the other one? Had a little accident did we?" Frank winked at Rod, who was standing beside Teller. The wink did not go unnoticed by either man.

"Well, you know how these things are. They get old, and need replacing. Got one or not?" Scrycher was playing with his rifle out of habit as he spoke and looked around the room, trying to spy the part.

"How's we paying for that now?" Frank placed another large piece of meat into his mouth, this time, waiting to lick his fingers. "Mmmmm?" His head angled as he emphasized the question.

"We have three barrels of water on the ship, which are yours if you want them. Just get me the gun." Scrycher was normally into haggling, but not this time. He had thrown all his cards on the table. They needed this part, and they needed to get out of here.

"Mmm, hefty offer. I would normally accept without question, but I have something else in mind. What we say, you give me that rifle of yours in exchange for the parts?"

Scrycher's eyes fired as Frank spoke. He had been trying to get the gun for years, but Scrycher had always worked a way out of it. "No," Teller chipped in, "I have something of more value." He unbuttoned his cloak to reveal a golden necklace with a pendant on it. The pendant was carved in the shape of a felines face. Teller walked to the counter, showing it to Frank as he drooled over the jewelry.

"Pretty, but I am not into pretty. Rifle or nothing! 'Pends how bad we want it I suppose." Frank smiled a greasy smile.

Scrycher ripped his rifle from his shoulder, throwing it down on the counter. "You had better throw in an extra canister of coolant while you are at it then."

Frank giggled to himself, his large belly wobbling like jelly, in excitement. "Oh yes, we can do that, we can." Scrycher cringed as Frank handled the gun with those slimy hands. It will take me some time to get the parts, but if you come back later, they will be here. Say, three hours."

"Be ready by then, or the deal is off." Scrycher stormed out of the room, swearing under his breath as he tried to flip his hood over his head. However, in his anger, he ripped the hood clear off. He swore again, as he entered the rain, and it smashed into his uncovered face.

Ten minutes had passed, and Scrycher had not spoken a word since trading his gun. He stopped suddenly, turning to Teller and spoke loudly to be heard over the storm. "Thank you for offering your pendant. I understand that it must mean a lot to you." Teller did not have time to respond, as Scrycher slammed his palm upon his temple in frustration, and pulled something out of his pocket. "Oh crap! I forgot to give him these connectors to make sure we get the right ones." The two men turned back quickly, the storm masking their entrance as they entered the shop again.

"We don't want to get the wrong part aft-" The two men looked up as they re-entered the shop, and stopped at the entrance. The picture before them unbelievable. Rod was stuffing what seemed to be a large sum of money into his pockets. He stood at the counter, laughing with Frank.

Scrycher cautioned Teller to be quiet as they approached, trying to hear the conversation over the storm.

"Scry…. did not kn... wh... hit him. Funny man th... one. See th... Lo... on his f... when I t... him . w….. it. Great plan Rod." Frank slapped Rod on the shoulder, and both men laughed.

Scrycher exploded in a fit of rage, as a luminescent redness flooded his face, lighting the room, as he ran towards the men. "What do you mean Rod? You sabotaged our ship, and you were the reason that Jaxter died… could have died?" Scrycher's face was such a deep red, his head looked as though it was about to explode. He stopped in front of the men, yelling at Rod, his body still emanated a faint glow.

"Ah, if I can interrupt? He was following my orders, after all, that gun of yours is worth a life or two." Frank spoke, as he fondled Scrycher's gun. "Oh, and she is a beauty, isn't she?"

"You went to trade a life for this gun? You filthy swines." Scrycher leant back to punch Rod in the face, but overbalanced in his anger, missing completely as Rod nimbly ducked. However, the punch did land, accidentally smashing into Frank's face. As Scrycher regained his footing, Frank swung the rifle at him, which Scrycher grabbed easily, and a struggle ensued. As they fought, the rifle started to glow. With a final pull, Scrycher dislodged the rifle, and with a fluid movement, swung the end of it in an attempt to knock Frank to the floor. Scrycher's assault attempt was thwarted, as Frank kicked him backwards. *Sssswwwww.* A black blade protruded from the end of the rifle, its edge glowing in power, as it effortlessly sliced through Frank's neck. The head stayed there for a second, before it dropped to the floor with a splat. As Scrycher fell to the floor, he realized what he had done, as did Rod.

"You are dead, Scrycher. The Syndicate will hunt you." Rod turned and ran, disappearing into the darkness of the streets.

"Teller, get out of here, now." Scrycher could not believe his misfortune, or luck, as he grabbed the duffel bag of Gatling gun parts, that were, for some reason already on the counter. He flung it to Teller, who effortlessly caught it in mid-flight. Both men ran out the door, and down the street. As they neared the fence, the sirens sounded, and the gates started closing. "Quick. If we don't get out, we are as good as dead." Both gates were almost closed as they dodged through them. Scrycher's jacket caught on a barb, and tore as he swore. "Damn you, Rod!"

Rod, and several other men, came running through the crowd behind them, only to be stopped by the closed gates. "Gregory, they're there. There's Scrycher and the Teller."

"Get these gates open! Now, men!" Gregory gave the orders and his men left quickly, leaving only Rod and himself standing at the gates, to watch Scrycher and Teller flee.

Profitor popped his head over Rod's shoulder, asking inquisitively. "R-Rod wh-what's going o-on? H-Has there b-been some k-kind of a-accident?"

"Well, well, what do we have here?" Gregory turned around, the light catching his silken sleeves, as he grabbed Profitor by the scruff of his neck. The duffel bag Profitor had been carrying, slid from his grasp. The sound of the smashing glass was drowned out by the rain, as his legs flayed helplessly.

"If we cannot have the master, we will have the slave. SCRYCHER!" Gregory's voice boomed over the sound of the rain. Both Scrycher and Teller stopped to see what the commotion was about. "When I catch you I will do this, and worse, to all your crew."

Gregory threw Profitor into Rod who grabbed the scared man. "B-But R-Rod I-I th-thought w-w-we w-were f-f-f-friends."

Rod pulled his knife from its sheath. He looked at Scrycher as he pulled the knife across Profitor's throat and yelled. "I have no friends." As he dropped the lifeless body; Rod's eyes glazed ever so slightly. He removed the snot from his nose with his sleeve. Bending down, he spoke into Profitor's ear. No one could hear but the wind itself, as he wiped the blood from his knife on Profitor's shirt.

"I thought I told him to get back to the ship. I made that friggin' clear, did I not? The friggin' imbecile." Scrycher nostrils were flaring, as he reached the ship. The comment was rhetorical. He did not waste time, waiting for an answer. He just stormed off to his quarters. "Get us out of here, and in a hurry."

"What 'bout Rod and Profitor, Boss?" Chelsea questioned quietly.

"They are dead Chels... They are dead!"

Chapter 10

The volley of cannon fire hit the side of the ship, the force making it lurch sideways, as Chelsea failed to dodge the onslaught. "Captain, they're too powerful for us. We need to run."

Scrycher had no time to respond before the next explosions. Scrags was thrown from his crate, to slam into the Gatling gun's cage. Teller wasted no time, bolting to the station, arming the gun, and shooting at the next volley of cannon fire. His aim and response were impressive, each volley being blasted before it reached them. Scrags had managed to get to his feet, as Scrycher reached him. Grabbing the young boy by the arm, he swung him out of the gun pit and onto the deck of the ship. "Get to the escape pods, and make sure they are ready to launch. They may be our only way out of this mess." Without question, Scrags ran through the cockpit door and into the galley, towards his destination.

"Go through this again, Jaxter. They just sat there and watched while you installed the Gatling gun? Then we came aboard? They started firing without a warning?" Scrycher was holding onto the cage around the gun, watching as Teller's precise aim took out another set of cannon volleys.

"Yes, Boss, just like that."

"We had better hail them again." Scrycher struggled over to the communications console, grabbing hold as Chelsea performed another hair-raising maneuver. "Whoa, Chels. I want to be alive at the end of this."

"If I don't keep flying like I'm doing, there'll be only one end to this. Us all dead!" Chelsea was grimacing as she concentrated, pulling the pilot stick this way and that, the ship responding fantastically under her control.

"Unknown ship. What do you want? We have done nothing to provoke you."

The firing stopped. The crew went silent. The humming of the engines brought a strange calmness to the chilled atmosphere, only broken by the hissing of steam, as Teller's sweat fell on the Gatling gun's hot shaft.

"Scrycher."

"Rod?" Chelsea's concentration was broken by Rod's voice over the speaker. She turned to Scrycher to scorn him. "Boss!"

"Long story."

"Miss me, sweet Chelsea? I haven't slept the same without you. That's why I told them where you were going." Rod's voice was full of the sick pleasure of someone on the winning side. He knew he could not lose.

Scrycher thought back to the co-ordinates he had given to Rod to input into the computer. The ones to the planet they were just on. *I am a fool*, he thought.

"Shut up, worm. Out of my way… Scrycher. This is Gregory; did you think you could get away from me, after invading my world? And for that matter, where did that planet below us come from, and what the hell were you doing on it?

Scrycher flicked a switch on the console, took two quick steps to Chelsea and whispered something into her ear. Just as quick, he leapt back to the console and flicked the switch back. "Well, why not take a look for yourself, but be quick, as I can only hold the planet in this realm for another... say twenty minutes. After that it is lost, and with it, all its riches." Scrycher and Chelsea locked eyes, not daring to breath as they waited for the response.

Murmuring could be heard over the com, but no real words as Gregory contemplated. "Alright. We will not kill you. Yet! Just wait right there; we have unfinished business, and we will be back." The battle cruiser started slowly towards the planet. As it stopped, two shuttles exited, heading towards the planet below. "Oh, and do not try to run, or we will be forced to blow you out of the sky, and that would be unfortunate for both parties." There was no emotion in the voice.

Scrycher nodded at Chelsea and then turned towards the galley, momentarily forgetting Profitor was no longer with them. "I hope your theory on this planet is right, for all our sakes." Chelsea threw the ship forward, violently accelerating, so all but Teller were thrown to the floor. The large battle cruiser opened fire on the tiny ship. The cannon fire exploded all around them, Teller blowing them out of space before they could get too close. Teller was hanging upside down in the Gatling cage, shooting behind them. He did not see the meteor storm in front of them. Neither did the others, only realizing their mistake as the first meteor hit.

Chelsea's attention was forced back to the task in front of her, as they were ravaged by the storm. Rock after rock smashed into the failing hull, sending the ship this way and that. They did not have time to observe the ships behind them. They did not see the syndicate ship, The Enforcer, get pulled at by the planet that needed matter to fill its void as it shifted realms. They did not see the planets wake rip the two smaller ships into pieces as it exited out of this realm. They did not see The Enforcer break free, and limp towards them, the remaining guns blazing until, finally, it stopped, the meteor storm too dense for a ship of its size to enter…

The small ship limped its way out of the meteor storm. Many of its hull plates were torn from its body; but its bulk, for the most, was space worthy. The crew stood in the cockpit, a deathly silence over them as they looked around, listening to the hull creaking as they tried to gauge the extent of the damage from their encounter.

"Scrags, you can stand down the shuttle pods now." Scrycher turned around searching the cockpit area. Walking into the galley, he turned as he spoke towards the table where Profitor always sat. "Prof. Have you seen Scrags?" His heart weighed heavy, as he remembered that Profitor was no longer with them and the betrayal that had caused his demise.

Scrycher looked around the Galley; it was empty. This difficult time took its toll on him as he searched behind the food preparation benches in the galley, a cold reality starting to set in. He had lost two of his crew, and was searching for a third.

He started to panic as he continued to search the rest of the ship. His heart beat fast, as though he had run a mile, but really he had only searched the cockpit and the galley. *Th-thump, th-thump th-thump*, his heart beat faster as he burst through the first prison cells. Into the crew quarters he went screaming, "Scrags! Scrags, where are you?" *Th-thump, th-thump.* "Scrags, Scrags, Scrags." Blink lifted his sleepy head as Scrycher ran, crazed. Not realizing the extent of the situation at hand, Blink lay back down. Scrycher ripped the covers from the bunks. Nothing. *Th-thump, th-thump, th-thump.* "Scrags, Scrags, Scrags." He opened the pod. Nothing! No Scrags. Running again through to the other room, he opened the door. *Th-thump, th-thump, th-thump.* "Scrags, Scrags, Scrags." The pod was there. No Scrags. He broke through the door to the storage area and stopped. Crazed, he looked, searching erratically, his lips and mouth dry. *Th-thump, th-thump.* He could still see no sign of Scrags, as his heart felt as though it would beat from his chest. He tried the door into the last two quarters. The door was jammed. He could not open it. Standing at the door he listened, then screamed. *Th-thump, th-thump, th-thump.* "Scrags, Scrags, Scrags, you in there?" His fists beat on the door, trying to open it, but to no avail. His stomach felt as though it was turning inside out as he dry retched. Turning, he ran through the quarters he had just traversed, and back into the cells. This was the only other entrance to the crew quarters and escape pods. *Th-thump, th-thump, th-thump.* "Scrags, Scrags, Scrags." Scrycher burst into the room. The door opened inwards. The air gushed out, ripping the door and his body into the room. In desperation he grabbed the doorframe, his fingers slipping as his heartbeat deafened him. *Th-thump, Th-thump, Th-thump.* Agonizingly, he managed to pull himself back in so his shoulders were level with the doorframe. But to no avail. The emergency door across this doorway slammed shut, ripping the door from its hinges and sending it into the coldness of space…

Scrycher lay on the floor, his ghostly white face in a pool of vomit as his heartbeat slowed. *Th-thump, th-thump, th-thump.* Teller's life-saving hands rested on the floor beside him. He had pulled Scrycher back through the doorway, just in time.

"Aaargh! Scrags! What have I done?" Scrycher wailed into the pool of vomit. He realized that Scrags must have been sucked into the dead of space with the missing pod. In a fit of rage, he raised himself, grabbing the stools from the table, smashing them across the bars of the cells; one after the other, until all that was left of each was crumpled metal. Smashing the last of the stools, he staggered, almost toppling. He fell to his knees, looking around, searching, searching for something, anything to smash. Hands covered in his vomit, now covered his face. Tears streaming as his body and mind, so worn and tired, crumbled. Falling to the floor, his cheek splattered on the deck, drool, spilling out as his face fell sideways. Teller stood and reached for him, trying to push away the *th-thump, th-thump...* *th-thump, th-thump* of his own head. Scrycher lay there, his eyes looking, but not seeing, as though his soul had died in this one moment.

Teller's mind fogged as the, *Th-thump, th-thump... Th-thump, th-thump...* drowned out the present. Blink screeched within his skull, deafening him in his anguish over the loss of Scrags'. Teller focused on this, the feeling of loss, as he tried clawing back, his mind splintering through the time lines as he made one last effort to call out through the fog in his mind... "Scrycher?" He called out as he slipped into his past self.

"Yes, Teller, what is it?"

Pulling his way back through the fog, he continued, concerned about Scrycher's well-being. "Are you alright?"

"Well if this damn hood had not ripped off, and I was not getting soaked, I would be much better... Oh, and thank you for offering your pendant. I understand that it must mean a lot to you." Scrycher spoke loudly to be heard over the storm, "Oh crap, I forgot to give him these connectors to make sure we get the right ones."

Teller did not move for a second, dumbfounded by what had transpired. He waited, as the rain fell down upon him, drowning out the drumming of his own head. "Oh. You had better let me give them to him, while you get out of this weather." Teller took the connectors off Scrycher quickly and stepped away.

Scrycher grinned, "Now what did I do before you came along?" he said as he continued to hurry away, and out of the weather. Teller quickly walked around the corner, looking into the shop, watching as Rod filled his pockets with money and the two men laughed heartily. *What should I do?* he thought to himself, as he moved into the cover of the shadows, waiting for Rod to leave.

Chapter 11

Rod used the darkness well, concealing himself as he slithered through the narrow streets. The lightning silhouetted his hooded figure, as he turned his head back. His eyes darted around the area he had just traveled, to ensure he had not been followed. He did not see the two children come out of the alley in front of him. One boy was plump, and the other deadly thin. They looked into their hands, rushing away from the alley, eager to spend their meager wages for the week. They were taken unawares as they walked into this hooded man, the coins of the plump boy falling to the ground, as he bumped into Rod's skinny frame.

"Sorry, Sir." The young boy of maybe ten years, his face still carrying his baby fat, awkwardly knelt on the ground, searching blindly to find all the precious coins.

"We're on our way to the arcade, Sir, sorry, bit excited, and weren't watching where we were going and we want to get there before our friends leave." The skinny boy, maybe a year or two older, now knelt down to help his friend find all the coins as he babbled.

Rod stood his ground, his throat swilled with saliva and he gulped while forming a wicked smile. His head swirled with all the options of what to do now. As he contemplated, he slid his dagger out of his pocket and sniggered. "No problem, boys, I am sure I can take it out on your hides."

The plump boy stood up, trying to run as he regained both feet on the ground. He was not going to be this man's bitch. He did not have time to think, or move further, as Rod plunged the dagger into his stomach. As the warm blood flowed over Rod's hand, he twisted the knife, the boy's body twitching slightly as it dug in deeper. The warm sensation stimulated Rod; his senses were heightened, and he inhaled deeply as the sweet smell of blood attacked his nostrils. He savored this for a moment, then, grabbing the boy's soft, chubby face in his hands, twisted the knife deeper as he watched the glint of life drain from his young blue eyes.

The thunder roared and lightning struck, lighting Rod as he swallowed hard and cradled the lifeless body; not allowing it to fall quite yet.

"Sorry, Sir, we will be on our way, won't we Nat?" The skinny boy grasped his friend's arm, pulling him away from Rod as he tried to navigate around him. Nat's body fell from Rod's grasp as the thinner boy tried to lead him. He overbalanced at the extra weight, trying to steady his friend, but to no avail. The body weight forced him to the ground, pinning him. "Nat! Nat!" The boy panicked, shaking his friend vigorously. "Nat get up."

Rod smiled wickedly as he slowly removed his hood from his head, his crooked teeth and smile, lighting in the next lightning strike. The young boy froze as he observed the face before him, pure evil, glinting in this man's eyes.

"Sir! Sir! What have you done to Nat?"

Thump. That evil smile, and those eyes, were the last thing the boy saw.

Slosh, Slosh, Slosh. Rod dragged the children to the end of the alley, taking his time as he pleasured over every cut and bleed. He did not see the figure in the street observing him , watching, and waiting. The figure felt disturbed, but not sick. The cold reality was that there was no hope for the children, no possibility of recovery for their broken bodies, so he did not intervene. The figure knew that they had never felt what had been done to them, and that they would never again feel the pain of this world. He also knew that Rod would not be around long enough to do this ever, ever again…

Satisfied, Rod rose from his knees, the ground around him now stained with blood. Replacing his hood, he left this place, the bodies mutilated beyond recognition. As he walked, he smiled, a sick, satisfied smile. He reached the end of the alley, stopped and knelt down to pick up the coins on the ground before him. The blood was gone; the bucketing rain had washed it from the ground, rinsing the scene clean.

He stood, but was knocked down by a large figure who seemed to walk directly into him. He checked his money as he regained his footing, pickpockets being common in this area. Feeling that the money was still there, he turned to view his assailant. There was no one there! He made his way to the next alley; entering the door he had gone through a hundred times before.

Teller smashed into Rod, knocking him to the ground. Rod fell hard, hitting with a *thump*. Teller had to hit him hard to cover the real act, the removal of the knife, replacing it with the one he had bought moments earlier. As Teller slipped Rod's knife into his coat, he strode off quickly, knowing what he had to do. He had no reservations. It had to be done.

Rod inserted the coins he had just stolen from the young boys and waited. Raising his legs so they were now resting on the table, he waited, thinking of his recent accomplishments. It had been an hour or so before the monitor in front of him lit up. With a start, he sat up.

"I thought I told you to take out their weapons? You damn near killed us." The Gunnery's voice betrayed the anger he felt for Rod as his face reddened.

"I've done it." Rod was casual, still not removing his feet from the table.

"'Bout bloody time. Thought you had done it before?"

"They were a little more resourceful than I thought. But not this time! I sabotaged their gun, causing it to explode and then got them to buy another part from a friend of mine. It will now only function at a quarter of its potential." Rod's smiled sinisterly.

"And I bet you made a few quid on the side too?" The Gunnery's tone was almost envious.

Rod fondled through his pocket, and ran his fingers through the cash, his smile broadening. "Of course, brother, you wouldn't have it any other way, now would you?"

Teller hastily made his way back to the shop. He was driven, knowing what he must do, as he thought of the young boys that Rod had just mutilated. *Could I have stopped them from being killed if I was earlier? he thought, Did they really need to die? Would they have died if I had not changed what should have happened?* This last thought plagued Teller's mind. He himself was a man of peace, yet he let an act like that take place, and he was about to perform another. One much worse!

"Hey, we forget something? The part is not quite ready yet, if you get what I mean. We still have to conceal the sabotage of it." The chubby man did not look up as he lovingly placed more meat into his mouth, while patting the Gatling parts on the counter.

Teller spoke, brandishing Rod's knife in the air. His voice was harsh and demanding, not at all like himself. "Give me the parts! Give me your money!"

"And the money?" As Frank spoke, he shivered, filling the duffel bag beside him with the Gatling gun parts.

Teller was aware the man was looking at the cameras across the room. He had walked into the shop. He looked shorter as he entered; lowering his frame so that it resembled Rod's small stature, not his own, larger profile. He now gestured crudely, as Rod would have done, leaning over the counter and pulling the money from the till, stuffing it into the duffel bag. This action covered the real act of removing Scrycher's gun from the counter. The man tried to grab the bag, and money from Teller, in a last attempt to stop the theft. Teller acted irrationally, brandishing the knife again, raising it high in the air, so it could be seen by all. Teller's own hand, the fur now jet black, blended with the room as he swung it down harshly. The blade sliced through the man's hand and into the counter. Teller made it look awkward and clumsy and with a great deal of effort as he pulled the knife from the table, using his full body weight to dislodge it. This was only done for the cameras as in reality, he could have pulled the knife with little, to no effort at all. For this plan to work, it needed to be flawless. So far his acting was exceptional.

"You will not get away with this. You will be killed." Frank was yelling as he grabbed Teller's hand.

Teller had given himself to the blood lust, and looked deep into Frank's eyes. The horror of Teller's blood red eyes caused Frank to freak out as he spoke to him, "Rod says thanks for all the money you are going to donate to his cause."

"Rod!" That was the last word Frank spoke before Teller plunged the dagger into his chest. To the camera and those watching it, it appeared as if it was indeed an act of passion. An act that was trying to stop Frank from speaking his assailant's name… 'Rod's name'. As the man lay there on the counter, Teller cut. He got the knife and methodically and systematically cut like he had seen Rod do in the alley. Finally, the blood red died out of his eyes, white replacing it as calmness returned to him and he stopped. All the time, he ensured that he kept the persona of Rod. Throwing the knife into the bag, he zipped it up and left.

As Teller stumbled through the alleys, his head throbbed, *th-thump, th-thump, th-thump*. Crashing into the wall, he threw up, grasping at his temple. Retching, he thought of the three killings he had been part of. However, he knew, he could not stop now. He had come too far. He had to finish this, and finish it now. He lowered his hands from his face, imagining the blood of innocents upon them. There was none. No blood, no hands! He could not see them at all. Panicking, the thumping in his head got louder until he pulled himself back, thinking of Profitor, and the relaxation technique he had taught him. *For Profitor,* he thought. *I must do this for him to live.* His death in the alternate version of this life had only brought sorrow, an uncontrollable chain of events and the loss of so much life. This is why he had to do it, why he had to push on. Feet heavy…legs heavy…chest heavy… In and out, his breathing calmed him, cleared his mind and cleared his soul. With clarity, Teller dropped his clothing, his naked body now covered in a fine fur as black as the night. Teller watched himself in amazement as it blended in with his surroundings. Like a chameleon, like Blink! He wandered the streets; no one knowing that he walked beside them, next to them, in front of them. The only part of him visible was his white eyes as they canvassed the area before him, his normal black eyes gone for now. Blending into his surroundings, he thought, *now this makes things easier,* as he made his way back to his belongings.

"S-Sorry, S-Sir." Profitor struggled to raise himself from the ground as he looked around. No one was there, but yet something or someone had knocked him down moments earlier. Looking around, he searched for his duffel bag. "D-d-damn, s-someone st-stole it." As he spoke, a small tinkle of glass echoed from the alley behind him. Shivering in fear, he turned and walked down the alley, nervously looking around him. "I-I-I-s s-s-someone th-th-there?" Not getting a reply, he walked further forward and sprawled over his duffel bag. In fear, he raised himself yet again. He grabbed the bag and ran, with all his strength, he ran. He did not notice the extra weight in the bag, nor did he bother to check the contents, as he did not care. He just wanted to get back to the ship.

"Dogny. Dogny. Dogny." Lallone stood over him, yelling. No one else saw, nor heard Lallone, and no one bothered with Dogny. The dog man thrashed for his life on the ground. He looked like every other crazy homeless man, scared out of his mind. Lallone grabbed Dogny's face, looked deep into his eyes, and searched; but he could find nothing. Dogny's mind was always so full. The emptiness sent alarm bells ringing in Lallone's mind. He turned to the stall Dogny had been manning, and pushed a small button on its side. The stall *wrrrred* for a second and then folded upon itself, again and again and again, until all that was left was a small suitcase-sized box, with a small handle on top.

Lallone lifted the petrified Dogny to his feet, grabbing the box as he started to walk, never breaking his gaze into his friend's eyes. Then it came. A flash! A spark of sanity, and then the words; "Help, Dogny. The dragon. The dragon. The dragon."

Lallone found a secluded alley, and placed Dogny down as he spoke, "Be patient old friend. I am coming. Be patient." He held Dogny's head taut as he looked deep into his friends eyes. Another's thoughts, a person unseen by him, bombarded his open mind. Filled it with the emotions of guilt, betrayal, hatred, love and fear. This mind, that of Teller, was an open book, showing Lallone what he had done and what he was about to do. He was pulled to this openness, probing further until he was shown what had been and what was about to become. "It is not possible. It cannot be. No one has that much power. To change the past, in order to change the future; we must protect him, nurture him, help him. Wait, Dogny, my friend. I must do something now, before the others find them, before his plan, falls apart."

"Freesh meet, beest meet on a steek." The little man stood still, his constant calling stopped as a thought popped into his head. *Freesh meet, two young children, too good to pass up.* As the little man was forced to think these thoughts, he walked away from the blue figure of Lallone who had implanted them. Turning, Lallone wasted no more time. He dropped to the earth, his knees buckling at the collision. He needed to return, he had to focus his whole mind on the one task he had not done for centuries. His mind cleared, his legs started moving and he was running, hoping he was not too late to aid his friend Dogny, who was still fighting for his life in that dark alley.

Rod smiled as he came out of the alley, thinking of his accomplishments. He had done all that he could hope for today and it could not get any better. As he contemplated what to do next, he heard screaming from the alley beside him. He walked closer, peering around the corner as he heard a high-pitched feline hiss. He stood there confused as a final scream, and two men came out of the alley, almost knocking him over in their haste. "Ghost!" They screamed as he felt something bump into him. Looking around, he could see no other, no one around to have bumped him. He waited, ensuring the two would not return and then stepped into the alley before him to study the scene. Seeing nothing of interest he turned around to leave. He spied something out of the corner of his eye. Turning back, he moved back into the alley and into the shadows. He leant down, looked closer and as the lightning struck, he saw an open duffel bag. Pulling open the top so he could see inside, his face gawked. It was full of money and that money was now spilling onto the metal decking around it. *Those fools must have left it in their rush to escape the ghost.* He smiled, thinking of his day and how it just kept getting better as he stuffed the money back into the bag. *My rendezvous with Frank will have to wait till later,* he thought as he sneaked off quietly, to return to the ship.

As they neared the ship, the sirens sounded and the gates started closing. Teller placed his hand gently on Scrycher's shoulder and ushered him on. "Let's get out of here, Scrycher."

"Teller, what was so important that we had to try and leave now? I have not got the Gatling gun parts yet." Scrycher looked to Teller for an answer, as the two men hurried to the gates.

"I have taken care of it. No need to worry." Teller was sure Profitor had made it back to the ship and the parts were safely on board. All they needed to do was leave before the gates closed, and they would be home free. As the two moved themselves through the gates, Teller stopped, frozen in fear.

"R-Rod, wh-what i-is all the f-fuss about? I w-was b-buying s-some more j-jars t-to r-replace the b-broken ones wh-when th-the s-sirens went o-off."

Rod slapped Profitor on the back, and spoke heartily over the storm and sirens. "Nothing to worry about, unless you stole something from, or killed someone from, The Syndicate."

Teller now stopped dead in his tracks. He turned back, squeezing through the gates with Scrycher following close behind. Teller headed directly to Profitor, and grabbed him by the collar, dragging him to towards the ship. Teller's eyes darted around, his fur matting to his temple as he slammed into the gates. Letting Profitor go, he hissed in rage and scraped his nails down the rusty bars. It was to no avail, the gates were locked tight.

"Well. What do we have here? In a hurry are we?" Gregory emerged from the crowd with several of his men. "Sound down the alarms, he is here."

Rod tried to hide his face from Gregory. He knew who Rod was, and he could blow his cover. "Well Rod, now what do you have there?" Gregory pointed to the duffel bag that Rod was carrying.

"Funny story. Found it in an alley, with a ghost. Two men left it there." Rod was jovial in his recollection of the events as he spoke.

"The bag, boys." Two of the men took the bag from Rod, as he let go freely.

"Nothing to hide, you will see." Rod was grinning, but could not hide the fact that he was uneasy about being identified. His eyes darted to Scrycher, trying to gauge his expression.

"And your knife." Gregory laid out his hand.

"Certainly. Rod reached in for the knife, only to come out with his hand covered in blood. Rod's face flushed in dismay, this was not right. He had washed all the blood off in the rain.

As he looked at his hands, the men sorting through the bag spoke. "This is the stolen money. It still has Frank's blood on it."

Rod clutched for a lifeline. He knew if he did not come up with an answer and quickly, he would be dead. "The blood is from the boys I killed."

"R-Rod? Wh-what are y-you s-saying?"

"Soorry, Siir" The little man peddled his wagon past the men as they entered the alley.

"Well, there is nothing here. It is a pity Rod had to make up such a tale to gain him some extra time. I thought that he was better than that?" The well-dressed Syndicate operative spoke strongly to the other man so he could be heard over the wind as he walked out of the alley. Heading back to the gate, he noticed the wagon that he had passed earlier. "Hey you, yeah you, stop."

The little man stopped suddenly, the hairs on the back of his neck rising in anticipation of the next question. "You got meat on a stick for me? I heard you were the best on the planet."

The little man let out a deep breath as he removed two of the meat sticks from his stall, giving them to the men. "Meet on the Steek for you, Siirs. Free from mee."

The two men could not believe their luck. They walked back to the hanger area of the planet, eating their meat on a stick, and discussing Rod's unfortunate predicament.

Rod could not believe his ears. How could they not have found the bodies? They must be there. Who would have removed the two children's bodies? The terror in his eyes was evident as he tried to run from the group before him. His escape attempt was short lived. His eyes glazed slightly and he reacted, holding his stomach with both hands. He looked down, blood spilt over his fingers. He opened them slightly so he could see between them. His shirt was sliced open across his belly and as he lent forward to check the damage, his insides sprawled out into his hands.

Gregory spoke as he wiped his blade on Rod's shirt, before re-sheathing it. "I took you in, and this is how you repay me? I thought that even you, you greedy son of a bitch would be smarter than this." As Rod fell to the ground he looked up at his assailant.

"But I did not kill, Frank." Rod's eyes pleaded as he gasped for breath and cradled his insides, throwing up on Gregory's shoes. Gregory laid a boot into his head, knocking him to the pavement below, now mixing blood with the sick in his mouth.

"You are free to go, Scrycher. Do not let me see you again, or I will kill you just for being there." Gregory turned and walked away, as Scrycher grabbed the shoulders of his two shocked crewmates.

"Let's go now." Scrycher did not turn around. He did not see the other men using the end of their weapons to smash Rod's failing body. He did not see Rod soil himself, or the hand stretch out for help. He did not want to see. He just wanted to get out of there as fast as he could.

Rod knew the drill. After all, he had spent years informing for these people. Gut the traitor, then smash every bone in his body. Pulverize him until every part of him was mush, until no blood remained and no form. This way, there was no evidence of the betrayer. Just a pool of mush! The only parts of Rod to have remained untouched was his heart, which had somehow been shielded against the onslaught and the organs, now lying on the pavement before him. He knew nothing. Not blackness. Not heat, not hell, not light. He just knew the nothingness and emptiness of not belonging. Like he had known all his life, he now knew this in death.

Teller turned to see the Syndicate men walk away from the mush that was once Rod. Two of the men were still chewing on the kebab sticks they had purchased from the meat man earlier. The steamers moved quickly. Two of them moving to Rod's carcass. They knew it would take some steaming to remove this one. Their actions were slow and deliberate as they swept over the body. The flesh and bone melted together with the steam as they worked. Teller turned back to the ship. As the doors closed, only he looked back. Only he knew the truth, and he had to keep it that way. His thoughts were interrupted as Scrycher spat under his breath. "Damn."

"What, Scrycher? We escaped with our lives."

"Yes, but where am I going to find another Syndicate informant that is dumb enough to relay all our false information through?"

Chapter 12

"Oh, freesh meet. Leeve meet for me. Stop, stop!" The man peddling his little wagon stopped near Rod's body and waved his arms at the Steamers as they worked. Both men looked at each other, laughed and then continued. The small man bent down, cutting away the organs expelled from Rod's abdomen. Standing up, he moved slightly away from the Steamers as they finished their work. Satisfied he could not salvage anything else, he stuffed Rod's internals into the top of his wagon.

The air became cold and icicles formed around Rod's body. The steam from the machines iced up until they both stopped working. Their steam was now frozen in and around the pipes.

"Waste. What a waste of meeat." the small man mumbled to himself, as he made his way from the back to the front of his wagon. As he placed his hands on the handle of the cart, he froze. His eyes were wide in disbelief. He shook his head to make sure what he was seeing was true. The meat from his wagon, his meat, was lifting itself from the cart, into the air and slowly disappearing, as if it were being eaten, stick and all. He stood there gawking as his whole wagon was depleted of its goods. He then ran screaming, pushing his cart down the road and away from the bloody corpse in the gutter, his little wagon creaking under the pressure of the quick movement. The two Steamers, who had been frozen in fear until now, followed suit. Dropping their canisters, they ran screaming into the multitudes of people.

"Mmmm, mmmm, mmmm. What a lovely snack." The voice was that of the Creator. As he knelt down, he nodded his head from side to side, clicking his tongue in disbelief. "Tsk, tsk. You were a bad one, weren't you?" Slowly he placed his hands on the remains of Rod's body. Rod's mass was now just one big pile of mush. Squishing his hand through the mess, the Creator searched. "Hope. Hope is all we have, my child." Finding the heart still intact, he sighed in relief. "Ah, we have a live one." Concentrating, he navigated Rod's DNA, looking for the image of his body before it was damaged. The Creator now used Rod's own genetic make-up to try and rebuild him out of the pool of mush. The putrid pile slowly took shape, then, quicker and quicker, as more of Rod rebuilt. As the Creator removed his hand from Rod's chest, the wound closed up. Not like flesh healing. More like water replacing itself after being forcefully displaced.

Rod's eyes flicked open, those black eyes, absent of all feeling. He was parched and he needed something to drink. His face was pale, as though no blood was present in his thin frame. After being singed and seared to his flesh, his clothes were covered in his blood, and useless. His figure looked so fragile and frail like a young, thin boy, not the cunning and cruel man he had once been. He searched with those black, soulless eyes, searching for his first victim. Kneeling, he gazed blankly around him. Seeing forms before him, he lunged, grabbing the first of the steam canisters. He placed the nozzle in his mouth, the ice melted slowly as he sucked upon it. Pulling the trigger, the remainder of the ice melted and he sucked in the hot steam that now flowed from it. Rod knelt this way for some time until the hissing of the steamer died down. With no more steam in the canister for his consumption, he looked around like a crazed beast. He spied the other steamer. This time, he ravaged the canister in seconds.

As Rod finished his second meal, the Creator spoke, "Come, my Son, we have work to do."

Rod's head twisted completely around to address the Creator; not needing to get up from his knees or re-position as he spoke. His voice was raspy, as though his vocal cords had been burnt, or crushed. "Am I in Hell?"

"Not yet, my Son, not yet. Now, let us get away from this place." The Creator gestured towards Philippe, who was standing near a small ship that looked like it would barely house ten crew.

Rod's head twisted back in place and he sniffed the air like a wild animal. Raising himself to all fours, his nose twitched, as he searched; "Not yet, I have business to attend to." Catching the scent he sought, Rod stopped sniffing, and bounded down the streets before the Creator could respond.

Philippe started to run, gaining momentum as his legs pumped strongly, but the Creator raised his hand to stop him. Philippe stopped suddenly. Now standing beside the Creator he looked at him with a question in his eyes, "Father?"

"He will be back my son. He will be back."

Rod bounded through the streets as he hunted; his sole purpose, revenge. He could smell the blood like he was there. Back there in the alley, cutting those boys, drinking in the blood as he flourished under the smell, and taste. He would have his revenge on those that did him wrong, but for now, his purpose was to find his kill, to devour the bodies and revel in their taste. He did not know what had happened to him, but he liked it. He was exhilarated, the animal in him now completely at the surface. No longer did he need to hide his true nature, and this made him feel powerful. Hunger gripped him; a hunger he had felt many times before, but had restrained himself from acting on. He could feel the pull of it, as though he had never eaten. This hunger, he knew could only be filled with the taste of flesh ripped from the bones of a kill. To this end, he sought, and now he was there. The smell was so strong, he could taste it on his tongue. His heart beat as though it was speaking to him, loudly, powerfully. He looked up into the night sky, howling an eerie call as he went in for the kill.

The little man had kept running. He was not about to stop and be eaten, like his cart full of meat. He had seen some weird things in his time, but this was different. He had felt the presence; the power exuding from the creature that he could not see. It had been debilitating, and he knew he had to get away. As he rounded the corner, he slowed and brushed his hand over his forehead to remove the beads of sweat from his brow. His eyes darted from side to side, in anticipation of something bursting from the shadows. Relaxing a little, his brow and shoulders dropped. He had been running for what had seemed an eternity and now, he needed rest. Letting go of the small wagon with his other hand, he bent forward, placing both hands on his knees in an attempt to catch his breath.

Between breaths, the small man spoke to himself. "Phew, theet was heiry. End my meet. Theet wonderful meet gone. Lucky me got the other ones." As he looked towards the hidden compartment of the wagon a spine wrenching howl echoed through the streets. "Oh sheet, theet is close. Sheet, sheet, sheet." Raising himself, he grabbed the wagon again, pushing it quickly through the streets. The thunder roared, and the streets lit up as the lightning struck. The small man looked around as he ran, the lightning allowing him to see many shadows and outlines, which all looked menacing. As he rounded another bend, he heard footsteps. They came closer and closer. His eyes, panic-stricken, looked as though they were about to pop out of his head. Stopping his cart abruptly, he grabbed for the filleting knife at the top of the wagon and turned to attack the assailant. There was no one there, the footsteps were now gone. Turning, he made his way slowly to his destination, knife in hand as he went, his head turned so he could see and hear most things around him.

Clop, clop. Clop, clop. New footsteps came towards him. *Clop… clop… clop… clop… clop…* The footsteps were getting quicker, as they made their way closer. *Clop, clop, clop, clop.* The footsteps were running now. Looking out the corner of his eye, he could see the figure. The small man's head was covered in sweat as he turned and swung the knife at the oncoming man.

"Whoa, man. Just wanted a snack, but if you'd rather skewer me, then no thanks." The lanky man walked away quickly, turning to yell at the little man, "Drive away all your customers, you will if you try to stick them like that eh."

The little man watched as the lanky man walked away. He watched and wiped copious amounts of sweat from his forehead, while allowing himself a small smile. "Foolish little men, mee no bother, mee fine." Thunder deafened him as he turned back to his little wagon. The lightning flashed showing a skinny, pale white figure before him. His clothes, if you could call them clothes, were drenched through with blood, and barely covered his essential parts.

Rod smiled as he looked at the little man. Leaning forward, he placed a hand on his shoulder. "You have somethin' of mine, yes?"

"No, siir, mee nothing of yours," the little man shook as another lightning bolt lit Rod's sickening grin.

"Nooooooo!" Rod's voice boomed at the little man as his head spun completely around to end up back where it started, "I think YES!"

The little man could not believe his eyes. This man's head had spun all the way round and he was still talking. Not taking another second to try and comprehend this, he ripped his shoulder from Rod's grasp. Rod grabbed deep into the shoulder blade, tearing the flesh. The little man winced as he ran. He knew he had to run for his life, which he did. As the rain pummeled onto his weary body, the wind carried Rod's voice to him.

"Run, run, run little man. Run, and I will seek. Run, run, and I will chase. Run, and I will eat."

"Uh, uh, uh," out of breath, the little man stopped at his door, fumbling with his keys as he tried to unlock it. He placed the key in the hole, only to have it hang for a second then slide out and drop in the puddle of water below. The look in his eyes showed fright beyond belief, as he turned to scout the area around him. His face was pale, as he searched the ground below. Finding the key, he turned back, concentrating on the lock.

"You're no fun. Run and hide. You need to run. Not hide inside," The voice was eerie as it sailed along the wind.

The small man smashed through the door as soon as the lock turned. He quickly spun around, trying to close the door behind him. The door jammed as though a foot within the doorway had stopped it. He could feel breath on his face as the voice whispered melodically.

"Knock, knock. Who's there?"

He opened the door slightly again, to slam it closed. He rested briefly against the door and then scrambled madly as he slid the three locks across. Breathing deeply, he lay against the door again, now safe inside the walls.

"Knock, knock." A large knife protruded through the door, just above his head. He panicked as the knife barely missed him and he dropped to the floor, scrambling to the other side of the room. Knocking over pots and pans, the man's face froze in fear, his mouth wide open.

"Knock, knock. Who's there?"

The little man's feet worked in overdrive as he tried to push himself through the wall and out of this place. Then everything went silent...

A voice whispered quietly, almost childlike, "Knock, knock. What's there?" Then the voice boomed, as though breaking through the door. "Not the door! It's on the floor!" The door exploded inwards as if being hit with gale force winds. Ripped from its hinges, the door slammed to the floor, barely missing the small man.

As he leant forward to examine the human shaped indentation on the door, he stammered, "H-H-h-how theee?" He did not have time to count his blessings that the door had not crushed him. He watched in dismay as Rod's misty shape appeared above the door and stood before him. The figure shimmered for some time before completely reintegrating itself and walking towards him. Rod's eyes drooped and looked down as he got closer. He reached the small man, and looked up evilly, speaking in an almost comical tone. "Mmmm. Being dead has its advantages, wouldn't you say?"

The little man tried to scream. His mouth opened, but no voice came out. Rod stood above him, feeding on the scream, the fear, the chase. Rod knelt before the man and spoke, "A knife for me. A cut for you. I don't know what else to do." As he plunged the knife in slowly, the small man winced, his life flashing before him, as the blood drained away...

"Well, what we waiting for? Let's go." Rod strode back to where he had been reborn. He walked tall and proud, but wore a cynical grin on his face. He moved towards Philippe, and the Creator, who were sitting on two crates, waiting patiently.

Philippe looked up with little care, as Rod strode to them. Rod's stance gave the appearance as though he thought he was invincible, as he now stood there. "Skinny thing isn't he, Father? I thought a night out on the prowl would have at least made him a little plumper."

The Creator turned, looking Rod up and down as he spoke. "You are a skinny little thing now, aren't you? Have you eaten?"

"To my heart's content, and then some." Rod waved around to the area behind him as he spoke. "Their world, is my playground."

"If you were as big as your ego, you might not look so ridiculous in that dreadful clothing." Philippe was sarcastic, and cutting in his tone, as he got up, ready to walk away. Rod did not seem fazed at all.

"If I was as big as my ego, which would be a damn site smaller than your oversized mug, then I wouldn't fit into these fine threads." Rod spun around showing his entire outfit to the Creator and Philippe.

"Oh my child, what bad fashion sense you have. Those clothes do nothing for your frame. You look like a black, skinny twig, waiting for someone to snap you." The Creator gestured up and down Rod's length.

"Can I Father? Snap this worthless, skinny man, like a twig?" Philippe was sick of this game and was ready to snap this man in two, if it meant they could leave this place sooner.

"Black leather pants, black boots and a silk black shirt. How can you go wrong with that? The young whelp I removed this from looked ever so sweet in it. Right up 'til the time that I drained him. Oh, that one was so sweet. Savored him so much more than the rest, so, so sweet, I sung him a song. Hush little baby go to sleep, hush little baby not a peep."

"You mean you ate more than one? One was more than enough for me." Philippe looked concerned as he spoke.

"Muscle man. Now let me put this in terms you can understand… You eat the flesh. I eat the soul!" Both the Creator and Philippe looked at each other. What kind of monster had been created? "Now to our ship." With a dramatic wave of his hand, Rod started walking to the ship. Philippe trailed behind, his thoughts on the small ship that was positioned fifty meters away. As they approached the ship, Rod stopped abruptly to look at the

Creator in dismay. "Is this what you call a chariot, Father?"

The Creator looked at Rod. He had not told his son about this ship being his chariot, how did he know?

"Don't worry, pops. You gave me a few talents you probably don't know about. Anyways, how 'bout that chariot?"

"What is wrong with this ship?" Philippe was insulted; after all, he had acquired this ship himself.

Rod turned. Wheels screeched in the distance, as a lone figure peddled a large wagon, covered with black tarps. The strain on the wagon, its wheels and the person pulling it was evident. "Well, it isn't big enough for my luggage. Unless you are offering to stay behind to make room?"

Rod stood in front of the Syndicate man. He shifted sideways to peer around the man and into the corridor. "Can I come in?" He gestured into the entrance of the large vessel. At the end of the corridor stood another well-armed man who lifted his rifle up and down in a menacing action, as he looked back at Rod.

"Leave now and I will not have to kill you." The man standing before Rod was at least four times his bulk and carried a large machine gun, which he now had pointed at Rod's chest.

"Oh I will get in, one way or another." Rod was grinning at the man, taunting him.

"Over my dead body." The Guard did not care who this man was or how indestructible he thought he was, he was not getting in.

"Well I prefer my meals fresh, but if you insist." Rod's smile was lost a little as he thought of a cold meal. The guard's face reddened as he lost his patience.

"I would suggest you re-think your use of force to remove me." Rod stared directly into the man's eyes, reading his thoughts and replying to them.

A shiver ran down the man's spine as he swung his machine gun around, smashing the flat of it into Rods face. Like putty, Rod's face absorbed the force of the blow. He stood his ground, not flinching.

"Gobble, gobble, time to eat. Gobble, gobble, don't try to retreat." Rod's speech was slurred as his face slowly flowed into its original form. As the man raised his gun to fire, Rod disappeared. "Oh, you didn't try to retreat. Oh well, boooooring." Before the man knew what was happening, his neck was snapped from behind. Rod's lips now embraced the man's mouth as he sucked out the last breath. Rod flicked his head back as his body glowed slightly, shivering with the power as his eyes glowed blood red.

The second man was not going to be another victim; he sprayed Rod and the other guard with a burst of bullets from his machine gun. Blood splattered the walls and the platform leading onto the ship. Rod let go of the corpse, the second guard stared in horror, his eyes bulging as Rod moved closer. Rod moved his tongue around his mouth as you would to get something from your teeth. "First step. Your friend is dead." *Thw*, Rod spat a bullet to the ground, the bullet clanking as it hit the deck. "Second step. Your friend hits his head." The body of the guard fell to the ground with his head hitting the floor as Rod stepped closer.

The guard raised his gun, spraying Rod with the whole clip from his machine gun. He was gob-smacked as Rod still stood.

"Now that's no way to treat a guest is it?" *Thw, thw, thw*. Rod spat out another three bullets as he took another step. Placing a finger into his shirt he poked it through one of the bullet holes. "And I liked this bloody shirt. Did you have to go and fill it with holes?" As the guard looked Rod over, he stared at his legs, he was sure he had sprayed his legs full of bullets too. Rod followed the guard's stare to his legs. "Oh man, not the pants, anything but the pants. You have done it now. I am angry." Rod stood still looking at the pants and shirt, shaking his head as his face reddened to match his eyes.

The guard was shaking violently as he tried to load another clip, dropping it to the floor in his haste. "Stop!" His complexion was white and clammy as he spoke, and tried to insert another clip, which also ended up on the floor.

"Now what you think words are going to do, that bullets can't? Back to the game shall we. Third step. You crap your pants." The guard dropped his machine gun as he turned to run, his eyes now wide with fear, as he soiled himself. "Fourth step. You run to hide." The guard has now turned around and had started to run, three steps on, he turned his head. Rod was no longer behind him as he retreated. The guard was confused. He turned back to focus on where he was running. "Fifth step. Your gun inside." The guard turned his head completely back to glimpse Rod's face as he pummeled the front of the guard's machine gun down his throat. Rod shook from side to side in ecstasy as he absorbed the life force of the man he had just killed. He allowed the body to drop to the floor, the front of the machine gun protruding out of the guard's head was now covered in brains. "Ooohh, much more fun when they run." As the sirens sounded and the blue lights filled the entry to the vessel, Rod disappeared. As he vanished, his voice trailed down the corridors "Two down, the rest to go. Ho, ho, ho…"

"Your chariot awaits you, my Father." Rod smiled as he bowed. The look on Philippe's face was worth the effort.

"What about her crew?" Philippe did not want any surprises.

"They have offered to hold a banquet in our Father's honor. They have even offered themselves as the main course." Rod sniggered as he called the small man and wagon to the ship. "C'mon man. What's taking you so long?" The small man slowly pulled the wagon, the large load creaking as it moved.

"Soorry, Siir."

"What is it man? What did you get me out of bed for?" Gregory was barely dressed, and a beautiful woman draped herself over his naked shoulder, rubbing her hands over his chest. A second woman also came to the door, groping at his silken night robe, trying to coax him back to bed. "This had better be good." As he spoke, he looked up from the hands now caressing his chest. Pushing the hands away, he stepped through the golden doorway, marking the front of his house. In front of him was a cart; the little man's meat cart. On top of the cart to either side was a child's head; one thin, and one chubby. Both heads were mutilated and displayed on a spike for all to see. Under these heads, lay bodies. How many there were, he could not tell. Sweat poured from his forehead as he looked on. Piles of bodies were surrounding the cart. The only thing he could see for sure, was that all these bodies were wearing syndicate colors. All were his men. All were dead. He lifted a foot from the ground as he felt the coldness on his feet. Raising his slipper, he could see the red, gluggy liquid that had soaked into it. His face cringed as he realized, he was now standing in a pool of it. It was blood. A moat of blood that surrounded his house.

His voice was shaking as he spoke, "Wh-who did this? How many men? Was it the Company?"

"Sir, look closer, at your feet." Looking down, Gregory noted there was actually an arrow painted, pointing from his door to the wagon. He slowly followed the arrow of blood. Clipped to the wagon with someone's finger bone, was a note. The note wrote in blood, read:

You killed Rod

so we killed your men

We are even

Scrycher

"How many, and how?" Gregory's face was white and he was shaking as he clenched and unclenched his fists. He did not know whether it was fear or anger, but he was pumped with adrenalin. He wanted revenge.

"A hundred or more, Sir. We don't know what happened. They just disappeared, then they were here."

"Get me, 'The Enforcer', I want my best ship to hunt down this animal and his crew.”

“Sir, The Enforcer has disappeared, as has her crew.”

“Get me the next best ship. These mongrels will pay.” Gregory looked as though he was about to explode, as he spat out the last order and the redness filled his face and body. The young women now slinked back away from the entrance to the house, seeking a place to hide from his wrath.

Chapter 13

"Mogly want food, now. You give food Mogly, or Mogly take it!" The short, furry animal looked aggressively at the small female that was cowering. Mogly's stance was erect and threatening, while the others of his kind around him, became submissive. She passed the small fruit along the ground, before running to hide in the trees. Mogly lowered his stance, all the time watching to ensure no others approached. Turning away from the fruit, he glanced towards the temple. "Mogly says thanks." A long tail darted from behind him to grab the small fruit, as his legs and arms moved him towards the temple, and upon a blue, stone statue. The stone column had been carved in the form that could have only been one being, the Creator. Sitting on the Creator's face, Mogly raised the fruit to his mouth, biting into its thick skin, spraying himself in the face with the sweet juices. One of his feet peeled the fruit, while he used the other to keep his footing. He was also keeping his eyes peeled on the mass of furry creatures fooling about on the ground below, ensuring none would try to take his food. The final juices of the fruit dripped from his mouth and his round ears rotated, their tips pointed skyward as he heard the intruders.

He spat out the pip with a *thwattttt,* into the crowd below. His head rotated to listen as he cocked his leg, soiling in the Creator's open mouth.

"Hey, Boss. Ain't this where you got li'l Blink from?" Chelsea walked in front of them, scouting ahead for any danger. The bushes in front of her rustled as she got closer. In response, she cocked her gun, only to see a small rat-like creature run from the bushes. *Grrrrrrrrrrrrrrrrrrrrrrrrrr. Whock, whock!* Mogly needed no introduction to the sound of the gun. Alerting the others, he ran inside the temple walls and hid in the shadows by the lone-cloaked figure.

The dark shadows concealed Jarel, as he leant against the pillar to the ruined temple. He reached forward to pat Mogly on the head, whilst he contemplated. He had no idea how these people had been locating this planet, or for that matter, how they were ripping it from its proper place in time and space, to this realm. Unlike Mogly though, he did not mind. He preferred this realm, with the warmth of others, and the feelings and emotions that came with it. How he longed for the closeness of another; but he also dreaded it. This place could be so cruel and cold as well. He had seen his world, his race, destroyed. His family, friends and followers were now all gone. All this was because of his actions, and his alone.

The Founders had forbidden his order, The Order of Dutanium, from interfering with the conflict between his people and the Company, but he had ignored them. He had thought that he was helping his brethren fight their revolution, by performing an open attack against the Company and their Councill. He had been swift and cunning, taking out twelve of the Councill in the shadows of the first night. No one knew what had happened until the next morning. That was his mistake; he should have killed them all! The remaining members fortified themselves, were guarded day and night. They also found witnesses, even though, he was sure there were none; found witnesses to say that a Stray had killed the members. The news spread fast; that it was a Stray assassin who had slaughtered half the Councill in the cold of the night. The Councill feared that if the Stray people were not all destroyed, the Councill would perish, and with it the empire of the Company.

Jarel was not sure what had scared them most, realizing their own mortality, or the realization that others might also start questioning, and killing off the Company and Councill members. Either way, it was fear that made them act so mercilessly. They attacked without warning and without compassion, making an example of his race. The result being the planet—his planet, his home—burning before the next day had ended. He told himself the Councill must have planned to attack his planet, whether he had assassinated the Councill members or not, as their ships had to be close to the planet to launch an attack so quickly. However, he still could not shake the guilt he felt for his people's extinction, but guilt had no purpose for a warrior like himself. He had carried this indecisiveness within himself for two thousand years, give or take, as he had no use for time and it had no use for him. They existed in each other's realms from time to time, but neither bothered the other.

Once his planet was destroyed, he had no purpose and he dared not seek revenge, fearing further repercussions, though he could think of none worse. So he had found this place, or this place him, he could not remember. There was no reason to carry on the bloodshed, so he learnt to call this planet home.

"Yep, found Blink in those ruins along that path," Scrycher looked at his surroundings, breathing in the atmosphere as though for a first time, and with added vigor. He could somehow see more, and appreciate the world for what it was, wondrous and full of life.

Blink, who had been resting happily in Scrags' hair, lifted his head groggily and disappeared for a second, before reappearing to drop something into Scrags' open hands. Scrags jumped, flinging his arms in the air as the slimy fish started flapping around, beating its wings in an attempt to escape. As the large fish straightened itself in the air, it flew towards the pond, slapping Scrags in the face with its tail as it went. Laughter roared through the glade, as Scrags wiped the fish slime from his red and embarrassed face, and wet hands. Little Blink's tummy jiggled as he giggled on top of Scrags' head, falling off with a plop on the ground to continue rolling around giggling in the lush blue grasses.

"Oh, pickle me rat's balls, what is that doing here?" Jaxter jumped up from under the Gatling gun cage and ran to the control stick in anticipation of the need to try to escape. The large vessel—The Enforcer— stopped above him, its engines powering down before a series of shuttles departed to the planet below. Jaxter held the flight stick with one hand whilst he wiped the sweat from his forehead with the other. "What the?" Looking at the panels on the ship, he concluded what had happened. While he had been working on the re-wiring for the new Gatling gun, he had realized they had been supplied with a faulty part. This part would not allow the gun to work at full capacity. His only resolution had been to suggest that all other crewmembers leave the ship, whilst he performed the repair. This allowed him to turn off all systems to the ship, but only allowed enough oxygen for one person, for several hours. This was the time he needed to jerry-rig the part into the ship's systems to get its full potential. The fact that the ship was not emanating a power signature, could possibly have just saved his life, now he hoped Scrycher and the rest of the crew were as lucky.

"My Son, are we at the destination yet?" The Creator's querying tone was directed towards Philippe, as he sat on his throne-like chair on the bridge of The Enforcer.

"We are coming upon her now, Father," Philippe returned the questioning tone, speaking further as he steered the large vessel, "How do you know of this place?"

"This planet, this world, was once my home. It was the place in which my second child was born, and subsequently my third. It is also from where I left due to my disagreement with one child. My children, how would you say, fought like cats and dogs, which I did not appreciate." Stroking his small, blue chin, the Creator reminisced.

"Where did you go?"

"I took my favored child and created a new world, one of beauty and wonder," A tear fell from his eye as he spoke.

Philippe was so enthralled in the conversation that he did not see Scrycher's ship as he lowered his own vessel into orbit, barely missing the hull of the smaller ship. "Father, who were these children?" Philippe was fascinated, and it showed on his face.

"Come with me to the planet and you will see. At least, you will see my second child, if you like." The Creator looked at Philippe with passion in his eyes, as though a father conversing with a curious child.

"But what about the vessel, Father? I must stay to man it." Philippe did not want to pass up an opportunity to see this planet for himself. However, he did not want to return to this part of space, to find his vessel had been stolen.

"Leave some of the disciples, they will know better than to steal this vessel." The Creator stood, walking to a scraggy man cleaning the floors. The man was skinny and pale, but he worked desperately hard and kept his head down in an effort to go unnoticed. Turning, so all those on the bridge could hear, the Creator spoke strongly. "If I, your God, leave you in charge of this vessel, you will defend it with your lives. You will not be blasphemous, and you will not run." Looking at the man on the communications console, he spoke more softly. "If we do not find our chariot here when we return, this fate will befall you all." With a sharp movement, the Creator's hand ripped through the floor cleaner's chest. He tore out his heart and held it in the air to emphasize the act, before eating it whole. He looked down at the man's crumpled body, watching as the blood pooled on the floor, then he spoke in a very worried tone, "Now whom are we going to get to clean this mess up now? It seemed like a good idea at the time, yes it did. Mess… no cleaner; it is no good. Note to self. Rip out the heart of the communications man next time." He looked at the communications man who had wet himself in fear. "Nothing personal, I just need someone to clean this mess." At this, the communications man ran from behind the console, grabbed the mop and started mopping the blood. The Creator grinned at the man's action. "Son, can you please get us another communications man?"

Teller walked uneasily as he studied the ruined temple from afar. "I thought you said this place held secrets to our ancestry? It just looks like a ruin to me." As Teller spun slowly around, taking in all his surroundings, he spoke in slight awe. "These ruins would have to be tens of thousands of years old, or more, what could we gain from them?"

"O-O-Older th-the better I say." Profitor was rummaging through his duffel bag to find a specimen jar. Scooping into the bushes with the open jar, he spoke in a soft voice; closing the lid as he did so, "Nice little arachnid." He placed the jar into his bag as they entered a clearing. He looked around in awe at the beauty of the glade, that was positioned directly in front of the ruins. Large pillars lay strewn around, fallen from the framework of the ruins. Moss and creeping plants covered the black stone that the temple was constructed from, and small creatures scurried from place to place, avoiding each other. A large pond lay to the side of the temple. Flying insects buzzed over the pond, only to be engulfed by huge fish, which hovered, once out of the water. Their large wings fluttered as they hung in the air, only to close, to allow them to drop into the pond in a splash. The crystal clear water sparkled in the light as its droplets became airborne.

Profitor was fascinated by the light that displayed a myriad of colors through the drops of water. Looking up, he observed a light emanating from the top of the ruins. A light that looked and felt familiar. Looking closer, Profitor noticed a crystal that he had not noticed before. It was positioned in an enclosed, black metal cage, positioned on top of the temple's roof, lighting the area around them. The crystal was surprisingly similar to the one that Teller possessed, even though it was many times the size. "T-Teller, th-that one's l-like yours?"

Teller turned to where Profitor was pointing and looked up. Stepping forward, he entered the temple. He did not see the figure in the dark corner, nor did he see Mogly, cowering into Jarel's cloak. He kept walking, oblivious to anything around him. He stopped in a pool of thick mud. In the middle of the pool were a pillar and a metal cage. The cage was the same as the one that housed the crystal on the roof. Teller, for no apparent reason, and without hesitation, placed his crystal in the cage.

Jarel breathed in deeply at the sight, almost giving away his position. The room lit up in brilliant lights, momentarily blinding all who watched. As the white fog cleared from Teller's eyes, he looked at the images projected into the air before him. They did not make sense to him, as they were all just images with no order or reason. What he did see though was a planet, his home planet, projected close to the far wall. Several other planets were also shown in the same area. As he studied the star chart, Chelsea came stumbling into the room. "Hey Teller what you doin'? Tryin' to blind us? If you wanted to have your way with me, I told you before, just ask. You don't need a fancy light show to impress me."

"Sorry, Chels. You know, I have to take any chance I can to get you under the influence." Teller pointed to the planets he was observing. "But before I take you on the floor, what do you make of this?"

Chelsea's face glowed a little red in embarrassment, and her jaw dropped. Her mouth stayed open as her eyes followed to where he was pointing. "How'd you get a picture of the planet we on, up there?" She pointed at the planet as she spoke, showing what she was talking about. "See, that is us, but what are these planets, never seen them before? Boss!"

"Hold on woman, never get a moment of peace with you, do I? No sooner am I blinded by the Teller over here, then you start hollering at me." As Scrycher walked through the door, his demeanor changed. "That is it. That is the last piece of the puzzle we were looking for." Running over to Teller, he laid a big kiss on his hairy cheek. "Home sweet home."

Teller pulled away quickly, giving Scrycher a look that could only mean. 'What the?'

"Sorry, got a bit carried away." Scrycher turned to look at Chelsea. "Do you think that you can get us there?"

"Can't see why not Boss." Chelsea leant over, giving Teller a small peck on the cheek.

"What is that for?" Teller looked confused.

"Thought I'd get in while the going was good."

"Now let's see what you can do, baby," Jaxter pulled himself up on the cage so he was now standing up, his large mass making him look much like a caged rat. Moving the gun slowly from side to side, he frowned, the screeching metal, unbearable to his ears. "Don't do this to me baby. I need a sweet song." Caressing the shaft of the gun, he stooped to squirt some thick, black liquid into the mounting point. Standing, he replaced the container back on his belt. "Alright, let's dance baby." Jaxter swung the gun gently again; this time the screeching was quieter, lessening with each movement. Smiling, he started swiveling it around, then dancing with it as it moved more freely. With no sound other than the stomping of his feet, he sung out of tune, a song that did not entirely make sense.

"Lead my baby to the door. So we can dance on the floor.
Dance merrily into the night, and hope we don't get in a fight.
But if we do, she'll see us through.
Then when it's over we'll eat rat stew.
Then lay in bed. I lay my head, thinking of you."

At the last note, Jaxter settled the gun to rest in its holding position, before giving her a big kiss on her shaft.

"You are right, Profitor. This does seem to be an archive of planets that we have not charted before. But we should have seen them around this planet. Here we are. Why are they not there?" Scrycher stroked his stubble whilst contemplating the issue at hand. If they could find these other planets, even one, it would make their job of finding a way to the home planet much easier to plot.

"A-ah. I-I see what has happened. This planet, as you so pointed out, is not anchored to this time. It seems that these planets seem to, play between realms, so to say." Profitor was in his element, barely stopping for a breath as he touched the floating image of the planet they were on. As he did, the others shimmered and disappeared, leaving only two other planets in the image. "This is the Stray home planet, as you have said. They all seem to anchor around this other one. Almost like it was there first and the others came later."

"But how'd we find that one?" Chelsea had never seen a series of planets before, except in the heart of the Company territory; and those planets that were not completely barren or depleted of resources. Well, there were none that she knew of.

"S-Scrycher, remember how I told you I thought that this planet was somehow attracted to someone, or something from this realm, and I thought it was you?"

"Yes."

"W-Well I think I was wrong. Look at how Blink has kept blinking in an out since we have been here. Blinking is a form of dimensional travel. Once blinked out, he travels into another dimension. One that I think is between the one we live in, and the one that this planet occupies normally. B-But, B-Blink's anchor point to this realm seems to be Scrags, as he is drawn back to Scrags, and only Scrags. I think, Scrags is somehow the anchor point the planet needs to come back to this realm. Without Scrags, or a similar attraction, the planet, as before, is ripped back into its own realm. A realm that needs this planet's mass much more than our realm does. The big decisive factor is, and this is a beauty; as I said before, the void needs to be filled on this side, or that, wherever the planet has come from. It does this by ripping matter from the surrounding space or displacing it, which is why we are buffeted by displacement waves every time we cause the planet to appear. When it blinks out, it causes sort of a black hole that sucks everything in and crushes anything caught in its way." Profitor looked at the others, proud and tall, as he finished.

"So you are saying as long as we have Scrags, and possibly even Blink, we can call this planet, and maybe others, forth, so we can use them as markers?" Scrycher thought he had followed this line of deduction from Profitor's speech as he had heard much of this before. "And now we have the crystal, it will possibly give us another anchor point which the planets will be attracted to?"

Profitor blushed. Looking at the ground, as he walked over to the other side of the room, through the holograms, to lean against the wall as he responded, "W-Well i-if you want t-to simplify i-it th-then, th-that is about it." His lip quivered, a little annoyed that his punch line about the crystal being another anchor point, had been taken.

Drawn into the conversation, everyone had listened so intently to this hypothesis, that they did not see what was happening by the entrance. Blink giggled, as Jarel tickled under his chin, and Scrags laughed as Mogly lay on his tummy, to be tickled as well. "Sir, what is his name?"

Mogly jumped up onto his feet, startling Scrags and Blink, Blink blinking away in panic. "Me Mogly. Me master of this castle." Mogly stood up, straight and proud, pointing at his chest.

Blink re-appeared on top of the small cage with the crystal in it. Frightened, he acted on instinct, spinning himself and the small cage around.

"Wh-what th-the? S-Sccccccrrrrryyyycheeeerrr." Poor old Profitor, who had been leaning on the wall, fell backwards down the staircase and into the secret tunnel, Blink had just opened.

Scrycher yelled behind him as he ran through the entrance, following Profitor. "Scrags!"

Teller grabbed the crystal from the cage and followed Scrycher, leaving Chelsea standing at the entrance, raising her hands impatiently as she spoke. "Well, Scrags?"

Patting the boy on the head, Jarel spoke. "Better be off, boy, before your mum and dad tell you off."

Scrags left, waving as he went. "Bye." Mogly stood, waving back until Scrags turned, then he scurried so quickly that you could not see him until he had returned outside to play.

"Who were you talkin' to?"

"Ah, just a nice man and his pet."

Chelsea patted Scrags on the head, as he walked through the entrance, looking around the ruins and shaking her head. "Boys and their imagination," she murmured as she followed behind.

Crystal formed from his breath, as the Creator glided along the lush, blue ground, and dropped, as he peered through the trees, smashing upon the grass, and freezing it. His eyes opened wider, screening through the wondrous vegetation, his head shaking as he stopped. Turning back to Philippe, he spoke. "This is not right. Where are my children? Did they not leave any? Those selfish fools, what gives them the right to take what I created, what is mine? Why would they disrespect their father like this?" The Creator grinned mildly as he thought of his revenge. "They will pay soon enough." Years of isolation had twisted his perception of reality into his own sordid ordeal, in which everyone had worked against him. In his mind, they had all plotted against his favored children, his perfect creations.

Rod skulked behind, sharpening one of the many knives now hanging from his leather belt. His new clothing of silken pants and shirt, worked to cover his tiny frame, making him look much more menacing. His tone was blasé as he spoke, "Maybe they just left 'cause they were sick of waiting for Daddy to come home?" and he lifted his attention, just enough to get his point across, then went back to cleaning his nails with a smirk.

The Creator did not respond, he either did not hear, or did not care to respond, as he approached the clearing. His posture tensed, his arms rising above his head, and his throat constricted. The ground below his feet crackled as it iced-up. It was then shattered beneath his weight as he stopped gliding again and his feet locked onto the ground before him. He glared at the fallen monument. His monument. It lay there on its side; broken. It was his monument; it was a statue of him! Monkey crap soiled his face. It was hard to tell how much of the statue was damaged as it was sporadically covered with native mosses and plants. The offending occupants played, flinging shit and stones, food and other items at each other. Buzzing could be heard over their chatter, as fish jumped out of the beautiful pond, hovering to eat small insects. Many other beautiful things filled the glade, but he did not see them, he only saw the statue. With hatred in his eyes, he glared at the statue, then dropped to the earth on one knee, as his hands rested upon his temple. The only thing in his vision was the statue! He could not take this, anything else but this. How dare they? "AAAAAAARRRRRRRGGGGGGGGHHHH"

Snapping, he screamed and flung his hands into the air. The occupants of the glade fretted, trying to bolt away at the noise. As the Creator's hand smashed into the earth below him, everything changed. The world they were in slowed, and almost every creature saw the ice, felt the ice, but they had no time to react. The earth shook, a large crack opening from where his hand had smashed into it. The crack traveled small and shallow, as it traversed to the pond. Once there, it ran deep into the bed, under the water. The water flowed up against the natural forces, through the crack and into him. He expanded, a little at first, then grew larger and rounder. The water drained out of the pond, filling him as he grew. He became a large, squat creature, a body full of water and little else. The water stopped flowing as the pond was bled dry. Raising his hand awkwardly from the ground, he stammered, but did not falter as he raised his head to look upon everything. His eyes were so small and insignificant, yet burnt red in a powerful rage as he screamed. "You dare defile my sanctuary? Now you will become my slaves! You will, worship me!"

He commanded the power through the ground as he punched. The ground shook violently as it splintered, a multitude of fissures forming around him; each one feeding along the ground, finding their way to all that lived.

"Grrrrrrrrrrrrrrrrrrrrrrrrrrr. Whock, whock… whock, whock!" Mogly had heard the scream, seen the commotion, and watched as the pond was drained almost instantly. He had managed the call to evacuate, to alarm his kin, but he was too late. As he screeched, he climbed the statue; his statue, in the shape of the Creator. Standing atop of the head, he beat his chest again and again. He could see that his warning alarmed all creatures as they tried to break for the trees and cover. Their attempted escape for freedom was short lived, as they all stopped, frozen in their tracks. The frozen fissures originated from the Creator, his mass shrinking as quickly as it had increased. The ground started to freeze around him, then the plants, and, finally, all life within his extended reach. The air misted with the coldness, the chill filling the creatures, and drowning out the screeching and horror, until only one remained.

"Grr. Whock! Whock, whock, whock." Jumping up and down, Mogly screeched and hollered at this man. He did not know what had happened, and turned towards Jarel, who reached out his hand to help, but did not dare reveal himself. Mogly saw the chance he needed. Running back down the length of the statue he stopped, directly in front of a frozen kin. Horrified, he turned to the Creator. "Grr. Mogly not like you. Nasty, nasty. Mogly not like you, nasty one." Turning, he bolted back up the statue, his focus on leaping as he reached the summit. Slipping on a pile of crap, he sprawled out, arms, legs and tail flailing as he sailed through the air. "Monkey crap. Mogly not happy!" As he reached out, so did Jarel, their grasp short as Mogly hit the ground, the momentum sending him rolling towards Jarel's hiding place.

As he regained his footing, Mogly could feel the power emanating through the ground, and the coldness that came with it. His small feet had barely hit the ground before they started freezing. The cold worked its way through him quickly. The sadness in his eyes was the last thing Jarel saw before he turned and headed down the entrance to the caverns. He must find the others. His thoughts were focused on this one thing, and one thing alone. They must be warned, saved from this mad being. Hurrying, he left, pulling his hood over his head and covering the tear he shed over the fate that had befallen his small friend.

He did not turn back as he made his way stealthily into the temple's depths. He did not see the Creator's frail body walk through the masses of frozen creatures, nor did he see the two men looking around in awe as they walked behind him.

"Not quite what I had planned when I came upon this place. These are not mine, but they will do just fine. I did not create these vermin, but I will certainly make them my minions. Mold them into beautiful beings." As he walked, the small furry creatures within his aura started to move. The blood in their bodies thawed, allowing their hearts to restart, the beating allowing their lungs to inhale and exhale, to breathe once again. The eyes of these creatures stayed cold and frozen, with no form of life apparent, yet they walked in unison behind the Creator.

A torch lay to the side of the temple, one that had not extinguished in the cold. His eyes sparked up in a red blaze as he saw the flame. "This will do fine." Raising a hand, he extinguished the torch. He drew the flame into his palm, throwing it from hand to hand, as he increased its size. "Nice." Walking past several of the creatures, he touched them on the head, transferring this fire. As the creatures absorbed the fire, they started to thaw, their eyes burning fiery red. Philippe's eyes burned red in turn as he walked behind, delicately touching each of the small animals on the head. The water dripped from their bodies, forming puddles by their feet before they ran screeching with their fur alight, the flames engulfing their small bodies. The aroma of burning flesh wafted through the glade.

As the creatures stopped running, they looked at their hands, feet, legs and finally tails. They were completely alight, but not burning, the aroma of searing flesh in the air was that of the others they stood near. Turning to another of his kind, one of the furry creatures pointed, flames flowing from his fingers to slam into the other's chest. One after the other, the small creatures experimented like this, until they all had projected a flame or two. Climbing into the trees, they screeched in joy, as they burnt at will, whilst Philippe looked on, smiling as his children played.

"Food! I need food." Gingerly, the Creator leant on the statue of himself, lowering his body to sit. Rod turned, looking to where they had traveled from. As if by answering his call, the rat men came trudging along the trail. A large wagon, piled to its extremities with bodies, also came creaking through behind them. Many of these bodies were dead, but some were dying, while others just murmured. The creaking and murmuring was drowned out by the small man's voice as he walked behind the wagon, screaming at the top of his lungs as if he wanted all on the planet to hear. "Freesh fleesh. Beest meeat on the planeet. Freesh fleesh, come and eeat."

"Aaah lunch, and then back to work." The Creator smiled as he watched the rat men bring him a squirming man. "Oh, still fresh. You have outdone yourself today, chef Rod. Outdone yourself indeed."

Rod could not hide his excitement at the praise from the Creator.

"Thanks, Father." He walked closer, his smile was replaced with a look of cunning as he raised his head, flicking it as he sniffed the air. He breathed in deeply and then spoke cheerily, "I smell a pussy or two. Well what am I to do?" And he was gone, not giving anyone a chance to respond.

"We have come down so far. Sure there's somethin' down 'ere Boss?" Chelsea had her rifle drawn, walking backwards while searching from side to side, protecting their rear.

"Yes Chels, I am definitely sure there is something down here." Scrycher stepped down the last step of the steep decline into a small cavern and stood, looking at the fluorescent markings on the walls, his eyes sparkling in delight. "Hey Prof, what do you make of this?"

As Profitor walked down the last few steps, he looked at the wall, his jaw dropped and his foot slipped on the last step. He fell, losing his duffel bag in his panic, only to have it rescued by Teller's quick reflexes, the jars clinking as they were saved from smashing on the rock floor. Profitor tried to throw out his hands as he screamed, somehow getting them caught up in his multitude of other items attached to his outfit. "Craaaaaaaapppppppp." The ground traveled quickly towards him as he fell, closing his eyes as his nose met the floor. Or did it? There was no pain, no blood. Opening his eyes, he noticed that his nose was not smashed. Turning his face sideways, he snorted in the dust from the floor. He looked directly into the eyes of Scrycher, who was kneeling beside him and had hold of the back of his shirt.

"Need a hand?" Scrycher laughed, as he raised himself and Profitor off the ground. "Watch that last step. It is a real neck-breaker."

The embarrassment was evident in Profitor's face and voice as he spoke, but he did not look away from the fascinating artwork on the wall before him, "Th-thank you S-Scrycher."

Profitor studied the pictures covering the walls from afar, as if afraid to touch them. "W-Well, they seem t-to be paintings from some ancient race.

I would not even guess how old they are. Th-they depict worshiping of this blue idol, or man, throughout these pictures. Mmmmm." He walked along the wall, not taking his eyes from it until he got near the end of the paintings. Turning to Scrycher, he continued, "This one depicts the blue idol performing some kind of ancient ritual, creating one of these dog-like creatures." Walking another step, he continued, "Here is th-the same ritual but look at this. T-Teller, do these people look familiar?"

Teller walked up behind Profitor to look over his shoulder. "You tell me. Are these my people, my ancestors?"

"Could well be." Profitor walked to the end of the paintings. "Oh. Y-You are not going to like this… These pictures stop abruptly." The picture was that of a Stray in a cage and the dog-like creatures were around the cage with sticks and spears, threatening it.

"Gives a new meaning to fighting like cats and dogs, don't it?" Chelsea moved closer to get a look at the painting, gently brushing Teller's fur as she leant in.

"Well, I am sure we could have a little rough and tumble of our own, if you would like." Teller raised his hand, using the back of it to caress Chelsea's blushing cheek. The actions were not completely concealed in the dim light, evident by Profitor's face which matched the iridescent paintings on the wall.

"No probs. Prof, don't worry, we'll be sure to close the curtains." Chelsea let out a little giggle as she winked.

Awkwardly turning back to the paintings, Profitor continued, "W-Well, i-it w-would s-seem th-that the dog people sort of won. The next picture depicts the blue idol leaving through a portal of light with the Stray and what looks like, Teller's crystal. And the portal is about there." Profitor pointed down the corridor to what looked like a lush cove inside the cavern, with a small pond in the middle.

"Have you seen Blink?" Scrags walked beside Scrycher, asking him the question in a soft voice.

"No, Son. However, I am sure he is all right. He never gets in too much trouble." Scrycher patted the boy on the head, "Let us have a look ahead, maybe he is there."

Profitor hurriedly walked into the garden like an excited boy. He stumbled slightly, finding his footing at the last possible moment. Circling around he squealed in excitement. "This is fascinating. I could study this for years."

A large hand clasped down on his shoulder. "Better settle or you'll be studying more than the ground." Profitor looked down at his feet; they were on the edge of the pond.

The crystal Teller was carrying started to increase in intensity, drawing light from every corner of the cove. The pond reacted in turn, raising droplets of water into the air. Each droplet combined to form what became an archway. This archway in turn, was lit by the crystal. As the crystal grew brighter, the portal became clearer, the light giving way to something behind it. A chill filled the air as snow smashed through the portal opening, and whirling winds came crashing through. Profitor shivered as the wind battered him.

"Quickly, you must go." Jarel came crashing down the stairs towards Scrags. "Now. Get going. What don't you get?" Jarel grabbed Scrags' arm as if to lead him away, and down the opposite corridor. Teller saw the assailant grab Scrags and took two steps to cut him off, following through the motion to plant his shoulder into his chest. Scrags and Jarel sprawled to the ground. Scrycher let go of Profitor and grabbed for Scrags to try and break his fall. Profitor stepped backwards out of fright. He stuttered something inaudible, and fell back. Snow swept across the room, engulfing his scream. Jarel rolled and jumped at Teller, who had continued his momentum. *Thump!* The two Strays met each other's charge, the sound echoing through the chamber. Teller's crystal became airborne from the impact, and Chelsea dived, catching it, just before it would have hit the ground. As Chelsea caught the crystal, its brightness dimmed. All those in the cove stopped. Their jaws dropped as the water from the portal crashed to the ground, drenching all in the vicinity. The portal, and Profitor, had disappeared.

"Prof. Prof." Scrycher screamed as he ran around the pool of water looking for a way in.

As if in reply, Rod's voice carried through the caverns, sending a chill down their spines. "Pussy. Here pussy, pussy. Here pussy, pussy."

Jarel pleaded with Teller as they wrestled. "You must go now."

"Teller, what are you doing?" Scrycher had stopped dead in his tracks at the sound of Rod's banter, and was staring at Teller as he struggled, apparently with himself.

"Oh." Jarel stopped wrestling, and loosed his grip; this action was reciprocated begrudgingly by Teller. Jarel dropping his hood and his outline started to shimmer, his body's shape forming before Chelsea and Scrycher's eyes. "My apologies. I am not used to company that cannot see me."

"What you want?" Chelsea, although shocked at the sudden appearance of the Stray, barked the question, as Teller moved away from Jarel, and towards Scrycher and Scrags.

"You need to get out of here. There are several men out the front of the temple that are doing some pretty nasty things to my friends. You need to get away before they do it to you." Jarel's eyes were full of remorse, but not sorrow, as he spoke.

"We need to get to our pod." Scrycher spoke in a commanding, non-threatening tone.

"You cannot get to your shuttle pod. You must take my shuttle. It can be cloaked; just hit the big red button in the center of the console, and that will help you get to your ship, if you have one. Go down the end of the tunnel and into the glade. Once there, use this." Jarel handed Scrags a circular disk of Dutanium with crystals and dragons engraved into it. "It is all you need to command my shuttle."

"But what about Profitor?" Scrycher was still looking into the pond for any signs of him.

"He is far safer where he is, than you are where you are." Jarel covered his face with the hood, disappearing again. He headed back to the stairs as the footsteps coming down got louder.

"Here pussy, pussy. Don't run and hide. I want to play!"

"What about you?" Scrycher knew that by taking this person's shuttle, he would be leaving him stranded.

"I have a score to settle for a dear little friend."

"Mmmm, what do I have here? A big Pussy?" Rod raised his nose in the air as he sniffed Jarel, circling him as a predator would its prey. "And not any old Pussy." Rod signaled down-wind of Jarel, towards the entrance where the others had left. "Familiar scent," *sniff, sniff.* "Oh, I believe you are little Scrags' daddy." Rod's smile was cynical as he continued circling.

Jarel took his eyes from Rod to look down the passage. *Could it be? Was I so blinded by my self-exile that I did not realize I had met my own son? But how—* These thoughts were torn from his mind by the searing pain in his shoulder, and the sound of clashing metal as the blade lodged in between his shoulder bones. He flailed his other arm around as he tried wrenching the blade out, but it was wedged too tight.

Rod appeared in front of Jarel as he winced in pain. Jarel's arm was dropped to his side, useless in its current state. "Now what I do to you, I can do to your son too. How I will pleasure over every cut, every…" Jarel shut Rod up mid-sentence as the butt of his rifle smashed into Rod's jaw, dislodging teeth, which clinked to the floor with the splatter of blood. Rod's face was misshapen, the rifle damage severe. As he knelt down, he mumbled something, then, one by one, he picked up his teeth and placed them back inside his mouth. He replaced the last tooth as his face finished remolding itself. Looking up with a menacing grin, he stared into Jarel's shocked eyes and, whispering softly. "A cut for you. A smack for me. A cut for you. This time it's free." Rod launched himself at Jarel, who nimbly avoided the slashing of the knife. With a backward swipe of his rifle, he smashed Rod towards the wall, sending him sprawling into it.

"A cut for you, or maybe two!" Rod's voice boomed through the tunnel as he hit the wall, disappearing in a cloud of mist. Jarel did not have time to react; he dropped to the floor, clutching at the knife now in his back. In an exaggerated gait, Rod walked from behind to place himself directly in front of Jarel, gloating all the time, yet conscious of the possibility of another attack as he smiled. "Another knife for you, that makes it two, oh what am I to do… Stuff it; I don't have time for you. I want to kill the others too. Kneel before me you Stray bitch. So I can watch your body twitch." Rod pulled a third knife from his belt. He knelt down next to Jarel and grabbed his hair in one hand, while slicing the knife across his throat with the other. "Shhhiiiiiiitttt!"

Rod's body was flung into the wall again by the power of the rifle that was offloaded into his stomach. Jarel, still on his knees, emptied the entire clip into him before dropping it, allowing it to swing from his damaged shoulder. Desperately, he tried to stem the bleeding of his throat.

Thwat. "You fight well for a Pussy." *Thwat* "It is a shame I have to," *thwat, thwat, thwat* "kill you." The bullets clanked to the floor as Rod spat them out and, as he twirled his hand, he was gone. "What rhymes with cat? Maybe… SPLAT!" The tinkling of many bullets hitting the floor echoed in the tunnel as a gigantic gust of wind and moisture smashed into Jarel's body, picking him from his knees to smash him into the wall. An eerie howl sounded from Jarel's mouth as he hit the wall. The knife in his shoulder tore the flesh from his arm as it fell to the floor with the force of the blow. The handle of the second knife snapped off, leaving the blade in Jarel's body as he continued his momentum into the wall. The flesh of his body pounded into the rock. His body dropped to the floor, and Rod looked on, amazed; he had not heard the sound of cracking bones that would normally have been associated with a blow this powerful. Jarel managed to stay kneeling, even though his head and body wanted to fall forward. He did not have to hold his head for long as Rod moved forward grabbing his hair again, this time pressing the knife deeply against his throat.

"Now where were we? A knife for me… A cut for… Ahhhhhhhhhhhh." Rod looked at the hand that had been pressing the knife against Jarel's throat. It was squirming around the floor, unable to find its body, unable to take orders. Rod continued screaming in pain as he let go of Jarel's head. He dropped down, grabbing his hand, while screaming like a little girl. He got up, turned, and ran back towards the Creator. The whole time, he was screaming and trying to place the hand back on his arm, but to no avail.

"Blink. There you are. No time to play. We need to leave." Scrags tried to push away the little dragon's nuzzling as he returned. Blink, blinked away as they entered the last room before the cove. The room was much smaller than the others, or so it seemed. The room was not small; it was instead covered from floor to roof on both sides with items. Shiny, shiny items. Teller, although in a hurry, walked over to the collection. As he reached down, Blink exploded aggressively, his hackles and head up, hissing, as he appeared before Teller to ward him off.

Teller jumped back, still looking at the large piles of shiny items. "This is his horde."

Scrags walked up to Blink and placed a hand on his head, to pat him affectionately. "Now, now. We don't want to steal anything." Blink nuzzled the hand, wagging his tail contently and was then gone. The smashing of bodies and gunfire echoed down the cavern, only to be replaced with silence. Stopping dead, they looked at each other. Tremors traveled down the passages and through the cavern, causing rocks to fall from the ceiling as an eerie howl echoed.

"Out now! Let's get out of here!" Scrycher grabbed Scrags by the scruff of the neck and ran, sprinting down to the exit of the tunnel.

"Blink." Scrags fought to break free from Scrycher as they left.

Scrycher replied as he continued carrying the boy who was screaming emotionally for Blink. "He will find us. You can never keep him out of trouble."

Jarel used his rifle to lift himself up; the large blade which had protruded from the butt to sever Rod's hand had now retracted. As he limped towards the exit to the tunnel, he could not help but shiver. *What kind of abomination is that, and how is he so strong?* He did not have time to think further as he shuffled himself, and his broken body, from the tunnel and into the small cove that Profitor had disappeared from. As his bleeding body slumped forward into the pool of water, he thought. *Peace at last, peace.* He did not feel the teeth upon his shoulder, or the scraping of claws on rock as he was dragged through the cavern and into the clearing where his shuttle had departed from moments earlier. He felt a long tongue on his cheek as his eyes opened to blink. Then he was gone as he drifted back into darkness.

"Father, Father, help me, help me." Rod was hysterical as he ran from the ruins, waving his severed hand in the air.

"All in good time, my son, all in good time." The Creator turned as he spoke, looking at the vast beauty of the land before him.

"Mogly want food, Mogly need food." The hideous little beast spoke though its manacles, and between drooling, as it scuttled to the Creator. In turn, the Creator threw to Mogly, or what mildly resembled Mogly, the carcass of a man. Rod looked around and smiled; forgetting the pain of his wound as he watched his brothers and sisters. Flying monkey-like creatures covered in fish scales darted in and out of the trees and ruins. Spider-like monkeys scuttled around, chattering to themselves. Flaming monkeys ran through the forest, burning everything they could, and the cold frozen monkeys just sat, unmoving, uninterested, yet to find a purpose.

The Creator stood, throwing his hand and several carcasses into the air as he yelled. "Rejoice, my children. Rejoice and eat' cause on the morrow, we shall reclaim more of what once was mine."

Gregory paced the ship deck. "Have you found them yet?" His fingers fidgeted behind his back as his question echoed through the bridge.

"Sir, the sensors suggest that we have to be less than a few hours out, at most." The Syndicate man spoke in a definite tone as he studied the array of writing and lights on the complex console before him.

"Get me as soon as we get to The Enforcer. I want to be here for Scrycher's demise." As he removed himself from the deck, he was followed by several half-dressed women. One of these women shivered in delight as she walked, gently rubbing her breast against his shoulder as she passed him.

"Well, what are you doing? Do not slow down, get after them." Lance was at the edge of his seat again, trying to show off his captaincy to the bridge. "Are you trying to lose them again?"

"If I recall… Lance, it was you who let them go in the first place. It was your bravado that got us stranded on the pitiful excuse for a station, and you who held up our departure. Any corrections yet?" Lance sat back uncomfortably in his chair. "And it was me who had an informant who managed to get us these co-ordinates." The Commander was calm in this situation, even though his voice allowed all to hear his disapproving tone.

"What are they doing? And where is Scrycher and his ship?" Gregory stared outside at the large vessel, The Enforcer. "And where the heck did this planet come from?"

"Sir, sensors show that there are many life forms on the planet, but only a few on the The Enforcer."

"How many on the planet?" Gregory's voice was very matter-of-fact as he spoke; his thoughts now focused on revenge; nothing else seemed to matter.

"Way too many to tell from up here. It is showing up like a large blip. The weird thing is, the reading for their life forms are off the chart."

"Who are they?"

"It is more like, what are they, Sir. Their life force seems very erratic, not at all familiar."

Gregory lowered his head. "Board The Enforcer." He lifted his head; his eyes were red in hatred. "Kill all aboard. If and when you find Scrycher, save him for me. The rest, do with as you wish."

The vessel pulled up beside The Enforcer, her crew hustling around to get their weapons as they prepared for the boarding.

"Sir." The voice was high and concerned as the man spoke.

"What is it, man?" Gregory had not lost the fire in his eyes, and the anger had spread into his voice.

"Another ship, Sir. It has just started moving away from The Enforcer." Looking at the console, his fingers pointed towards the small blip next to The Enforcer's large one.

"Why did you not see it before?" Gregory was fuming.

"It was not there before, Sir, it is almost like they had no power before now." The voice sounded strained as he spoke, terror evident in his eyes. You did not make mistakes in the Syndicate, or you were never heard from again.

Gregory looked out the front screen as the little ship edged its way from the planet, also removing itself from under the cover of the much larger vessel, The Enforcer. "Blow out their engines. I want them alive, to gut them myself."

"Yes, Sir."

Chapter 14

The volley of cannon fire hit the side of the ship, the force making it lurch sideways as Chelsea tried to dodge the onslaught. "Captain, they are too powerful for us. We need to run." The crate beneath Scrags' feet went sprawling along with him. He hit the floor hard, winding himself. Teller had been observing the actions around him. He bolted to the station, armed the Gatling gun, and shot at the next volley of cannon fire. Teller's aim and response was even more impressive than Scrags', each volley being blasted before it reached them. Scrags got to his feet as Scrycher reached him. Grabbing the young boy by the arm, Scrycher swung him out of the gun pit and onto the deck of the ship. "Get to the escape pods and make sure they are ready to launch. They may be our only way out of this mess." Without questioning, Scrags ran through the cockpit door.

Teller's body glowed brightly and he screamed, "Noooooooooo! Don't go!" not taking his eyes off the cannon fire before him. Scrags stopped in his tracks, only making it into the galley, now frozen by Teller's commanding voice. Scrags looked back at Scrycher in a questioning glance.

"Do as he says, Scrags, give Jaxter a hand." Turning to Jaxter, he continued his line of questioning. "Now go through this again, Jaxter. They just sat there motionless while you installed the Gatling gun, until we came aboard? Then they started firing without a warning?" Scrycher was holding the cage around the gun, watching as Teller's precise aim took out another set of cannon fire.

"Yes, Boss, just like that, except that I never had no power on until you came aboard."

"Crap, we should have stayed silent; we've given away our position." Scrycher struggled over to the communications console, grabbing it as Chelsea performed another hair-raising maneuver. "Whoa! Chels, be careful. I want to be alive at the end of this."

"If I had not restarted the power, we'd all be dead anyway." Jaxter's tone was annoyed as he flicked switches to give Scrycher a line of communication to the other ship.

"Unknown ship. What do you want? We have done nothing to provoke you."

"What do you mean? You killed my men, took my vessel and then have the audacity to leave me a letter saying, we were even." The voice was strong and aggressive.

"Who are you?" Scrycher did not recognize the voice.

"Who am I? Are you that stupid? It is Gregory, the head of the Syndicate. Hand over my vessel, now!"

"Aren't you the one firing at us?" Confused, Scrycher ran his fingers along the console and watched as only one light blipped before him. Another blip started at the extremities of his console, and then the one close to them split into two, traveling apart. "That's it. Chelsea there are two vessels and another on its way. Get us out of here. We don't stand a chance if we stay." A shuttle exited the planet's atmosphere and headed towards The Enforcer, causing a smaller light on the screen, which went unnoticed by all.

"Gregory, we are not in control of any ship, other than our own." Scrycher's voice pleaded to be listened to.

"Then who is in charge of, The Enforcer?" Gregory's voice sounded conflicted but his question was soon to be answered as, The Enforcer opened fire.

"Scrycher, get out now while I hold them off."

"Philippe? How the... I saw you killed!" Scrycher's voice was almost teary as he spoke.

"Long story, old friend. Now get out of here, and now!" Philippe's voice was full of sorrow, and pleading as he repeated. "Get out of here now. Please."

"Captain? What is happening? When was Philippe killed?" Chelsea's eyes were bold as she spoke, demanding an answer.

"Later, get us…"

The ship was rocked by another set of cannon fire exploding close to their hull, this volley projected from the third vessel, the Company vessel. Several outer plates were wrenched from the hull, shaking the ship violently; Scrycher did all he could to hold on. "Get us out of here Chels. NOW!" Then he turned towards the galley, momentarily forgetting Profitor was no longer with them. "I hope your theory on this planet is right, for all our sakes." Chelsea threw the ship forward violently; accelerating so fast that all but Teller and herself fell to the floor. The Company vessel continued to fire on the tiny ship, while the two other vessels, The Enforcer and the Syndicate vessel, fought between themselves. The cannon fire exploded all around them as Teller blew them out of the sky before they could get too close. Teller was hung upside down in the cage, shooting behind them but quickly spun the cage to the unseen meteor storm in front of them. Pulling the trigger, he fired, yelling out as he did, "Chelsea!" and hitting the first meteor before it could collide with the vessel.

Chelsea's heeded the warning, her attention removed from the fight behind them and now focused the task in front, as they were ravaged by the storm. Rock after rock was shattered with the Gatling fire, breaking them into smaller fragments before they had a chance to smash into the failing hull of the ship. *Th-thump, th-thump, th-thump.* Teller's fur radiated as he absorbed the heat from the gun, converting it to energy. All were oblivious to his energy conversion, even though the brightness caused them to be temporarily blinded if they looked at him. He continued to destroy every meteor before it hit the ship. Jaxter looked at Teller in awe of his skill, his eyes blurring as he pulled away. Looking at his console, he could not see the blips of the Syndicate vessel and The Enforcer's ongoing battle. He did not see the blip of the planet shimmer slightly as it tried to exit out of this realm. Or catch the shimmering out of the corner of his eye as the planet stayed where it had been, in this realm. But as his eyes regained sight, he did see the blip of the Company vessel as it continued hunting them with guns blazing until it too stopped, disappearing from his screen as the meteor storm was too dense for a vessel of its size to enter…

"Scrycher. What are you doing here? And how the hell did you get me into this mess." Philippe had made his way to the deck in extremely quick leaps, as he raced to defend the vessel against the oncoming fire. He now stood on the bridge, breathing perfectly normally and not at all out of breath. *This new body has its advantages.* As he looked on at the fire-fight before him, he could see Scrycher's little ship had little chance of survival. "Communications, open a channel…" The atmosphere was grave, with no one operating the communications station, all the crew on the bridge looked down at the deck in complete silence, trying not to be noticed. Walking to the console, he flicked a switch. He did not act; he reacted, as he performed his next action, fueled by loyalty and friendship. "Scrycher, get out now, while I hold them off."

"Philippe? How the? I saw you killed." Scrycher's voice sounded weak to Philippe as he spoke.

"Long story, old friend. Now get out of here, and I mean, now!" Philippe's voice was filled with pity as he spoke, *these poor, poor people. They do not stand a chance, as they do not even know they are the inferior species.* "Get out of here now. Please." Philippe knew he could not hold onto his friendship forever, and that the day may come when he would have to fight the people he once called friends.

"Captain?"

The communications went dead. At the sound of Chelsea's voice, his heart melted. As big as his heart was, it did not feel right today, so he turned his thoughts elsewhere. "Fire on the large vessel, and now!"

The Commander continued his scolding of Lance. "And it is me who will get us around this fire fight, so we will not have to then fight a Syndicate vessel, or two."

The Gunnery sniggered as he lay uncomfortably back in his chair. His fingers were white with the strain of holding his trigger in anticipation of the fight to turn their way. This Captain was making his secret mission far too easy, however, those two syndicate vessels were making him very nervous indeed.

"Stop your sniggering and earn your keep. Fire at them, and take out those engines. And make it better than the last time." Lance threw his frustrations at Gunnery, who responded as if he were a proud teenager who had been challenged.

Swinging his sight around, he lined up the ship. "A little closer, closer, closer. Now." As his fingers pulled on the trigger, he gasped. What had he done? The cannon fire drifted for what seemed an eternity before he watched it explode near the hull of the small ship, tearing off hull plates.

"Well done, Gunnery. I did not know you had it in you. Now just one more trajectory like that and their ship and crew, is ours."

The Gunnery froze. He did not want to jeopardize his retirement. Thinking quickly he fired, ensuring all the subsequent shots were aimed slightly away from the hull. The gunnery on the other ship made his job easy as they blew the shots out of the space before they reached the ship.

Then it came, a meteor storm. Firing at the meteors, the Gunnery tried to make enough room for them to follow, but it was just too dense.

Lance stormed out of the room, yelling back as he left. "I suppose it would be too much for me to ask for you to follow them through the storm, and put us all out of our misery?"

The small ship limped its way out of the meteor storm; many of its hull plates torn from its body, but its bulk, for the most part, was intact. The crew stood in the cockpit, listening to the hull creaking as they tried to gauge the extent of the damage from their encounter. They did not see Teller until it was too late. The Stray's light dimmed now, so low it was barely a glow. *Th-thump, th-thump, th-thump.* Teller's head beat so hard that the fog entered, and concealed all else in his mind. He tried to claw his way out, but to no avail. As the room started spinning, he leaned away from the gun, attempting to walk away, but crashed to the ground heavily. "Jax, get him to the crew quarters. Chels, get us far, far away from here as quick as you can. Scrags, get some wet cloths, and go with Jax. Prof, are you alright? " Scrycher barked orders as he wiped the sweat from his brow. Not hearing anything from the galley, he walked in. "Profitor?" His voice softened as he remembered. "Oh. Where are you, dear friend?"

"Scrags!" Jaxter grabbed the boy by the scruff of his neck, as the door to the crew quarters was sucked open. With his hold on Teller and Scrags slipping, he gripped tighter. A ripping sound was sucked out with the atmosphere as Scrags' top tore. The breach doors slammed closed. Dropping Teller to the floor, Jaxter fell to his knees, sweat pouring from his brow.

Scrycher turned sharply to see Jaxter on his knees, the commotion, over in seconds. Pleadingly, he looked at Jaxter, a scrap of Scrags' top still in the large man's hands as he lent forward and wept into it. "Scrags! Scrags! Scrags…" Scrycher screamed as he searched hysterically for any hope.

"To the crystal, quickly." The panicking creatures ran in circles as the planet tried to shift back into the other realm. The Creator was yelling at them and pointing atop the ruins at the crystal in the cage. "To the crystal, quickly."

"Mogly go, Mogly go now." The long spider legs scuttled up the ruins as the planet phased slightly, all around, shimmering as it happened.

"Now little one. Now, before it is too late." The Creator was calling at Mogly, making him very nervous as he reached the top of the ruins. Grabbing with his hands and tail, he wrenched at the metal cage that was housing the crystal, with no effect.

"Whock, Whock. Mogly need help. Fly ones, here now." Mogly's tone was harsh and decisive and the panicking flying fish creatures stopped circling in the air, buzzing up to where he was sitting. "Whock, whock. Tail now. Here, here, here, now, here." Mogly pointed at the creatures' tails as they shimmered again.

"Now! Get it now or we will be lost from this realm." The Creator was still yelling at Mogly, between mouthfuls of flesh, as sweat poured from his blue brow. He stuffed another carcass down his throat, swallowing it whole as his mass expanded, filling him with more energy.

The flying creatures grabbed the bars with their tails and they all flew out at the same time. The first attempt was a failure as they smashed into the temple roof, the cage bars not moving at all. "Again." Mogly barked the order as the creatures buzzed above the temple and tried again, this time, he helped with the pulling. The bars ripped apart, sending the crystal into the air. Mogly's tail stretched out as he headed towards the Creator, grasping the crystal with it as he leapt. A small thread of crystalline webbing shot from his anus area, attaching onto the side of the temple as he plummeted to the earth below. His body traveled fast, as if to splat on the ground below. He knew time was short so did not control the descent until he was a fraction above the Creator's head. He stopped suddenly, bobbing up and down on the thread. "Mogly got you crystal. Now take it." Gently he dropped it into the Creator's hands.

"Anchor to this realm. Anchor now." Grabbing the crystal and thrusting it high in the air the Creator's voice boomed, the sheer volume of his voice causing parts of the ruins to crumble. The raised crystal drew forth power from all those around it, small wisps of energy could be seen being pulled from all who were near. The crystal's intensifying light burned all those around; the Creator's own flesh was cooked by the intense heat. "Anchor now!" As the crystal's light became unbearably hot to all in its vicinity, he slammed it into the ground. The wave of light exploded into the ground, flowing like a tidal wave across the planet, anchoring it to this realm. The planet then shimmered slightly before the crystal's light diminished; the planet was now fixed in its position in this realm.

"Dogny not want fix Jarel. Dogny not like Jarel or Jarel's bastard child. Dogny hurt." Dogny cowered in the corner of the ship, looking at Jarel's seemingly lifeless body.

"Now, my old friend, that is no way to treat our guest. And I am sure that the boy did not mean to put a Dragon in your head. Lucky enough I removed it before it could do too much more damage to that frayed mind of yours." A pungent odor filled the cabin, as Lallone leant over Jarel, tending the wounds with some unusual colored paste.

"Dogny exiled Jarel's kind from our home. That when Father left. Left us, left me, Dogny. We not want none to do with them now." Tears ran down Dogny's cheek as he recollected the day many millennia ago. "Dogny just like master. Master save Dogny, and Dogny's kind. Dogny like serving master. Give Dogny purpose."

Lallone turned Jarel to his side. He dug his fingers into the bruised, swollen flesh across his back, and yanked out the blade. Applying the paste he mumbled to himself. "Lucky for Jarel we went against the Founders wishes, and infused his bones with Dutanium." He stalled momentarily as he thought back to his wife, Paleen, and the joining they had done with Stray, Dragon and Dutanium, and its unseen side effects. All who had gone through this procedure had gained immense power, and great strength. The Dutanium acted like a conduit for the crystal's natural energy, but at a cost. The same cost that the Founders and their species had lived with every day since their awakening; they could not reproduce. This was all done in order to fulfill one of the prophecies; One day a Stray born of flesh, combined with Dragon and infused with the strength of Dutanium would save their people from a dark death.

To a race that had out lived all others and could not die, this was blasphemy. The Founders would need no help, no saviors, so they banished Steller—the Teller of this fate—and the two she had confided in. Lallone, Paleen, and Steller were all to live out their long existence, exiled from each other, and others of their kind.

On hearing what Jarel had done to the Councill members, the Founders were afraid for their own lives and recalled Lallone, and Paleen. They forced them to put the rest of the morphed Strays into stasis. Begrudgingly they were put in stasis, and Paleen was exiled again. In some weird show of appreciation, The Founders had allowed Lallone to stay, though he never felt that he belonged.

Jarel had escaped the fate of stasis, as he had not returned home. The order was executed; the others did not know what happened, nor would they as long as they slept. Lallone knew now why they had not been able to find him, or, why the others thought he was dead. The planet they had removed him from was also in a sort of stasis, somewhere between two realms, barely entering this one. How Scrycher and his crew could call this planet forth was a mystery to Lallone, a mystery he would love to solve.

Jarel grabbed Lallone's cloak, pulling him down to his mouth. He was in a trance like state. His breathing was raspy as he croaked into his ear. "Is my son alright? Did he escape?"

"Dogny, you were not hallucinating; but how? How is that boy, his son and who is the mother?"

"Steller, but why, do not make me leave. We are alone. Lonely." Jarel was talking to the roof, blankness still in his eyes as he spoke.

"Steller, the Teller of our fate, the Teller of the Fabled three? Could she be the mother of his son? But how? We cannot bear children, we cannot, should not, could not." Lallone's blue complexion paled to a white and its glow diminished. He sat in shock as Jarel started screaming again.

"Steller, Steller, Steller!"

Scrycher dropped to the floor, his senses reacting in slow motion as his tears dropped from his cheek to hit the deck with a deafening clunk. Jaxter just wept, his large body heaving as he raised his head. "Noooooo!"

The Clanking of a pot in the galley surprised both men. Curiously looking at Jaxter, Scrycher got from his knees and walked to the preparation bench to gingerly peep over. "Profitor?" His eyes widened, his top lip quivered, and his heart beat faster. He did not waste a second as he scaled the bench; knocking everything of the side and grabbed Scrags in a huge embrace, almost crushing the small dragon, Blink, beside his feet; now rummaging through rat bones. Scrycher sobbed, shaking uncontrollably as he hugged Scrags tighter. "I thought I lost you. I... I... I do not know what I would do without you."

Blink, blinked, disappearing to avoiding Scrycher's feet as he whirled the boy around in joy. Seconds later Blink was on top of the counter, and proceeded to try to remove a piece of Scrags' shirt from his claws. "Blink, Blink. You have come back. Oh, Blink." Scrags broke Scrycher's hug by ducking under it and grabbed the small dragon in an embrace that made the little dragon raise his head in question. His little eyes opened wide, bulging from his head as Scrags hugged him tighter. "Don't leave me, Blink. Don't leave me." Scrycher lifted little Scrags onto the counter, and Scrags softly cuddled his head on Blink's chest; using his soft belly as a pillow.

Wiping his tears away, Scrycher turned to Jaxter querying. "What the heck just happened, Jax?"

"Sorry Boss. The pod must've been smashed off in the meteor storm and the breach doors didn't close till we tried to open the door here."

"No need to be sorry, big man, no need to be sorry." Scrycher walked towards Jaxter, without letting Scrags from his sight. As he got close, he turned to Jaxter, whispering so the boy could not hear it. "Blink must have transported him as he was sucked out. If... if Blink was not here..."

Chapter 15

Jaxter was holding desperately onto the flight stick as he yelled. "Nuuuuuuuutttttttssssss. Hold on to something." The warning came too late for Scrags and Blink, who were thrown violently to the floor. Jaxter also went sprawling after them as he failed to wrestle with the flight stick, which had been thrust backwards from the external force on the ship. Blink's hackles were up, and his eyes bulged as he grabbed with his claws, anchoring himself to the decking, while he hissed, guarding the ship from the unseen force. Jaxter's face pushed into the grating and slobber dripped onto the deck as he grumbled. "That's right, Blink, you tell them. They sure did not listen to me."

Chelsea had made her way from Teller's side, to the cockpit, at the first sign of trouble. "Stay down, big man!" She leapt through the doorway, Jaxter started to raise himself, she skipped slightly as her foot planted on his back.

"Whaaaaaat?"

She caught hold of the flight stick and his face met the deck again, with a salivary slap. "Do I have to do everything myself?" She held on tight as her body impacted the stick with enough force to almost level the ship again before the next wave of spatial distortion hit them. "What you done Jax, put us in the middle of spatial eddies?"

His words were obstructed by the grating, as he had not bothered getting up again. "Nope, Chels." He smiled as he watched Scrags and Blink lose their grip again, rolling back onto the floor, as a new wave hit the ship. "I just found us one of those planet thingies that you said Prof was talking about. And by the feel of it, it's a big one!"

The waves of space buffeted the small ship as though they were trying to smash it into tiny pieces. Chelsea steered the sheep into these waves, riding in and out with them, losing precious distance every time she did. Chelsea looked up as the ship creaked. "If this planet does not show up soon, we'll have to leave before she gets ripped apart." She grimaced as she surfed another spatial wave. "She can't take much more of this."

"No problem, Chels, you have done well and there she is." Scrycher was holding the communications console while he reached out, pointing at the gigantic mass appearing before them. The planet was many times the size of the other one that they had so easily found and explored. Another wave, this one much larger, exploded from the space in which the planet now occupied. Scrycher was thrown forward over the communications console and then flung back into it as the ship settled, and the space around them became calm.

"Am I the only one that can stay standing? You men!" Chelsea laughed as she helped Scrycher to his feet. He rubbed his head, accepted the gesture and in return, walked over to help up poor Scrags, who was battered and bruised. Jaxter lifted his criss-crossed cheek from the floor, but before he stood, Scrycher spoke.

"Jax. You reckon when we get out of this mess, that you can install some seats for us all? Starting with the Captain's chair of course." Scrycher allowed himself a little smile as he spoke.

"Only if you promise not to throw it against the wall again." Jaxter was upright now, and listening to the creaking of the hull as he spoke. "But Captain, if I don't do some repairs to her now, then she ain't gonna need seats."

"Chels?" Scrycher queried her as she pulled out buttons and turned knobs on the communications console.

"We're in luck. By what I can see, this good old planet will allow us into the atmosphere, without crushing her hull… too much.

"You sure you can fix her?" Scrycher was standing on the soggy grass, yelling up at Jaxter as he climbed the hull. Jaxter looked down. "No problems, Boss." He took another step and swung his large hand to his neck. Splat. "Bloody bug…" Jaxter's large body faltered, his arm still on his neck as he slumped. He rolled down the side of the ship, slid off the wing and hit the soggy grass with a *Splosh.*

Scrycher stepped quickly to him, grabbing his shoulder as he spoke. "What the heck, Jaxter? This is no time to take a nap. We need you to fix the ship." Scrycher rolled him over; he could not see the large man's face through the mud. Scrycher wiped the dirt from Jaxter's mouth and eyes. With no response, he pried open his eyelids. His eyeballs were rotating back and forth in a rhythmical pattern. Peeling Jaxter's large hand from his neck, Scrycher gasped. "Tsetse."

"Bless you." Scrags spoke as though Scrycher had sneezed.

"No, Tsetse."

"Bless you."

"No, Tsetse."

Scrags looked confused. "Bless you."

"It is a Tsetse fly." Scrycher delicately plied the squashed, little bug from Jaxter's hand to show it to Scrags. "This little bug, as Profitor would put it, is the most wondrous of all insects. With one little bite, it puts a grown man to sleep." Scrycher could not help but laugh at the irony of such a little insect, putting such a large man to sleep. "Oh, Prof would have loved this planet, he really would have." Black clouds started seeping in from around them, seemingly coming from the swamp that they were yet to explore. The clouds quickly concealed Scrags, Jaxter, Scrycher and Blink, who was atop Scrags' head. The clouds continued to move until they had encircled the ship. Then the clouds seemed to halt, no longer seeping from the depths of the swamp.

Blink's eyes opened. His little ears rotating as though seeking out something. His ears stopped, drooped and then he dropped from Scrags' head. He tore at Jaxter's shirt, snarling as he signaled that he wanted to drag the large mass up the platform, and into the ship. Scrycher and Scrags looked at each other, shrugged their shoulders and complied. Wiping the sweat from Teller's brow, Chelsea looked up. "What the? Another patient. A girl would start to think it was something she'd said or done."

"Will you be alright with these two sleeping beauties?" Scrycher's voice was more telling than asking. "We need to go." He felt the pull of the dark cloud around the ship as though it was calling to him, drawing him into its body to engulf him and lead him to something, someone.

Chelsea waved him away, winking as she spoke. "I've handled more than two before." They placed Jaxter on the other cot, and left the room as Chelsea whispered under her breath. "Take more than these two to wear me out…"

"I look silly." Scrags was looking at the outfit Scrycher had placed on both of them. "I don't want to wear this."

Scrycher laughed. "What, you do not want to look like your old man?" He patted him on the head gently. "If I do not mind looking this stupid, why should you? Especially when you never brush that mop you call hair." Blink was rolling around the floor giggling as his tummy jiggled, "But why?" Scrags pleaded with Scrycher. The giggling stopped, replaced by Scrags gawking and pointing at Blink, who was running around the inside of the large netted hat that had been placed over him.

"You too, Blink, me boy. Prof said the only way to get through a swarm of insects hungry for your blood was to catch yourself." Scrycher waved his hands up and down, modeling his silly looking outfit. He had dressed himself in a large jacket with a massive pocket in the front of it and the rest of his body was concealed by a large net, as was Scrags'. "Do you think this is what he meant?"

Blink disappeared. Surprised, Scrycher jumped up, banging his head on the roof. Scrags broke into boyish laughter, rolling over in fits of joy at the sight. Blink looked up from inside the large pocket in the front of Scrycher's jacket, only his large eyes visible. Scrycher looked into those eyes with humorous disapproval. "Comfortable now, are we?" Blink's response was quick, as his little head popped completely out of the pocket, and shook up and down. "Yep, comfortable indeed. I hope you do not think I

am going to carry your lazy ass all around this rock? Get this hat on now."
Scrycher bent down, grabbing the hat and pointing to it. Blink just looked
up at Scrycher, grinning and shaking his head no. Scrycher's voice raised as
his face flushed. "I do not have time for games little one."

Chelsea removed her trinket box from below the bunk. "Well, if I have
to spend my time with you two, I may as well make me smell pretty." She
opened it; memories flooded back as she removed the shiny bottle.

*"Hello, little Scrags. What you want?" Chelsea looked at the little boy, Blink
on his head and looking around cautiously. Blink had not been with them long
and either had Scrags, so neither was completely comfortable in their new
surroundings.*

*"Thank you for saving me." Scrags placed a small shiny trinket in Chelsea's
hand, closing it before running off with Blink still resting on his head. Chelsea
opened her hand; she observed a small cylindrical, shiny bottle. The bottom of
the container was glass. It was capped with a metallic lid containing a picture
of an unusual flower of some forgotten time and place. Its petals were positioned
so they were closely bunched, and colored deep, deep red, with green leaves
coming off the stem. Chelsea thought she had seen nothing as beautiful as this in
her life, and held it to her breast, closing her eyes as she did so.*

*Tiny claws probed at her hand; startled she opened it and her eyes. Blink's
own eyes were wide and curiously affectionate as his little clawed fingers slipped
the container from her hand, his claws flipping off the lid. With a subtle pop,
the lid came off and the perfume wafted into the air. The scent was unbearable
to her, its smell so sweet and innocent. As Blink placed the small container back
in her hand, she realized that this was Blink's trinket, one he had given freely.*

*Leaning over towards him, she placed a small kiss on his head, he shivered
in almost childish delight and was gone. Chelsea sat for some time, smelling the
sweet fragrance, daydreaming of what it would be like to wear such an aroma,
and maybe touch that flower. However, this time would never come, not while
the Company ruled.*

Chelsea opened the bottle. Except for the day she had received it, it had remained closed. She dabbed the smallest amount on her wrists, and nape of the neck, contemplating while observing both men now lying on the beds. Teller was screaming, moaning, and covered in a deep sweat, which soaked his fur, and Jaxter just snored, loud and strong. *Is this all life is to be? One horrific trial after another?*

"Lance, I have the co-ordinates of the vessel you are seeking," Lord Dragoon's voice was less than impressed as he spoke. "You are supposed to be chasing them, not letting them escape. You disappoint me Captain; I hope you can capture them this time."

The monitor switched off, and Lance turned, leaving the room. His palms were nervously sweaty as he handled the memory stick containing the new coordinates, but he still managed to scream down the corridors in a prideful voice. "Commander! We have some criminals to apprehend."

Scrycher was trudging through the swamp, his legs and feet wet and heavy, Scrags rode on his shoulders and Blink slept in the large pocket. "I still think I got the worst end of this deal." They had been traveling for what seemed a day or so, but they had no recollection of time in this place. "I think we have to head back. There is nothing here for us." Almost by the power of these words, the fog parted, revealing a large cabin in the swamp. Two little windows, one each side of the door, allowed an eerie light to emanate through to them. The light barely breached the darkness around the cabin.

"Mmm, maybe we should turn back." Scrycher did not like the look of this cabin, but could not help but be drawn into that eerie light.

A sweet voice floated out of the windows and into Scrycher's ears. "And go where, my hero, my savior?"

"And who may you be, sweet lady?" Scrycher assumed the owner of the voice to be such, as he walked cautiously towards the door.

"Some call me the Teller of fate, some the Teller of the future, some the Teller of what never should, or could become. But those close to me… that were close to me, call me Steller." The voice diminished slightly as she spoke the last words, but picked up again as she continued. "Enough of me! Why have you come? We were not destined to meet. Something is awry in these series of events. Have you come to find out more of you, and what you must do?" With the last word spoken, the door opened, the black smoke bellowing out through the doorway, but also filling inside the small cabin so nothing could be seen.

Scrycher talked in a proper manner, as he gestured towards the cabin. "May we enter your abode?" He asked as he walking up the steps. He placed Scrags down. The smoke attacked his senses. His eyes blurred as he moved, and he reached for his rifle.

"It will be over soon, do not fight it, or it will fight you." The voice was very reassuring as it spoke, like a mother comforting her child.

As he steadied himself, Scrycher noticed Scrags was not affected by the strange smoke and stood staring. He was speaking the same phrase over and over again; "She is beautiful. So, so beautiful." Scrycher tried to peer through the smoke, but could not see through it. *Was Scrags hallucinating?* His thoughts were soon to be answered as the black smoke cleared, revealing a humble abode. Large black stumps filled with some type of liquid metal, Dutanium, it seemed, glowed with an unusual light. This light emanated out of each of the crystals within each stump, the Dutanium billowed out of each in a cloud-like stream, almost dancing as it left the logs. Each crystal possessed a heart so dark, corrupted from within by the Dutanium itself.

In addition to all the other wonders in the room, one drew Scrycher in. The beauty, which once he had looked upon, he could not remove his stare. His jaw dropped as she stood, her legs so luscious and long, a small black skirt covering her shapely buttocks, but not much else. Her subtle but definitive cleavage was framed by an intensely perfect figure, which curved where every woman should curve. Her beautiful body was nothing in comparison to the beauty she emanated from her face. Her cheekbones were high, her nose small and delicately shaped and her lips the symbol of perfection. A blue aura radiated from her, framing her in a halo of soft and pale blue light, and her hair flowed, shifting this halo as it did.

"My hero, why should you be so taken by me? I am just a Fortune Teller. No more." Scrycher could not remove his eyes from her lips as she spoke. Softly and gently they moved, slightly wet, as she mouthed the words. Steller might as well have been telling him how to cook rat stew as he was so mesmerized by her beauty that he could not hear.

Scrycher's jaw had dropped open, allowing drool to drip out; Steller gently lifted it, to stop the flow. As she did, he made contact with her eyes and the spell was broken. Those eyes, they were black, lifeless and unseeing. No feeling resided within their sockets, no remorse, no love, and no lust, only blackness.

"Are you controlling the smoke?" Scrags was not in her spell. Because of his innocence, he only saw beauty and he was curious, so the question seemed appropriate.

"No, little one, it controls itself, it seeks, flows and shapes as it sees fit. I am but a conduit for its content. Now hush, little one. Your father and I must link." Looking deeply into Scrycher's eyes, Steller searched. The room filled with smoke again, this time it was not random. Images filled the room, those of dragons and ships. Of death! Firstly, Jaxter's, the images were clear, then Profitor's, those images made Scrags look away, and then Scrags'. This image was the worst. Scrags moved back, slamming into the wall, horrified at witnessing his own death.

Steller's head jerked to the side, her eyes not seeing, searching, but finding nothing as she spoke. "Hush little one, you did not die, do not die, not yet." The images became more intense, battles in space and then on land and a final showdown where none remained, not even Blink. Blink screeched at his death and tried to blink away from this place, but something kept him stuck. As he had tried to blink, Steller screamed, her mind taken to where Blink had tried to go, back to the ship, on the ship but in Teller's mind. "No. This one has changed too much. He is the reason we met. They must die. They should have died, what will happen, how will it end. Nothing is set! All is unstuck! Will need luck, much luck. He is here. So powerful, none should be such, the power too much for his body, his mind."

Steller's mind pulled back, her body's light dimmed and then the clouds menaced around her. Their shape was that of a man. The man looked around, as if searching, and then he, the smoke, reached, grabbing at her throat, grabbing her, and choking her. As she gasped for breath, Scrags lunged for the figure, clawing through the figure as the smoke parted. Scrycher followed suit, smashing the rifle into the smoke only to see it reform and continue the strangling. Then, as suddenly as he had appeared, the smoke man bent backwards. A scream came from him, so pained it shattered the small, partly open windows. The smoke fell to the floor, returning to a black mist. Scrycher drew the blade back into the butt of the rifle. He threw the rifle back over his shoulder, as he bent down to help Steller. Kneeling on the floor, she continued to gasp. Red hand and finger marks remained around her neck, where the smoke had latched on.

"You must go. The danger is near. Your power is great, but so is theirs. Beware the dark light, the cold heart and the revenge. Pit them against each other and you will prosper, let them side, and you will die." Steller pushed Scrycher away, and as Scrags walked to her, she waved her hand in dismissal, barely seeing into his eyes for a second before she stopped.

"Let me see you with my own eyes." Steller looked up at the ceiling, and then slowly back down at Scrags. The blackness drained from those lifeless eyes, replaced with a deepness of pale blue. Looking into these eyes you could see the life of someone who had seen and experienced too much, but had never yet seen such beauty as was now before her. "Oh my boy, how I have longed to hold you, touch you, kiss you; but it has never been before and will never be again. This is a gift, an omen, a future, one of many possibilities. One that should never have happened." Tears rolled from her eyes as she hugged Scrags and turned to Scrycher. "Please take care of my only child, and protect him with your life."

Chelsea spoke as she leant over Teller. "Jaxter, you sure you up to going out?" She did not look up as she mopped the sweat from Teller's fur, before draining it into the small bucket beside the bed.

"Well Chels, you got your hands full." Anyways see'n that I had such a good rest, I gotta work so much harder, or I won't get sleep tonight." Jaxter smiled as he left the room.

"As long as you ain't sayin' I didn't offer is all." The humidity from the swamp had made its way onto the ship, and Chelsea was uncomfortably soaked in her own sweat. As Jaxter left, she slipped out of the compartment as well, changing into more comfortable undergarments.

Th-thump, th-thump, th-thump. Teller awoke, wide-eyed like a trapped animal, looking into the distance, but not seeing. "Ah." Chelsea panicked, raising herself up and, smacking her head on the bunk above, as his body moved erratically. Every muscle in his body twitched in pain, as he was ripped from this realm, and through another. Chelsea's hand flew to her mouth as she stared in horror, watching as his body disappeared before her eyes, until only his clothes remained.

"What are you doing? You must make sure you do not fail! Others are now on their trail, and this will mean that they are more under threat than I had hoped. Ensure that you keep your mission secret, and soon enough you will have your riches. However, you must make sure they all do not die. I need their destination, as do you. Now go!" Lord Dragoon did not give the Gunnery time to respond as he dismissed him from the room, giving him one last direction as he left. "And if your Captain is going to jeopardize your mission, kill him! He is expendable."

Lord Dragoon delayed his exit, contemplating on how close they were from their goal, knowing that there were too many cards now in play. *Now what am I to do about them?* A chill ran down his spine, as the Gunnery left his sight. He could feel a powerful presence enter, it was on board, he could sense it. He could sense that the entity was strong, its potential to jeopardize their mission was great. However he also felt it changing, its transformation was not completed yet, he would make sure that it never was.

He searched the room like a serpent, his head darting from side to side. Looking directly at the spot where Teller stood, he reached out to the empty space, grabbing at the presence, strangling it as his eyes lit up, a dark light sparkling in them. This light in his eyes grew in intensity, illuminating his facial features under his hood. They were that of an insane killer, pleasuring over the last few breath of his victim as he gripped tighter, forcing an invisible foe to their knees. "You puny fools, you cannot hurt me." Dragoon voiced this with certainty as his body moved slightly, as though a breeze moved through him. His back arched, the feeling of sudden and excruciating pain was written over his face as he let out an ear piercing scream, that echoed through the room.

"Aaaaaraarrrrrrrrrgghgghhhhh." Dragoon contorted, reaching frantically for his back and then disappeared.

Lord Dragoon continued screaming as he was ripped back to his anchor point, his hands still grabbing behind him at the invisible weapon. His hands touched something familiar, and he stopped grasping. He stopped screaming, taking comfort from the touch of the tree trunk behind him as he finished materializing Blood spurted from the wound inflicted from Scrycher's blade, staining the crystalline tree. He grasped the tree harder as he grimaced in pain and the blood flow slowed. It diminished as he drew the healing power from the tree, until finally there was no blood flowing, only an open wound. His body glowed and the wound healed further. The dim light from the tree grew dimmer as it traveled through him, fixing his broken body. The tree's essence healed his body as best as it could in its withered state, and the cages rattled, as its branches strained.

Dragoon did not know what had hit him, what had caused the wound.

He had thought himself almost immortal, and untouchable, in the form he had taken. He was mistaken. It was a mistake that had almost cost him his life; a mistake he would not make again. In agony, he turned, dragging himself up, resting his palms, and head, on the tree. He allowed his body to drift off to sleep, as his mind filled with the moaning lullaby of the caged Strays, hanging from the tree. The tree was warped, the branches twisted and distorted, the light from it, barely lighting the lifeless eyes of the Strays as they cradled their malnourished bodies. This was a tree from the Stray home world. A trophy of the battle won and the reason the battle had started. In addition, it was the reason Lord Dragoon had lived so long. However, it was dying, it had been withering for centuries and its light was almost out. He needed a replacement tree, he needed eternal life…

Th-thump, th-thump, th-thump. Teller awoke, his eyes not seeing through the thick fog around his mind, but his mind was completely lucid. The dream that he thought he had been living, was fresh in his mind. He remembered the death of all he had grown to care about, and the fate they had all shared. Many were lying in the snow, buffeted by the blizzard, with pools of frozen blood beside them. Their hopes and dreams, like their shells, were frozen in time, with no one to care about, or acknowledge their deaths. He could not live with this fate. He had to change it. *Th-thump, th-thump, th-thump,* his head thumped as he pulled his thoughts back, heavy feet, legs, thighs, bottom, stomach. Oh, his stomach was growling, he was so hungry. *How long was I asleep?* He did not know. His mind cleared enough for him to feel it, the presence of the uninvited visitor.

He could feel the Fortune Teller probing his mind, trying to find a reason for his powers. His body tingled slightly and then his stomach felt as though it was being ripped from his body. The pain almost left him as suddenly as it had begun, now only a dull aching. Still disorientated, he looked around. He was standing on an unfamiliar deck, one belonging to another vessel. He was in a dark room, with the only light coming from a small table in the center. He watched as the powerful man spoke, his power obvious as he barked his will at the Gunnery. Teller felt his body chill as the submissive Gunnery left toward the door, right past his location. Shocked the Gunnery had not seen him, he looked down at his hands, through his hands as he could see the floor. *I must have camouflaged myself again out of instinct.*

Looking at the remaining man, he stood still. Lord Dragoon was looking directly at him, reaching towards him as if trying to strangle him. Teller did not know what to do, he panicked, closing his eyes and wished he was gone from this dream or this place…

"Commander, I am sure. I want our men deployed. In addition, I need you on-board with me. However, if your men are incapable of being able to perform without you, then I am sure one of them would trade places. You are aware that such an action would show you are not confident with your men, and their ability to get the job done." Lance had been working on this speech for hours and it had done the trick. The Commander had stormed off to get his men ready. This was why Lance was alone when he heard the scream. It was why he was the first to bust into the room, and, why he was the one that startled Teller. Teller clawed at him instinctively as he drew his weapon. Lance grabbed at his face, trying to dull the pain of the cleaved flesh as he screamed. His own screams now echoed down the corridor as he dropped to the floor in pain.

Teller jumped, as Lord Dragoon's scream wrenched him from his trance. The beating of his head had drowned out all but the scream. *Th-thump, th-thump, th-thump.* Until the *Click*. Teller turned, reacting to the sound behind him. He barely had time to think. Lance had already panicked and grabbed the gun from his holster, and the click had signified that the safety was off. He was now shaking as he pointed it menacingly at

Teller. Teller's reactions were primitive, like Blink's would have been. His claws extended, his arms moving lightning fast as he tried to swat away the immediate threat of the gun. He was unaware of the outcome of his actions, as in that moment, he disappeared from the vessel. So he did not see Lance drop to the floor, clutching his cleaved face, or hear Lance scream, as he was already gone.

Chelsea was leaning over the bed in a daze as, Teller reappeared. In her shock, she threw up her hands, losing her balance, and falling onto his naked body. Teller's gray fur smelled musty to her, as her nose fell into his chest. Gently, she turned her head, positioning her nose so it was not poking into his flesh. She could hear the rhythmical beating of his chest grow faster as her ear touched it, resting there for a second. His chest's expansion stopped, momentarily, as her touch stimulated him, his breath held, while he lost himself in her perfume and the moment. Grabbing her by the arms, Teller lifted her easily, as if to right her. He took in a large breath, basking in her aroma, the scent of some forgotten flower, from a forgotten time. With his primal instincts heightened, he could sense her arousal as she grabbed his arms in turn, the softness of his fur, feeling like silk in her hands. Gently she squeezed tighter, his fur parting, as she allowed her soft breasts to rest on his lower chest. Softly and subtly, he slid her upwards along his naked body, as he looked down towards her breasts. Catching her gaze, he felt like he was losing himself in her soul. Aggressively, he licked her bottom lip, then bit down on it, as their mouths met. Teller knew this act was not him, he had never had intimacy before, but he did not care. This was real and something to grasp onto in a world that had changed so much. This reality was what he needed, and he was going to take it. He ripped her undergarments from her body. Twisting her over and onto her back, he laid himself over her, licking intimately with his rough tongue at her other parts…

"Hey Chels, reckon you can give me a...? Oops." Jaxter's jaw dropped, as he saw the passionate bonding. "We do have doors, guys!" He turned, slightly annoyed, as he walked back out, blushing as he left.

"You can see very little down there, but our sensors show they are somewhere within the black smoke. Do not take any chances. Wear your protective gear, but do not kill them." The men looked forward as they spoke in unison. "Yes, Commander."

"And let us make this pompous ass of a Captain, eat his words."

"Understood, Sir."

The engines from the shuttle echoed through the swamp, amplifying the noise, until the sound entered the cabin in which Scrycher and Scrags still stood. "Let's get out of here, before we get trapped." Scrycher pulled Scrags away from Steller as he tried to get out the cabin in a hurry.

"I cannot guide the smoke now. You will be out in the open, and so will your ship. Good luck, Scrycher." Steller looked at Scrags again, a tear still in her eye as she spoke softly. "Go now, my son. I cannot protect you here. Go now."

"Will you be alright?"

"They are after you, not me. Anyway, it is not my time yet. Now go." Steller turned as the tears poured down her face. Scrycher threw Scrags over his shoulder, and ran from the cabin, his only thought, getting to the ship before he was cornered, caught, or worse.

"Sshhhhhh." Scrycher put his finger to his lips as he lowered Scrags to the swamp below. The voices before them were muffled, but the sound of sloshing steps as their pursuers waded through the swamp were obvious.

"They went this way." The voice was definite in its conclusion and Scrycher knew that they had been found. Three other voices chipped in.

"'Bout time."

"Better hurry, I want to get out of this crap."

And "They aren't going to know what hit them."

Scrags was covered to the waist in muddy water, and Scrycher was exhausted. Quietly, they headed away from the voices, lengthening their trek to get to the ship. They continued to trudge in misery, the dampness, seeping into their bones. He assumed that the Company men had not found the ship yet, and this detour meant, he was not about to lead them straight to it.

The sloshing water was deafening, and painful on their legs, as they rushed back to the ship. The Company men had heard them sneaking around the swamp, and now they were in pursuit. Blink's eyes were bulging as he was being thrown around in Scrycher's pocket, slipping upside down in the pocket, so his little feet and tail flailed outside it. Scrycher knew they had little chance. They were both tired and they could not outrun four Company men, but they were not about to go down without trying.

Scrycher fell to his knees, tripped by a log, or some other item hidden by the water. Scrycher pulled himself up quickly. Panicking, he placed his hand inside his pocket, grabbing Blink by the neck and righted him. Blink's head came out of the pocket, sputtering and spitting mud around as he looked at Scrycher, tsk-tsking him as he spat out more brown water. "Another time, Blink, my boy, another time, if there is one." Scrycher's optimism diminished as he heard the men behind him cocking their guns.

"Scrags, cover." He was too late. One of the men must have circled around them and found a perch high in a tree. He now had the advantage he needed, dropping down on Scrags and grabbing him from behind, before he could react. Scrags bit down hard on the man's hand, causing him to scream loudly, and raise his sniper rifle in the air; his aim to teach

Scrags a lesson.

Tooh, tooh. Scrycher's aim was precise, ripping holes through the man's shoulder, forcing him to drop the rifle and grasp his shoulder in pain. "Run Scrags, run!" Another man dropped from the tree behind Scrycher, but this time, Scrycher was ready. Swinging the butt of his rifle upwards with great force, the two collided before the man hit the ground, his helmet smashed and his nose plastered across his face. Scrags' attacker raised himself and grabbed hold of his rifle, which hung to his side. Raising his rifle, he shot blindly as his face shield was sprayed in mud and blood. Several bullets whizzed past Scrycher, lodging themselves in the tree next to the two men. Scrags acted irrationally, screaming as he jumped on the man's back, clawing at him and the helmet as he fought wildly for their survival.

Scrycher hesitated slightly, assessing his surroundings. He got his bearings, and then slammed the rifle backwards and into the face of the man who had attacked him. This time Scrycher made contact with his jaw and his helmet was smashed off. The force caused him to somersault backwards and into a tree.

The two men that had led them into the trap came running through the water. They watched, horrified, as they saw one comrade shot, collapsing to the ground, and the other violently assaulted, his body smashed against the tree. Looking back, they could see the first man get up, only to be hacked and clawed by the animal on his back. Battle hardened, these men disobeyed their orders, hatred in their eyes as they went in for the kill.

Scrags screeched as the shot hit his shoulder, the force throwing him clear of the man's back. His head hit the stump of a tree, causing him to lose consciousness, and to let go of the visor of the helmet he had managed to rip off. His head was now submersed in the water. Scrycher bellowing something that resembled a war cry, ran towards Scrags. Once by his side he did not stop, grabbing him by the back of his shirt and throwing him over his shoulder. He kept running, his adrenalin fueling him.

Blink had been partially watching, his little paws covering his eyes at all the beating, and hitting, shivering at each painful blow. As Scrags hit the stump, something inside Blink snapped. He became enraged, his scales hackling, his tail darting inside the pocket in deadly strokes and his eyes

Scrags a lesson.

Tooh, tooh. Scrycher's aim was precise, ripping holes through the man's shoulder, forcing him to drop the rifle and grasp his shoulder in pain. "Run Scrags, run!" Another man dropped from the tree behind Scrycher, but this time, Scrycher was ready. Swinging the butt of his rifle upwards with great force, the two collided before the man hit the ground, his helmet smashed and his nose plastered across his face. Scrags' attacker raised himself and grabbed hold of his rifle, which hung to his side. Raising his rifle, he shot blindly as his face shield was sprayed in mud and blood. Several bullets whizzed past Scrycher, lodging themselves in the tree next to the two men. Scrags acted irrationally, screaming as he jumped on the man's back, clawing at him and the helmet as he fought wildly for their survival.

Scrycher hesitated slightly, assessing his surroundings. He got his bearings, and then slammed the rifle backwards and into the face of the man who had attacked him. This time Scrycher made contact with his jaw and his helmet was smashed off. The force caused him to somersault backwards and into a tree.

The two men that had led them into the trap came running through the water. They watched, horrified, as they saw one comrade shot, collapsing to the ground, and the other violently assaulted, his body smashed against the tree. Looking back, they could see the first man get up, only to be hacked and clawed by the animal on his back. Battle hardened, these men disobeyed their orders, hatred in their eyes as they went in for the kill.

Scrags screeched as the shot hit his shoulder, the force throwing him clear of the man's back. His head hit the stump of a tree, causing him to lose consciousness, and to let go of the visor of the helmet he had managed to rip off. His head was now submersed in the water. Scrycher bellowing something that resembled a war cry, ran towards Scrags. Once by his side he did not stop, grabbing him by the back of his shirt and throwing him over his shoulder. He kept running, his adrenalin fueling him.

Blink had been partially watching, his little paws covering his eyes at all the beating, and hitting, shivering at each painful blow. As Scrags hit the stump, something inside Blink snapped. He became enraged, his scales hackling, his tail darting inside the pocket in deadly strokes and his eyes

"They went this way." The voice was definite in its conclusion and Scrycher knew that they had been found. Three other voices chipped in.

"'Bout time."

"Better hurry, I want to get out of this crap."

And "They aren't going to know what hit them."

Scrags was covered to the waist in muddy water, and Scrycher was exhausted. Quietly, they headed away from the voices, lengthening their trek to get to the ship. They continued to trudge in misery, the dampness, seeping into their bones. He assumed that the Company men had not found the ship yet, and this detour meant, he was not about to lead them straight to it.

The sloshing water was deafening, and painful on their legs, as they rushed back to the ship. The Company men had heard them sneaking around the swamp, and now they were in pursuit. Blink's eyes were bulging as he was being thrown around in Scrycher's pocket, slipping upside down in the pocket, so his little feet and tail flailed outside it. Scrycher knew they had little chance. They were both tired and they could not outrun four Company men, but they were not about to go down without trying.

Scrycher fell to his knees, tripped by a log, or some other item hidden by the water. Scrycher pulled himself up quickly. Panicking, he placed his hand inside his pocket, grabbing Blink by the neck and righted him. Blink's head came out of the pocket, sputtering and spitting mud around as he looked at Scrycher, tsk-tsking him as he spat out more brown water. "Another time, Blink, my boy, another time, if there is one." Scrycher's optimism diminished as he heard the men behind him cocking their guns.

"Scrags, cover." He was too late. One of the men must have circled around them and found a perch high in a tree. He now had the advantage he needed, dropping down on Scrags and grabbing him from behind, before he could react. Scrags bit down hard on the man's hand, causing him to scream loudly, and raise his sniper rifle in the air; his aim to teach that would leave me, Snipe and Gordo, to do the searching. That would leave you, sitting comfortably on our Vessel, while the Gunnery baby sits you!"

"Suits me. After all, they are your men that you have lost." Lance put a new dressing on his face again, squirming in pain as he did. "Be gone."

"Scrycher, stand down and let us board. You are outmanned and outgunned." The Commander had been getting his vessel ready to land on the planet when he had received the communication, explaining that Captain Scrycher wished to negotiate. *This is a turn of events. They must be getting desperate*, he thought.

Scrycher did not recognize this voice, so he did not quite know how to play this man; yet! "Sorry, I want to talk with your Captain."

The Commander's voice was calm as he also tried to size up his adversary. "The Captain is pre-occupied. Injured by one of your crew, I believe."

Scrycher glared at Teller, and continued, "Yes, I know of this incident. Somewhat unfortunate, but not deliberate. Circumstances beyond our control were at play."

"Surrender now and we will not be forced to fire on you." The Commander's voice was growing a little impatient as they bantered.

Scrycher saw his opening. "Here are the conditions for our surrender…"

Lance and the Gunnery sat aboard their vessel as the Commander searched for his men. "What is taking them so long?" Lance was impatient, and his face seeped green ooze, the pain unbearable. He injected himself with the contents of a needle and syringe, his eyes rolled as he leant back and relaxed with a sigh.

"I believe, Captain Scrycher said that he had strewn our men and their clothing around the swamp so that it would be more fun for us to find them." Gunnery was amused. This Scrycher was cunning. Betting on the chance that Lance would choose saving his men from possible death in the swamp, over chasing him down. It was a brazen gamble; one that had paid off. The Commander had spent the better half of a day trying to find their lost men through the thick, black fog.

"Bloody bugs." Lance squashed another of the bugs against his neck as he was bitten. "Who left the bloody door open?"

The Commander looked up from the fog that was muffling his sensors. It now showed another twenty or so sites to look for his men. Luckily, he had chosen well, and had already found three, there was only one man to go. As he thought of this he saw the shimmering of the planet, saw the space above them change briefly, and then stood in awe. His jaw dropped as the sky above changed. Instead of the blackness he had been accustomed to, he saw small lights in the sky. Looking closer he could make them out, twinkling in the sky. They were stars, hundreds of stars, covering the sky above them.

"Let's get out of here Chelsea, before they turn back." Scrycher had a large grin on his face as they left. "This should keep them off our backs for a while."

"Where's the fun in that?" Chelsea winked at Teller, who reciprocated as she steered the small ship away from the planet, and thrust the stick forward to gain maximum velocity. The planet behind them shimmered slightly and then disappeared. Its removal from this realm was much quicker than its appearance days before, and the bulk of the planet left a large hole to fill. The force of the spatial distortion trying to fill the void was enormous as the small ship was buffeted. Trying to drag the ship into the hole, the forces peeled off the makeshift hull plates Jaxter had recently installed, sucking them into the void.

Jaxter was looking out the window, watching as all his hard work was torn away before his eyes. "Not my baby, I just fixed her. Chels, do something." His eyes and voice pleaded as he dropped to the floor. "Captain?"

"Chelsea, can you do anything? We are getting torn apart." Scrycher was holding the communications console, trying to keep himself standing.

"Your plan, Boss. Not mine." Chelsea spoke, her voice trembling over the force she needed to keep the ship steady.

"Did you forget, we need to be alive for the plan to work Chelsea?"

The Creator stood in the glade. The archway leading into the other planet was open above the pool of water and he had the crystal from the top of the ruins raised high above his head. "Go forth, my children. Go forth, my little General, and reclaim what was taken from me." The small frozen creatures did not need a second order; they followed their General into this cold and inviting world. This was exactly what they required, a sense of purpose. Piling through, one after the other, they traveled to land upon the snowy peaks of the once beautiful, home of the Strays…

Chapter 17

Scrycher bellowed at the top of his lungs, as he came through the shop door. "Yo, Nifty. Been a long time, how's you going?" He did not stop to acknowledge the stares he was receiving. "And while you are at it, give me a hug." Scrycher jumped up and slid across the counter, grabbing the tall man by his shoulders, as he landed on the other side.

"Don't touch the…"

Scrycher jumped back, and onto the counter, as a large black creature leapt at him from out of the shadows. The creature's size more than matched the bulk of Scrycher, and it was easily as nimble as it changed direction in mid-flight; its head landed square in Scrycher's chest and knocked him to the floor. Blink, blinked out of Scrycher's pocket and latched onto the tail of the creature as it wrestled his master. The creature was fiercely growling, as she tossed Scrycher to the side. He regained his footing easily, and rushed back in to the fray, grappling her, and then tossing her aside like a toy. She rolled, gained her footing, and then growled, teeth bared as she leapt into his arms, they locked each other in a death roll, knocking into shelving as they did.

Scrycher was overpowered, now laying on his back with the creature at his throat. Blink was still holding on tight to the tail, being slammed from shelf to shelf as he continued to growl, his hackles up. Grabbing his fist, Scrycher rubbed hard on the head of the creature, then grabbed her ears with both hands, muzzling into her cheeks with his face, while being lapped by her large tongue.

The large black dog stood over Scrycher, her tail wagging strongly. Blink calmed a little, his growling stopped, and his hackles lowered as he continued to be smashed into shelving on both sides as her tail swung to show her excitement. He let go, sending him screeching across the floor. The graying man behind the counter was slapping himself on the forehead.

"My customers." He watched his clientele attempt to leave. "No, please do not go. I'll throw in some free nuts and bolts with your order." Even with his offer of free goods, the customers left, unable to shuffle out fast enough. He turned to scorn Scrycher. "How many times must I tell you, Scrycher? Don't touch. Do not touch. How many times? I don't…" Nifty's voice trailed off as he spoke the last few words, inaudible to all who listened, even Teller.

"C'mon, Nifty, you reckon that Bones would have been able to forgive you if we did not have our tumble?"

"But my stock, my customers. How am I…?" Nifty's voice was high, an almost pleading tone, as Scrycher cut in.

"Mmmmm. Yes about that. That is why I am here. My ship took a real beating from a little accident we had. Barely ship worthy, she is. Jaxter and Chelsea are in the bays trying to repair her now. I was hoping you could lend us a hand."

"You know I am out of that business. Not good for the credits, and you are mixed up with some pretty bad sorts." Nifty buzzed around picking up the fallen items and placing them back on the shelves in meticulous order as he spoke. He paused to look Scrycher in the eye. "The Company and the Syndicate! What have you gotten yourself into? No thanks, to that type of publicity." He continued cleaning up, mumbling about the order of things.

Scrycher's pocket jingled as Blink returned, with him were some of the shiny wares from Nifty's shop. "Well, we need help. You were never one for letting a mate stay out in the cold too long." Scrycher patted Nifty on the shoulder, as he spoke solemnly.

"Don't touch, don't touch, and don't touch. Ahhhhhhh." Nifty picked up the last item and turned to Scrycher, a crazed look in his eyes. "If I give you the supplies you need, do you promise to stop touching?"

The grin across Scrycher's face lit the room. He continued scratching under Bones' large ear, who was lapping it up, as he replied. "Deal."

"Back." Scrycher pushed Teller back as they rounded the corner. "Crap. They have found us." He looked around the corner again. He could see at least a dozen of the Syndicate men scouting through the hanger bay. "They have not found the ship yet, at least that is good."

"Die, you Syndicate swine." Chelsea came running from the base of the ship with Jaxter behind, shooting up the crates in the quarantine bays, causing the Syndicate men to take cover as they returned fire.

"Double crap. That blew that one." Scrycher turned to Teller. "I believe you can do a little magic that may help."

"But Scrycher, I do not wish to harm anyone…" Teller was cut off, as Chelsea yelled.

"Son of a bitch. You just shot me." Chelsea removed her hand from her shoulder, revealing a flesh wound. "And I am bleeding!" Chelsea returned fire, with Jaxter following suit.

Scrycher turned back to Teller, opening his mouth to speak but nothing came out. His jaw dropped as he saw the clothes fall to the floor, and nothing else.

Thump, thump, two of the men were knocked out from behind, both bodies slumping to the floor. Other Syndicate men turned, firing at where they thought the assailant was. Another two men dropped to their knees, blood spilling from their smashed noses. Teller's eyes burned red, as the smell of blood sent him into a blood lust, going from man to man, now killing as he went.

Gregory saw the red spark that seemed to be killing his men. Drawing his rifle slowly, he aimed, and shot. Teller hit the floor hard, blood spurting from the side of his neck as he tried to get up. It was too late; he was uncovered. His body was now visible to his next intended victim. The man drew his knife and swung it at Teller's throat. The swing from the man stopped short as he grasped at his own face. Blink was sitting atop his head, clawing at his eyes and slashing at his face with his tail.

Another man pulled up his rifle, aiming point blank at Teller, and pulling the trigger. Scrycher's heart sank. He had been tearing down the path of fallen men that Teller had made, and was barely two steps from his friend when the shot went off. The body of the man who had just fired, sailed over the boxes, his throat being torn open as he lay there to gurgle his last breath.

"Grrrrrrrrrrrrrrrrrrrrrrr." Blink disappeared, only to reappear on the large dog's back as they tore their way through the rest of the men, Blink slashing and biting and the large black dog doing the same.

With Scrycher dragging the injured Teller back towards his ship, Gregory saw his chance. He raised his rifle and took the shot. Scrycher dropped to the ground at the sound of the rifle shot. His body now lay over the top of Teller's.

"Scrycher." Chelsea dropped her rifle and ran, dashing for her Captain.

"Gregory, I would leave if I was you. This is my station and out of your control." Nifty appeared from out of the shadows, carrying a platinum colored rifle. It was immaculately crafted and so polished, that his complexion could be seen in it.

Gregory stood from his crouched position, his rifle on the floor and a bullet wound through his hand. "You picked the wrong side, Nefal! You picked the wrong side." His voice trailed off as he left, walking up his vessel's platform.

"I did not pick sides. My customers did not receive their cargo yet. Can't let a paying customer be killed, you know." Turning to Scrycher who had righted himself, Nifty spoke more quietly. "Did you forget something, Captain?" He turned, waving their attention towards the crew of workers that had started entering, carrying every possible supply they would need to get their little ship space worthy again.

"But we cannot pay you." Scrycher looked up as though embarrassed.

"Oh, I have a feeling 'you will' find a way. Bones!" The large dog came bounding back, with Blink riding wildly on her back, holding onto the studded collar as he held on for dear life while giggling uncontrollably. Blink leant over the large dog as they stopped, hugging her, and giving her a big kiss on the head before blinking back into Scrycher's pocket.

As Blink jingled in the pocket, Scrycher's eyes lit up with an idea. "Well,

I may have something you might be interested in. Blink..."

"Come forth, my beauty." The Creator stood on the deck of The Enforcer as its large bulk was buffeted by the spatial distortions. As the planet materialized fully, he turned to speak to Philippe. "My son. This was my home. My first children reside here, and it is here that I will reclaim what is mine."

Philippe looked on, marveling at the large mass before him. He did not see the Company vessel escape this place and continue its chase. Even if he had, he would not have cared; he was home.

Chapter 18

Scrycher and Chelsea were leaning over the console, trying to pinpoint the exact location of where their goal may be, as Scrycher casually called out to the galley. "Jaxter, do you think you can take that little ship we used to escape the ruins, and give it a spin? See if you can handle a few laps around the ship, then we will both be going down to the planet and all."

Scrags jumped up and down, trying to get Scrycher's attention as he worked. "Can I? Please. Can I?" Scrycher acknowledged the request with a wave of his hand. Scrags dropped to the ground, placing his hand upon the racing Blink as he did circles in excitement around his feet. "No, not you Blink. You stay. We won't be long."

Jaxter grabbed little Scrags by his pants, lifting him in the air like an airplane. "Oh you wanna fly with me, do you?" He spun the boy around in the air as he left. Scrags laughed heartily as he was flung through the doorway, leaving Blink to sulk in the galley and gnaw at a rat's head…

"I think we got it, Captain." Chelsea felt something on her shoulder, and turned around to find Teller behind her. She gave him a long, hard, passionate kiss as her leg rose in the air.

"Fantastic." Scrycher stood away from the console, not sure where to look as he continued. "I will let you have the room, whilst I load the coordinates into the pod, and then we will be away." Scrycher grabbed for the memory stick, but Chelsea grabbed it first, grinning. As he gave her the, *Give me the damn stick,* look, he walked through the door; she playfully threw it at him as he headed towards the pod. Anticipating the catch, he turned, only to grasp at thin air. Blink intercepted the stick, turning it in his claws before realizing he was in the air and plopped onto the deck, the stick slipping out of his claws, to be caught by Scrycher as he knelt down. "They'll be the death of you, Blink my boy, those trinkets of yours."

Scrycher laughed with the jingling of shiny items heard from his pocket. "Oh, and Chelsea, call back our boys will you? That is, if you are not too busy."

Th-thump, th-thump, th-thump. Teller grabbed at his temple, the room spinning and fogging around him. Pulling himself back slightly, he thought of the relaxation technique Profitor had taught him, but he still slipped into the future, the present, and the past. He was unsure, which was which anymore.

He lived the horror of the first time they had visited this planet. Chelsea being seriously injured in their attempt to get off the ship. The fight on the planet below, with Lance and his men, the one that they would all, ultimately perish in. His own death, and finally Blink's. Blink's death was followed by the Three joining together to fulfill their goal; his soul, the crystal's, and Blink's. Then the emotions overwhelmed him, as he was flooded with the loss of hope felt by the crystal tree, and all that depended on it.

Then he was back on the ship. Although he had seen this before, he was lucid this time, it was not a dream. It was real, unlike the visions… dreams he had experienced whilst on the planet with the Fortune Teller. He had lived it all this time, and in full color, full emotion… The death, the carnage, his friends dying, it was all too much. He fell to the floor, screaming, and crying. Unknown to him, in his anguish, the crystal slid from his pocket, into the galley, and finally into the waiting paws of Blink. Blink, blinked away quickly as Teller screamed at the top of his lungs. "Why? But why? Is there no justice, no love, no higher being?" His thoughts turned to the cold realization that *at the end of this journey, they would all perish,* and worst of all, *Chelsea would bear, horrible, excruciating pain.*

"Teller." Chelsea lent down beside him, delicately brushing his fur from his eyes.

"Away from me. Away now. Leave me, you wench. Go down to that precious planet you have been searching for, and leave me in peace, to do what I want to do, what I have always wanted to do. Tell of our past." Teller struck out at Chelsea with words of hate, trying to drive her away from him, away from this horrible fate.

"Bastard." *Thump*. Chelsea punched Teller in the face as the first volley of cannon fire hit the ship, throwing her into his arms. Disgusted at his touch, she pushed herself way away from him, spitting in his face. "Pig!"

"Chels, what is happening up there?" Scrycher was using the internal communications from the pod when the next volley hit, ripping the pod from the ship and sending it and him, hurtling to the planet below.

"I know Scrags, I just can't find it!" Jaxter's distressed voice blurted over the com. "Chelsea, which one's cloak, the blue one, the green one, the… " The communications were cut off as Jaxter's small shuttle was also bombarded with cannon fire, it then followed Scrycher's, plummeting to the planet below.

"Noooooooo!" Chelsea screamed uncontrollably, as the Company vessel veered down upon them. Grabbing the flight stick, she yelled at Teller. "Man the gun." Even though their ship was in fantastic condition, Chelsea knew that their only hope was to take out their opponent's weapons and run for cover, cover she knew they did not have!

Teller climbed into the circular cage at the bottom of the room, as he had done so many times before. He knew the crystal window around the room separated him from the dead of space, and even that would not be enough to save him. But none of this mattered, as another volley exploded around him. He knew what he had to do, or they would die, right now, in the cold darkness of space. "I'm in, but you need to get me nearer to them before it'll do any good." The adrenaline kicked in and the dull, *th-thump, th-thump, th-thump*, of his head, petered out.

"You just be a pesky little mosquito, and I'll worry about the driving. Jeez it's worse than being married!" Chelsea pulled a hard right; the ship groaned and shuddered under the maneuver and the volley of cannon fire that hit the hull, ripping a hull plate away.

"If they do not kill us, you will," Tellers voice lowered, his voice affectionate and inaudible as he finished "my love."

"Shut up and shoot, you prick."

The Commander watched with curiosity as Lance paced back and forth, impatiently. He seemed almost poetic, as his polished boots clunked rhythmically on the metal decking, echoing through the bridge of the Company vessel. *If the sound of a mad man walking could be poetic.* The Commander pulled himself from the thought as the sound ceased for a second. Lance stopped to view the ship in front of them, and aggressively wiped the green seepage from the cut on his face. The Commander held back the sickness he felt at the disgusting act. *What had happened to the pompous, but proper man they had called their Captain not so long ago?* "Have we taken out their weapons yet?" The tension in the air was so thick that the crew could hear the ooze hit the deck. "I want them now!" Lance yelling his orders did not give them any more substance, but it had become the norm of late. The Commander's attention was drawn to the Gunnery as he answered.

"No sir, we have only managed two hits on their hull. No vital components hit, although I have taken out two of their shuttles. Obviously whoever is flying that thing is as crazy as hell, and wasn't in the pods, or I'd never have hit them." The Gunnery laughed to himself at this thought, *well, it is obvious that the one flying the ship wasn't in the pods, unless they could split themselves in three.* No matter, this Captain was crazy; he had come down with some type of swamp sickness and now he was out for blood. He would have no idea what the Gunnery just said, or even if it had made sense. He was thankful that they had not all been overcome by the sickness.

While deep in thought, the Gunnery did not see the smaller ship change course, nor did he realize that the ship was now headed straight for them. The small, fast moving projectiles hit the dome, *ping, ping, ping,* shaking the ship slightly. Surface cracks webbed outwards, the pressure lengthening them, forcing them deeper. The Commander responded to the threat, shouting orders to his crew, making sure the automated response system kicked in, and that the dome was repaired quickly, preventing compromise. Though he questioned if he was just delaying the inevitable. *I wonder which one will kill us first, the Captain in here, or the criminals out there?* He did not have to wait long for his answer.

"What are they doing? They know at this range they do not stand a chance. Are they trying to ram us? What are you doing?" Lance did not care for the capture of these people any more. As he wiped the seepage from his nose, he yelled. "Stop them. Shoot them down. Shoot to kill." The aggression slithered off his tongue, as he spat the orders.

The Gunnery Sergeant smiled, pulling the trigger and aiming at the oncoming vessel, trying to kill its occupants. The Commander just sat back in his chair, shaking his head at the incompetence that had become his crew.

"Oh ya, wanna play hard ball? I'll play hard ball!" heckled Chelsea. "Try an' hit me now." Teller had seen it all before. He saw everything, in his mind's eye before it happened. Chelsea pulled the ship into another hard turn, barely avoiding the weapon fire from the oncoming vessel. He could see that even though the ship had been extensively repaired, neither it, nor Chelsea, were faring well. He flinched as the scraping and moaning of the metal ship attacked his heightened senses, and he was forced to revert to Profitor's relaxation technique.

He gave himself over to the moment as he composed himself, knowing what was their only course of action if they wanted to escape. However, he wanted to do more than escape, he wanted to live! Focusing on the task ahead, he yelled over the cannon fire. "You are going to have to get closer than this if you want me to wound them," He knew at this distance, he was barely grazing them.

"Oh you care now do you? How 'bout this then, send you straight down the whore's throat?" Pride filled him, as Chelsea pulled back on the stick and aimed their small ship straight down the front of the Company vessel.

He knew she was crazy, and he wanted to show it.

"You're crazy woman, just crazy enough. Keep it coming, straighten up,"

Teller knew there would be a lull in the firing. "Chels, accelerate!"

She did not need the cue, she had taken the opportunity and had already accelerated the ship. "Just 'cause you bedded me, don't mean you can order me around." His nostrils filled with a scent, his primal urges kicked in overdrive and he turned quickly. He knew he shouldn't have turned from the fight, but the sweet smell of the blood on her lips as she bit down was too intoxicating for him to ignore. His eyes glowed red as they searched her figure intimately, he could see her muscles tightening on her body as she strained. "Now…" Teller faltered, he had taken his mind of the target, his head started thumping again. *Th-thump, th-thump, th-thump.* "Now!" Chelsea was yelling this time, her heart sinking as she could see their opportunity pass by.

He turned, pushing the throbbing of his temple from his mind. He must focus. He pulled the trigger, then again and again, he kept pulling the trigger until his fingers went white.

"Enough Teller, enough." Chelsea's tone had softened, her concern evident as bullets crashed into the glass dome of the Company vessel and then the oncoming projectiles, as they were fired from the Company vessel's own cannon.

Teller did not have to watch, as his bullets hit their targets, he could tell by the intense coloring of the cockpit walls that he had hit his marks. The cannon exploded from the side of the Company vessel, the vessel pulled away from them and limped away, but all he was worried about was Chelsea.

"Oh yeh, who's the man?" He saw Chelsea mouth the words, her delicate lips making them seem like poetry and then, he was beside her. He grabbed her by the hair, kissing her aggressively and then letting her be, to stare in shock, steering their little ship out of harm's way, as he whispered to her. "I am the man. I believe I proved that some months back. " Affection breaking its way through the bloodlust in his eyes.

Chelsea tried to compose herself, looking at Teller, as he continued to walk past her. "What, the?" Teller continued walking, and as Chelsea did not know what to say, she reverted to shop talk. "Those last few tricks really screwed with her, she won't be doin' that again. We need to get her down there." Chelsea still had a bewildered look on her face as she gestured to the planet. "We won't last another attack."

Teller recalled the pain and the suffering that he had felt only minutes earlier, all this pain was apparent as he replied and headed to the escape pods. "We won't last long down there either, if we don't find what we are looking for."

Tired and exhausted Scrycher stopped again, resting his weary muscles as he leant on the butt of his rifle. He had not seen Scrags' and Jaxter's small vessel after he had seen them forced to the planet below. The pod he had traveled in had been damaged on impact, preventing him from pinpointing where he was, where they were, or where he needed to go. Scrycher's chest and nose were burning from the continuous inhalation of the cold air, and his sense of smell was all but gone. He looked back through the hills and valleys, looking at the pod, its shell crashed and broken on the ground before them. He wondered if he would be better to stay in its shell, as he turned back to the way he had been traveling. No! He must go on.

He wondered how Chelsea and Teller were faring as he looked up towards the sky. It was lit in a blended procession of fireworks as if in response to his question. The planet's upper atmosphere, and the white snow covering the landscape, acted together to amplify the light above into a brilliant display. "How beautiful..." A large explosion that further lit the heavens interrupted his thoughts.

Blink screeched, throwing the crystal from the pocket, as it lit up. Scrycher bent down quickly at the sight of the crystal melting instantly into the snow. He picked it up, scolding Blink as he did. "Blink, this is not yours! Did you steal this from Teller?" The crystal in his left hand became brighter still, as though feeding off the explosion above. Scrycher was so focused on this he did not see Blink's look of embarrassment, or even realize he had left.

A light shone out from the crystal, bright and narrow as it pointed the way. Scrycher's hope returned as he followed the direction of this light.

"Not far, I hope." He mumbled through his cracked blue lips. His tongue probed, trying to lick his lips but there was no feeling, it was far too cold. How he longed for Teller, and the rest of the crew to be with him now, to feel the warmth of their smiles. Alas, he needed to stay focused as he trudged along again.

"Yes, Sir, the hull has almost finished repairing itself. Also the compartment that was ruptured has been repaired, so we have got power back to navigation." The Commander went to raise himself from his seat, to come to the Gunnery's aid, then he rethought this, as Lance replied in an aggravated, and overly loud tone.

"What about the cannon, did you fix the bloody cannon?" The Commander watched in dismay, holding his hand to his head as Lance continued to rant. "How did they evade us again, they must have nine lives?"

He turned his attention from Lance, to the Gunnery. The Gunnery's head was beaded in sweat and his voice trembled. *Even the useless, incompetent Gunnery does not deserve this*, he thought. "No, sir! None of the cannon was left on the hull. As you know, we require part of the object to be left intact to be able to replicate it back into place. The resulting explosion of that last shot removed half the hull."

Lance started spitting out more questions as his face reddened. "Can We!" his arms flailed around, as the Commander got to his feet, placing a hand on Lance's shoulder. "Start!" Lance turned, glaring at the

Commander, while spitting out the end to his question. "Moving Again, Gunnery Sergeant?!"

"Shortly, Sir, we can." The Commander looked Lance directly in the eyes, as the Gunnery answered, making sure Lance knew that enough was enough. "I'll just need to double-check a few systems before we head off." The Commander's neck whipped around at the answer. *I thought that we had finished the repairs*, he thought, his curiosity piqued.

"Dismissed!" Lance screamed into the Commander's face, removing him from his line of thought. "Wake me when you are ready to finish the hunt." *Well, he can still make an exit*, the Commander thought, as Lance strode out in his normal pompous fashion.

The pain was still excruciating, as Lord Dragoon stooped slightly. His body was not yet fully healed, but he needed to get his message across, and in person always worked best. He looked at the Gunnery as he fidgeted with his jacket buttons, bile sticking in the back of Dragoon's throat as he thought of the Gunnery's insignificant existence. *It would soon be over*, he thought.

"Your orders are rescinded. Kill the Criminals. I have had enough of this game!" Lord Dragoon's hood did well to cover his features as he spoke, explaining to the Gunnery his new orders and his demise. He stopped talking, lowering his head as he waited, only to hear the Gunnery quietly clear his throat. "Do you understand?" Dragoon did not wait for the answer, the Gunnery's eyes showed that he did, but the Lord finished with a line he knew would have no rebuttal. "All must die at whatever the cost. Your payment will be deposited into your account, waiting for your return home." He did not wait for the Gunnery to answer, he knew he had him in his grasp and he lowered his head, signifying the conversations end.

"Yes, Sir." Gunnery's mind filled with ways he could spend all the riches he was to receive. His thoughts went to all the women and booze he would be able to afford.

"Like taking candy from a baby." The words echoed to the Commander's ears as the Gunnery left the dark room. *Now what was he doing in there?* the Commander thought. He waited for a second, before slipping around the doorway and entering the room. He thought he could hear a slight snigger as he did.

"Fool, you won't last long enough to spend what you receive. There are to be, no witnesses, no survivors!" But when he looked around, there was no one to be found. *This is turning into one heck of a mission*, he thought to himself as he shook his head, and left the room.

The Commander found himself on the bridge yet again, this time, in the middle of what he knew would be a reckoning. Lance spat out more orders. "Well, get searching, I want them killed by the end of the day!" The Commander and the Gunnery's necks snapped around together. The Commander's thought's flooded his head in confusion, *I thought that was a heat of the moment order, Lance has never wanted them dead before.*

"Killed, Sir?" The Commander could see the same question on the Gunnery's face as he must have had on his own.

"Killed!" The Commander could not believe his ears, *Lance just said it again, Killed.*

"Killed." The Commander's jaw dropped at the conversation between the two men as the Gunnery's last comment gleefully exited his lips.

"You heard me, Gunnery, get to it." *Lance just said what?* The Commander blinked in surprise, only to be shocked further by the Gunnery's quick and decisive reply.

"Yes, Sir, whatever you say."

What? The Commander was confused as he went from face to face, Lance obviously out of his mind, and the Gunnery just sitting there, the cogs ticking, thinking about something the Commander knew would not end well for any of them.

Teller lent over Chelsea, as she worked feverously, taking in her subtle scent as he playfully fondled her hair. She was trying to pinpoint Scrycher's exact location, but without luck. Teller did not seem concerned, taking this time to appreciate his surroundings, his demeanor almost blasé as he spoke. Try triangulating Scrycher's life sign with the crystal! His eyes flared as he said the last comment. The crystal. He reached into his pocket frantically, checking to see if the crystal was still there. "Blink..." he smiled

"I would never have thought of that." Chelsea input the separate energy forces and watched as the beeps got closer together. "But what about Jaxter and Scrags? We haven't found them yet." For the second time, Teller was stunned. *So I do not know everything, things can be changed, so she won't die.* Grabbing Chelsea hard by the head, he kissed her, and took several steps, before he slid into the Gatling gun compartment. With new found vigor, he started to load in the new belt of bullets.

He spoke affectionately. "Do you remember…"

Teller's comment was cut short, he had forgotten a key factor to the fight, the Company's weapons rained down upon them, stripping more hull plating from the failing ship, as Chelsea waited for the co-ordinates to download.

"Got it!" Teller could hear Chelsea jump up from her station, the clinking of two memory sticks as she grabbed them from the console, and then the clunking, as she was thrown to the ground. The sticks clinked again, and she was off, the sticks between her breasts, while she ran towards the control stick and their destiny.

Teller grabbed the gun before him, his own voice screaming in his head as blood lust and his thoughts fueled within him again, *I will change our destiny!* He remembered that in this time line, the gun was not faulty and sprayed bullets across space, removing the Company's canon fire before it could do any further damage. The ship was leveled, Tellers unusual angle,

233

corrected, as he continued to fire.

"Now let's give 'em hell." The words echoed through Teller's head as though he had heard them many times before, then they were drowned out as the, *th-thump, th-thump, th-thump* of his temple echoed through his head and he tried to make every shot and every second count…

The Commander felt sorry for the criminal's crew as they bore down upon them again. Both Lance, and the Gunnery's faces, beaming as the unsuspecting ship was pelted with cannon fire. *Where is the sense in this?* He thought to himself. He would have normally welcomed a quick and decisive end to his prey, but not today, not this way, and not after three months of chasing the crew half way across the galaxy. He clenched his fists, as the first volley hit the little ship, wrenching hull plates off, and sending it sideways. *The gunnery's aim has improved considerably*, even if he was firing at a stationary target. *Where the heck is the crew?*

The Commander felt a weight lift from his chest as his question was answered and the ship took off erratically, but it was moving and he felt a whole lot better about hunting a moving target.

"Gunnery, can't you just kill them, so we don't have to do this all day?" The Commander covered his mouth as he listened to Lance and the Gunnery interact, trying to stem his need to laugh. What had moments earlier been a massacre was turning into a game of cat and mouse. "We have got them on the run. They can't maneuver like that forever, especially in that heap." Failing to keep the chuckle to himself, the Commander choked, coughing uncontrollably as Lance spat more useless orders, and the Gunnery sprayed cannon fire half way across the galaxy.

Sporting the appearance of an oversized snowman, Scrycher stopped again to look high in the sky at the fireworks. A dumbfounded look was on his face as he asked himself questions aloud. "Had they survived? How had they survived?" His hope was increased by the fact that his colleagues must still be alive, for now… He continued trudging, his speed quickening with every step; driven on by the thought that if he could reach their goal. There was still hope for them all. The fireworks continued above, and unknown to Scrycher, powering the crystal as it fed from the energy.

Teller was optimistic. The barrel of the large gun, now red hot, as he swung it back into position. "Get on the side we took the cannon out on. That one has not repaired itself yet; I know that we got them real good." He was not concerned with his slightly unusual wording of the sentences he just spoke. His fur was slicked down by his sweat, sticking to his flesh and emphasizing his strained muscles. He was not concerned with this either, as he knew, it had been much hotter in the past time-line.

"First you bed me, then you hate me, then you want to tell me how to drive. Can't take you anywhere." Chelsea's mind was on the job but she could still feel the sting of Teller's earlier words.

"I'd prefer to be taken to bed again, if you were going to take me anywhere. But you just seem to only be taking me into fire-fights. I did not think I was that bad, but on the other hand, you've not asked me for seconds." Tellers had given up trying to keep his distance, and everything blurted out. His shock of living the deaths of every one he knew was gone for the minute as the fog lifted from his mind. "If we are going to die, we may as well have some fun while doing it." he joked to himself.

Chelsea questioned, "Huh?"

The Commander had only just got his composure back as the next lot of antics unfolded before him. The little ship running rings around them.

"Get out the laser. Make it count, Gunnery, we only have one shot."

The Commander's jaw dropped in laughter again, he knew it was not professional, but he could not help it. If the Gunnery's performance of late was anything to go by, he would be barely able to hit the planet on the other side of that ship with the laser, let alone that one, tiny ship. Lance's hand smacked him across the head as he lost his composure. Holding his head and looking up, he looked into Lances eyes as Lance barked the next order. "Shoot them down!"

Lances eyes flared like that of a mad man, sweat sprayed across the room as he wiped it from his forehead and flicked it away; and the laser cannon extended out of the vessel. The Commander could hear the Gunnery input his coordinates, and see the bars on the console, increasing as it charged. The Gunnery beamed a smile of a man who had already won. Who had already decided that those pesky criminals that the Commander had grown so fond of, deserved. 'Death!'

Teller knew it was almost time as Chelsea dodged the volley of cannon fire and the Company vessel swung around for another pass. He could hear the ship moaning and creaking, the sound only mildly tearing at his soul through his heightened hearing. He felt comfort in the cycling of the Gatling gun spinning in harmony, as he sprayed another wave of projectiles. Instinctively, he ducked as a rivet poppet from the hull, the sound telling him that his time was close. He readied himself, loosening his grip on the gun to conserve energy for the task ahead.

Teller ducked again, the panel expelling itself from the hull, sounding like a roaring shuttle to him, *th-thump, th-thump, th-thump,* Chelsea's sweet voice brought him back. "We can't do this much longer; she'll have a major breach soon." Her voice sung to Teller, drawing him from the fog that had returned. He continued clawing through the fog as she continued. "You'd better get to the pods, before she does."

"I'm not leaving you, we'll get through this together." He was determined. He knew the outcome. He had seen it. Lived it. He now pushed to the extremities of the fog, using Chelsea as his anchor. He allowed the events of the next few minutes to play repeatedly through his mind, as he sought a better path, worked out trajectories and sought out collisions and injuries along their exit route. While processing this all, he was ignoring the cannon volley before him as he knew, *it did not matter.*

"If I leave this station, we'll be shot out of the sky before we get to the pods. We'll be sitting ducks." Chelsea pulled him back out of his thoughts, he did not know how much time had gone by, but he knew, he must act now.

"Do as I say, when I say. Do not question me!" His voice was abrupt, cautioning Chelsea not to question him.

"Turn the ship into the planet, Chelsea!"

She had to know why, what Teller was asking of her was insanity. "Why, Teller?"

He yelled, as he leapt effortlessly out of his gun pod, becoming a blur of movement before he hit the deck as he had scrambled on all fours. "Just do it woman, and do it now!"

He could feel the ship being pulled towards the planet below, the ship lurching already as its hull buckled and then it was upon them. He leapt, taking a path closer to the laser than before, trying to gain valuable seconds. He passed by the laser, not a second too soon, The burning smell assaulted his nostrils as his fur and clothes were singed in the blast, but he pushed on as the air started to be sucked out of the cockpit.

He felt the anguish as Chelsea's head dropped, tears rolling down her cheek, as she gave up all hope of survival.

"Bend over." Teller screamed, over the noise, as his body dropped lower, only seconds had passed, but it seemed like days.

Chelsea reacted as he had hoped, dropping her upper body in turn. "No time for s…" Chelsea's words were cut short, as Teller's shoulder crashed into her hip, winding her as he did. He made sure that he clasped her by the bottom, his aim for her hip had stopped the broken ribs that he knew she had originally sustained, but, he did not see the memory stick as it fell from her cleavage. Chelsea reached for the stick, grasping at it, but it slipped through the grating below. A small shiny reflection was caught out of the corner of his eye as he cleared the room, and the blast door shut. "The stick!" Chelsea yelled. He knew the control room was now shut off completely, stopping the ship from becoming depressurized further, for now. It also stopped them from controlling their descent and retrieving the memory stick. But he did not have time to worry about this, his path ahead clear to him through the fog, or so he thought.

The dizzying spiral of the ship did not affect Teller, as he continued bounding, *th-thump, th-thump, th-thump.* He did not stop, he knew that he had to continue as fast as he could, gaining as much advantage as possible, as he used his legs and his free arm to increase his speed. He raced towards the pods, knowing that their survival depended on it.

The ship was like one big, mind blowing puzzle as the floors twisted and turned, filling Teller's ears with painfully loud noises. It only lessened in intensity as he clenched up, in response to the explosive sounds of furniture, and other items, as they smashed on the inner hull. Teller's eyes burnt red as his long claws ripped into the ribbed decking, the smell of his own blood fueling him with more adrenaline as some of those claws were torn from his flesh. Teller's head flicked sharply to the sound of the movement of rusty hinges, holding the doors on the gun cabinet. He played it through his mind again as he watched, in slow motion, as the doors were torn off, the hinges screaming and the cabinets contents flung around the room. Nothing was erratic to him as he checked their locations, and dropped his head, dodging an incoming rifle. He sighed, raising his head, only to be forced to bend backwards as a shotgun appeared at his chest. He could feel it as it touched his clothes, ruffling them and reminding him that he was not infallible. Distracted, he faltered, and his upper body kept going backwards, Chelsea's weight over balancing him. His hand hit the deck, his legs still moving forward, and then he was up, his body flipping forward with new found agility as the rifle hit the deck, sending ringing through his ears.

Teller paused, the near loss of balance would have cost him his and Chelsea's lives. *I need to see more,* he thought as he probed the fog, but only for a second. He reached for the closed doors before him, knowing that the worst was still to come. "Teller." He did not hear her soft voice, barely squeezed out of her aching chest between breaths. He had his whole weight upon the doors as he focused. With one mighty heave, he pulled them open, the ship lurching and sending him off balance as if in response. *Th-thump, th-thump, th-thump,* his head became clouded again as he barely avoided the cans and utensils that flew through the doorway. *Heavy feet, legs...* He reacted, quickly remembering, and forcing one of the doors closed again. The door became a shield, deflecting many knives from their original path. He glanced back as these knives pierced the steel lockers, doors and the walls. Turning back to the task at hand, he swung through the doorway as the ship lurched again, this time leveling slightly. *Th-thump, th-thump, th-thump.* Veering left, he avoided the small frying pan.

"This is fun, Teller." Chelsea laughed as he spun around again. "Just like a joy ride."

He tried to focus on her words, he had heard this before, but, the tone was different. The *th-thump, th-thump, th-thump,* of his temple drowned out the sound of her voice, the buckling hull, and smashing items. Focusing on the table bolted to the floor, he leapt, his claws ripping into the steel framework as he prepared himself for another leap.

His hands grabbed at his ears as he went to leap, the ship roaring as it hit the atmosphere and stunning him. He opened his eyes, a large frying pan upon him, he dodged, sighing a deep sigh as it passed. *Th-thump, th-thump, th-thump,* Chelsea panicked as she slipped, gripping Teller in a frantic effort not to fall. Her nails bit into his body as she grabbed frantically. Using the pain, he focused, grabbing her again and stumbled. The knife stuck deep, its blade clinking on the floor as he ripped it from his chest. Faltering again, the ship lurched, his claws shredding the table beneath them as he struggled for a perch. *We are losing valuable time!* He cursed as he steadied himself again for the leap.

His increased strength sent him further than anticipated, smashing through the door into the brig with his shoulder, and clearing the doorway in one leap. He rolled, distributing the force evenly, as the ship leveled and Chelsea hung to him, frighteningly tight. He took advantage of the next scene as he played it in his head, "Chels, hold on!"

"What ya-?" she had no time to finish, Teller was swinging on the rusty bars to the cells, both arms making fast work of the distance as he cleared the room. The door slammed behind them as the ship screamed, lurching as its wing cracked, straining under the pressure of the uncontrolled descent. Teller tore clothes from his face and body with one hand, while he batted personal items and toys from his body with the other. The items seemed to come alive, trying to trip and tangle him and stop them from escaping.

Teller's fingers were becoming numb, as his remaining claws ripped through the walls of the ship. He could not feel the blood leaching from where claws had been torn from his flesh, and he did not care about the blood splatter that he left in his wake. But he did care about the drumming in his head, that made it harder to concentrate on the escape at hand. *Th-thump, th-thump, th-thump*, he bounded twice more, the fog clearing to allow him a vision of the escape pod before him. With clarity returning, and their escape guaranteed, he allowed himself a minute to slow down. He lowered Chelsea to the floor, opening the pod door and gesturing, "After you." with a big smile on his face as he saw her relatively unscathed figure bending over and entering the pod. With a smack on her behind, he helped her in. Slightly bewildered, she reached out her hand, which he took affectionately and allowed himself to be led inside as if for a weekend rendezvous.

Th-thump, th-thump, th-thump, he pulled away, his hands grasping his ears as he tried to drown out the excruciating pain, as the ship lurched and the wing was ripped off. He stumbled as the metal on metal contact continued. He was slammed to the floor, and screamed as the ship shifted. It was not the impact that pained him but the screeching of the metal lockers as they were sucked along the decking and out into space. He could hear the whooshing of the air as it was sucked from the ship, and anything caught in its path followed out of the huge breach. The screaming of metal attacked his sense again, as he tried to push past it. Struggling, he dropped his hands from his ears, raising himself to his knees. Then one knee, standing and he stumbled, one step, two. Chelsea screamed for him to get inside the pod. *Th-thump, th-thump, th-thump,* he reached out, their fingers touching and the blast doors of the brig closed.

With his head ringing, and his senses shot, Teller did not hear the straps of the cargo bay start to give way. He leaned forward, only to react, turning completely at the ripping sound that was to follow. The singing of the metal rode on the air, as the buckle was sent across the room. He ripped his hand from Chelsea's. His palm now open and in front of her face. The metal stopped hissing. The buckle lodged in his hand and he yanked it back close to him to stop her being slapped in the face by the force. He howled as the pain attacked him and the ship lurched further and then, he was in the pod.

Chelsea had yanked at Teller, pulling him backwards and into the shuttle. "Get in here, and make love to me!" She laughed aloud, oblivious as to how close the buckle was to ending her life. Teller did not wince at the sound of the crates, as they broke free from the cargo curtains and smashed upon the walls. He did not flinch, as he tore the shrapnel from his palm. He just sighed in relief as his head cleared the pods entrance, and he fell into it. *The ordeal was over,* he thought, this thought shattered, like the crate splintered into pieces at the pods entrance. Frantically, he looked for the lever as Chelsea kissed him passionately and pulled the lever to the pods door in the process. Another crate crashed into the door as it was about to close, spilling its contents and soaking them in the brown murky slop they called water.

"Didn't know I was that good." Teller laughed wiping his wet hair from his eyes.

"Don't get too cocky now." Chelsea jumped onto Teller, his back soaked in the pool of water now on the floor. "My turn to be on top." she teased as the pod jettisoned itself from the downward spiraling wreck. Teller barely heard the, *hisss, thump* as the pod ejected aimlessly, continuing behind what was left of the ship as it descended to the planet below. He pulled Chelsea tighter as he kissed her passionately, the blood lust leaving his eyes and the fog, his head. "Patience." Chelsea teased as she placed her finger on his lips and pulled the silver memory card from her bosom. The light on the wall panel lit the room in a romantic ambiance as she inserted the stick into it. "I hope this is the right one she whispered into his ear."

Neither Cheslea nor Teller were concerned as the computer panel recognized the data as descent patterns and immediately activated, giving the pod a purpose.

They were oblivious to the pod's tiny engines firing up, adjusting its trajectory as it attempted to reach its location. Teller howled as the debris from the failing ship smashed into one of the engines, sending the pod spinning out of control. Chelsea looked up, her eyes rolling into the back of her head, as she threw up over Teller. The movement was too much for her as the pod spiraled out of control. "Bit of an extreme reaction, would you not say?" Teller jeered, but Chelsea did not hear him. Her last action before losing consciousness was to activate the air cushions, protecting their bodies as they now plummeted to their deaths, and Teller screamed, holding his temple... *Th-thump, th-thump, th-thump.*

The Commander bit his lip as he lent forward in his chair. The Gunnery had hit the target.

"Well done, Gunnery. You are not a completely incompetent fool after all." The Commander turned to see Lance's face beaming, and the side of his face glowing florescent green, now plastered in a sickly grin in anticipation of going home.

The Commander held his head down in a moment of silence, his conscience telling him it was the right thing to do. This silence was interrupted rudely by a crew member speaking out of turn. *Fool, you will be disciplined,* he thought as he turned to see what the fuss was about.

"Captain. Captain."

He turned to see the man speaking, trying to get Lance's attention, but not wanting to feel his wrath. He looked to where the man was pointing as Lance praised the Gunnery for his kill. "When we get back I will see that you get a commendation for this!"

"Captain… Captain!" The Commander did not hear the second plea, did not see Lance's face as he briskly walked over, grabbed the man by the collar. Lifted him up from the chair and spat into the man's bruised and swollen face, as he screamed.

"Shut up man. I am sick of hearing your whining." He did not see the man point over Lance's shoulder. Lance glance back and drop the man as his eye caught the movement of something small in the wake of the ship's debris that was now plummeting to the planet below. "How the…?" He heard the frantic running, the switch being flicked again and again. *Click, Click, Click, Click, Click.* But he did see the shock in Lance's eyes as he, the Commander, turned and yelled at him.

"Lance, you idiot! What are you doing? The laser has only one shot." Apart from the raised level, the Commander's voice was calm, as he watched Lance's face returning to blood red, and his nostrils flare.

The Commander went to turn to watch as the escape pod make its way into the atmosphere, but was concerned as Lance let go of the trigger. He focused on Lance, as his face became so red, he looked about ready to explode. Grabbing the back of the Gunnery's chair, Lance tried to rip it from the floor. He heaved, once, twice, three times. His muscles and veins seeming to pop out of his neck as green ooze was expelled from his nose. His face reddened further as he continued his efforts. The crew stared at their Captain, and his lunacy. Exhausted, Lance fell to the floor, speaking quietly. "Commander, get me a search party. We are all going on a mission." Turning to the Gunnery, he spoke louder, his voice full of venom. "Even you, you useless…"

"Lance is not answering my communications. I fear the worst, but we must wait. I will contact you when I hear from him." Slight agitation edged Lord Dragoon's voice, as he spoke.

"I will wait. However, do not make me wait for too long, Father. I need this world as much as you."

"Garath, you forget who you serve." The monitor blinked off.

"No Father, I do not. I serve you. Until I claim your throne for myself." Garath sat back into the chair in the dark room, contemplating his rise to power.

"Brother, how long must we wait? I do not like waiting." Zackory paced erratically in the room as he spoke into the dull monitor before him.

"Patience, my brother, good things come to those who wait."

"And good things come to those who take them!" Leaning forward Zackory turned off the monitor, red faced and fuming at the delay.

"Steller, my beautiful daughter, my first born. What have they done to you?" The Creator was standing in the small cabin, looking through the smoke at his child, love swelling in his eyes.

"Father. They have done to me, what they did to you; banished us for our beliefs, for the fact that we care for others than ourselves. But enough of me; why have you come here?" Steller chose her words well as she spoke, The Creator hanging on every syllable.

"Oh, my daughter. You know all too well. I have come to reclaim my place as your Father, your God!"

"But Father, what about your favored children?"

"You know as well as I, daughter, that they were destroyed, and my other children did nothing to stop it." The Creator's eyes flared red as he spoke.

"But Father, they still live. Not all, but some. You must help those that seek them. Seek to release your favored ones. Journey to give the home world a rebirth, and to awaken the ones in stasis." Steller slumped to the

244

floor in anguish as he left; he was her Father, her salvation.

She raised her eyes as the hidden figure spoke softly; "You have done well Steller. We may have a use for you yet…" With that said the figure was gone, leaving Steller to her lone exile again.

"You do not know what you have done. He will be back, and with him, death!" Steller sobbed into her hands as she recalled the future that had changed to the one that she now saw…

Chapter 19

The crystal responded to the large flash of light that filled the sky, its light becoming more intense as it fed off the power from the air around it. It could sense Scrycher looking up, partly in awe, partly in horror; over the glow above that was getting brighter as it moved closer to them.

It could feel his heart sink, as he saw his ship make its way into the atmosphere. It bathed in the energy as the ship fell like a sun, falling out of the sky, a red tail, trailing it as far as the eye could see.

It acted in this moment, feeling the power inside itself needing a release. It caught Scrycher's attention, causing a little discomfort at first as it tried to get through his skin. He felt an intense tingling on his left hand, and his attention was removed from the burning mass. The crystal increased the discomfort, willing him to change hands. Its power and will to change him became so severe that it started burning his hand. He juggled the crystal, swapping it to his right hand to ease the discomfort. The crystal made contact, inserting much of its life force into him in one steady flow, causing his body to arch. The crystal felt comforted as his hand clenched, and all his muscles tightened, his muscles so tight that he was unable to let it go. It knew it was causing him pain, but it could not do what it had to without the pain.

The crystal continued to send its power into his body, through the wound. Falling to his knees, the pain burnt through his blood, working its way to his veins, finally following them to his heart. It changed his heart, and sent the new found power to the rest of his body, spreading it as though it were a disease.

It could sense Blink's emotions over that of Scrycher's. The primitive animal huddled in fear, as it listened to the howling of the wind, and wild animals. It felt Scrycher's body drop sideways, as he clutched his arm. His eyes still open as he fell, watching for both of them, as the great ball of fire headed towards them. The crystal continued to change his body, as it called out and it made its way through him.

It knew it would probably survive, but not the vessel in which it resided, it hurried to finish its task as the ship got closer, continuing to search for help. And then it found it. It held him there as it worked, burning through every part of him. As it reached his brain, it realized its mistake, this one was not made like the others, its power too much for him to take. His breath quickened, trying to expel the power, but the crystal needed this power to call out. It had made contact, it was waiting for a reply. And then it came, the call from its mother, the tree in which it was born. As Scrycher's head rolled into the snow, it looked through his eyes, saw her working, felt her power. The ship redirected by her large hand as it protected both her child and her savior. And then it was gone, his mother's spark, and Scrycher's as the ship crashed into the mountain behind them.

The crystal searched, taking Scrycher's consciousness with it as it went. To have come so close and to have lost its mother again, it cried out in pain. It saw the pod that had followed the ship, as it slowed in its descent and level out, landing with a light *thud* in the snow. It stopped momentarily for Scrycher, studying the pod, seeing no movement it continued. It felt the wonder that Scrycher felt, as it flew along the snow to find a cavern into which they traveled. It flew through the tunnels, but stopped, allowing Scrycher to walk slowly to a glowing crystal shield. It allowed him-them to stand there, pulsing with the shield until they pulsed together, then they walked through. They continued through the caverns, searching for their mother, the crystal's mother! Finally, the crystal cried out. But its' cries were that of sorrow, as its mother lay dying, her energy expelled when saving its life, Scrycher's life. Exhausted, they lay down to rest at the bottom of the huge crystalline tree, bathing in what may have been the last moments of her life. The tree's light dimmed, dimmed into nothing, exhausted by this ordeal. All that was left of the tree's life force was directed to the barely lit capsules around the room. But one was lighter than the others... Scrycher and the crystal looked together at the capsule beneath the tree. They both jumped at the sight; they were inside. It was housing them, comforting them, beckoning them...

Hungry for its next meal, the Snow Leopard crept around Scrycher, observing its prey, and waiting for the kill.

Blink had worked his way out of Scrycher's pocket and was sitting on his back. His wings and spikes extended, trying to make himself more menacing, while he screeched like a frightened bird. As the Leopard dashed forward, Blink lurched forward with fangs barred...

"Raah!" The Leopard hesitated, growled and then slinked off as Teller ran screaming, behind Blink. Blink had not heard Teller through his own hissing and screeching, and strode up and down on Scrycher's body as if in a procession for his own bravery. At the slight sound of Teller's movement behind him, Blink screeched, his hackles down as he blinked back into Scrycher's pocket.

"Company vessel will be 'ere soon. We'd better get moving." Chelsea was looking into the sky for any signs of a descent.

"Well grab hold, Chelsea. I can't carry him myself." Teller placed the crystal on Scrycher's unconscious body and grabbed one end of the stretcher where Scrycher now lay. "Show us the way, my beauty."

"No probs, Teller, but I might get us lost." Chelsea giggled as she flirted, struggling slightly with Scrycher's large mass, as she lifted the front of the stretcher.

"Well as long as you don't throw up on me again, I think I can take it..."

"Can't you fly any faster?" Lance was sweating profusely and his face was bright red as he used his crumpled uniform to wipe away the snot from his nose.

"Do you think you could use a handkerchief for that?" The Commander had finally had enough of this behavior and wasn't going to hold his tongue a second more.

"I'll use a handkerchief when you learn to fly!" Lance yelled at the Commander, spraying him in the face with spit.

"Well if you can work out how to control this blizzard, then I will learn to fly fas..." The Commander pulled back hard on the flight stick barely missing the large mountain that appeared suddenly in front of them. "Another one like that and we're walking."

"Chelsea, are you alright, you don't look so good?" Teller walked strong, his heavy steps sinking deep in the snow as the blizzard buffeted them. Scrycher was thrown over one shoulder, and Chelsea over the other. Blink sat atop his head, crystal in hand, pointing the way.

Chelsea, blue from the cold, shuddered as her teeth chattered. "Nothing a little cuddle couldn't fix. H-how 'bout it?"

Teller was about to respond when Blink started jumping up and down on his head, causing his open mouth to clamp shut as he bit his tongue. "You little..." He stopped mid-sentence, looking before him in awe.

"Captain Dragoon. As your first plan did not work out so well, then I believe we should follow mine. After all, I am the senior military man in this command."

"Certainly, Commander! I would not want to cramp your style. After all, crashing into that mountain range was so tactically impressive I cannot wait to see what you do next."

"Prat." The Commander spat the insult at Lance as he walked beside him. *Smack*, Lance's fist landed square in the Commander's jaw, jolting his head sideways. The Commander stumbled, but did not fall. He glared at Lance whilst he probed his cheek with his tongue. "You get one, but Captain or not; the next time you hit me will be your last." The Commander spat blood as he walked off, dreading the several days trek ahead of them.

Teller watched as the shuttle crashed in the blizzard, spreading snow clouds high into the air. He jumped down from the vantage point above the cave entrance, and turned towards Chelsea inside. "It is almost show time. You know I have seen this end, and they will kill us all when they find us." Blink shuddered as Teller spoke, blinking off to some unknown location.

Chelsea was cleaning her pistol, caressing it up and down as though a lover, but Teller could see her hands shaking and knew that behind her tough exterior, she was petrified of the upcoming conflict. "I'm not waiting 'ere for them to corner and butcher us, like animals. I am ready! We end this now. We kill 'em all. Are you up to it?" Chelsea's voice was very serious as she turned. Teller's lips embraced hers, he purred, pulling her body to his in their last act of passion before the end…

"Snipe, veer off, and ensure we do not get taken unawares." The Commander's voice was barely audible over the wind which howled ferociously and pelted them with snow. Snipe broke off to the right to scout ahead as they headed towards the large cave before them in the mountain, his small body disappearing in the snowstorm.

Chelsea was tending to Scrycher with the warm water and rags Teller had prepared. Teller had managed to find a large shell of some kind to put the snow in, and enough kindling that they could start the fire. Chelsea had removed all Scrycher's clothing except his undergarments, as his body was boiling. Light from under his skin lit the cavern even over the fire's flames. How he was so hot in this cold, she could not understand. She turned, wringing the sweat out of the rags and onto the blackened soil, as Teller entered.

"And he called me sleeping beauty!" Teller had walked in from the middle tunnel behind them, carrying what appeared to be a large spider's leg. "He's forgotten that sleeping is supposed to make you more beautiful." He threw the leg into the fire, allowing it to spark up, the smell of cooking meat wafting through the cavern. Teller pulled the crystal from his pocket, its' light so bright it almost blinded them. From a ledge in the cavern's wall, Blink's eyes widened. The crystal was so beautiful, he had to have it.

"We need to keep this safe at any cost. We can't let them get it." Teller pointed to her half covered breasts. "Can you hide it?"

"Yep. Unless you have another use for them, Teller?" Chelsea smiled playfully as Teller sat down beside her. "What 'bout Scrycher?"

"He can watch if he wants, but I am not having him join in." He slid over to her, pulling up her tank top, licking and caressing her breasts as they made love yet again.

The Leopard had been observing the three on their trek across the snow. With too many to attack at once it waited, it just needed one. It did not have to wait for long, and it closed in…

Snipe walked through the snow to scout ahead, as he had done a hundred times before. The only thing of interest was the menacing cliffs and cave looming in front of him. Its large mass was foreboding, as though a warning for them not to venture too near. The storm had all but deadened his senses so he could not see, could not hear, until it was too late. The frozen monkey-like creatures stalking him had waited for the right moment. He did not see the web before him attached between rocks, or Mogly, waiting for his trap to be sprung, until it was too late.

He stopped suddenly, his body unable to move as he got stuck in the web. He panicked, trying to see around him; glimpsing the movement, he opened his mouth to scream. The scream echoed through the landscape, heard over the storm. Then suddenly it was silenced, as Mogly opened his mouth wide enclosing Snipe's head. *Crunch...*

"Feed, my brothers, feed; as we have work to do."

The Leopard, slunk off, these were not of his planet; yet he sensed a danger. This prey was not worth the risk.

The Commander held up his hand, cautioning everyone to stop their mindless chattering. The scream echoed, then nothing. No scream, no sounds of struggle, nothing! He signaled to two of his men, sending them around the back of the cave. The other two, he sent to the other side. The remaining man he positioned to guard the entrance.

"Well, where did you want me? I've got to be of some use to you." Lance yelled over the storm.

"In your condition," the Gunnery looked at Lance in disgust, "You are of no use to anyone. Not even yourself."

"The cavern goes on and on," Teller said, "branching off all over the place. It will take days to explore all of the different tunnels."

"The crystal kept lighting the middle one. You can't get through?"

Chelsea and Teller had been questioning this for days; the crystal had been right until now, to come so far and to be stopped by a wall seemed ridiculous to say the least. "Yes. A large wall blocks our way out of here, maybe if we had time..." Teller was cut short by the screaming that echoed through the snow.

They were here...

"You keep the crystal safe Chelsea." Teller handed it to her, their hands touched briefly then they locked in a passionate embrace. Teller pulled away, replacing the hood, covering his face and the determined look on it.

"Blink, look after Chelsea. Make sure she is kept safe." Teller's head nodded towards her as he finished getting ready, by slinging a large shell over his back.

Blink paced up and down at the entrance of the cave, his wings and ears upright, patrolling the area. This signaled to Teller that he would not let anything pass.

Chelsea laughed slightly, as she placed the crystal between her breasts. "You sure you don't want one last romp before going into battle?" Her movement was sensuous as she reached for her pistol.

Teller shook his head, "Sorry, my love, no time. I will hold you to it once we are done."

Teller looked back at the still unconscious Scrycher, as he skulked off into the snowstorm, knowing the Company men would be here soon, to kill them all…

Walking towards the cave, Lance's thoughts returned to the incompetence of his crew. *How could my father have employed such imbeciles? Oh well, it will be over soon!*

Nervously, the Commander walked beside him. He did not like this sense of dread that had come over him. *This place was too quiet.* He had already lost one man, and with this loose cannon of a Captain beside him, his job was all that much harder. He stopped dead still, catching a glimpse of something on the ledge above the cave. Looking harder, he queried that it was just his imagination.

"Oh crap." he mumbled under his breath. He bolted, knocking the Gunnery off balance, and face first onto the ground. He did not look back to see if the Gunnery was alright as the snow was making his job hard enough to get there in time to warn his men.

The Gunnery mumbled under his breath as he fumbled with his pistol, trying to stop it from melting into the snow. As his clothes became soaked, his thoughts turned to the many ways he could get his reward for killing the remaining criminals, and hopefully taking out the Commander in the crossfire. Making sure he remained safe, of course.

The two cautiously climbed towards their destination above the cave entrance. As they found level ground, they took a moment to exhale into their hands, trying to warm their numb fingers before placing them at the ready, near their rifles' triggers. They could see little in the storm as they made their way to get to their vantage point. This ledge above the cave was perfect for line of sight, they could sniper anyone moving to, or from, the cave. If they could just see far enough to do it! As one of the men went to lie down, the other fell, his throat ripped open. His blood spilled onto the snow below. The other man had no time to react. A squishing sound signified his death as his head was lopped off and it rolled to the ground and down towards the cave's entrance. Teller stood momentarily growling in anger, his blood red eyes assessing the battlefield before throwing the shell to the ground. Jumping upon it, he slid down the side of the mountain.

Chelsea heard the entrance of the guard and raised her gun with both hands steadying it. She waited, nothing, they came no closer. Then there was a splat.

"What the…! Gordo, go no further!" The Commander stopped his man, not daring to venture in. She swore under her breath. *Why had they stopped, was Teller OK?*

The two guards cut across the front of the cave moments earlier. They were close enough to see the entrance, but not to be seen. "This will be an easy kill." The leading guard snickered, as he quickened his pace in anticipation of flanking these criminals.

"Sweet. 'Bout time we saw some blood, other than our own. "

"I am just hoping that the little vermin from the swamp is still alive, so I can skin him."

The trailing guard licked his lips. "Well, you've got to have a goal."

The men continued their banter as they rounded the side of the cave, caught unawares as the snow came crashing down upon them. The shell and Teller's weight broke the first man's neck. As the second man reached for his gun, the sound of his heart beating confused him. *Th-thump, th-thump, th-thump.* Then it lay motionless in Teller's hand as he slumped into the snow.

Teller was not privy to the Commander's presence, as he stepped in behind him, cursing loudly as he clobbered Teller over the head. "You animal." *Thump*!

With both hands, Chelsea raised her gun, trying to steady it. She was nervous, as Teller had not returned. She waited yet again. Nothing. They came no closer. Then, Teller's limp body was flung into the cave.

"If you want him to stay alive, drop your gun and come out now." The Commander walked in with his guard circling behind Chelsea. The guard took her gun from her drooped hands as her head lowered. He pushed her violently, forcing the crystal from between her breasts and into the fire. She swore under her breath, as he pushed her again.

Blink saw all this from his vantage point, *too many* he thought. Watching the crystal fall into the fire, his ears pricked up as if hearing something. He waited, waited, and then he blinked. The men looked around. Seeing nothing of interest, they turned and left.

The Leopard had stalked its prey; had waited for Scrycher to be alone, and now it was time for the kill. He had slunk past Teller, and Chelsea, whilst they were being forced out of the cavern and into the snowstorm. Traveling under the cover of the snow, past the guards and then into the warm cave. He could sense his prey as he cautiously stalked it. He followed the smell coming from the scuff marks Chelsea had left whilst dragging Scrycher's body to safety. Chelsea had hidden Scrycher within the cavern, and out of harms way. As it rounded the corner, the Leopard's eyes lit up, he was starving, and now it was time for a feast.

"Hiiiiiisssssssss" Blink appeared on Scrycher's chest, raising his hackles, and hissing at the Leopard.

The Leopard continued circling his prey that had been hidden further down in the tunnels, and was not threatened by the attempted distraction. It was after a feast, not a snack. Making his move, he darted in and grabbed at Scrycher's hand. Blink intercepted, clawing at the Leopard's eyes with teeth bared. Then Blink was gone. The Leopard who had been caught off-guard, growled as he went in for his kill again, now that the pesky little dragon was gone. His fangs pierced the soft wound that had not healed on Scrycher's hand, transferring some of the energy across. Then the Leopard was blinded by an intense light; the crystal Blink had retrieved from the fire touched him briefly before falling to the ground, the mere touch enough to start the change!

Blink lurched forward again with fangs bared, hissing another warning. The Leopard took notice this time. He could not see, and as he pawed aimlessly around him, Blink, blinked to his back, biting his ear. Roaring, the Leopard ran down the cavern, and away from this unseen attacker.

Blink returned to Scrycher's side. Gingerly, he lay on Scrycher's belly, favoring his blistering paws; the crystal, now diminished in light, was of no further interest to Blink. With the pain of the fire fresh in his mind, he trembled as he slept.

Scrycher felt the little dragon shivering in pain on his chest and willed his eyes to open. After failing, he mumbled, his throat sore and dry, his voice inaudible over the fire. "I know, I know."

Chapter 20

Scrycher awoke to the echoing sound of men, loudly discussing what they should do with the prisoners, where they should be taken, and whether there were any others alive. This last point was driven home by two equally angry individuals arguing the point, and asking questions. Scrycher gulped; he knew by the commotion, his crew, or what was left of them, had been captured, but little else. Grabbing a handful of water from the shell beside him, he gulped it down, its pure essence burning, as it filled him. His stomach rumbled, churning as it informed him that it was empty. Blink raised his little ears, his eyes wide, and his stomach growling in response. "I know Blink, my boy... But death waits for no man!"

Scrycher's voice was strained as he stumbled towards Teller. "He is innocent!" His throat was dry, giving him a raspy sound as he breathed. He was still not fully functional, and the fogginess that surrounded his head clouded his thoughts. "He has done nothing wrong. I took him prisoner, forced him to work for me. You must let him go. I will surrender." His voice lowered at the end of the sentence as he knelt down to place his rifle at his feet. He had no idea what was going on, but he could not quickly assess and work a way out of this situation in his current condition. So he took his time, still kneeling as he surveyed the scene before him. He could see that both Teller, and Chelsea, had been apprehended, so he had to think smart. Scrycher's sudden appearance from the cave had given Chelsea enough time to turn the rifle on the guard holding her arms, crashing it across his face.

Click, click, click, click.

Scrycher's instincts kicked in, he saw the scene before him turn into chaos, saw Chelsea gunned down, Teller to follow, and himself forced to the ground in a hail of Bullets. "Chels!" Scrycher nodded towards her, letting her know he had objections to her actions and may have just come up with a plan.

"As will I." Chelsea lowered the guard's gun to the ground and raised her hands above her head again. The guard bent over cautiously, picking up the gun.

"Cow!" He said in an all too aggressive tone, as he spat out two teeth, and smashed the gun into the side of her face. Chelsea collapsed forward. Raising herself, she spat blood.

Teller's eyes burnt red, his words slow and methodical through clenched teeth as he growled. "Bad move!"

"You shut up, you murdering scum." Lance spat the words at Teller, before turning to Scrycher. "Innocent, my ass. He is murdering scum the same as the rest of you and will be killed, the same as the rest of you."

Scrycher moved forward in an all too slow and non-threatening way. "But he has killed no one except for need of preservation. Blink!" Blink poked his little ears out of the pocket, then his eyes, his head and, finally, the crystal was lifted out. Scrycher took this crystal, leaning towards Teller with it. If Teller were released, he would need this crystal to get to their goal. Scrycher was going to make sure it damn well happened. He grasped the crystal in his right hand, the tingling sensation of the crystal's energy coursing through his open wound and into his blood again, as he swaggered as though drunk.

Through the fogginess, he slurred his words. "This man is but a Story Teller for his people, he uses this crystal to tell of their past. You would not deny them of that now, would you?" Holding his temple, he pointed the crystal towards Teller.

Lance knew that this Teller, a Stray, was not a part of his original orders, but he did not care; he wanted revenge as he stroked the scar on his face.

Scrycher staggered towards Teller, his arm outstretched as he attempted to hand the crystal to him, its glow diminished greatly as it had now deposited much of its energy into him. "I hand you back your lineage, use it wisely, and find what you are looking for." Scrycher knew this was their best course of action now. Teller may just get out of this to finish what they started, even if they did not.

Teller stretched out his hand.

"Bravo!" Lance stepped forward and clapped, before the Commander could speak. "Now if you do not mind. Would you please step away so I can kill your disfiguring, fortune teller, was it?"

Scrycher gently lobbed the crystal to Teller, but overbalanced and fell forward. *Bang.* Lance's gun went off. His aim was true but Scrycher had stumbled out of the way. Rising up, Scrycher placed his hand up and showed his compliance. "Whoa. Itchy trigger finger, I meant no harm."

While this was happening, Teller caught the crystal, cupping it in his hand and protecting it from any unwanted observations.

The Commander was nervously raising his hands in a submissive gesture as he pleaded. "Captain, calm down." There were too many variables thrown into this situation and he wanted to get out of it alive. He turned to Scrycher, hoping to diffuse the situation. "I accept your surrender. The Story Teller can go once you are, cuffed, or dead. Choice is yours!"

Lance looked at the Commander, his eyebrows raised and his eyes fuming red. "I want him dead, not released. Why negotiate at all? We have the control."

"No. You are a loose cannon, and I do not want to end up dead because you have ideas of grandeur. Once this is over, we can all go home, safe and sound, and you can go back to daddy Dragoon." The Commander hoped he could convince Lance to follow his lead, however if it came to it, Lance was no longer his main objective. He was not willing to die for stupidity.

Lance was quick and cutting in reply. "I do not care about my father! Why should I go home, when I can do as I wish out here, in the depths of space?"

Scrycher had been struggling to follow the conversation through the haze inside his head, however he saw this as the opening he required and took it, pushing his way into the conversation. "Well, we do have something else you may want, other than our capture."

Lance spat aggressively as his head spun towards Scrycher. "What?"

As Scrycher made eye contact, he realized he was talking to a mad man. "Captain Dragoon! I feel there is no love lost on your father, so I put this to you. On our ship we had information leading us to believe your father is performing a great deal of illegal activities."

"So? Do not test my patience. What are you saying?"

"You spent three months chasing us across the galaxy, and your father is the real one you should have been chasing."

"How do you know this?"

"We have been collecting information on him for years"

"Like what?"

"Like the slave trade of Strays, the hunting of them and the senseless butchery of Stray children. In all this, we have information pointing directly to Lord Dragoon!" Scrycher could see the doubts going through Lance's mind, on his face, and in his eyes, but the aggression was still there, the desire for bloodshed.

Lance's temper simmered down a little, as though Scrycher was getting through where no others could. "And where is this information now?"

"Can we make a deal? Let us go in exchange for the information?" Until he got a definite answer, Scrycher had presented all he was going to.

Lance turned to the Commander, talking abruptly, and loud enough for all to hear. "Do you reckon they are bluffing?" The Commander had been on the Company ship long enough to know this was more fact than fiction.

He shook his head. This would have been bold even for a criminal to boast this without some real hard evidence. "No I reckon they might just have it."

"Show me this information."

Scrycher looked over to Chelsea, giving her the nod. "Sorry, Boss, the memory stick fell out on the ship."

Lance looked at Scrycher, slight admiration in his face. "Played well for a criminal, but alas you have nothing to barter. Take them into custody. All of them, until we pass sentence."

"Hold your own there, young man…" Scrycher remembered that his pocket had got somewhat lighter for a short time while the fireworks were in the sky. Maybe. "Blink!"

Blink recognized that tone; he knew he was in trouble as he poked his huge eyes and tiny head out of the pocket he had been hiding in. His little clawed paws fumbled with the shiny memory stick he had removed from the ship earlier. The one that had fallen from Chelsea's breasts, when Teller had got them safely off the decompressing ship. Shaking, he brought the stick to the top of Scrycher's pocket.

"Thank you very much, little boy." Scrycher raised his hand to take the memory stick from Blink. Blink looked around nervously at all the guns pointing at him and fumbled with the stick, dropping it in the snow beside Scrycher's gun. Scrycher bent down, innocently trying to get the memory stick before it melted its way into the snow.

Teller grabbed at his head, the intense pain was intoxicating, and the fog flowed into his mind. *Th-thump, th-thump, th-thump.*

The Gunnery had had his pistol trained on Scrycher for the whole situation and now it was time to use it. He pulled the trigger, as if in response to Scrycher's movement.

In his nervousness after dropping the shiny stick, Blink scoured the armed men with his beady eyes. One caught his attention; the Gunnery. He had his gun trained on Scrycher and sweat was beading down his face. No one else noticed; their attention diverted by the play unfolding before them. Blink did not take his eyes off him. The Gunnery pulled the trigger. Blink, blinked from the pocket to the Gunnery's gun, knocking off the aim and immediately blinking back into Scrycher's pocket.

With its original trajectory changed, the bullet crashed into Scrycher's shoulder blade, shattering it on impact. Scrycher spun, his body trying to cushion the impact of the bullet. Spinning, he dropped his body low, lowering his center of gravity to allow him to remove the dagger within his boot with his right hand. His motion carried him a full circle to stand up, but he faltered slightly as he flicked the knife at the Gunnery. As he let go of the dagger he felt the power from his blood follow it, engulfing it. A bright energy ball was released from where the dagger had been.

The Gunnery's stomach took a direct hit. The smell of burning flesh was intense. All gagged at the stench. Gunnery stood with his eyes wide. *What had happened?* He dropped the small pistol, clutching at his stomach. Unable to find his stomach, he dropped to his knees. Where it had been was now a burnt hole. The flesh cauterized into place, with no blood flowing. His eyes were still open as he fell forward, into the snow, where he was to sleep forever… dreaming of beer wenches, and riches.

The snow filled the hole in the Gunnery's stomach briefly and then melted.

The Commander had not seen anything like this before, *who is this freak? How can he do this thing?* Those were the last things he thought before all hell broke loose.

Chelsea saw her chance again; she dropped to the floor, grabbing the knife from her boot. Her reflexes were quick as she rolled to the side, the knife ready to throw.

The Commander did not waste a second, shooting at Chelsea twice before she could throw it. He did not see Teller arch his back; however, the guard that was behind Chelsea did, shooting at Teller's chest.

Teller saw in disbelief as Chelsea's body hit the snow. He saw the Commander move his aim to Scrycher. Still holding the crystal, Teller arched violently, hissing as he did. He did not feel the bullet as it passed through him, his body blinking at the precise moment that was required. All he could feel was the acid rise from his stomach to spit at the Commander. His body arched forward completely, projecting it so fast, the Commander had no time to react.

The Commander dropped the acid ridden rifle and clutched his face in agony. His face and hands burnt, in agonizing pain, the overwhelming smell of his burning flesh, mixing with the Gunnery's. The acid attacked his face. It ate through his skull, to his brain as he held his head, his fingers now corroded to bone, falling apart as he screamed for mercy. No mercy came, just the cold dark sleep of death, a horrifically painful death.

Scrycher's pain was pushed aside, as he saw Teller's clothes drop to the floor, the crystal in the pile. Scrycher reacted, and grabbed his gun from the ground. Still kneeling, he had the perfect vantage as he aimed at the guard that had been behind Chelsea, the one that had just shot Teller. The guard did not react, his eyes glazed as he fell to the snow, a victim of the Commander's two shots meant for Chelsea. Scrycher's rifle did not fire; instead, he swung it towards Lance. The Commander was gripping his face. An agonizing scream was coming through his fingers as the flesh melted from them, the bones dropping in the snow beside his feet. He saw Lance grab his weapon and reacted by flipping his rifle and activating the blade, slicing at Lance's calf from the kneeling position he was in. He could feel the cold blade cut deep and saw the blood, the shock in Lance's eyes, and the shaking of his hands.

Vomiting, Lance's head flew forward, covering the snow in his sick. Confused and crazed, he raised himself shakily, and drew his pistol, adrenaline making him react rather than act. He did not see the footprints in the snow moving stealthily towards him. However, he did see the blade from Scrycher's rifle extending from the butt, and felt the cold of the blade as it bit into his flesh. He pulled the trigger of his pistol repeatedly, aiming into Scrycher's chest. As he pulled the trigger, his body felt the impact of Teller crashing into him, and he let his body become one with it as the blow knocked him to the ground. The blackness above him was the last thing Lance saw, before his body crashed to the snow.

"Well, Captain, do you want to live or die? The choice is yours."

"I would rather burn alive than side with murdering scum like you. You killed my men, and tried to kill me."

"Correction, Captain Dragoon. You and your men tried to kill us. You have been chasing us for months. We merely defended ourselves." Scrycher walked around Lance, who sat awkwardly by the fire, then whispered in his ear as he finished his sentence. "And if I wanted you dead, you would be."

Sweat poured from Lance's forehead. He moved with a tiredness that crept into his voice. "What do you want of me? Can't you just let me die?"

The shiny memory stick reflected the fire's glow as Scrycher waved it in front of him. "I just want you to do what is right."

"How do I know what is right?"

"Teller, would you so kindly show Captain Dragoon what you showed me earlier?"

Teller moved in front of Lance, as he removed the crystal from his pocket. Concentrating, he drew forth an image from it; the one of Gunnery and Lord Dragoon's discussion. As it ended these words echoed in Lance's mind, "And if your Captain is going to jeopardize your mission, kill him! He is expendable."

Lance was gawking at the final image of his father. "What about a crew? You killed mine."

"We have business here. Once we are finished, we will escort you back, using your vessel, of course. Our ship was destroyed by some egotistical tyrant's son! All I ask is that we go free with your…our, NEW vessel at the end of the journey."

"It won't replace her, Boss, nothing will." Sorrow filled her voice as Chelsea spoke from the shadows.

"Bloody vessels, don't even need mechanics. A freak of nature, I say." Jaxter's comment hung in the air as silence filled the room…

Lord Dragoon's posture had improved as he re-appeared in the room in which he had met the Gunnery many times before. But still he fidgeted, trying to find a better position in which his aching back would be less debilitating as he waited impatiently. Barely minutes had passed before he grew impatient and grasped at the table beneath him, letting out a sigh of pain as his back twinged. *This was becoming a chore*, he thought to himself. *I would much rather be healing my wound than coming to this vessel.* But the reward was too great, eternal life was within his grasp. A compartment had already opened in the middle of the table, as he was lost in thought. A little taken back at his lack of perception, he questioned how much the wound in his back was really affecting him. He shook his head, tsk, tsking himself, as he removed his black gloves. He placed his palms, bare of skin, upon the box, the power from the crystal that appeared, calming him, and helping with the pain. He felt more connected this time than he had before, maybe there was a useful side effect to his injury. The corrupted crystal, its core blackened, filled the table with a black smoke. As he concentrated, Lord Dragoon transformed this smoke into images on the planet below. He breathed in deeply, then held that breath as he saw the crystals on the ground, many of them sticking out of the ships wreckage scattered across the planet. *These will come in useful*, he thought, as he let his head tilt back slightly "Finally!" He breathed out, expelling an eerie laugh, as his hood fell from his head.

His shoulder-length blonde hair flowed around him, as he continued to laugh, framing his young face. His eyes glowed, as his voice took on a menacing tone of a mad man. "Finally I have found you! After two hundred years of searching, you were here all the time, the Crystal Planet, my destiny!" He walked around the table, stooping slightly to peer into the vast surroundings as they changed, getting more excited as he searched, trying to locate a crystalline tree. "I will be back to claim you, once I convince the Councill to let Lance take my place as the head of the Company. A reward for finding this place! I will assume his..." Dragoon's smile was that of a madman, as he waited to deliver this last word, the exact same smile that Lance had worn in the past few months. Lord Dragoon finished his sentence dramatically, as he laid out his plans to assume his son's "identity."

He did not think twice, as he now searched for his son's body, he had no remorse. After killing his first born from every partnering, and assuming their identity, why would he, he had been doing it for close to five hundred years. The tree would have to wait until later. After all, he would have much time to search once he returned, but for now, he needed to confirm their deaths. He laid his palms on the crystal again, changing its location to where the battle had happened earlier. As he searched the bodies, making sure all were dead, he spoke softly as if to the crystal planet itself. "I will bring him, no... me, back to claim you as my own."

"Your own... Father, what about the Councill? Never cared for anything but yourself, did you?" Lance's voice projected across the room from within the shadows.

"Lance, you are alive. Oh. I had given up hope."

"Save it for the Councill, Father!" Lance's tone dripped with venom as he continued. "All my crew is dead, men, unlike myself, men I should have befriended. But no, I became you. Egotistical and evil."

"But Lance, we can return together as heroes, why the venom?" Lord Dragoon was scanning the room, searching the shadows as he tried to pinpoint his son's location.

"You know all too well Father. You will kill me the first chance you get."

"But it does not have to be like th-"

Lance walked from the shadows; Lord Dragoon acted quickly, and with unnatural strength, as he rushed for him. He held his throat, trying to strangle the life from him. Lifting him from the ground, Lord Dragoon laughed as he looked upon his own reflection. Their features identical bar the length of their hair. "You puny weakling. You wonder why I want to kill you. You are a disgrace. Now die and leave me to use your life for a purpose."

Lance did not struggle. He was too tired, and did not care. The sickness he was carrying allowed him to act, not react. Slowly, and cautiously, he raised his hand, his small pistol in it. Aiming carefully he pulled the trigger. His body fell to the ground, and Lord Dragoon's scream echoed through the ship, as though he was being pulled apart. Slowly, Lance dragged himself up, and walked to the table. He picked up a shard of the broken crystal, he had just shot, turning it in his hand, before he threw it to the floor in disgust. "Die, Father. Die!"

"What are we still waiting for?" Zackory was impatient.

"I agree brother, I am sick of waiting for father too. We must venture to the last co-ordinates shown on my tracker, and see for ourselves. I just hope that wench Cheslea did not uncover it before they reached their final destination." Garath spoke with an air of distrust, as he continued. "Be careful, brother, do not cross me when we get there." The monitor blinked off.

"You know me too well, Garath. Far too well."

"Mogly want them. Move them now." Mogly swung his arms toward the corpses as he ordered his frozen minions to move the bodies. As they finished hiding them in their lair, he spoke with satisfaction in his voice. "Father be proud. Two more generals for his army!"

Chapter 21

Grease dripped from Profitor's mouth, as he feasted on the cooked leg in his hand, speaking between bites. "So, th-there I w-was... stumbling th-through the s-snow... trying to find a crevice, or cave, to keep w-warm... and trapping r-r-rabbits, or s-s-something that resembled them anyways... I s-saw th-the shuttle crashing... S-So I th-thought I'd take a l-look. A-And you w-w-would not believe it, I f-f-found these t-two wa-wa-andering aimlessly in the sn-sn-snow." Profitor looked up from his food, curiosity in his eyes. "Hey J-Jax, I f-forgot to ask y-you, I th-thought Scrags mentioned th-that the sh-shuttle had a cloak? So how did y-you get sh-shot down?"

Jaxter glared, asking bluntly. "You caught lots of bunnies, Prof?"

"… sh-shut up and p-p-p-pass me some m-m-m-more s-spider."

Scrycher grinned at Jaxter's uncomfortable mood, and thought he would add to it as he recalled another little adventure. "Hey, Prof. You would have loved the swamp we were stuck in. There were so many insects you would not believe it. We had to catch ourselves, and Jax over here, just went to sleep. Just like sleeping beauty in there.".

"Wh-what do y-you mean, c-catch y-yourself?" Profitor queried Scrycher.

"You know, we had that conversation and you said; only way through a swarm of hungry insects was to catch yourself." Scrycher patted him on the shoulder in appreciation.

"O-Oh th-that. I w-was m-making a j-joke."

"And I bet you are going to tell me the Tsetse fly's bite does not put you to sleep?" Scrycher laughed aloud and Jaxter joined in.

"Good one, Boss. Real good one." Jaxter bent over bellowing out laughter that echoed through the caverns.

"W-Well, that is a myth. It actually deposits a parasite into the blood that causes sleeping sickness with very severe symptoms." Profitor was grinning as he spun off the facts.

Scrycher's smile turned to a frown of concern as he asked. "What happens?"

"I-In the beginning you may think you have the flu. High fevers and hot sweat are common. Your joints may ache, and you may even have itching. Once the parasite reaches your nervous system, you are pretty much a slave to your emotions. You become vulnerable to all types of fits of rage, and aggressiveness, especially in times of stress. But the worst is that once your body finally succumbs to the sickness completely, you fall into a sleeping coma, and eventually, die." Profitor stood up straight, smiling from ear to ear and grinning, proud of his recollection of the facts. Scrycher swore, fumbled through his large pockets, offloading their contents onto the floor.

"Th-there is no problem, Scrycher. The Tsetse Fly has been extinct for over two thousand years." Profitor spoke candidly, as he tried reassuring Scrycher who continued to frantically go through his pockets.

Finding a small specimen jar, Scrycher threw it to Profitor. "Are these your extinct Tsetse flies?'

Profitor turned the jar around, the insects inside were dead. "W-Well, I'll be damned. One of these is. Th-the other one. I-I am not sure. It seems to be a much more developed. Look at its structure, its thorax and abdomen, it is much harder."

Scrycher leant down, picking up the items that were in his pocket and placing them back. As he was doing so, Blink returned, hissing loudly. "Whoa, Blink, just putting them back." Scrycher continued placing the items back in his pocket as Blink paced back and forth in front of him, hissing, his frills up. Scrycher stopped for a second, looking at Profitor, then at Blink. "Prof, does this affect animals as well as humans?"

"W-Well, if bitten, I s-suppose." Profitor followed Scrycher's stare to Blink, as he got more, and more, aggressive. "Oh c-crap."

"Can you make an antidote?" Scrycher did not take his eyes from Blink.

"Not here, Scrycher, and it will be too late by the time we get to a space station."

As Scrycher put the last item back in his pocket, Blink disappeared. "Well, we have two problems then, don't we?"

"Boss?" Jaxter had got lost in all the conversation.

"Blink and Lance. They must have both been bitten by the flies." Scrycher pointed to the smaller, less developed fly.

Jaxter's concern showed in his eyes as he threw his hands in the air. "But what about me, I got bitten too?"

"Wh-when did you say you got bitten?"

"I was the first."

"N-No symptoms?"

"Nup, fit as a fiddle. Except falling straight to sleep of course. Best sleep me had in ages."

"F-Fascinating. Evolution is a fantastic thing. Y-You must have been bitten by the more evolved fly, a different strain of parasite. One that does exactly what you thought; puts you to sleep. Oh this is marvelous! I must study it further!"

Scrags was out of breath as he spoke, "Profitor, Scrycher, you must come now." He did not wait for a response as he rushed back the way he had come.

"What about me, do I not matter?" Jaxter skulked behind, mumbling as he followed Scrags to his destination, leaving Blink hissing, looking blankly at the bare ground his items had been laid out upon.

"So that is what we were missing? A handprint in the wall. What is the big deal?" Scrycher had not got his breath back. He was talking between breaths and wondered why this was so important with all the other problems they now faced.

Teller raised his hand that had been holding his crystal, placing it in the hand print indentation. The wall shifted and disappeared. Scrags bolted through, calling behind him, "We must hurry. It does not last for long."

"Hey, Prof. Why's Teller and Scrags glowing so bright? We don't need no torch down 'ere with 'em around." Chelsea ran up to the two, laughing, as she slapped their bottoms, and continued past them. Stopping, she turned to look from one to the other, heckling them. "Reckon it's 'cause they have bright futures ahead of em?"

Profitor walked up behind the two Strays, and placed his arms around them, as they pulled faces at Chelsea. The three were a very funny sight, as Profitor reached on tiptoes for Teller and stooped for Scrags. "W-Well." He stopped suddenly, pulling a hair out of the back of each of their necks.

Both Scrags and Teller turned, fuming. "What did you do that for Prof?" Scrags was rubbing his neck.

"Yeh, you had better have a good reason." Teller did not bother with the small amount of pain; the thumping within his head was more of an issue.

Profitor grinned from ear to ear. "L-Let me s-show you." He had made sure both hairs' roots were facing towards the ground. Both of these hairs had a faint glow to them. "W-Watch closely." Turning his hands upwards, he raised the roots of the hair into the air. Nothing happened.

"Well, Prof, if you try that trick with me hair, I'll swat you like one of those insect thingies of yours." Jaxter had turned to look, but, unimpressed by what he didn't see, turned away. As he turned, small wisps of energy drifted from within the hairs and into the air, sitting for a moment before they disappeared.

"S-See, your fur is hollow. Y-Your body absorbs the energy, amplifies it, and then your fur allows the energy to sit within it. Your fur then expels the energy slowly back into the environment. A-A very nice arrangement, if I do say so myself." Profitor stood up straight and proud as he dropped the two hairs and dusted his hands together.

"If I find out that I've sprung a leak cause you plucked one of my hairs, I will skin you with my bare claws." Teller looked angrily at Profitor who quickly ran behind Jaxter to seek refuge.

Looking around Jaxter's large bulk, Profitor spoke nervously. "B-But I-I-I d-did n-not m-mean a-anything b-by it." Profitor's red face hid behind

Jaxter again, as Teller lost his serious face amidst his laughter…

"Th-this is fascinating. Look at the s-size of these arachnids. They are huge." Profitor looked in wonder at the cavern before him. Spiders the size of small rats ran from side to side, trying to avoid them as they walked.

"Ah." Chelsea jumped high in the air as a spider fell onto her, its fluffy legs, brushing her arm.

"We have an audience, my love. Maybe it would be better to do this later?" Teller placed her back on the ground after he had quickly moved to catch her in her fright.

Blushing, she spoke softly. "Another time, then."

Scrycher cleared his throat. "Enough around the child. And the answer is no, Teller; I do not want to watch. Days of listening were enough for me. I don't know where you two found the energy."

Chelsea face blushed deeply, as she realized Scrycher had heard everything while he was in his coma. "Sorry, Boss."

"Not as sorry as me, Chels." Scrycher grinned as he walked out of the cavern. "Let's get to work."

"Y-You just go on. I want to study some of these specimens."

"I'm not going any further, in case these spiders get any bigger." Chelsea was nodding her head, forgetting about the momentary embarrassment.

"Th-they can't get any bigger than this. It is anatomically impossible."

"As long as you say so, Prof. Coming, Boss." Chelsea ran to catch up with Scrycher as a spider ran across the floor, and was splattered by her foot. "Eeiiik!"

Profitor walked over to examine the squashed spider. Turning it over, his voice became high pitched in excitement. "W-Wow the chelicerae has been replaced with a pincer, how fascinating."

"English, Prof." Chelsea called back as she continued, scuffing her boot on the floor as she tried to scrape the goo off her boot.

"Th-the jaws are extended out like a pincer, look rather sharp too, don't let them go to bite you, it might hurt, l-l-lots…"

"Look at these, Teller. These crystals seem to be better formed than the ones further along the tunnel." Scrycher was studying the crystals with so much interest that he did not see that the end of the cavern he was in, stopped abruptly. The exit was sealed by a large spider's web.

"It seems that this planet is in various stages of repair. Scrags was saying there were many fully formed crystals in the peaks of the mountains where they crashed, the same mountains that they had found Profitor walking aimlessly through… Scrycher stop!" Teller had been studying the room whilst he talked, stopping abruptly at the sight of movement. Something very large scuttled along the roof above them, although he could not make out what it was.

Chelsea screamed as she walked further into the room, the smell of rotting flesh attacking her nostrils. "Scrycher… look." She was pointing at the web. No, not the web. The Stray that was trapped in it, murmuring as it pleaded for help.

Scrycher ran to her, drawing his blade from his rifle and cutting down the Stray. As it fell to the floor, Teller spoke, his voice airing his concern. "This is like no Stray I have ever seen. Where is its fur, and why are its eyes so black? It is almost like it can't see." The Stray moved its head as if it was following the sound of Teller's voice. It retched its head back and forwards to spew acid from its mouth. Teller barely had enough time to escape its spray, as Scrycher severed its head.

"Nasty bugger, wasn't he?" Scrycher wiped the blood on the cocoon type webbing the Stray was wrapped up in. Looking up at the remainder of the webbing, he continued to cut it down. Several more Stray bodies in different levels of decomposition fell to the floor as he did. "Well let's get going."

"Boss!" Chelsea looked terrified as he turned to see what she wanted. A large spider, twice the size of a human had dropped from the roof on a thick thread and was scuttling towards her. Chelsea froze in terror, barely able to get her words out. "Help… Teller."

Scrycher opened fire, the bullets from his rifle splatting, as they hit the thick hide. The spider turned, aggravated. It looked at him with many eyes before it scuttled towards him; its pincer like attachments in front of its mandible clicked hungrily as it did. Scrycher offloaded his complete clip into the spider, and it kept coming, scuttling faster until it was upon him. Blade extended, Scrycher slashed as he was knocked to the floor, severing several legs as he did and covering himself in sticky goo. Kicking desperately, Scrycher could feel the claws on the legs, ripping through his jeans, tearing holes so it could get to his soft flesh. Scrycher screamed, as he fought to stay alive, breaking Chelsea from her trance. She steadied herself as she moved so that she could get a clear shot, offloading her clip into the spider's head as soon as she was in position. Eyes splattered and dropped to the floor, but this did nothing more than anger the spider, turning again on Chelsea.

Teller jumped between the two, slashing with his claws. His body was battered away by the spider, as it continued to scuttle towards Chelsea. His crystal hit the floor, skidding to land beside Scrycher, as he tried to regain his footing. Raising itself high in the air, the spider stopped momentarily, before crashing down upon Chelsea, its pincers clicking together to sever her head.

"Chelsea." Teller's scream echoed through the corridors, as he saw the spider's mass consume her.

The spider reared itself again, and then its head was gone with one fell blow from Scrycher's blade. The head now rolled across the floor, to Teller's side. He sighed, relieved at this miracle. He kicked the head away, as he tried to get his bearings, *where is Chelsea?* Scraping his feet for some perch, he panicked, trying to stand and find her. He glared in shock as a much larger spider hit the floor, looking for a victim. Scrycher scrambled for the crystal, grabbing it as he made his way to Teller's side, trying to lift him from the ground. *Th-thump, th-thump, th-thump.* "It is too late, my friend. We are no match for this one." Teller sunk back to the floor, his body and mind exhausted from the constant fighting, and death.

"I'm not about to give up that easily." Scrycher dropped the dull crystal from his hand, much of its energy now absorbed into his body. Running at the spider, he slashed with his blade, piercing its hide. He slashed repeatedly and the spider lost legs, flesh, and other parts as he frenzied. Scrycher started to get some hope back, Teller was now on his feet and slashing beside him, the spider was confused and darted from one to the other. And then Scrycher fell over a stalagmite, that lay broken on the floor. The spider saw her chance. She raised herself up, clashing her pincers together. He grabbed for the stalagmite, removing it from under his back to thrust it upwards. His power transferred from his hand to the stalagmite so it sliced through the hide of the spider with ease. The spider arched backwards, as she screamed in pain, attempting to slash her way to freedom. Scrycher flipped himself off the ground, holding the glowing stalagmite that was now charged with his power. As she lurched forward he forced it into her. The spider was caught off-balance, and was thrown back onto the dead carcass of the other. The cavern was filled with a brilliant light, and then a splatter of parts, as both spiders exploded over the room.

"Lunch and no one invited me?" Scrags walked in the room, grabbing one of the spider's legs from the floor to munch on it. "Mmmm. My compliments to the cook."

"Th-this is m-magnificent. L-Look at the size of this thing."

"And it's tasty." Scrags wiped the spit from his mouth, taking another bite.

Jaxter followed behind the two men, looking at the carnage and asked the only question that came to mind. "Where's Chels?"

Scrycher and Teller continued to rip parts off the spiders, throwing them around the room in a frenzy. "Under here!" they yelled in unison.

Jaxter ran to the pile, followed by the others as the room became one big mess of spider parts.

Tears welled in their eyes, as Chelsea's crewmates uncovered her body. They could barely hear her as she croaked through her burnt throat. She lifted up her hand gingerly, placing it upon Scrags' head, as Teller knelt down to lift her up. "Don't eat me, Scrags. I don't think I'd taste that good." Her hand rested upon his head momentarily, falling to her side as Teller moved out of the spiders' remains.

"Chels. How did you survive the spider?" Scrycher was standing over her.

"Which one?" Chelsea coughed out the words, and then lost consciousness, as Teller stood upright, cradling her to his chest.

Scrycher removed his tear, as Teller moved away from the carcass. He stared down at where Chelsea had lain, realizing that an indentation in the ground had saved her life. She must have fitted into it to avoid the first spider, only to be cooked by Scrycher's energy blast. "Why?" He screamed as he fell to his knees, covering his eyes as more tears streamed.

Th-thump, th-thump, th-thump. Teller's heart beat faster as he tried to reassure him. "You could not have known, Scrycher. You could not have known."

GRRRRRRRRRRRRRRR. Everyone turned to glare at Scrags, as his stomach growled, possibly giving away their position. "What? It must have been the cook," he whispered as he raised his hands and his eyes rolled into the back of his head as if to say it was not his fault. Scrycher placed his finger on his lips, then quietly turned back to watch the mass of Strays in the cavern before them. They shifted slightly, but did not respond to the sound. Relieved, Scrycher wiped his brow, but Scrags bowels failed him again and he let out an echoing fart.

"This is so bad." Scrycher turned to Teller who was standing determined beside him.

"We've been through worse."

Scrycher raised his brow. "Have we?"

"Nope. But it sounded good at the time." The two men stood shoulder to shoulder, waiting for the onslaught of Strays they knew would follow.

The Strays looked up as they heard the large, echoing sound, smelling the air as they did. The first Stray caught their scent, running crazed towards them to drop at their feet, a bullet through its skull. Scrycher did not remove his stare from the masses before him as he cautioned. "You know I can only shoot ten, or so, before they rush us?"

Teller flicked his hands downwards, releasing his claws. "Yes. I am ready. Rest of you, back. This is going to get messy."

The mass of blind Strays rushed them, Scrycher putting down many with his rifle before they were upon him, biting and scratching, trying to rip him limb from limb.

Scrycher's blade bit deep into a Stray's neck, severing it as he spoke. "Oh well, better to die together than alone."

Teller snapped a neck as his eyes flared red with blood lust. "Better to die amongst friends, than live alone for an eternity."

The Strays kept coming. Scrycher ducked, slicing open the stomach of one that had tried to jump over them. "Get back!" he yelled, "They are trying to get past. Get back now!"

Scrags stepped back, mesmerized by the slaughter before him. He jumped in fright as the claw grabbed at his shoulder...

"Blink. Oh you scared the crap out of me." Scrags looked down at his pants. Blink's eyes still blazed red, but he was calm as he pulled Scrags into the tunnel in the side of the wall; a tunnel they had overlooked on the way in. It was large enough for Scrags, and maybe Profitor, but not large enough for the rest of the crew.

"Get your ass in there boy, and take Profitor with you." Jaxter had hold of Chelsea and fed her body in after them, her breasts making it hard to get her very far into the tunnel. "That will have to do. "Get going, there is no point in us all dying." Jaxter called to them, as he removed his shotgun from his shoulder, and ran back up to his exhausted comrades.

"Boss, have a rest." Jaxter exchanged places with Scrycher, blasting the Strays back with his shotgun as he moved into place. Soon the Strays were upon their own kind, tearing the flesh from their fallen brethren. Jaxter, now out of ammunition, started using the rifle to batter the Strays, whilst Teller continued to tear throats and limbs from his assailants.

Scrycher grabbed his knees, puffing and out of breath, as he heard the roaring from behind. Turning, he saw more of the Strays. They had been alerted to the fight and had now closed them in. He managed to talk between breaths, "Thanks, Jax. Last time I swap with you," before running into the group, swinging his blade above his head.

The Leopard heard the screams, felt the pull, and knew he was needed. His joining with Scrycher, and the crystal, was complete; and he slinked through the tunnels, answering their call. Finding a small, narrow tunnel, he traversed it quickly. He knew time was not on his side, as he heard Scrycher yell, a Stray claw ripping at Scrycher's arm as he tried to block another.

"There are too many. We cannot hold out." Scrycher's arms were heavy, as he yelled to his companions. Severing an arm, removing a head, slashing a throat, and still they came, in their unlimited numbers.

Then came the screams. Scrycher was so exhausted; he dropped his shoulders as he heard them. "Not more." His arms dropped as he allowed another Stray attack to rip into his flesh. Then the Strays started falling in front of him. They were grasping at their legs, backs and arms as they were torn or sliced off. The Leopard's powerful claws and jaws made fast work of his prey. As the last Stray fell, Scrycher and the Leopard locked glances. Neither moved, neither spoke, nor growled. The Leopard just left, dragging one of the bodies off for a snack.

Heartened by what had transpired, Scrycher raced back to his companions just as Jaxter fell to the floor with a Stray's fangs at his throat. The head severed easily, spraying Jaxter in blood. "Thanks, Boss." As Scrycher stood over him, Jaxter crawled out, wiping the blood from his eyes. "Gives a new meaning to blood bath, hey, Boss?"

"As long as it is not our blood, I do not care." Scrycher was slashing and jabbing, taking out Stray after Stray, and gaining back some of the lost ground with his new found vigor.

"Good to see you back, Scrycher." Teller was covered in his own blood as well as that of the Strays and was trembling with exhaustion. "No offence, Jaxter.”

“None taken, it's good to take the back seat again.” Jaxter slammed the butt of his shotgun into a Stray as it launched over Scrycher's head, and yelled, “Got it,” as he smashed its head into the ground.

“Company vessel. Please respond.” Nifty Nefal sat forward on his silken tapestry that draped over his Captain's chair. He picked up his silver cup, and drank the wine he had just been poured. “Things I do for you, Scrycher. Where the hell are you? I haven't got all day.” Nifty's voice trailed off as he mumbled about the injustices in life and how he was always waiting on one person, or another.

Lance lay in the Captain's chair of the Company Vessel, exhausted from the ordeal. He did not hear the beeping of his communications console or see the small vessel attempt to board. He just lay in the chair, dreaming of the day three months ago when his life was changed forever…

Lance awoke, his head throbbing violently as if he had just lived a bad dream. Looking through unfocussed eyes, he tried to make out the figure that talked to him as they walked his deck.

“Where is Scrycher? What have you done with him?”

The conversation was too much for Lance's punished mind to cope with, as he drifted back off to sleep. Nifty Nefal's voice also drifted away as he did. “No problem. We will still be here when you awake…”

The rocking of the vessel stirred Lance. His head was clear, and his instincts sharp. “What are you doing on board my vessel?”

“Well, he finally awakens. Please take charge of this vessel, while I make my way to mine.” Nifty ran out the room, screaming behind him. “You owe me your life. Do not forget it.”

Lance looked around the room, people of various races stood around operating their stations. His instincts kicked in. "Who is attacking us?"

"The Syndicate…"

Lance wished that he had never woken from his dream and entered into this nightmare, as another set of cannon fire hit his vessel. "Shoot left." He yelled as they took a beating from the Syndicate ships that now had the smaller vessels, commanded by Nifty and himself, outnumbered and out gunned. "How many systems out?"

"That would make it four, Sir."

Nifty's voice boomed over the communications console breaking the silence that had taken over the bridge. "You are getting creamed up there. Get your game together. I can't take on four ships by myself." Although the best in its class, Nifty's little ship was only small, and had nowhere near the arsenal of the Syndicate ships. Its main advantage was speed, and Nifty used it well, but he knew he could not evade them forever. "Flank left, right, between the two, fire!"

Explosions radiated through the fleet, ship and vessel almost colliding, as the Syndicate moved in on Nifty and an all too familiar voice graced their bridges. "You do not have to hold them off on your own, Nifty old friend. I have come to even the odds." Philippe's voice echoed through the bridges, drowned out by explosions, as he commanded The Enforcer to fire at the Syndicate vessels.

"What a mess." Gregory pushed away the women that were draped over his barely covered chest and raised himself out of his Captain's chair as he spoke. "Crap. I only wanted Scrycher, and now I have three vessels that want to die." His mood darkened as he saw the vessel firing before them. He strode to the viewing window. His eyes lit up as he pointed aggressively and yelled to his crew. "Attack The Enforcer, I want my ship back."

Gregory cursed, as one of his Syndicate vessels exploded before him. "Where the hell did that weapon fire come from?" The question was rhetorical, and he cut off the crewmember that attempted to answer as he yelled. "Open coms!" He realized that he was not going to win this fight without a great deal more casualties, but he was hoping he could increase the odds back in his favor again. "Company ship. We have no fight with you. Stand down."

Lance stood, straightening his shirt as he pushed out his chest and spoke strongly. "Well, you should have thought of that before you fired on me. You stupid fool." Lance was partially back to his normal self, enjoying the exhilaration of the fight, as their cannon fire damaged another Syndicate vessel.

"What's wrong Gregory? Can't stand the heat?" Philippe was holding his own in command of The Enforcer and doing severe damage to the other Syndicate vessels. "Now if you told me which sh…"

"Fire on that ship, now." Philippe was ripped from his jest, his focus torn from the fight before him, as he pointed at one of the two vessels that had just appeared at the outer reaches of the battle.

"What the? Zackory gripped his Captain's chair in order to keep his footing as the cannon fire hit his vessel. "Who the hell is firing at us?"

"Remember me, you thieving prick? You took something from me!" Philippe screamed down the communication console as his vessel veered down upon them.

"Who the hell are you?" Zackory did not know. He had no enemies, well, none that were alive.

"The one you severed two arms from, you prick. Now feel my wrath." Philippe cut off communications as he yelled to his crew. "I want that ship destroyed, no matter how you do it."

The Creator stood smiling proudly as he watched Philippe work. "Revenge is sweet, my son. Revenge is so sweet."

"Why should we help, Lallone? They have done nothing but cause us grief." Jarel stood aboard the small ship, wanting to do nothing but disappear again.

"Because Dogny know your son there." Dogny spat the words at Jarel. "But Dogny don't care for bastard child. Dogny don't care at all."

"We should help, because Steller asked it of us." Lallone spoke softly.

"Steller! When?" A spark lit up in Jarel's eye as he spoke.

"While you were recovering. You slept for a very long time."

"Dogny don't be lazy, sleep all time like Jarel. Dogny work hard, keep Lallone happy." Dogny's smile beamed from his place by the console.

"Well Jarel, the choice is yours. Do we turn back, or join the fight?"

"Sorry father. I have disappointed you." Philippe sat disheartened as The Enforcer was pelted again by another set of cannon fire.

"Good tactic, Zackory."

"Same to you, Garath. We make a good team when we work together."

"What the! That little prick. After all this time, he is here." Garath looked at the shimmer in space to the side of him. The shimmer's trajectory headed straight down to the planet to assist Scrycher and his crew. "Change of target. Shoot there." Garath's gunnery turned the cannon, firing blindly where Garath had pointed.

As the small ship lost its cloaking, Lallone turned to where the cannon fire had originated. "What the?" Seeing Garath's vessel, he put his hands over his eyes and sighed. "Oh no, not again."

"Dogny not like this. Dogny wanted to fight on ground, not up here." Dogny was below in the depths of the ship looking for anything to get the cloak back on. "Well, you wanted to fight. Here we are. Let's fight." Jarel's eyes sparked up in anticipation.

"Be my guest." Lallone stepped away from the console, allowing Jarel access.

"What about you?" Jarel looked concerned.

"Oh. We do not fight. It is not in our nature."

"Great." Jarel fiddled with the knobs before him, the engines stopped and the ship sat motionless in space. "Crap! What have I done now?"

"Dogny have to fix another of Jarel's mistakes." Dogny came bounding up the stairs and to the console, his hands moving so quickly that Jarel could not understand what was happening. As the cannon fire neared them the ship jerked out of the way, knocking both Jarel and Lallone to the floor. "Jarel. Thought you wanted fight. Get off floor." Dogny passed his hand over a compartment that opened, revealing a weapons stick and targeting system. "Dogny hope this works."

"Why wouldn't it? How many times has it failed in the past?" Jarel was looking a little worried as the ship was buffeted by cannon fire again.

"Never!" Dogny smiled at Jarel.

"That's good then, isn't it?" Jarel smiled as he grabbed the stick, lining up the oncoming vessel.

"S'pose. Dogny never used before. Not sure was installed."

Jarel closed his eyes then opened them. "I hope I never have to deal with you two ever again." He pulled the trigger…

"Why don't you use this weapon? It is magnificent." Jarel spun the stick around again locking onto Garath's ship and pulled the trigger. Small bursts of laser fire lit the space as they made their way towards the vessel, smashing into it and dislodging another few hull plates. "Repair that, you evil…"

"Do we have any auxiliary power left?" Garath sat on the chair, laying back in a casual manner, as he asked the question.

"Yes, Sir. I can route it from life support."

"Route it all to 'Laser control'."

"But, Sir, won't that overload the crystal?"

"Not now it won't. I made a little modification after our last encounter." Garath smiled. All these years of waiting and finally his plan was going to be fulfilled. "Fire!"

Garath's gunnery flicked the switch; the crystal powered, and cannon fire from another ship hit their hull. The laser shot out at Lallone's small ship, but the cannon fire exploded, shifting their vessel and the shot to barely miss its target. Shy of its target the laser continued, smashing into the atmosphere. Much of this energy was absorbed by the planet, the ice starting to melt and the crystals below it began to glow, their light increasing with every passing second. The laser, although weakened, continued as it crashed into the mountain that Scrycher and his crew now inhabited. Ice vaporized on impact, and rocks and debris sprayed in all directions.

"No, no, no, no." Garath stood. The laser shot missed as it shot past the ship and continued to the planet below. He sat again, his ship dead in space until it re-powered itself. "Too late." He mumbled, closing his eyes and welcoming the death to come.

"You won't take another man's arms, I will see to that. Shoot him down, I want him dead." Philippe was reaping the rewards of persistence. With Garath off fighting his own battle, Zackory stood no chance against The Enforcer. Zackory's ship was now badly battered, and barely space worthy.

Lance stood on the bridge; everyone seemed to be fighting their own battles, so he watched the Syndicate vessels. Nifty and he had made fast work of these vessels after Philippe had wounded them, disabling their weapons and then their propulsion. Now all he needed to do was wait; wait for the outcome of the other fights, his vessel repairing as he did. If anyone dared to attack him, he would be ready, and it would be a quick fight.

The cavern lit as the laser hit the atmosphere. The room behind the blind Strays also lit up, the shield covering the entrance pulsing as if calling someone. The remaining Strays dropped to their knees, as if in worship of the light. Exhausted, and in agony, the three defenders used this to their advantage. Teller returned to the tunnel in the wall. Seeing no others, he whispered. "Scrags?" hearing no reply he removed Chelsea's battered body from the hole, and carried her protectively, while the others walked either side, protecting them. As they moved through the Strays, not one moved, all of them focused on the light in front of them.

Scrycher touched the shield; it shimmered but did not let him pass. Jaxter touched the shield, and there was no change. Finally, Teller laid his hand on the shield, and it shimmered, but still, it did not let him pass.

"Teller." Scrycher signaled Jaxter to take Chelsea. As he did, Teller and Scrycher joined hands, touching their free hands to the shield. It shimmered, and then faltered, allowing them to enter.

"W-Well this is magnificent. I-It is centuries in front of our technology." Profitor was studying the consoles surrounding the large crystal tree in what looked like a bridge to a ship. A small, glass chamber lay at the base to the tree, and others lined the walls.

Scrycher walked in, blood stained and exhausted, with Teller beside him, and now carrying Chelsea again.

"What do we have here, Profitor? I hope it was all worth it?" Scrycher limped over to one of the coffin-like chambers, and wiped the dust from it. Startled, he jumped back. In it was a skeleton of what could only have been a Stray, its fur-covered flesh wrinkled around its bones. Moving to another chamber, he wiped the dust. This time he stood, mesmerized at the beauty he saw before him.

Jaxter stood guard at the doorway they had just entered, nervously calling over his shoulder. "Boss, the shield is not replacing itself."

The laser hit the mountain causing rocks to crash through the caverns, squashing one or two of the Strays as they kneeled in their trance. Then the Strays raised themselves, the blood lust back in their eyes as they ran crazed, knocking Jaxter to the floor and running for Scrycher. Two of the Strays hit Scrycher square in the chest, forcing him into the glass coffin he was looking into, and smashing it, causing air to hiss out.

Scrycher fell to the floor as the Strays assaulted him. The others were also attacked, all knocked to the ground, as the Stray's blood lust fueled them.

An unbearable heat tore through the room, Scrycher could feel it even beneath the Strays that continued to tear and rip at his flesh. A roar so powerful it made his hairs stand on end blasted the room. Then there was a silence, a deadly silence; even the Stray's screams of blood lust had quietened. An unfolding sound echoed through the room. He could only place this sound as a sheet being flung onto a bed, but one thousand times more powerful as his ears started ringing. The wind generated by this movement gushed past them all, as though a great force had ripped the roof from the room. A large shadow filled the room, he could barely see the shadow as it moved outwards on the ground before him. He could not look up, the Stray's weight too much for his broken body to throw off. There were more sounds, deafening, as the shadow flapped as though going to fly, and then there was crunching, followed by screams.

Scrycher could feel the weight lift from him, as the screams got more intense, the roaring and tearing sounds that followed cautioned him to not dare look. The Strays continued shrieking and screaming, as their limbs were ripped from their bodies, and thrown across the room, thumping as they fell to the floor. Scrycher was frozen, unable to move as he continued to look at the floor. He could see and feel the blood as it splattered over him and the room. Then there was silence…

Scrycher removed his hands from the back of his head, blood dripping from his wounds. He looked around the room as the others dragged themselves from their protective positions on the floor. He then stopped, looking directly at Scrags, and Blink, who were standing in the center of the room with not a scratch on them. Scrags' innocence showed through his eyes as he spoke. "Are you alright?" Blink just perched on Scrags' head, laying his own head down to sleep.

Scrycher turned, remembering the chamber that had been damaged in the scuffle. The air had completely gone from it and the beautiful woman's chest dropped for one last time. Grabbing his rifle from the floor, he extended the blade. Quickly he tried to pry open the lid. In his weakened state, he could not. Jaxter ran over, leaning his large bulk upon the rifle, the blade slipped, and the lid popped open. Scrycher did not bother with the blood as it gushed from his hand, and the open wound caused by the blade. He grabbed the body out of the coffin, and lowered her to the floor. Her long, curly brown hair, pale skin, and supple breasts lay lifeless. Placing his wounded hand on her chest, he pushed, stopping only to blow air into her lifeless lungs. His life force traveled through his blood to his hands, then to her. Slowly, her chest rose and fell, and her eyes opened. He was lost in those brown eyes for a second, and then he collapsed. As his vision blurred, his last thought was, that out of the corner of his eye, he saw a figure sitting up in the open chamber, beneath the tree…

Chapter 22

Scrycher awoke, panicked, as he smashed his hands against the glass chamber. He felt trapped, confined and anxious, but not in pain. A head popped itself over the chamber, seeing him awake, the chamber opened. Scrycher sat up, gasping for breath, in his distressed state.

Chelsea laughed at his reaction; he looked shocked as he watched her standing before him. He shook his head and pinched himself. Was he dreaming again?

"Welcome, Scrycher. I am Zavier. I welcome you with open arms to my vessel, and my life's work." The short Stray walked over to him, placing his hand in Scrycher's. "It is an honor to meet you, Sir." Then he bowed…

"This vessel was only days off of being complete when the planet was bombarded. On seeing so many dead, we decided that we had no stomach for deep space exploration. Especially if all the species were as evil as the Company. With so much damage to the planet, and the Company guarding us, we did not think we could get this deep space exploration vessel into orbit without being destroyed. We assigned a sentry to keep the ship responding, and repaired. As you can see, that plan did not work. After several sentries, one died unexpectedly, and even though I was in an awakened mental state, I could not wake another.

Therefore, the secondary plan had to come into play. I had sent your grandfathers and fathers off with a different piece of the puzzle, so if either were trapped, we would not be found. Teller, your father was my son. Scrycher gasped, *that means Teller is, how old?* I did not expect it to take so long to get your lineage back here, though. I have been sending out messages, and searching for the minds of the chosen, for almost a thousand years with no response, and the tree, as you can see, is almost exhausted. Many of us have perished but you are here now, that is all that matters."

"Teller, may I have the crystal?" Zavier asked nicely, but the look in his eyes told them he was going to take it if it was not given freely.

Teller walked to him, placing the crystal in his hand as he knelt before him. "Yes, Grandfather Zavier."

Taking the crystal, Zavier walked to the large crystalline tree and reached over the coffin. It had been used to save Chelsea's and Scrycher's lives by regenerating their bodies. He placed the crystal into the gap in the middle of this tree. It fitted perfectly as it slid in and reintegrated. The tree responded with a mild illumination, its branches glimmering in what now was obviously a large crystalline dome. The glimmer then shimmered slightly, and fell dark.

"No, not after all this time. It can't be." Zavier ran to the consoles madly flicking switches as their lights dimmed. "They will all die."

"S-Scrycher, r-repairing you, and Chelsea, must have drained the crystal tree's energy to a point that was too low to sustain itself. It then used its remainder energy to re-integrate the smaller crystal back into itself.

"What do we do, Prof?" Scrycher was watching the chaos around him, as other coffins lining the walls started to release the air within them. Scrycher raised his hand to his face, what had he done? He did not wait for Profitor's response; the wound on his hand began to glow, pulsing in the dark. He turned; Teller, Scrags, and Zavier all glowed too.

He turned to the tree, reaching for it in desperation, with not a moment to waste as more of the hissing filled the room. "I give my life freely. My life to continue the rebirth of our once proud brethren." His body arched backwards as the tree gripped him, ripping his energy from him, his eyes glowing in pain as he screamed. Jaxter ran to his side, trying to pull him from the tree, but to no avail, the tree would not release him.

"It will kill him, get him away." Zavier was working frantically on the controls, trying to save his people as he yelled, seeing the events unfold out of the corner of his eye.

"W-Will his life force save them?" Profitor directed the question loudly over the sounds of screams and hissing, as he gestured to the thousands of coffins throughout the room that were still de-pressurizing. The answer from Zavier was simple and precise.

"Yes."

Profitor walked slowly to the tree, its light marginally brighter as it sucked Scrycher's life force from him. He was now close enough to see Scrycher silently screaming and the pain it caused. He gulped hard as he slashed his hands upon the crystal coffin, Profitor reached forward grasping the tree with both hands, standing proud and strong as he spoke. "It has been an honor, Captain. I die amongst friends." His head was thrown back violently as the tree gripped his life force, tearing it from his frail body, his features shrinking before Teller's eyes.

Teller, who was standing beside the tree, moved slightly and quickly, re-enacting the series of events that Profitor had just performed. Looking at Chelsea with compassion, and love in his eyes, he whispered. "I die amongst kindred spirits, those who became my family." Teller forced his hands upon the tree, *th-thump, th-thump, th-thump,* its dim life force now exploded through its branches as all who looked upon it were blinded.

The Three forced their way back out of Teller; they could not go back to the realm from where they had come, nor stay here. They knew his damaged body could not house them for much longer without falling to the stress of their combined power. Their task was complete. Their only choice was to enter the tree itself! They knew this could be their death, but they decided together, simultaneously, and explosively.

"Deliver the final blow." Philippe was standing at the front of The Enforcer, thrusting out his hand and grinning at his victory. His thoughts were focused on the fact that the next shot would mean the end of Zackory, and his vessel. He turned, jumping slightly at the soft touch of the Creator's hand on his shoulder.

"Steady, my son." The Creator raised his hand slowly, pointing to the large mass that was now exiting the planet.

The Captains all stood in shock, as the large crystalline ship headed towards them. It was magnificent. A crystalline dome surrounded a brilliant crystalline tree. The tree and its branches supported the dome to its extremities and filled the space around it in an awe inspiring white light. Many small creatures, humanoid, Strays worked feverishly inside the dome, their own fur glowing brightly.

This vessel was a grand design, and well thought out. The tree exuded energy; energy used to power the ship. The energy that was not used by the ship was recycled by the Stray crew, their bodies amplifying it and increasing it ten-fold, then releasing it back. So pure, no waste and so powerful. The beauty ravaged them all, even Zackory, as he stood from his chair to look in awe.

Their disbelief heightened as they saw the short Stray, Zavier, projected onto all of their bridges.

"On behalf of the Stray people, I reclaim this planet and this space. This is our home world and we will protect it. If anyone has an issue or a claim to this planet, please speak now."

Beep. "Shut it up, man. What are you doing?"

"The communications console is damaged, it is not respo…"

With one massive pulse from the Stray vessel, the Syndicate vessel was gone.

"Anyone else?" All vessels and ships sat quietly, not one, daring to move…

Chapter 23

"Father, I have failed you. How will you ever forgive me?" Philippe, shook his head in disgust over their inconclusive battle. No one had really won, only delayed the inevitable. He had wanted to see Zackory, and even Garath, pay for their actions against him, but even they had escaped as he watched, slinking off as everyone else was occupied. As soon as The Enforcer was repaired, and running smoothly, Philippe had bid Scrycher farewell and left. However they had not gone too far.

"You worry too much, my son. Lest you forget that Mogly, is amassing our army as we speak. Patience and all will fall into place."

"Welcome, Nifty. You have something for me?" Scrycher grabbed his friend, giving him a large hug.

"Don't touch, don't touch, and don't touch." Nifty jumped up and down as Scrycher hugged him harder, and laughed.

Letting him go, Scrycher spoke again. "Well?"

"If you'd stop hugging me, then we could do this a lot quicker." Nifty opened a silver case. "Remember that secret weapon you gave me? Sleeping flies I think you called them. Well one of them carried a deadly parasite. I had my techs make you a batch of the antidote, as I thought you would require it." Nifty looked serious as he spoke to Scrycher.

"Always the hero, hey Nefal? That's why we call you Nifty Nef, after all." Scrycher laughed as he was injected with the antidote just in case.

"Blink!" the little dragon materialized on the bridge, between the two men, his eyes blazing red and his tail flailing madly around him. Nifty looked in slight disbelief, lobbing Scrycher a syringe as Blink started snarling, and then, he backed away. Scrycher's eyes lit up as the large black dog, Bones, bounded through Blink and slamming into him. The three rolling into a ball of fury. "Holy rat's balls!" he screamed as they smashed into the consoles and crew.

"My ship, my crew... Scrycher!" Nifty yelled.

There was a yelp, as Blink was injected, the three breaking their formation, and standing off. All three snarling at each other, Scrycher included. Blinks eyes flared red, and then he was gone, his disapproving growl left behind.

"Now that is done with, we have some business to discuss. Firstly, can you get that antidote over to my crew at Lance's... oh, my ship? I am sure Jax would appreciate the peace of mind, knowing that he will not go mad. And secondly, how do you feel about a little, 'water trade'?" Scrycher grabbed Nifty by the shoulder, leading him away to discuss the particulars, as Nifty mumbled.

"Don't touch, don't touch. How many times must I tell you, do not touch?"

"Pickle me rat's balls, Teller, what we supposed to do now? This self replicatin' tin can is no place for us!" Jaxter stormed back and forth in the cargo bay of Lance's vessel, kicking at the scrap that lay strewn across the ground. "And what's you lookin' for?"

"You will see soon enough, my friend." Teller flicked out his claws again as he tore open the next crate before him. The room was now littered in broken crates and various bits of equipment in different conditions.

"Oh, baby, I luv it when you do that!" Chelsea walked over and stroked Teller's arm as he pulled the packing from the box.

"Well pickle your rat's balls, Jaxter. It seems that I have found what I was looking for." Teller stood up straight, his fur and face, illuminating the room.

"What the?" Jaxter had walked over to the crate, looked inside and almost fallen over in excitement. "But, how we supposed to get her-?"

His thoughts were cut short as Scrag's jumped up screaming, "Blink, Blink, Blink, we found it." he was erratically throwing all the stuffing out of a box, one half the size of the box that Teller had opened. Blink was not concerned, he was raging, his claws and tail shredding the contents of an undeserving box next to Scrags'.

"Found what?" Jaxter was torn between the boxes, as he watched Teller walk to Scrag's.

"The pint sized version of my beauty over there." Courtesy of Gregory and the Syndicate. Unfortunately it seems that he was in such a hurry to get reinforcements, that they did not have time to unload their cargo. Unfortunate for them, fortunate for us." He lifted the barrel out of the box, its casing shiny, and brand new. "Now we can defend our people together, young man. Together." Teller smiled as he laid the Gatling gun down on the floor, admiring the sheer beauty of it.

"Now we got us some more ships, I reckon we stand a chance. Funny that, Gregory, givin' us his spare ship, and all. It wasn't as though 'is life depended on it, much!" Chelsea laughed, allowing her face to fall onto Teller's arm. She breathed in his musty smell as she tensed a little. "Too bad 'em goon squads escaped while no-one was looking."

"Ah, Chels, but Lance is sayin' that we'll be seein' his brothers again. It's a family thing, I s'pose." Jaxter was not really paying attention as he answered, his mind already working out the requirements on how to attach the guns to the Company vessel.

"This is Captain Lance Dragoon." the loud speaker boomed. "Can the chef, or chefs, please make their way to the galley?" Another voice could be heard in the background as Lance received an incoming communication.

"Sir, we don't have a chef." Lance went silent as he contemplated his dilemma.

He answered the outside com, not realizing that the internal com was active. "Well what the hell am I going to eat? I am starving! Oh, sorry, Captain Scrycher, no that comment was not meant for you. Um, yes I

understand, we will be ready for the package, and I will relay the message...
Com on please."

"Sir, the com is already on, you forgot to turn it off."

"Um, I knew that. Can," he paused for an instant. "Scrags, and Jaxter please report to the galley? It seems, you are our new chefs. And Captain Scrycher says, please do not forget to add 'two nuts' to the stew." Lances voice trailed off, not understanding the joke he just relayed.

"Pickle me rat's balls!" Jaxter yelled out again. "Boss!"

Chelsea laughed as she slapped him on the back. "C'mon big man, let's go pickle us some rat's nuts."

Lance allowed himself a moment to rest, his head weary after the long days, and the sickness still within him. He was unsure about the dream that became so vivid as he fell under sleep's spell, pulling out his gun he focused, "Die, Father, die!"

Lord Dragoon gasped, as his body was wrenched back to the tree. His head was thrown back from the pain he felt as the bullet, shot by Lance, had shattered the crystal. Opening his eyes, he yelled "Not again!" as he grasped blindly at the tree. His eyes were dead, that lust for power gone as he looked around the room. Something else was there with him and not just the Strays, starving in the cages. These figures, he could not account for. They were dark and ominous, shapes that made him shudder. Moments passed, and the presence did not lessen. Catching another glance, he realized that he had pulled a darkness with him, as he was ripped back to the tree; a darkness he had never felt before. With the initial fear gone, he grew to like this darkness, welcome the power it offered as it coursed through his veins.

It had found its way into his eyes, whirling in a black swirl. He laughed, throwing his head back in that same cynical laugh that he had moments earlier, when he had thought the crystal planet was his. *With this new found power it may just be*, he though as he blinked; and then it was gone. Desperately he tried to find it, but he could not. It had disappeared, where he did not know. He allowed his head to fall to the tree, as he whispered softly. "Come home, my son. Come home to die!"

Chapter 24 (Three months earlier)

"Do we have to get him?"

"Only if we want to keep our jobs."

"What about our lives?" Fumbling with the keys, the guard stopped at the cell. "Stand back."

The second guard spoke as he stood beside the cell, fear in his eyes and his voice shaking as the large man raised himself from the steel bench. "Hammer. Come quietly."

Hammer cracked his neck as he stood. "Why?" His booming voice made the guard drop his keys.

Fumbling, the guard tried picking them up, constantly looking back into the cell, which caused him to fumble more. "Step away… please."

"Why?" Hammer repeated the question.

Click. The guard slid the key into the lock as he mumbled into his hand. "You are to be hung."

"Well why didn't you say so. I've been waiting all day." Hammer walked to the cell door as the key was turned, holding his hands before him and smiling. "Hope the weather's nice out there today. Wouldn't want a dreary day to ruin a good hanging, now would we?"

To Be Continued…

Teller fan art by Jon Dei Goon

http://deidarags.deviantart.com/

Fan art by Shelley McCaw

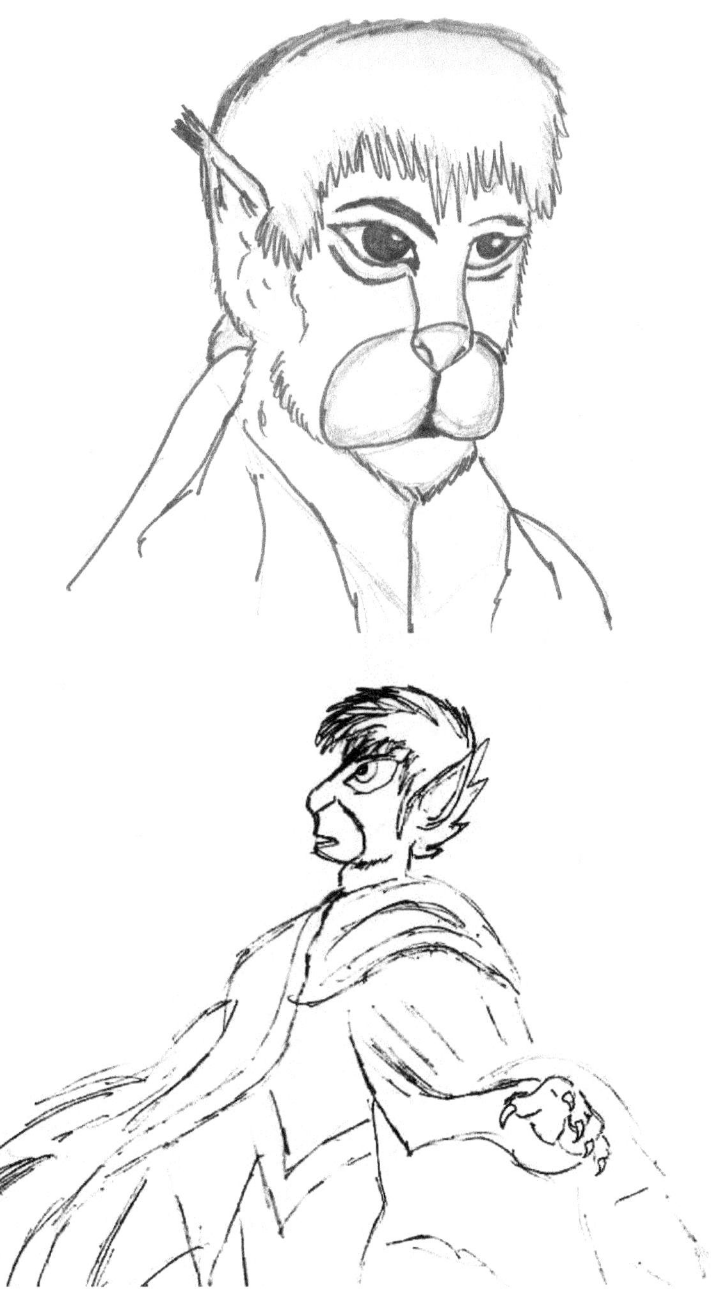

Artwork by Stephen Landry

www.Facebook.com/StephenLandryArt

Artwork by Stephen Landry

Other Works by DC Daines